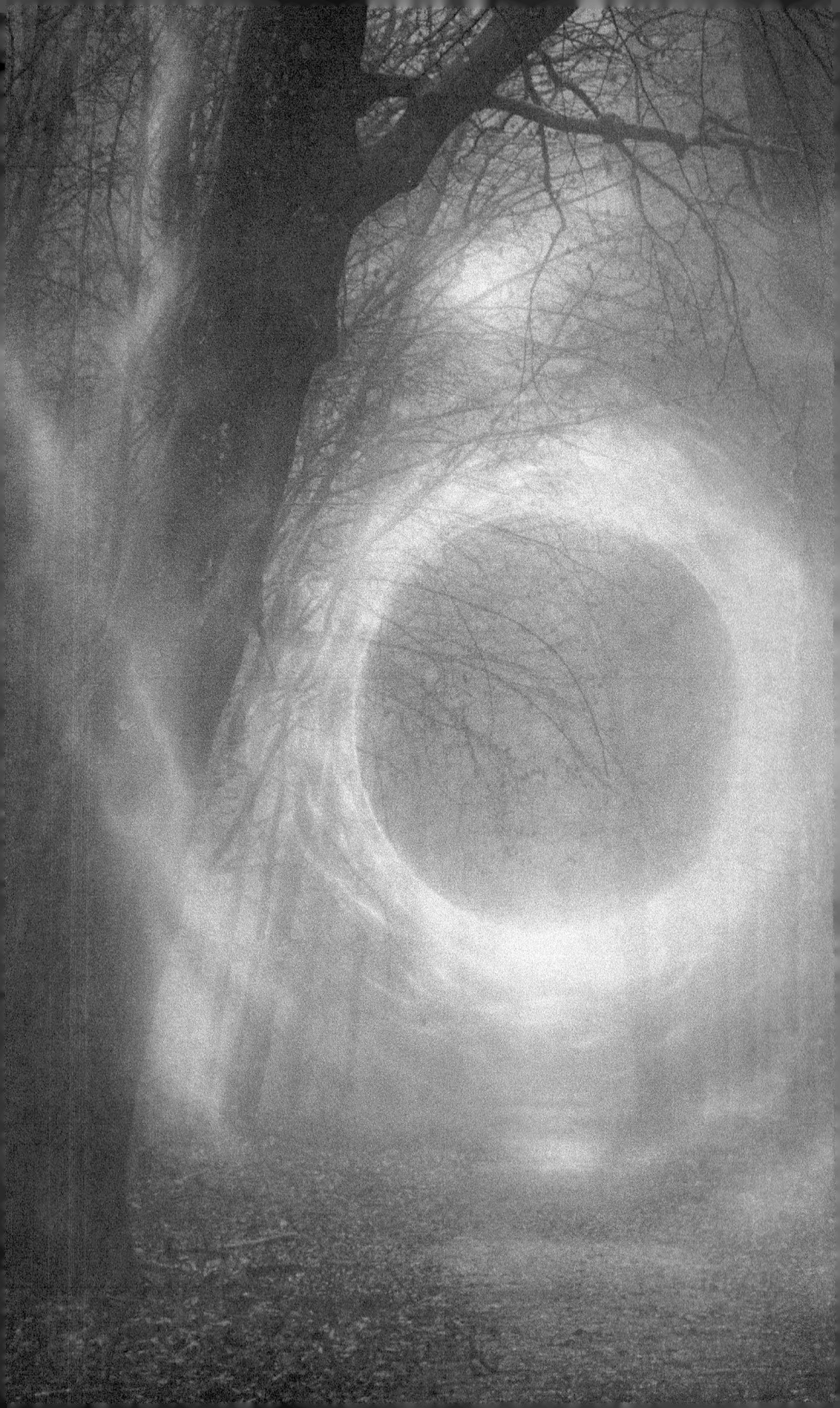

Kingdom of the Forsaken Saint

MELANIE CARDONA VÉLEZ

Cover design: Danielle Greaves

Character Illustration: Marina Ceban

Map Illustration: Danielle Greaves

Formatter: The Nutty Formatter

AUTHOR'S NOTE

Kingdom of the Forsaken Saint is a New Adult Fantasy-Romance. It contains explicit sex scenes, swearing, torture, physical and emotional abuse, death of a loved one, and religious culture. This book may be unfit for anyone under the age of 18.

For Rocky, I hope that they're treating you well up in doggy heaven.

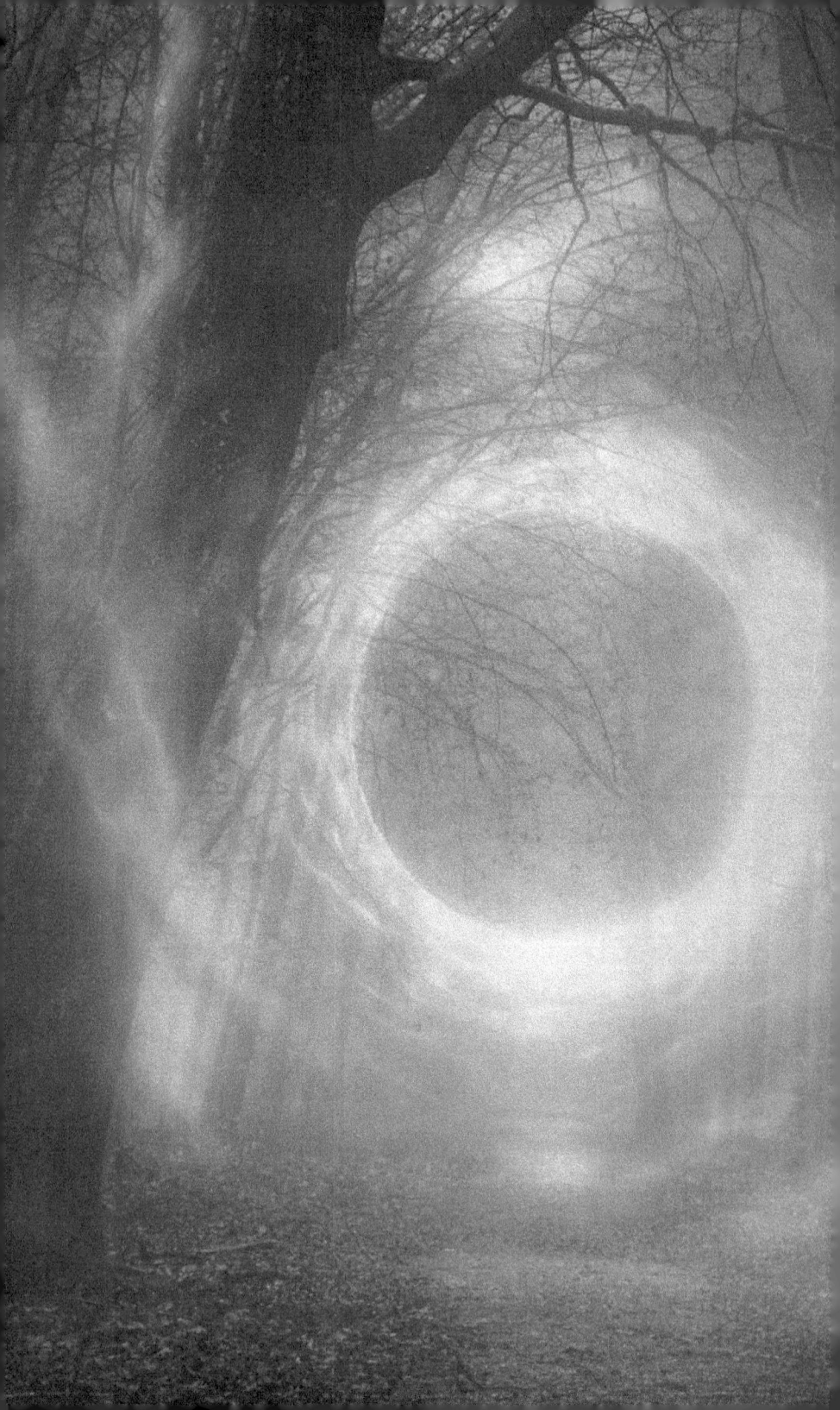

PROLOGUE

THE PAST

It was the most important day of all. Dominus held his staff erect. Seven angels stood before him with heads bowed. All waiting to hear who would be chosen as the one lucky angel to become his right hand. All seven angels were already bestowed with the highest of honors: to be chosen as gods to serve beside their lord and savior. But to be chosen as the Lord's second meant you were the holiest of all, that even Dominus himself considered you an equal to him.

That was the day Valec was chosen. A moment forever planted in his memory.

It was the beginning of a new life.

A life that was sadly short-lived.

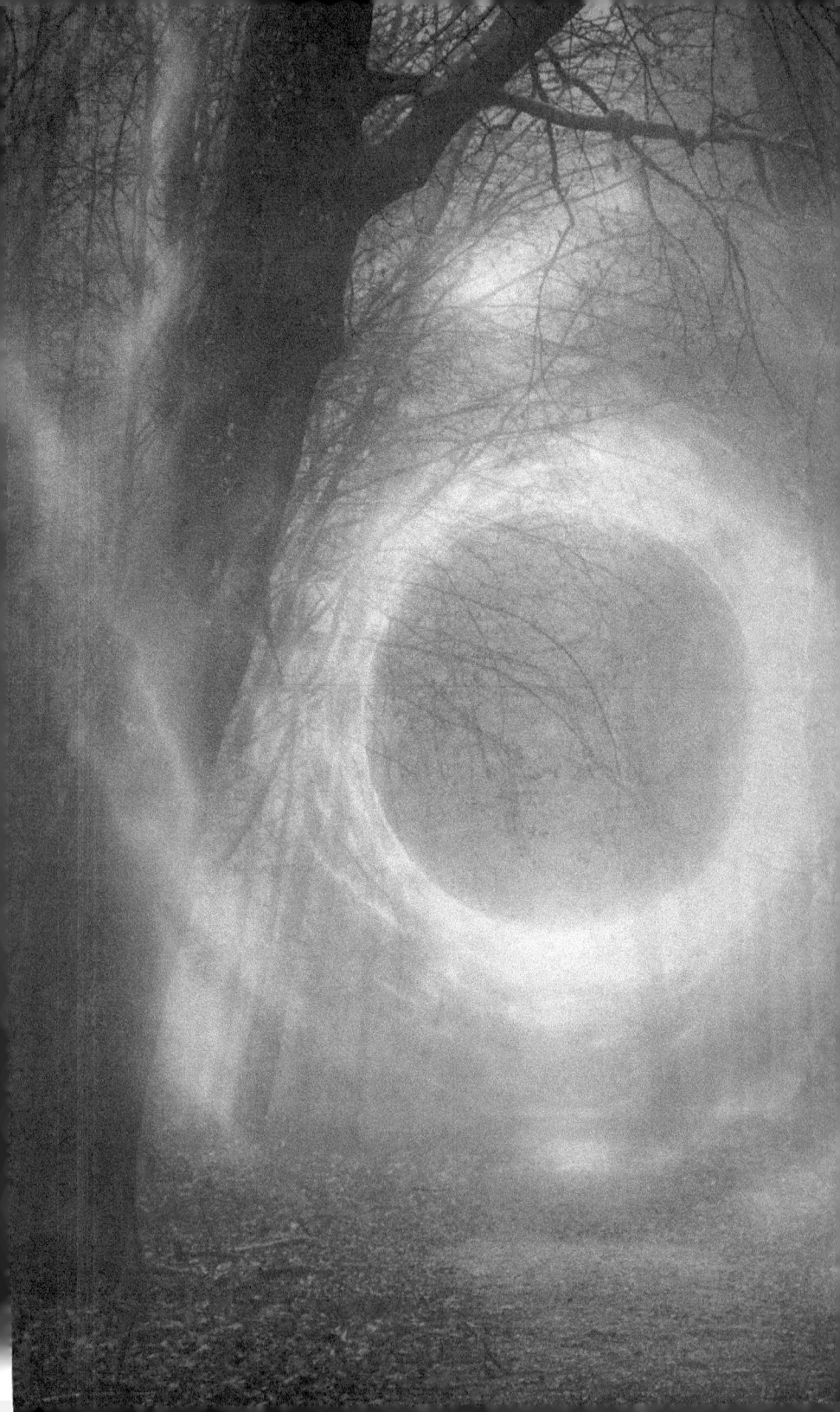

CHAPTER 1

A WAY

Year: 15: After the Fall

VALEC

Valec seems like a long-forgotten name. I wish it were so. But because of Julius, my older brother, I can no longer forget it, even when I've already been given many names by others. The Devil, Your Majesty, and my least favorite, Lucifer. The one who deceives. Me, the former god and second-in-command to Dominus, now the forgotten and perished. He who lives in this land as a forsaken saint.

Fifteen years ago, my brother and I were wrongfully cast down from Caelesti, the holy land where there is no pain, and pure joy abides within every angel who resides there. A place of rest for the dead who pass on to their second life. It was my home.

I now call Inferis home. A land established inside massive interconnecting caves where stalagmites and stalactites are considered the only decoration.

Life has not been the same since then.

From the moment my brother and I began establishing our new life here in Inferis, so did others. I was shocked the day someone else appeared in this land, as if by magic. They were confused and afraid, with no idea where they were. The last memory they had was of their death. That's when things began to make sense for me. I knew that these people had died. But instead of arriving in Caelesti for their eternal rest, they arrived here in Inferis. Without anyone having to voice it to me, I understood that there were now two lands for the dead, and this happened because of Esveld, the god who tricked me and caused my downfall.

As I exit the small home Julius and I made from the very stones of the cavern walls, I spot my brother racing through the dusty dirt pathway that leads to the larger caves farther out. He always keeps busy tending to his garden. There may be no sun down here in Inferis, but the plants still manage to grow. The garden may not be like the one he had in Caelesti, but it keeps him happy, and that's all I can ask for, given the circumstances.

"Val!" Julius is out of breath when he reaches me, his grayish-blue eyes wide in alarm. When Julius and I were younger I used to believe we looked alike, though our appearances are very different. For instance, his blue eyes are a lighter shade than my own. His jaw is less sharp than mine, giving him a youthful look despite him being the eldest. Now when it comes to our hair, we share the same shade of chestnut, but his is slightly wavier than mine.

"Yes, brother, has something occurred?" I ask him, intrigued as to what has caused him to run all the way from the garden to our house. I take notice of his stained tunic and trousers. His boots covered in mud up to the ankles. A fruitful day of planting, indeed.

"A woman has arrived," he announces. "She is insistent on speaking with you."

"With me?" I wonder why. "Where is she?"

"She's at the veil. Come; I'll take you to her." I follow Julius up the pathway, thankful to be wearing an extra garment under my own tunic to keep out the harsh cold of the caverns. From our home it's about a ten-minute walk to Julius's garden, which so happens to be where the veil resides.

On our way, we pass over houses that were carved from the inner walls of the caves as well. Each one belongs to someone who's taken up residence in the land. And some are kinder than others. But I guess that's what happens to some humans who let themselves be corrupted by sin.

My curiosity grows with each step we take through the winding path of damp tunnels. I can tell we're almost there when the light smell of roses and midnight blooms fill my nostrils. Julius's gardens loom ahead in all its beauty.

It's been a while since I came here. "Wow, Julius, you sure have outdone yourself." I follow behind him as I admire each flower, we pass. It's an entire field of fresh color. These flowers are what give Inferis life. If only there were a blue sky and a shining sun above us right now. I close my eyes, remembering what it was like in Caelesti, surrounded by nature. I can almost feel the warmth of the sun on my face—

"Valec?" Julius calls, drawing me out of my memories. I open my eyes to find him standing a few feet away from me. A woman I've never seen before stands next to him, while I still remain in the middle of the flower field. Behind them stands the veil in all its luster. A perfect oval of shimmering onyx—our very own picture frame carved from stone.

It's the only thing separating us from the mortal realm known as Einalem.

"Valec, allow me to introduce you to Soela." Julius gestures to the woman beside him. I walk toward them. Her wet, fiery mane is the first thing I notice of her appearance, followed by her light bluish-gray eyes as they bore into my own. Her alabaster nightgown is slightly damp and ripped at the bodice.

"Your Majesty." She bows before me. An act I wish did not need to occur at my presence. I am no king and I will never consider myself one, despite all who believe I rule upon this land.

"There's no need for that. You may call me Valec," I offer.

"As you wish, Valec. Please allow me to tell you a little about myself."

I nod my head slightly, letting her know that she is free to speak. Julius moves to my side so that we can both face her as she continues.

"I was a member of The Circle of Impure." The Circle of Impure is a community of human worshipers in my name. They place their faith in and pray to me. I am their lord the same way Dominus is the lord of Caelesti. He also has his community of followers in the mortal realm of Einalem, known as The Order of Divine, which is led by the high priest and priestess.

"I was also a black nun," she adds. Now, a black nun—those are rare. They're the women of the black veils who stalk the nights, chanting my name and lighting candles in my honor as a sign of their devotion. It's a vow that can never be broken once taken. Like selling one's soul. If you choose to be a black nun, much the same as a white nun, one lives a life of utmost dedication towards that land of the afterlife and its ruler.

I nod, avoiding her stare as a spike of dread courses through me. *Is this woman here for some malicious reason?* As if taking notice of my discomfort, Julius speaks up. "What is it you wish to discuss with my brother, Soela?"

She shakes her head, some of her messy locks falling over her face. "Forgive me. That came out wrong." She quickly tucks her loose strands of hair behind her ear. "What I mean to say is that in my life, I dedicated myself to your cause, but not as you believe it to be."

I'm confused.

Soela continues. "I had a family member who saw what the angel Esveld did in the mortal lands. She saw you and your brother fall." I freeze at the reminder of such a day. Julius was punished for the sole reason of being my brother. Nothing more.

"Since that day onward, my family has dedicated the past fifteen years to finding a way to free you from this land," she says.

I take a step back. Could this be true? Are there indeed people out there who know the truth? *My truth?*

"My family and I are not evil. We prayed to Dominus every day. We prayed for justice and your wellbeing. We prayed for the return of simpler times. We joined the Circle of Impure as a way to gain more information on you and your brother." She looks from me to Julius at my side.

It's as if all my prayers have been answered, and yet I can't help the slight feeling of apprehension taking over me. "And what did you learn?" I ask, needing to know more.

"They were trying to prove a discovery that would supposedly allow you to walk on the land of Einalem during a blood moon."

Not uncommon; blood moons tend to occur twice a week, rising between seven in the night, mortal time, and setting by midnight. Except during the period of a lunar eclipse.

"Apparently, the veil between Einalem and Inferis is thinner during a blood moon," Soela explains. "Easier to penetrate."

"Do you think it could actually work?" asks Julius.

"I believe it's worth a try. Especially now, before any member of the Circle of Impure tries to weaken it further to get you out for nefarious reasons. This could be your opportunity to plead your case to the mortals, to the high priest and priestess. Since they are the only ones who can summon Dominus willingly."

I'm in shock yet again. "Valec, this is what we've been

waiting for." Julius turns to face me now. Our opportunity, indeed. We've waited all these years for a miracle to occur and now there's a chance it might become a reality.

"When's the next blood moon?" I inquire.

"Tonight," Soela answers quickly.

"How will it work?" I need to know all the details.

"Allow me to show you." Soela moves to the side no longer obstructing the full view of the veil. "I'll need something to draw with."

Julius walks away only to return a few minutes later with a claystone in hand. "Will this do?" He places the stone on Soela's outstretched palm.

"This will do perfectly." She lowers herself to the ground near the veil and begins to drag the stone against the floor, drawing various symbols.

Julius and I stare at each design she creates. The drawing is mostly a pattern of swirls interconnecting with other lines. In the end, Soela has created what she calls a pentagram.

I fix my gaze on my brother, who lost interest in what Soela was drawing a while ago and has since been staring at the veil. "Brother, I can assure you the veil will not get any thinner from the countless times you've looked at it."

He laughs.

"You're quite right, Valec. Perhaps it's the anticipation that's got me on edge."

"The moon is just about to rise," Soela announces, tossing what's left of the rock onto the ground. "And I'm done." She finally gets to her feet. "Are you ready?"

"We're ready!" I announce.

Soela frowns. "I'm sorry, I forgot to mention this before. But only one of you can cross the veil at a time."

"We can't go together?" Julius's eyes flash with hurt.

"No, only one of you can leave the veil."

6

"Then I'll go," Julius volunteers, closing the distance between him and the veil.

"Are you mad?" I pull Julius back. "I was wrongfully accused, brother, so I will be the one to fix this situation."

"I'm your older brother, Valec." Julius lightly claps me on the shoulder. "And it's my job to protect you."

"I know. But I need to be the one who appeals to Dominus, not you."

His hand drops from my shoulder. "I couldn't save you from this." His face falls. "I couldn't save you from Esveld, from any of it. I failed you." His lip quivers slightly and I avert my gaze. I can't stand to see Julius like this.

Soela steps away, retreating further into Julius's garden, giving us the space we need.

"There was no saving me from this, Julius. This was nothing more than a stroke of bad luck. But now I've been given an opportunity to make things right and *I* will be the one to do it." I grasp my brother's arm and pull him close to me. His arms press around my back in an embrace.

"I love you, Valec." His voice comes out broken.

"And I love you, Julius. Trust me on this."

"I do." He pulls away and then we're both facing the veil. "Crazy to think after all these years of poking around the veil, trying to see what it could do, now we finally have our answers."

"I know, despite everything, I'm considering this a gift from Dominus regardless," I say, beaming.

Soela returns a few minutes later. "Alright. I'm assuming you both decided on who's to cross?"

I step forward. "I will."

"Good, then I'll need you to stand inside the pentagram. The symbols around it represent the seven virtues." Seems fitting. "In order for the veil to grant you access, it will need to extract the virtues from your being and into the pentagram, which will act as an anchor into the mortal world." I shoot her a concerned look. "Don't worry, as soon as you pass through, your virtues will be delivered back into your body." That eases my tension, though not entirely.

"Remember, the veil is meant to keep the dead in," Soela adds. "You are not dead; you are an immortal former angel. Thus, at its weakest, the veil will be able to tell the difference and therefor allow you to leave this land. But don't forget it is only while the blood moon is still in full. Once the clock strikes twelve in the mortal realm, the veil will close off and the pentagram will have lost its power, and you will be ejected from Einalem and thrust back here to Inferis."

"I understand the risks."

"Good, then let us begin. Close your eyes and focus on the seven holy virtues. Name them in your head if you'd like. You can even recall a few cherished memories from your time living in Caelesti." I do as told, starting with the virtues one by one in my head.

Chastity.

Temperance.

Charity.

Diligence.

Kindness.

Patience.

Humility.

"It's working, brother," Julius informs me. I'm about to open my eyes when Soela warns me against it.

"You will lose concentration. Just know that the pentagram is glowing."

I can only assume that's a good sign. Soela begins to speak in the ancient tongue of the ancestors: those who walked the lands way before Dominus. I'm surprised anyone knows how to speak it, though it is rumored that tongue is still used in other continents.

While she chants, I continue to recall the day I was chosen to become a god, and later when Dominus chose me to be his second in command, when a rush of cold wind hits me.

"It's done, Valec, open your eyes," Soela urges me.

My eyes fling open on command, and I look forward to the veil. It's no longer shimmering, nor is it the usual color I'm accustomed to. Instead, it's like looking through a window; a window between realms. I can see directly to the other side. A clearing of oak trees greets me. Carefully, I stretch a hand outward and come into contact with a shadowy wall of air. My hand tingles as it passes all the way through. I'm at a loss for words when I see my hand on the other side.

I turn to face Julius. "I will save us, brother. We will return to Caelesti. I promise you."

Julius takes my free hand in his. "Good luck, brother. I'll be praying for your safe return."

"Thank you." I glance towards Soela now. "And thank you, truly. To you and your entire family."

She bows and this time it does not bother me, because I know it's out of respect for the truth. "You're welcome. Tread carefully."

"I will." I step through the veil, leaving all of Inferis behind me for the first time in fifteen years.

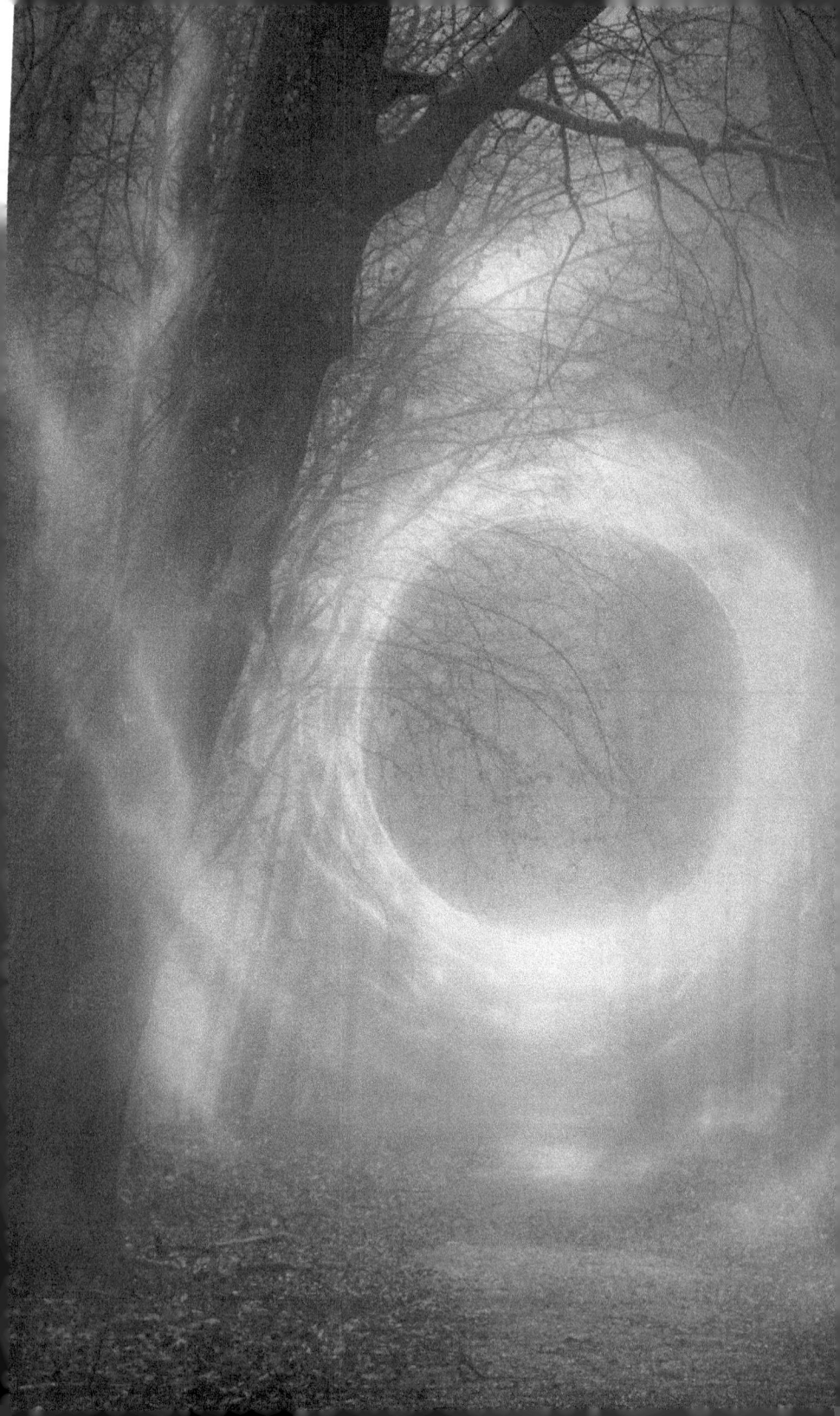

CHAPTER 2
NEW EVIL

VALEC

It is a strange feeling to walk on grass again. I forgot how soft and pillowy it feels under the weight of my old boots. The oak trees engulf me from above with their rich earthy scent. Impossible to forget such a smell. Even the night sky is as I remember, with more stars than I can count.

All of it seems so new to me in a way, yet everything is exactly the same. My mind and heart can never forget. No angel forgets their time in the mortal lands. And being here now feels like a dream come true, even if the land of Einalem is not truly my home. The fact that I can now walk amongst mortals again... it's everything I've longed for.

I take my time trekking through the forest, taking in every magnificent scene. Even under the light of the blood moon everything looks spectacular. As if touched by Dominus's very essence. As a god I had the pleasure of descending to Einalem a few times at his Lord's side. And each time was a whole new experience for me. I got to meet new people, see forests much like this one, help those who needed aid. They were always so pleased to see me. I wonder if there are any more out there like

Soela's family. Those who know my story and want to see me free.

Though finding said people is not what I've come here to do. I've come to speak with the high priest and priestess to convince them to allow me a hearing with Dominus. If that first part goes well, then my only worry is whether or not he'll listen to what I have to say. It's been fifteen years; surely he must see reason now if I appeal to him.

I've reached the end of the tree line, now arriving at a cobblestone road. I'm startled by the sound of an oncoming carriage trudging through the street. Two ladies poke their heads through the window, one of them smiling at me. Their carriage comes to an unexpected stop.

"Hello, sir, are you going to the celebratory ball as well?" a young blonde woman greets me. The other simply stares at me from head to toe, taking in my worn-out tunic.

"Don't be silly, Mera." The brunette woman swats her friend with her fan. "He's not dressed for a ball."

"There's a ball?" I ask.

"Why, yes," the blonde named Mera chimes in. "The high priest and priestess are celebrating their ten years of service to the church. Do you need a ride somewhere?"

"Yes, I'm going to the ball too," I announce. This is my chance; these women are going exactly where I need to be.

"Not like that you're not. Come, we know a place that can get you a decent attire," Mera's friend exclaims, all excited.

"That would be very much appreciated. Thank you. But I'm afraid I don't have any coin."

The brunette frowns while Mera grins at me.

"Not a problem." She ushers the footman to open the carriage door for me. Now getting a full look at their attire, I take in the elegant, white lace gowns they both wear. "Besides, it's not every day we come across a handsome beggar on the side of the road. It's a blessing from Dominus." I nearly burst into laughter at her assumption.

We arrive outside a large brass gate nearly an hour later, after having stopped at a local town shop for something for me to wear. I settled on a white embroidered tunic, along with a pair of long tan fitted slacks and matching crakows.

Behind the gate stands a mass structure elegantly clad with intricate golden designs. Carved by the angels themselves. The purest celestial white. The Grand Church. It's the same as when I last saw it during a brief visit with Dominus and the rest of the gods. It's as if nothing has changed. Its signature golden cross adorns the very top of the church.

The women exit the carriage, their footman helping them get out. I follow close behind. We are greeted at the front door by an elderly man wearing white robes. "May Dominus bless you all." He speaks in a low voice. I offer him a smile as well.

As we're led inside, the women disappear into the crowd. I can't help but gaze towards the altar. At the very top, sitting on some intricately carved wooden chairs, are the high priest and priestess of Einalem. They both seem to be engaging in their own conversation. I know I am short on time, but I take a few minutes to walk around the church, taking in the scenery. The pews have been taken out, and in their place are various tables and chairs for the guests to use during the celebration. Each table has its own flower vase full of lilies at the center. The whole room is covered in lush beige curtains that descend from the top of the glass windows all the way to the floor.

I walk slowly towards the altar and the priest is the first to notice me. "Good evening," I greet them both.

The priest stands from his chair. He wears the same robes as the man who greeted us at the entrance. As does the priestess beside him, who rises from her own seat as well. "Good evening, may the Lord bless you."

"Amen." I answer. "I know this is a celebration to commemorate your ten years of service. But I was hoping to have a word with the both of you."

"Of course." It's the priestess who speaks. Getting a closer look at them both, I assume they're in their third decade of life, which is quite young to be in such high service to the Lord.

"Please tell us what's troubling you, young man," the priest says, offering me a seat at the altar steps. I sit on the top step, and they do the same. As if this were nothing but a conversation amongst old friends.

"What I ask is of great importance." They continue to listen, their eyes never wandering. "I would like a word with Dominus." Now their expressions change though they aren't as shocked as I expected them to be. I mean, it isn't every day that some random man comes asking to speak with the Lord.

"May we ask for what reason?" the priestess questions. "Speaking to Dominus is no lesser thing. Only those in his direct service have spoken to him. What business do you have with the ruler of the skies?"

"I have been wrongfully accused of heinous acts," I start off. "And I must set things straight with him. I've waited too long for an opportunity like this to present itself and now that it has, I am asking for your permission to speak with him. He must know the truth. That I was deceived."

"Deceived by whom?" the priest questions, an eyebrow raised.

I take a long, deep breath. *Here goes nothing.* "By Esveld, the Lord's now second, second hand."

Now their expressions have morphed into shock. The priest rises. "This is impossible," he shouts. "You couldn't—he's locked up." The priestess also rises, keeping close to the priest.

"You're Lucifer." His voice echoes through the church.

I flinch at his words. "I am Valec. My name is Valec."

"You mean you were once known as Valec." It's evident that there is anger now coating his words. "How on Einalem did you get out?" He raises his hand to stop me before I can speak. "I don't want to know. You have no business here. All you say are lies. I ask that you leave at once."

"Pardon, but I am not who you think I am—"

"Yes, you are," the priestess interrupts. "Leave this realm, now! Be gone, Lucifer."

"I am not leaving without a word with Dominus." We've now drawn a crowd as people watch us, having lost interest in the festivities.

The priestess inhales, her eyes bunched in concentration. "Very well, then I banish you in the name of Dominus." I've always known that just those simple words said by a high devotional would be my ticket back to Inferis if I ever managed to get out. It is a powerful spell that was given to the church by Dominus himself after my downfall.

The banishment takes hold of me, as if invisible hands are slowly tugging me backwards.

As I'm pulled back, I catch the stares from everyone at the event. Their faces carry nothing but fear.

I'm almost at the archway near the entrance to the sanctuary when something snaps inside me. The banishment spell releases me for the smallest of instances, and I feel a slight tingling in my body. My emotions start acting up. Changing for the first time ever, anger takes hold of me. My memories surface. From Esveld's trickery to my exile and downfall from Caelesti.

Now, as I witness the hate and fear in these mortals' eyes, a dark feeling engulfs me. A foreign emotion. Something that never existed within me until Esveld changed all of humanity. Pure unadulterated wrath.

Tethering myself to the blood moon's effects, I try my hardest to keep the banishment spell at bay. For now, the moon seems to be acting in my favor.

Somehow, I manage to find my voice. Though they are foreign words that slip past my lips. "If I cannot convince you of my innocence, then perhaps I can convince you of my fury." And just like the Lucifer they think me to be, I unleash my full force. "Mark my words: you will regret the day you banished me from this realm."

Black smoke starts to seep from my hands. I am even startled by it. People move away, the priest and priestess stepping back.

My fingers swirl the smoke in the air. Everyone seems bewildered by the fact that the banishment has not yet taken effect. *Oh,* it's pulling. But I'm resisting.

"You believe yourselves to be so clever. Falling for a false story instead of the truth, and for that I curse this land. Beware my successor who will be the death of all. Born on the night of a blood moon, much like tonight. Within them they will carry the seed of hell. The very power to destroy all mortal life as you know it. And with it, they will break free the seals of Inferis.

"Their age of maturity will mark the commencement of their descent and my rise to power. So even banished as I am, I *will* collect my successor. If not by my hand, then by someone else's."

The banishment fully takes hold over me and this time I can no longer resist. The expulsion from this land throws me out of the church, hauling me across Einalem at lightning speed, until I'm flung through the veil and back to Inferis.

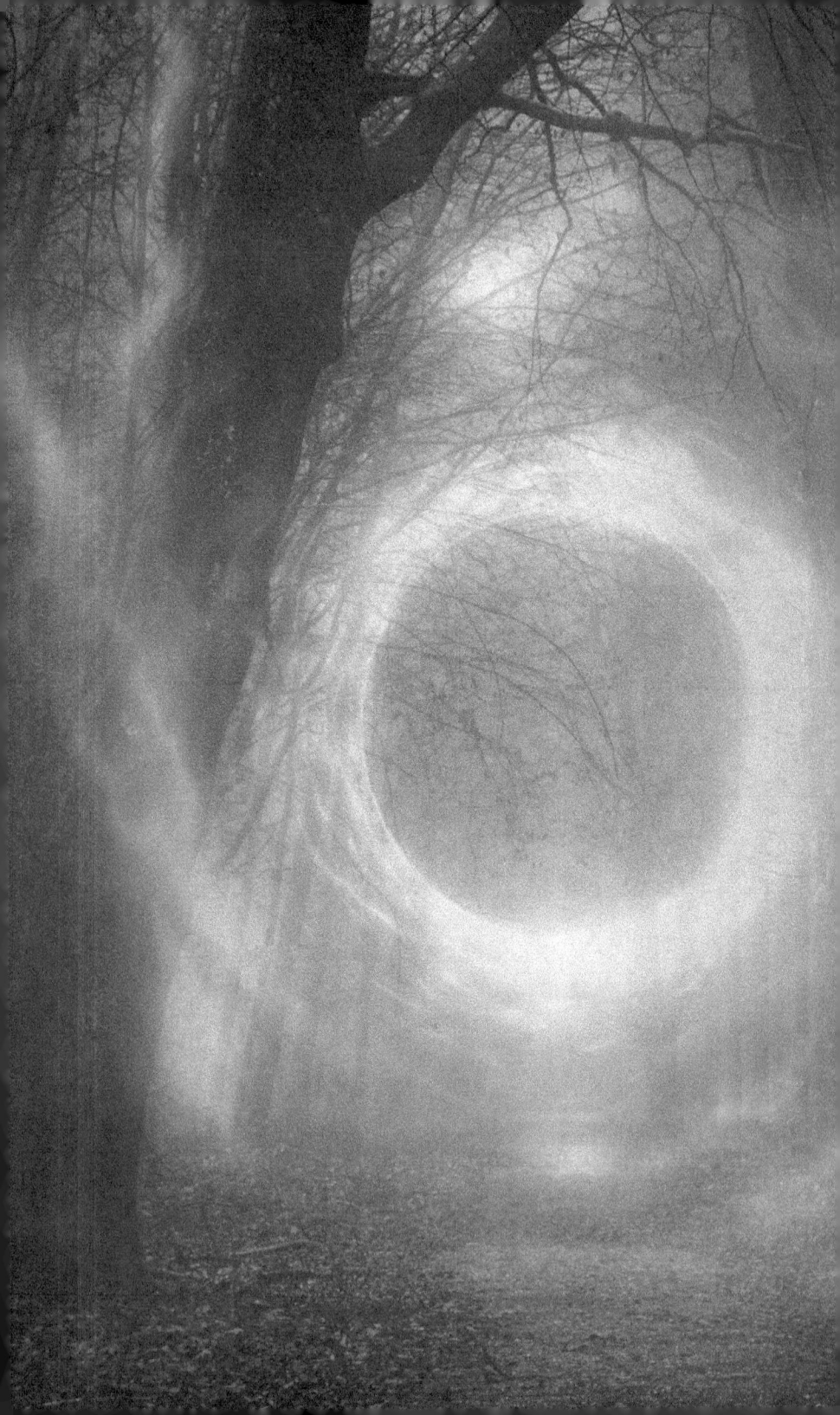

CHAPTER 3
THE FALL

Year 100: Before the Fall

JULIUS

Yesterday was my birthday, and Valec came over to my place after his choosing ceremony to celebrate. As if angels need to celebrate aging after they no longer age. But Valec likes keeping the tradition. Both Valec and I were created by Dominus when he first made the land of Caelesti, one hundred years ago. I stopped aging after my thirtieth birthday, while Valec no longer aged after his twenty-ninth birthday.

However, my birthday is not the only important day this week. Today is Valec's first day as second-in-command to Dominus. The highest honor an angel-turned-god can ever receive. And I couldn't be prouder of my little brother for achieving the holiest of accomplishments.

Just past a clearing of clouds, the golden temple of Dominus comes into view. I've never set foot inside because I'm not allowed to. Only the seven gods and Dominus himself are allowed, so I will remain at the top steps while Valec receives his orders for the day.

He reaches the foot of the stairwell when two of his fellow god-brothers point two piercing metal objects at his throat. I've never seen an object sharper than a knife. Maybe it's some form of gardening tool I've never heard of before? No, that's not it; this instrument, whatever it may be called, screams danger.

"What is happening? Brothers, what are those instruments you carry?" Valec looks at both angels, eyes wide, a slight hint of fear in his voice.

"As if you didn't already know, brother," one of them says. He taps the tip of his pointed instrument with the pad of his thumb. "Do you know what this instrument is called?" he asks my brother, who shakes his head no. "It's called a spear. I've heard they are instruments of great use to traitors and liars." This cannot be good.

"Dominus wishes to speak with you," says the other god at his side. They pull back their spears, allowing Valec access to ascend the temple steps. I move behind him, stopping at the temple entrance.

There at the center of the sanctuary, just past the golden columns, sits Dominus upon his gold-encrusted throne, staff in hand. At his side stands another of Dominus's chosen gods, Esveld. He has the appearance every mortal assumes of an angel, from his snowy white hair to his light skin, and clear eyes. Everything about him is ethereal.

"I am disappointed in you, Valec." Dominus's eyes hold sorrow. What in Caelesti is happening? "You sinned upon my person and my people. Disgraced this holy land and the pureness of the mortal realm as well. By taking it upon yourself to create weapons of mass destruction and opening the eyes of all humans on Einalem to a world of suffering and cruelty."

"My Lord, I have done no such thing—" Valec tries to defend himself.

"Do not lie in my temple." His voice rises with power and authority. A voice Valec cannot go up against. "I was tricked by your innocence. You thought it clever to hide as one of my own in plain sight. Today, I see the truth.

"I visited the mortal lands yesterday, shortly after your choosing ceremony, only to discover that all chaos had broken loose in the mortal land, and I was forced to intervene. That's when I saw terror in their eyes and cruelty in others for the first time."

Valec remains as calm and composed as he can, but I can tell he's hurting.

Dominus continues to speak. "Shortly after my visit to Einalem last night, I noticed my staff missing when I arrived back at the temple. I immediately called for an emergency meeting, and you did not show."

Of course, Valec didn't show up; he was visiting me at my home, which is miles away from here.

"I sent the others to retrieve you, except you were not in your home. But the others did find something unexpected. A loose floorboard, at the foot of your bed. Baffled and concerned as they were, they removed it, and lo and behold, they discovered a latch that led to a secret room. Though it wasn't just any room it held an arsenal of weapons. To their surprise, there lay my staff. Magic flowed through it, as if it had been used by someone other than me, your angelic essence clinging in the air like sulfur.

"That's when it all made sense, The humans are no longer living in harmony, but through a shadow of despair and hatred, and it is all because of you."

"Dominus, I would never do such a thing—"

"Silence," Dominus cuts Valec off. "You wished so desperately to claim power, but I am your superior. You answer to me; I am he who created you." The Lord laces his words with anger, but his sadness overthrows him. "My disappointment is palpable. In all one hundred years of existence in this land and the mortal realm, we have lived in prosperity, and you have brought forward sin.

"Now." Dominus stands, and the rest of the angels move to stand at his side, joining Esveld. "Since you so desperately want to reign in Einalem, teach them warfare, hate and malice, show them truths that bring forth lies. And allow for their souls to waste before entering my lands, then justice must be served accordingly."

In that instant I notice something off: Dominus's eyes have a glassy sheen to them. Almost as if he is in a trance of sorts. From where I stand, I can tell Valec notices it as well, from the way he lets out a slight gasp. From the corner of my eye, I catch Esveld's smirk, and that's when I know he's the one who caused this. He's the traitor, not my brother.

In one swift movement, Dominus raises his staff in the air. "Valec, my second-in-command. Your actions have been heavily acknowledged and for that I hereby banish you from Caelesti."

I cannot tell if my brother's breathing. I sure am not.

"Since you want nothing more than to corrupt my people, so it shall be. You will rule in a land of your own making. And upon the seven deadly sins you will uphold your title. You will stand by those who seek corruption as you do. Any mortal who disagrees with my ideology will now answer to you in their second life.

"May your punishment serve as a reminder of your wickedness for all of eternity." The staff comes down, hitting the marble floor, magic pouring from it, and that's when I notice the clouds parting, creating a gap in the land. Before I know it Valec is shoved through.

I don't have enough time to register what has happened, not when I suddenly feel the floor beneath me vanish too.

I go down as well.

We are now both freefalling. Beside me, I hear a cry of pain. "Julius!"

I snap my head to the side, witnessing the most horrid thing I've ever seen in my life. My brother, yelling, as a trail of feathers fall onto my face. The wind blows them in my direction. I manage to grab one, and with one look, I know who they belong to. Valec's scream gets even louder as I watch in horror as his now barren wings burn at his back, and then crumble as if they are made of nothing more than paper.

The clouds continue to pass us by and all the beauty of Caelesti vanishes as we plummet further down. Like a blur, our home is out of sight. As we're descending, we both see it: the mortal land, Einalem.

Like something out of a storybook, we stare in shock as a new land takes shape. Deep below the caverns of Einalem. That's where we land.

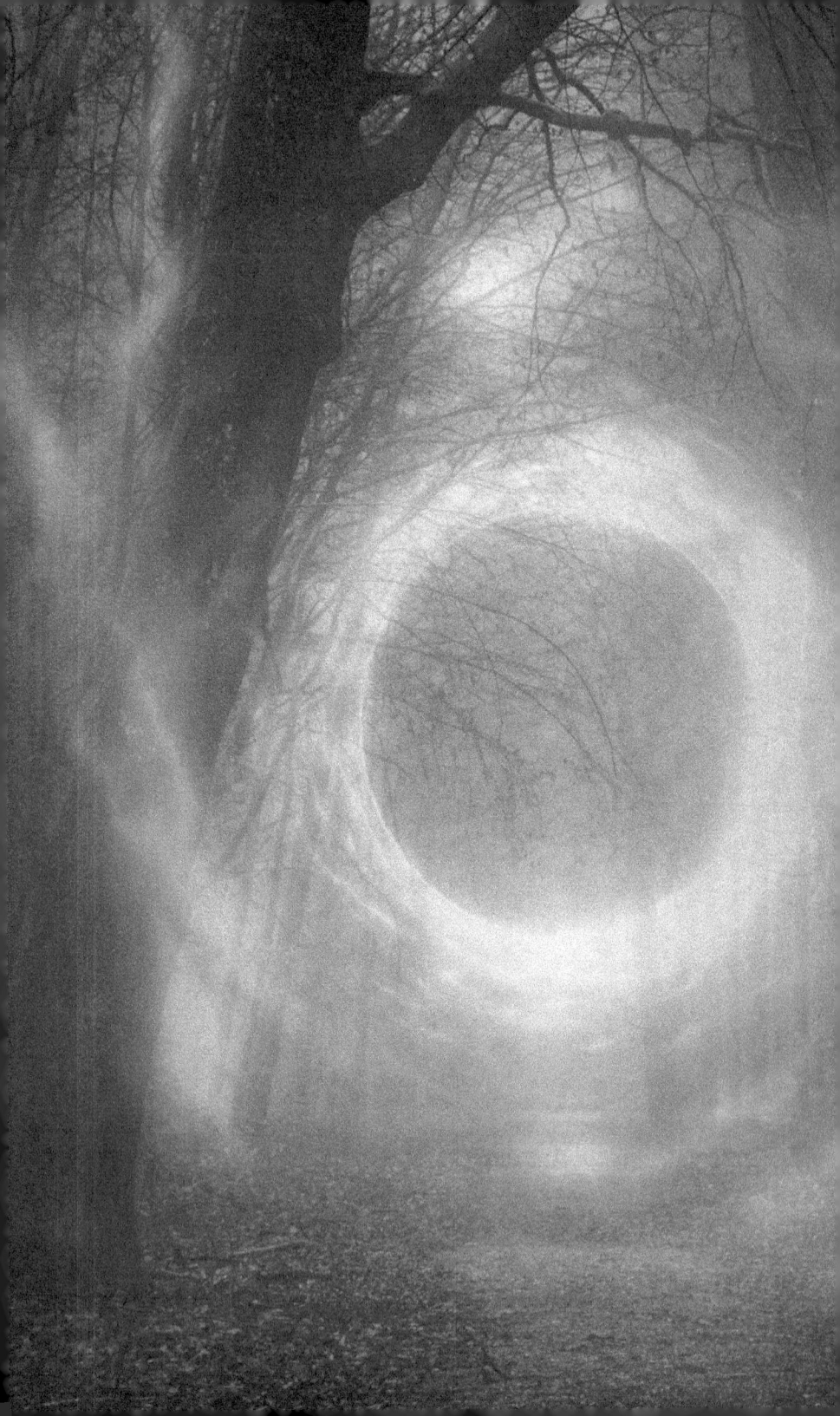

CHAPTER 4
THE CHILD

Year 26: After the Fall

JULIUS

I'm not the same man I once was eleven years ago, and neither is my brother. That night when Valec went to Einalem seeking the high priest and priestess, he didn't return the same. He looked like my brother, but I knew in an instant that he was no longer the Valec I cared for. Something changed in him, like a cloud of darkness had settled over him. For the first time there was evil in his heart, and since then I have feared I may never get him back.

I still love my brother deeply, but our relationship will never be as it once was. I now treat him from afar, as one would a stranger or an enemy. It's the only way I am able to keep some peace of mind, despite the new role in my life: Shade Hunter of Inferis.

Valec was not the only thing that changed that day, as the land of Inferis did too. We hadn't noticed anything amiss at first. It wasn't until one afternoon, when I was tending my garden, that

I saw it. A creature the size of a large dog, its body full of inky black scales that seemed to ooze liquid as it walked on all fours. And it wasn't alone. We called them shades, and from that day on, Valec tasked me with hunting them down. That's how I got my new job.

Soon after Valec demanded a better home for himself, and thus construction began on the mansion. Right where our old stone house used to be now resides a tall structure painted black as night. Glass windows adorn it from top to bottom. That is where we live now, amongst riches— us and a few others who have taken the liberty of working for him.

It's already seven in the evening when I cross to Einalem, the same time I have crossed twice a week for the past eleven years. I never know what part of Einalem the veil will take me to. It's a different exit every time. But if I concentrate enough, sometimes the veil leads me where I wish to go. With the banishment placed on Valec by the priestess all those years ago, he cannot set foot outside of Inferis. Thus, I was left with the task of finding this so-called cursed child, who is meant to free us all.

I cross through the small pine forest in a hurry. I know this forest. It's close to Eremat, the capital of Einalem. I've looked there in the past, but many more children have been born since then.

I stop by the nearest stables and ask the stable hand to borrow a horse for the night. I can make the trip on foot, but it will take me longer and I need to use the moon to my advantage in order to cover more ground. After handing the man a few coins and promising to have the horse back to him before midnight, I quickly pick up my pace, continuing the journey ahead.

I reach the neighboring town of Imar in no time. Dismounting, I walk through with the horse at my side. It may be night time, but the town is quite alive. Too early for anyone to retire to bed. I pass by a section of wooden houses and continue through the cobblestone pathway. I notice the people dancing on the sidewalks, couples kissing in dark corners, others coming and going through taverns and many other establishments. Kids play ball in the streets as their parents keep a close eye on them. I keep walking at an average pace. No one bats an eye at my presence. Good; the last thing I need is for someone to be suspicious of me.

I make my way further into the town, reaching the more lavish homes. Each one is constructed out of sparkling rock. The structure of these homes is what separates Eremat from the rest of the smaller towns. Every building here is made of pure stone, giving Eremat its grander look.

Guess it's time to start my usual routine. I knock on the first door I spot.

A woman answers the door. "Good evening, ma'am, my name is Sir Jules." I use my nickname given to me by my brother. "I am a soldier from the Einalem armies."

Lucky for me, this is customary of Einalem soldiers. Some soldiers are meant to knock from door to door every now and then, asking the parents of young children if they'd like to enlist to be a part of the land's armies. "And on behalf of the land of Einalem, I would like to know if you have any children who would be interested in joining our ranks."

The woman smiles lightly. "Sorry, sir, but it's just me and my husband. Well, for now at least." She pats her stomach lightly.

Oh, she's pregnant. "Not a problem, ma'am. Have a good night and congratulations."

"Thank you," she says kindly.

I repeat the same process at the rest of the houses within the area. No luck. I check my pocket watch for the hour. It's nearing ten at night—two hours left. I near the tree under which I left my borrowed horse before I started walking house to house. And to my surprise I find a little girl there. She's petting him from atop the tree. "Good horsey," I hear her say.

I approach her carefully. I don't wish to frighten her. She looks straight ahead, catching my presence.

"I see you've met my horse," I say as a way of greeting. She nods and I watch as she slowly descends from the tree, keeping a sharp eye on her in case she slips. Like a cat she lands with grace.

"I like all animals," she says, her light eyes shining. Due to the lack of light, I can't exactly make out the color; blue or maybe green? She has wavy brown hair that cascades down her back and looks about ten years old in her light violet dress.

"Oh, really." I crouch down so that she doesn't feel intimidated by my height. "Which is your favorite?"

She gives this good thought. "Dogs," she blurts out.

"I like dogs too." A few years ago on one of my outings, I came across a white Siberian Husky and brought him to Inferis after Soela told me that animals are the only beings able to cross between worlds. Because according to her, animals have no souls; thus, they cannot be trapped within the plane of the living or the dead. Something I knew nothing about. I named him Saint, and since then he has brought me a sense of calm after a hard day's work. "I actually have one," I tell her.

"What color?" she asks.

"White."

"Like a snowball." She giggles.

"Yes, much like a snowball." I laugh.

"Is it a boy or a girl?"

"A boy; his name is Saint," I tell her.

"That's a pretty name." She stares at me in wonderment.

"It is." From afar I hear the voice of a man and woman.

"Evalina, Evalina," they call.

I notice how the girl's expression falls. "I thought they'd stay longer at their friends' house," she admits.

I'm about to ask her who she's speaking of, but as the couple nears, I realize she is the spitting image of the two combined. They must be her parents.

"There you are," her father says, both parents stopping short when they notice my presence. I quickly stand, not wanting to frighten them. It already looks bad enough—a stranger speaking with their little girl. I don't want them to assume I'm some kind of predator.

I move away from the girl, and she happily walks to her parents. "Mom, dad, did you see his horse?" She points to the mare behind me.

"Yes." The mother smiles. Her father continues to stare at me with the same light eyes as his daughter. I should introduce myself.

"Good evening, my apologies. I'm Jules."

"A soldier from the armies," the man says, now noticing my uniform, courtesy of the Inferis seamstress. "My respects to you." The man brings a fist to his heart. "Thank you for your service."

You wouldn't be thanking me if you knew the truth, I say to myself.

"It's an honor." I stare down at the girl who continues to look up at me. "Your daughter seems to have taken a keen interest in my horse."

They both laugh.

"Yes, she has quite the affinity for animals," her father answers. "Also has the bad habit of disappearing when we least expect it."

The girl merely shrugs. "It gets boring whenever you visit the neighbors. They're boring."

Her mother caresses the back of her head. "They have kids your age you can play with."

"Yeah, but they're no fun. They're always playing ball in the streets. They don't read or climb trees; they don't like to garden or do anything I like to do," she complains to her mother. "That's why I left."

"We know, Evalina." Her father pats her on the head. *Evalina.* That's a pretty name. "And you are allowed to have fun as long as you don't go too far away from town. We don't want you getting lost or worse, that you end up kidnapped. Today, you were lucky a soldier found you."

"I know, Dad." Evalina rolls her eyes. "I know the rules."

"Good, now come on. We should get home. It was nice to meet you, Jules. I'm Evan, by the way. And this is my wife, Lina."

Evan and Lina...Evalina. They combined both their names to form their daughter's. How creative.

"Nice to meet both of you." I crouch down once again. "It was nice to meet you, Evalina." Being this close I get a better look at her eyes. They *are* blue, cerulean blue to be exact. I've never seen anyone with such a rich iris color before.

"Nice to meet you, Jules." She extends her hand out to me, and I take it. The moment I do a shockwave hits me. My palm suddenly turns hot. The girl doesn't notice a thing; she all but shakes it before I remove my own.

No, this can't be. She moves away, back to her parents as they return once again to town. I remain frozen, feet planted on the ground, for several minutes. Until I mount my horse and race back to the veil.

I never would have thought that poor young girl could be the Devil's Curse.

A week has passed, and though my search has finally ended— and all I must do now is keep an eye on the girl, make sure no harm comes to her until she is of age—I have Valec constantly breathing down my neck. He was overjoyed the night I told him I found the girl, and ever since then he has been extra demanding. With a need to escape I find myself heading to a local tavern in Zelev, a merchant town east of Imar. One I'm all too familiar with. It was in this very tavern where I took my first lover a few years ago.

Some of the men recognize me and extend their hands out in greeting, while others pat me on the back. The advantage of this tavern is that it's also an inn. Perfect for those of us looking to have a good time. The smoky taste in the air is always a fair welcoming, especially since their smoked meats are a must-try.

I order the usual: their homestyle beer and a helping of potatoes and boar meat. As I wait, I turn my attention to the live music. They're a local band if I'm not mistaken. And they're good. I'm not much for music like Valec is, but it's enjoyable. The upbeat tempo has a few people dancing around near the stage. There's a woman swaying her hips from side to side. Her eyes land on me, skimming over my frame from head to toe.

My order arrives and I eat without taking my eyes off her. She has a great figure, wide hips, and full breasts. Her hair is the color of rubies, and it falls down to her waist. She's beautiful and quite tempting, I'll give her that. I finish up my meal only to find her pointing at me with her index finger, curling it to beckon me over. I stand, her own swaying my motivation to walk up to her.

"Hi, handsome," she whispers in my ear once I reach her. "You looking to have fun tonight?" She winks at me

Hell yes. "Whatever you want. Name it," I respond.

"A submissive," she coos. "Gotta say that's a first for me." She inches closer, till our lips are only a breath apart.

"Sweetheart," I inch closer, "I never said I was submissive." And then I claim her mouth. She gasps, not having expected my sudden attack. She tastes of cheap beer and vanilla. It's a rather intoxicating mix. I part her lips with my tongue, and she happily obliges. Our tongues find each other, playing their own game of cat and mouse. I gently bite her lip and she loses herself in a breathy moan.

"It's true," a very loud man shouts through the room. "I saw them last night. Soldiers, near my home. They were looking for her."

"Find who?" someone else says from the crowd. The music has since died down. Everyone seems to want to listen in on the conversation.

"Who do you think? The Devil's Curse." Those words are enough to halt my actions. The woman notices I've stopped kissing her and opens her eyes. I step away from her. "The kid who's meant to be the savior of Inferis and the damnation of us all. Dominus, save our souls." Everyone looks at him as if he's deranged. "Does no one remember the story?"

"We all know the story. Thought I choose to believe it is an old folk tale," someone else answers.

"Fool. It's all a matter of time until someone finds the kid."

It's not the first time I've heard people whisper about the soldiers working for the priest and priestess. I've come across them a few times on my own excursions. Though now that I've found the girl I need to know if the soldiers are searching close to where she lives.

I walk closer to the bearded man who first spoke. "Where are they searching?" I ask him and all eyes land on me.

"Not sure," he answers. "Though some people say they saw some soldiers lurking by Eremat a few days ago." *Fuck, that's not good.* "Who knows how long until they search all of Einalem, but hopefully they find and kill the child before it comes of age." Some people gasp at his brashness.

"What?" He defends himself. "If that kid frees Lucifer, then we are done for. All of Inferis will reign upon us. Is that what you all want?" He gestures to everyone in the room.

Not caring what anyone else has to say, I toss a few coins on the counter to pay my tab and run out the front door.

I race through the streets of Eremat and knock on the first few doors, trying to guess where Evalina's house might be based on that night. I ask for Evan and Lina. No one answers. I knock on a few more doors; no luck either. I find a solitary home near the end of the road and knock, hoping this might be the one.

Evan answers the door. "Jules?" *Thank Dominus.* I'm glad he remembers me. Seeing my distressed state, he asks, "Is something wrong?"

"I need to speak with you and your wife. It's an urgent matter." He sees my worried expression and holds the door open for me to pass through. Their home is inviting. Light-colored walls and modern furniture surround an elegant fireplace. I remain by the entrance while Evan goes to retrieve his wife.

"Jules." She's just as surprised to see me as her husband was. "We must keep our voices down, Evalina is asleep."

"Of course." I had forgotten it's almost twelve, and I need to hurry. Evan makes a gesture for me to sit. I take my place on one of the single recliners while they sit on a loveseat beside one another. I take a deep breath. "This might sound odd, but I need for all of you to pack your bags and move out." If my arrival did not startle them, this surely does.

"Why on Einalem would we do that?" Lina asks.

"I know you probably have no reason to trust me. We only met a week ago, but I came here to warn you. You and your daughter are in danger. It's not safe to remain here in the capital."

"Is a war starting?" Evan asks.

"Something like that," I answer. "Look, I know I'm not here on official military orders." Considering my lack of uniform. "But that's only because I am not yet allowed to issue such warnings." Let the lies begin. "However, I do not wish to wait until my superiors give the orders to announce the evacuations. I rather you leave now. Before chaos ensues."

"If that's the case, shouldn't you be warning the rest of the citizens?" Lina makes a good argument.

"I'm working on it. Starting with all family units with children."

The pair exchange a worried look. "Where would we go?" Lina turns to me.

"Up north, where it's safest. There's a village called Nairedian. Ask around for it. It's about a ninety-minute journey by horseback. Pack tonight and leave in the morning." I bring myself to my feet and look out the window. I've overstayed my visit; I need to get back to Inferis.

"Thank you," Evan says. "For warning us. I've sensed something off in the past days, given all the soldiers I've seen around here recently."

So they are aware of their presence. Good. That's more than enough for them to believe me.

"You're welcome," I say as my final farewell before exiting their residence.

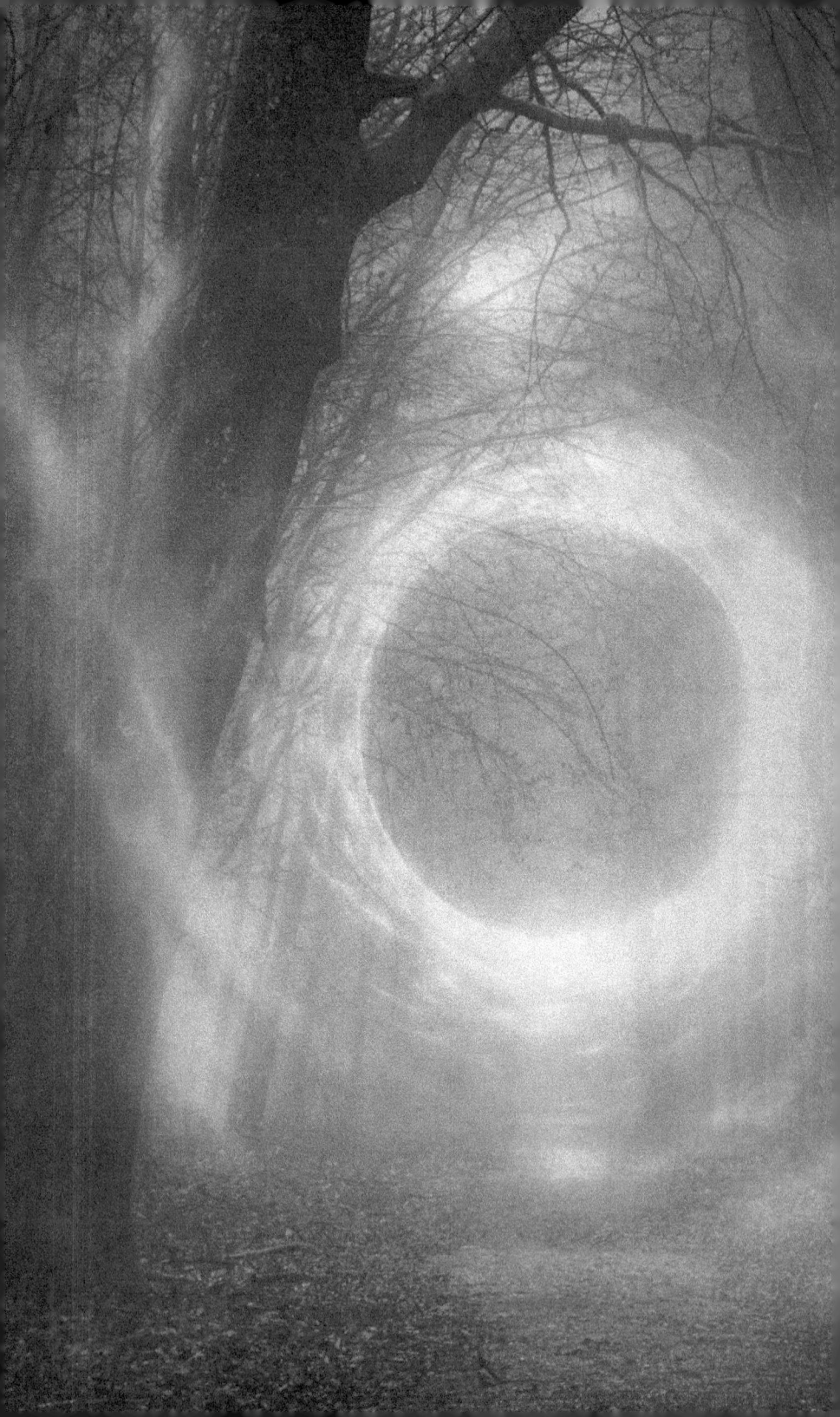

CHAPTER 5
MYSTERY MAN

Year 35: After the Fall

EVALINA

The wind rustles through the darkness. It's one of those full moon nights, where the wind wreaks chaos as if a storm's approaching. I can't sleep. The night sky is too bright and the whooshing air makes an eerie screeching sound that puts ghosts to shame. Though that's not the reason I am awake.

It's the wave of heat emanating from my body. It's never a fever; I know the difference by now. This is something else entirely. My body doesn't ache, it's simply hot to the touch. It started happening a few months, after my nineteenth birthday. At first I wanted to tell my parents, yet some gut feeling tugged me against it. So, I still have not told them.

I stand at my bedside window staring out into the forest far ahead. I can practically see through the trees, given how bright the moon is tonight. It's actually red. How interesting—a blood moon.

The leaves stir between the trees and that's when I'm certain my eyes are deceiving me. I wipe at them with my shirt sleeves. It does little to help; he's still standing there. This is absurd. *Who is that?*

My rational side tells me I should wake my parents and alert them to the man lurking in the forest. Though my irrational side tells me I should investigate for myself. Of course, I never listen to my rational side. That's why I quickly unlatch my window, opening it as soundlessly as I can. My parents' chambers are right next to mine. Any noise on my part and they'll be up in seconds.

The window springs open as I lift it up. Before climbing out I retreat back to my dresser and grab a pair of boots and a coat to put on. Prancing around in my night attire is not exactly ideal, even with my mysterious body heat. Without further thought I march over and climb onto my windowsill. The descent is nothing, considering we live in a one-story home.

Landing gracefully on both feet, I spring for the woods. I turn in circles, searching for the mysterious man. But he's gone. He was right here. I saw him. A leaf crunches behind me and I nearly scream when a warm hand presses on my mouth from behind. Maybe I did make a mistake by venturing outside in the late hours of the night.

He spins me around so fast that once we're face to face, I can't help the dilation of my pupils. He's...well, he's too hot to be a kidnapper or murderer. I mean, he's quite tall, for one, and leaning against him like this, I can feel all the hard muscles of his chest. There may not be that much illumination out here, but the blood moon allows me to see just fine.

"You shouldn't be out here," he says, keeping his hand on my mouth. He hasn't broken eye contact for a single second. And simply staring into his eyes is giving me a headache. They're blue, but not like mine. His are lighter, almost gray. I know I should be feeling some sort of panic right now; instead, I feel quite the opposite. Plus, if this man wants to kill me wouldn't he have done it by now?

We both hear it when a twig snaps behind us. "Shit," he says against my ear. "I need you to remain quiet and do as I say," he whispers.

I nod.

He removes his hand from my mouth. "Or else neither of us will make it out of here alive." So, I am right. He isn't trying to kill me.

"Get closer to me," he says. *Closer.* I'm already as close as I can get. Footsteps sound nearer. "Get on me."

"Excuse me?" I ask.

"Wrap your legs around my waist."

What? He doesn't wait for me to do it. The man lifts me up, tucking my legs firmly around his back and guiding my hands to his neck. My arms follow his request by lacing behind his head. He presses a firm hand behind me. Applying just enough pressure to get me to lower my head to his chest.

"Do not make a sound."

"I won't," I promise this man I don't even know.

"Good." We wait, both of us flushed together. The footsteps near and I lift my head slightly, getting a look at black robes approaching us. The man forces my head down.

"Do not look," he hisses. We remain flush together until the robed figures are long gone.

He keeps me close to him for a little while longer, looking in all directions. "I think we're good," he says.

"Who were they?" I ask. The man lets go of me.

"People you shouldn't be caught up with. I'm sorry for touching you like that."

"It's fine. No hard feelings. Thanks, I guess. For saving me." I present him with my hand. "I'm Evalina, by the way."

He shakes my hand eagerly. "I'm Julian."

"Nice to meet you, Julian. You know"—I place my chin on my fist— "you look quite familiar. Have we met before?"

"Not that I know of. Believe me, I would remember if we did." He takes me in from head to toe. "Anyway, it's quite late. I best be heading home." He shoves his hands into his pants pockets, taking a breath of air as he says, "It was nice meeting you, Evalina." Julian turns around.

"Are you from nearby?" I ask quickly.

"A little far out of town," he answers, no longer facing me.

I notice something small and leather-bound peeking out of his back pocket. "Is that a book?" I inquire.

He pivots, facing me once again, and pulls out the thin binding of pages from his pocket. I was right. "It is. Do you read?" he asks.

"I do. I actually own a bookshop here in town. Well, it belongs to my parents, but I'll be inheriting it once I turn twenty-one in two years." He suddenly blanches and I don't know what to make of it, but he seems to make a quick recovery. "Feel free to visit if you'd like. I work there most days and nights."

He smiles. "Tell you what. You keep this." He hands me the small book. "That way I'll have a reason to return for it. You can read it if you'd like."

"It's a deal." We shake hands one last time and then we're both on the move.

I race back to my home and climb back into my bedroom. I peek through the window again just in case Julian is still around. But when I look to the forest all I see is the outline of trees.

It's one of those tiring days where I go from spending a long morning in university classes to working the rest of the day at my parents' bookshop. I'm not complaining, though. I love being surrounded by books all day. It brings me comfort.

I graduated from the final grade at school almost three years ago. Ever since then I've been working at the bookshop as a part-time employee. I am now a Literature student at my local university. It's small and a little outside our village, but I am still able to get there on foot. It's a twenty-minute walk, though, and if I want to make it on time, I have to wake up early every day.

I'm finishing up with a customer at the register when the front door jingles with its familiar chime. "Good evening, welcome to Books N Baubles—" The rest of the words die on my tongue as I notice a tall frame standing in the doorway, dressed head to toe in a gray uniform.

It's Julian. My eyes widen.

I bid farewell to my usual customer and wait for him to leave. He bypasses Julian and says a quick "Good evening" before exiting. Once the bells jingle, I finally move away from the counter.

"You came." I can't believe he actually came. It's been two nights since our meeting in the forest.

"I said I would, didn't I? Plus, I also came to get my book." He smiles. His book: I completely forgot.

"I don't have it with me," I confess. "It's at my house."

"Don't worry about it. You can keep it if you'd like," he offers. "Did you like it?"

I move a little closer to him so that we aren't speaking from such a far distance.

"I did," I confess. "It wasn't what I expected, though."

He raises an eyebrow. "What did you expect?"

"I don't know, something more action-packed. I don't know any men who like to read romance."

"You didn't until now." He beams.

"There's a first time for everything, I guess." I clear my throat. "So, would you like a tour of the shop?" I offer.

"I'd like that."

"Great." I walk ahead, showing off the wooden walls decorated with knickknacks. It's a small but homey space. The smell of old book pages clings to you from the moment you set foot inside.

I start the tour at the back of the shop. "Here's the kids' section. Aka, my favorite section for the longest of times." Julian takes in all the cute chairs facing each other in a circle. "Those are new. We just brought them to do monthly storytime with the children of the neighborhood. I usually read to them."

"That's nice of you."

I turn my attention from the chairs and face Julian, who quickly averts his gaze.

Playing it cool and not wanting to bring up the incident in the forest just yet, I keep walking. "Moving on, this way." I guide him through the neat rows of oak bookcases. We pause at the center of the shop. "This is the young adult section, my second favorite section." He takes in all the shelves and the brightly colored books lining them.

"Come, we have one last stop. The adult section." We arrive back at the front of the shop. And right near the counter is the adult section. "My new favorite section," I add.

"And your favorite genre?" he asks me.

"Fantasy, always fantasy."

"Is there a particular reason why you gravitate more towards that genre?"

That's a good question; it sounds like something my university professors would ask.

"I think I can make a convincing argument on why I think fantasy is the best."

"Okay, then, shoot." He leans against one of the taller shelves, which kind of matches his height.

"Wait, give me a second to gather my thoughts." I clear my throat. "Okay, fantasy books have always called to me, because I love the feeling of being whisked away into a new world. Reading about creatures that don't exist, about people who possess magical powers, it's thrilling in the sense that you feel completely transported." I don't know if I should finish there, but I'm so passionate about the topic that I continue on as if I were giving a presentation.

"Typically, I'm a person who believes wholeheartedly in the concept of escapism. That's one of the reasons I love fantasy so much. There are no ties to my real life; it is its own complete story. If I'm having a bad day, I usually I don't feel inclined to read about a protagonist who's going through a similar situation. I want to read something fantastical and unique. To travel to a place that I can't actually go to in my real life. Because why read a book set where I live, or a place I have gone to and know, when I could read about fictional lands and people that have so many different things to offer? That's why I love the fantasy genre so much."

Julian begins to clap, and I can't help but giggle a little. "More people should answer questions like that. With deep meaning."

I shrug. "Well, what can I say? I'm an aficionado." I'm quite shocked that he enjoyed my monologue.

"I can see that."

"Did you like the tour?" I say, taking my post behind the register.

"I did."

"Would you like to purchase a book, by any chance?" I inquire.

"I would love to, but first I need to speak with you."

Guess the time has finally come.

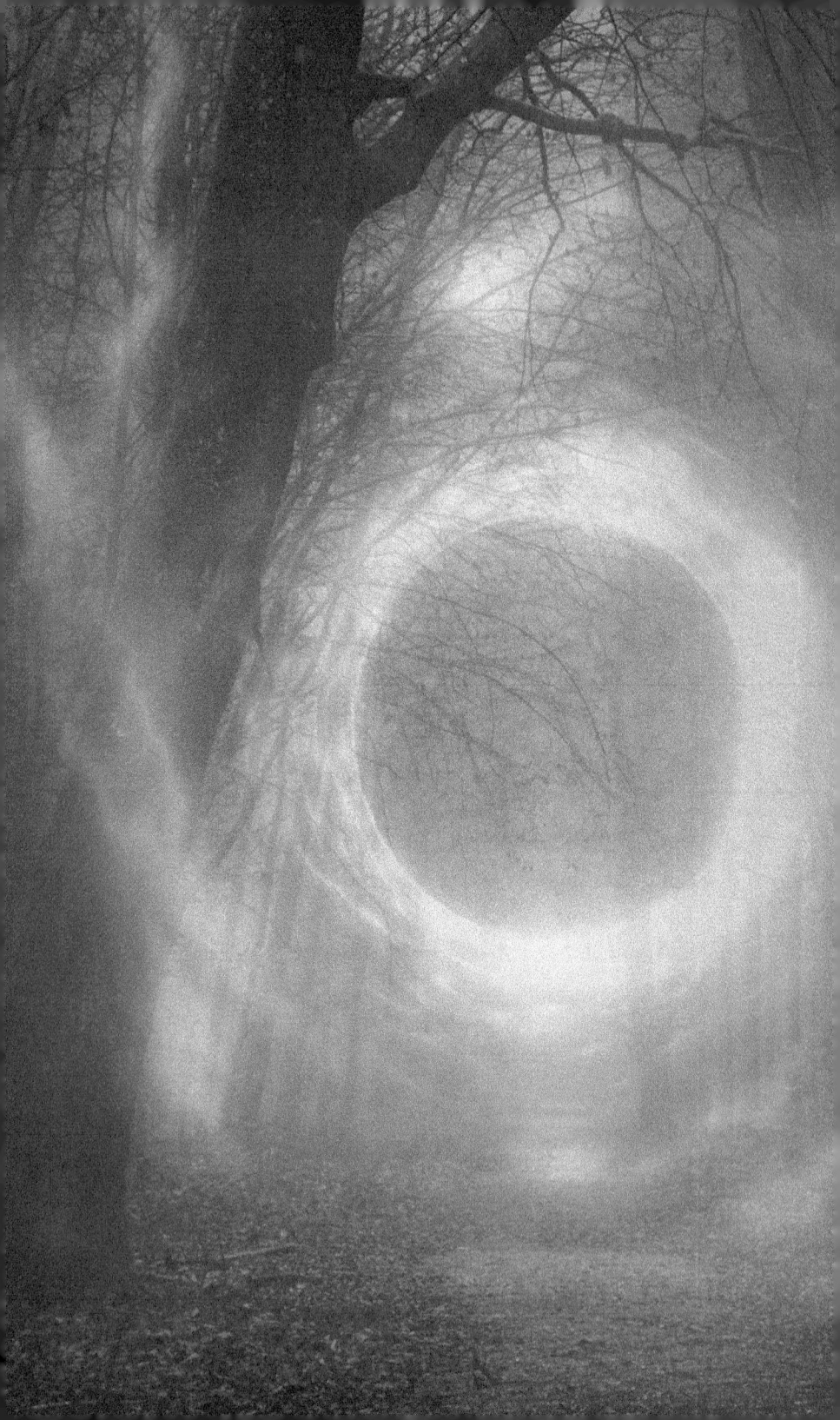

CHAPTER 6
TELLING LIES

JULIUS

"Alright, let me close the shop," Evalina says. I help her pull down all the curtains, and once the door is locked and the "closed" sign is in place, she walks us back to the children's section. "It's either this or the floor," she informs me.

I let out a loud chuckle. "This will be fine." I try my best to be casual as I attempt to sit on the small chairs. Thank goodness they are the cushiony kind, because I end up needing two and I must look ridiculous all the same.

She covers her mouth with her hand, suppressing a laugh at my expense.

"You find my current state amusing, don't you?" I raise an eyebrow.

"Very much. I've never had such a large man sit in the kids' section before."

"Guess there's a first for everything." I accommodate myself on the seats to the best of my ability. With no trouble at all, Evalina sits beside me.

I begin by saying, "I'm sorry about the other night. I can imagine you must have been frightened."

"I was for a second, but then I wasn't." Her expression says more than her words convey but I'm not about to ask her to elaborate on the matter. "May I ask why you were out creeping in the woods?"

"I could ask you that same question," I tell her.

"I asked first." She casually leans back on her seat.

"Sometimes when my job gets too stressful, I like to take walks at night to clear my head."

She adjusts herself better on the chair, picking up her loose waves and tossing them behind the seat. "What do you work in?"

"I'm a soldier for the Einalem Army." The lie rolls easily off my tongue, considering I've said it so many times by now.

"I imagined, considering your uniform." She motions to my attire. "That's no easy job. I bet it can get exhausting from time to time."

"Yeah, it can. But now it's your turn. What were you doing in the forest in the middle of the night?"

"I couldn't sleep and then I saw you through the window—"

"So, you went out to investigate," I interrupt her.

"Yes, I was curious."

"About what?" I probe her for more information.

She chooses her words carefully and I happily wait to see what she's going to say next. "You can imagine I was surprised to see an extremely handsome man standing in the woods near my home. I think I did what any impulsive young adult would do."

That was exactly the answer I was hoping for. "So, you think I'm extremely handsome, good to know." She picks up a cushion and places it over her face, but then quickly sets it down.

"You know what? I'm not going to be embarrassed about it. I said what I said, and I don't regret it." That's bold of her.

"Are there no men around here that look like me?" I wonder.

"Not like you. You put other men to shame."

"Guess that way I'll scare them off."

"Please don't. I'd hate to be seen with you to only lose the chance of finding love," she jokes.

"You don't have a boyfriend?" I find myself asking.

"No." She shakes her head. "No one. It's just me, myself, and my books." She waves at all the bookcases in front of us.

"Interesting." I didn't mean to say that out loud.

"My lack of a love life is interesting to you?" She raises a brow at me.

I try to defend myself. "I didn't mean it like that."

"Then how did you mean it—you know what? Don't answer that." She begins to wiggle her feet. "No one has caught my eye yet." I notice the exact moment her eyes veer from my own to my mouth, and then away. Or maybe I imagined it.

"Evalina." I shift a bit in my seat. "I think we should address the elephant in the room."

"Yeah," she says, breaking from her trance. "Go ahead." She straightens herself in the chair, now facing me again.

"I told you there were dangerous people out there in the woods and then placed you in a compromising position."

"Yes, I remember. I saw black robes. Who were those people?"

"Black nuns, and they enjoy stalking the nights. Doing ceremonies in honor of Lucifer. They are not a group you should be seen by, especially if you aren't devoted to the Circle of Impure."

"So, you were trying to hide me?"

"Yes. Getting close to you in that way, well, they wouldn't have batted an eye at us. They would have only seen a man and his lover."

Not true. They passed us by because my scent, the scent of Inferis, is a perfect mask to cover Evalina's. With people both in the Order of Divine and the Circle of Impure on the lookout for her, I need to be more vigilant. Especially if she's started showing signs of her power. Hellfire—that's what runs through her veins, and what she will be able to manifest upon the age of twenty-one. Both churches are more than eager to obtain her, each for their own reasons.

The Order of Divine, along with the priest and priestess, will most likely kill her if they get their hands on her. While the Circle of Impure will make her a part of some ritual in order to get her to my brother. Both options end with her death.

"Interesting," she ponders aloud, leading me away from my wandering thoughts. "And how old is this girl's lover?" she teases.

"Thirty," I answer. Now this is the first truth I've told her. Well, half-truth, at least. Though I may be 135 years old, I will always look thirty.

"I'm nineteen, by the way. Well, I'll be turning twenty soon, in just a few weeks. I'll be celebrating here at the shop. My parents will be closing down early. You can come if you'd like. I'll let you know the exact date once I have it." She stands and waits for me to do the same.

I cannot believe she invited me to her birthday party, after I just told her my age. Does that not bother her?

"I'll be there," I tell her, praying for a blood moon on the night of her party.

"Perfect." We make our way back to the front of the shop. "Thanks, for protecting me," she adds. "And for coming today. As I said before, my dating life has not been great and the very few interactions I've had with guys never work out well. I've been stood up a few times."

Whoever those jerks are, I hope they get what's coming to them.

"No problem." We both walk to the exit. Evalina turns off the lights before we step out into the chilly night air. We mostly walk in silence until we reach her house.

"Well, this is my place." She motions to the one-story

wooden cabin we've arrived at. It's cute and homey, with a small porch and a few potted plants adorning the entrance. "Good night, Julian," she says.

"Good night, Evalina." I wave once she's reached the front steps of her porch.

"You know, you forgot to buy a book," she reminds me.

I chuckle. "Remind me to do so the next time we meet."

"I won't forget." She waves and then turns to unlock her front door, glancing one last time at me before she disappears into her house.

The following morning, I prepare myself for yet another day of shade hunting. I need to speak to Valec, but he's busy entertaining his council. I pass by the four shaded figures in the hallway, trying my best not to even glance in their direction. The Wicked Four. They are the quartet to be feared. I may act as if their presence does not bother me, but in truth, it downright unsettles me.

I'm not the only one, though. Many staff members flinch when they're around, and some even hide if they have the time. Soela being one of them. Lucky for her she's too busy running the mansion, keeping an eye on the staff, and making sure they get every task done to notice the Wicked Four this time.

A year after Valec ignited the curse, these four individuals walked into Inferis. They had spent most of their mortal lives serving in the name of the Circle of Impure. Serving in the Devil's name, hoping to someday be of assistance to the real man himself. They got their wish, and Valec got a security and execution team at his beck and call. Each member of the Wicked Four is terrible in their own way. Though they each share one specific talent: exceling in the art of torture.

I make a quick stop by the training room to retrieve my sword. The familiar, black-painted walls greet me with various weapons attached and displayed. Ranging from all manner of knives, swords, throwing stars, daggers, axes—truly any weapon imaginable. They hang like paintings, decorating the wall with deadly beauty.

I'm startled by the sound of the entrance door opening. Lo and behold, there stands Valec in his traditional ebony tunic, his sparkling gold crown resting atop his head. Guess his last meeting was cut short.

He approaches me, scanning my appearance. "Getting ready for work?" he says with his usual blank expression.

"Yes. How did the meetings go?" I casually inquire, trying to seem interested in the matter.

"Uneventful. As can be expected." That's all the information I'll be getting from him. "Let us cut the pleasantries, Julius. I need to know if you are fulfilling your duties to me as promised."

I wish I knew exactly what he's speaking of. As if hearing my unspoken thoughts, he says, "Have you finally spoken to her?" He means Evalina.

"I have," I declare.

"And are you gaining her trust? Trust is key in order for her to return to Inferis with you on her twenty-first birthday."

"I know what my duties are, Valec," I huff, irritated. Ever since Evalina's family moved to the Nairedian village as I requested, I've been tasked with keeping an eye on her every blood moon. I've never been permitted to interact with her. Nor did I care to. Not until she was older. Those are the rules Valec set.

"Good, you cannot fail me. If you do, then I don't care if you have to drag her here kicking and screaming. As long as she's here, then all the pieces will fall into place. Understood?"

I nod.

"Perfect, then our little chat is over." He pauses, placing a hand on my shoulder. "Soon we will be free to reign hell on all those who misplaced their faith in us. They will pay, brother, every last one who pledged their allegiance to Dominus. Each one will fall." He gives my shoulder a tight squeeze before exiting the room.

I prepare to leave, strapping a sword to my back and adding a few knives to the holster at my thigh. I try to concentrate on my duties for the day, killing shades, which proves difficult when all I can think about is Evalina and how I'm deceiving her.

That afternoon, Soela and I sit together mostly in silence. I usually come to the garden alone or with my dog, Saint, but today calls for some guidance. From the very beginning Soela has always been there for me. That hasn't changed.

I stare up at the glowing wisteria trees. The garden is the only place besides the library that brings me peace within the mansion grounds. Sometimes it baffles me, how much it's grown. How many more flowers there are, ranging from every color in the rainbow. How now the seeds I'd planted years ago have sprouted into beautiful trees, some even containing fruits for our consumption.

"How is everything going?" Soela finally breaks the silence. She knows I didn't just bring her here for company.

"According to Valec everything is going as planned," I answer sincerely.

She shakes her head. "I did not ask you how things are going according to Valec. I want to know how things are going according to Jules." She uses my nickname to address me.

"I'm lying to her, Soela. How can she possibly grow to trust me?" I blurt.

"What have you told her?"

I stand so I can face her properly. "I told her that I was a soldier from the Einalem Army. I also told her my name is Julian, I—"

Soela holds up a hand. "I'm going to stop you right there. One, you have no control over what needs to happen. Why? Because the curse is already there; it was there even before she was born. What you're doing, lying to her, is the only way to soften the blow. Or would you rather tell her right now who she is and what her purpose is? I'm certain she wouldn't trust you after telling her that. Then you'd be forced to kidnap her once she's of age and bring her here. To the underworld with Lucifer and his brother..." She tsks. "I'm almost certain that won't sit well with her."

She's right.

"You'll have her full trust by the time she's twenty-one. And once she's here you can explain everything to her. It won't be easy, but it beats telling her the truth now," Soela adds.

"You make a good point," I answer truthfully. I sit back down beside her on the bench. "That solves one thing, but there's still a problem."

"And what's that?"

"She finds me attractive." The words haven't fully left my lips before Soela starts chuckling. "Stop that! It's not a joke. I'm being serious. She downright told me."

"What do you want me to say?" Soela clutches her stomach, laughter still bubbling inside her. "You're a catch, Jules. How could she not find you attractive? I mean, you literally had your body pressed against hers the night you two officially met." She makes air quotes when she says the last two words. "I'd be awestruck as well, after meeting a handsome stranger in the forest."

"Ugh," I groan.

She takes my hands in hers. "Look, there's no stopping the

fact that she's going to get hurt. The least you can do is make the lie memorable for her."

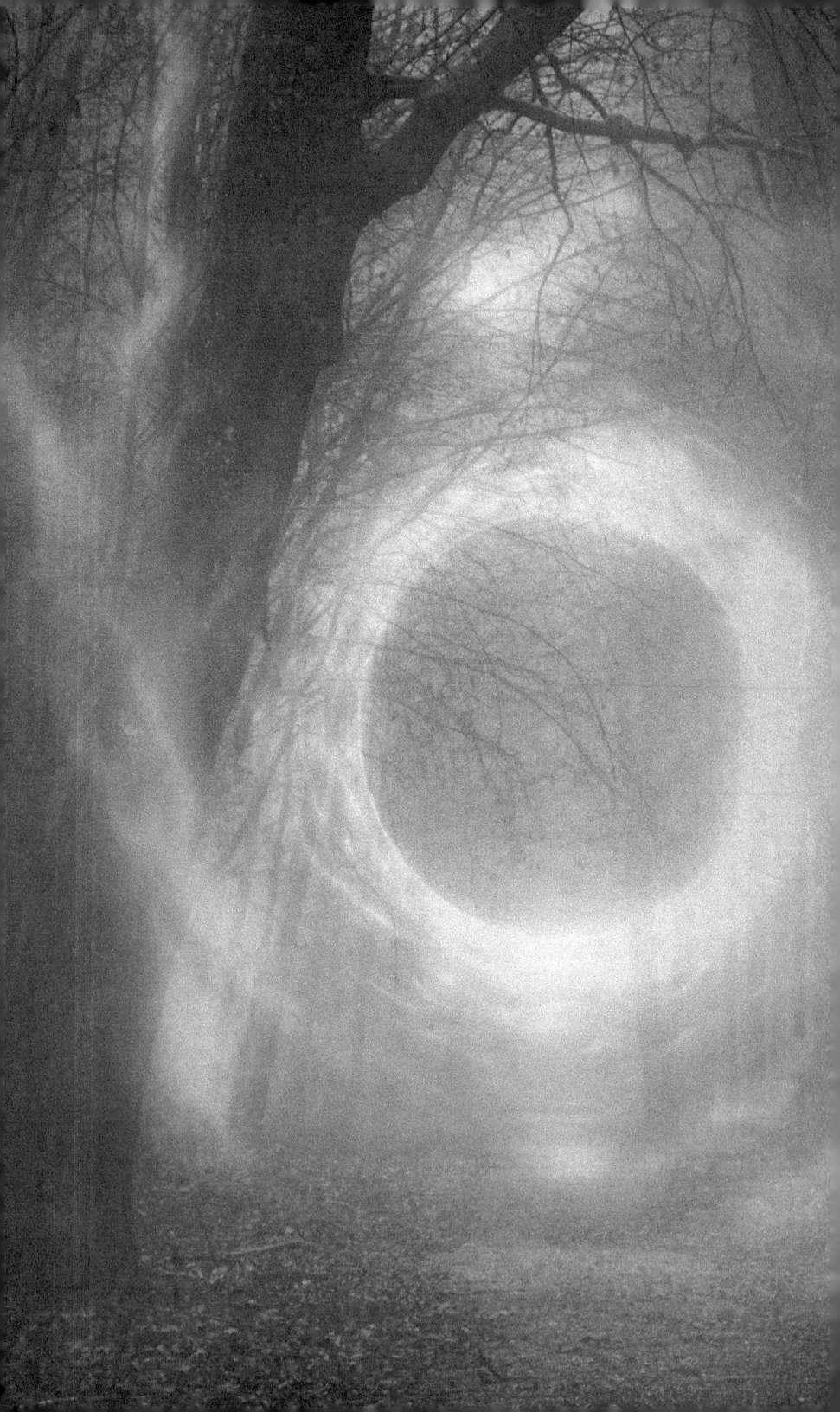

CHAPTER 7
KNOWING HIM

EVALINA

"Julian, can you fill up the watering can?" I ask him.

It's a week until my birthday. Tonight, my parents are spending time with some of their friends, so I'm doing the same. Julian surprised me a few minutes ago as I was about to start working in the garden, so now he's helping me tend to it.

I like to work at night because it means no sun and no heat—my two mortal enemies.

"Right on it." He disappears behind the house. "Here you go." He returns with the watering can full to the brim.

"Thanks." I've only just started with the first row of plants when I feel a droplet on my back. More begin to fall rapidly without warning. "Is it raining?" I ask him.

"It is."

Suddenly the droplets turn into a light drizzle. I look up to the sky. It's very hard to tell when it's going to rain in the middle of the night since there are no visible clouds to give you that information.

"I think we should go inside." As soon as Julian says that the drizzle turns into a downpour. I drop the watering can, all the water spilling to the ground.

"Let's go!" I yell and start running. Julian follows and, of course, my feet slip on the mud. I end up falling on my ass.

"Are you okay?" Julian is already at my side.

"As okay as I can be." I lift my hands up and they're coated in soil. "We're already drenched. What's the point in running away?" I throw my head back, landing on the cool ground.

"You're crazy," Julian says through the loud rush of falling water.

"Come on, Julian. Join me." I extend my hand out to him. "How long has it been since you played in the dirt?"

He lifts up an eyebrow. "Since never."

"All the more reason to do so now." I give his arm a light pull, and he's caught off-guard, nearly landing on top of me.

"Evalina," he yells the second his head hits the moist ground. His usual hazel locks are now a darker shade of brown.

"I love this new color on you." I lift a strand of his hair for him to see. I can only imagine how hard it will be to clean all this muck from my own strands, considering its length and wavy texture. A nightmare I am not looking forward to.

Julian rests on his side, leaning on an elbow and grabbing a handful of sludge that he smears on my cheeks. I gasp. "You did not!"

"Revenge," he tells me.

"Oh, if that's how it's going to be." I grab my own handful of mud and press it against his face. I didn't know how raspy, yet smooth Julian's face is. Granted, it's the first time I'm touching him like this. His eyes don't move an inch from my own as I rub the mud across his skin.

The rain magically stops. Guess it was a passing cloud.

"I have a feeling your parents might kill you if they see you like this," Julian says.

"Then we better go hose off," I announce, trying my best to stand back up without slipping. Julian places a steady hand on my back, and the cool feel of his palm makes me shiver.

I'm turning on the hose when I look back and—Julian is taking off his shirt and somehow I've forgotten how to breathe. *Dear gods, he's... Shit, I can't even explain it.*

I mean he looks exactly as a god would, mud and all. He turns and I nearly faint. Holy abs. I remember feeling those exact muscles pressed against me that night in the forest. He leans down to remove his braies as well. Suddenly, he faces me and catches my stare. I quickly raise the hose over my head, averting my gaze. I am so glad this man has no modesty.

"Here, let me." He takes the hose from my hand, raising it up to my head. The cold water hits me instantly. I untie my hair from my ponytail, letting it run free. The water falls all over me, but I guess it's useless trying to clean all this mess from my skin with my clothes still on.

As if knowing what I'm about to do, Julian turns around, taking the hose with him. I strip to my undergarments as fast as I can. I announce once I'm done undressing and he makes his way back to me, drenching me with the hose once again.

As I wash away all the dirt and mud, I catch Julian trying to look away from my body. There's no point, really. It's obvious we're both looking.

"Let me help you." Julian helps wash my back. A faint shiver passes through me when I feel his hands glide over my skin, rubbing slowly.

This brings me back to that damn forest again, to when I first felt his hands on me. I'm lost in his touch when I hear him speak, missing his words entirely. "Huh?" I ask, dazed.

He laughs. "I said, I'm done."

I move to face him, taking the garden hose from his hands. "Guess it's my turn to help you now."

He tries to object by saying the height difference will make it difficult. "I can stand on my tiptoes. Honestly, Julian," I say, letting the water fall over him, "I'm not that short."

He throws me a pointed look. "Okay, I am short, but not by a lot."

"Evalina, I'm almost an entire foot taller than you," he points out.

"No, you're not. You're, what, like five nine?"

"I'm five ten actually," he clarifies.

"Then that's not a foot; that's nine inches taller than me. Plus, I've still got a year to grow."

"Doubtful." I purposefully fling water at his face, startling him. "No fair." He wipes his eyes.

"Serves you right for making fun of my height." I copy Julian's movement, holding the hose with one hand while the other glides down his backside, rubbing the dirt off. I watch his back muscles constrict as I gently slide my palm up and down his spine "All done." Well, that wasn't as awkward as I expected.

Once we're both clean, we are left with one problem: our clothes are still a mess, and we have no towel to dry off with. "Simple," I say. "I'll run inside the house and get some towels really quick. We dry off and then we can go inside and get dressed."

"You want me to go inside your house?"

"Yes. Why, is there a problem?"

He lets his mind ponder for a minute before answering. "No, no problem, just…what am I supposed to wear?"

"You can borrow something from my dad, I guess." His eyes widen. "He's got some old clothes he hasn't worn in a while. There's bound to be something that will fit."

"Are you certain?" Not at all. My dad is more on the leaner side; Julian would rip straight through his clothes.

"At least let me get the towels, then we'll discuss the rest," I inform him before heading inside. I tiptoe through the house, trying my best not to get the floor wet. I bring back the first towels I find from the washroom.

"Here." I hand him one and proceed to dry myself with the other. "Alright, let's go in." I run in first, trudging to my room.

I search for the most comfortable clothes I can find while Julian remains somewhere in the living room. "Okay, now to find you something." I emerge dressed in nothing but a beige chemise. He takes in my appearance, scanning me from head to toe. I keep the towel wrapped on my head, making sure my hair doesn't drip onto my clothes.

"Evalina, there's no need. I'll wring out my clothes and return as is."

"Are you insane, Julian? I'm not leaving you to return to the army camps in your wet clothes. They'll think you had a crazy night out."

"I did have a crazy night out," he remarks. "You threw me into the mud."

"True, but that's not the crazy night they'll be thinking about. More like a steamy night dip in a lake or something with a few fine ladies." He laughs. "How about a robe? Those are one size fits all. My dad won't mind." I stop midway in the hallway. "What about a cloak as well?" I yell.

"Sounds good." Perfect. I pick out one of my father's robes and a cloak for Julian.

"Are you certain he won't mind?"

"He won't." I hand him both items. "This way you'll be double warm. The air is getting chilly."

"You sound like an overprotective mother," he tells me.

"I find that statement insulting. Now, dress." He puts on the robe, tying it up nicely. Then he drapes the cloak over his shoulders.

"Thanks," he says.

"There, look at that, clothes." I motion to his attire.

"I can still feel a breeze," he says.

"I bet," I say with a grin, knowing quite well the draft he speaks of. "Just be grateful you have underwear. Even if they are damp and cold."

"Perhaps I'll remove them while on my way."

I raise my hands in the air. "That's your decision."

"Well then, I think I better get going. Come here." I step into his outstretched arms. "See you in a bit." He kisses my cheek.

"Don't forget about my birthday party," I remind him.

"When is it?"

I flick his shoulder. "You know when it is. I told you earlier."

He grins knowingly. "I'll be there." He starts heading to the door but stops in his tracks. "Can I bring my dog with me as well?"

"You have a dog?" I question.

"I do; his name is Saint." Why does that name somehow ring a bell?

"By all means, feel free to bring him along," I encourage him.

He chuckles. "Alright, I will. Bye, Evalina."

"Goodbye, Julian." And just like that, I watch Julian exit my house.

"Happy Birthday!" my family and university classmates exclaim as I walk into the bookshop. It's finally the day I've been waiting for. My twentieth birthday.

"You guys." I'm all tears and smiles. "Thank you." The entire shop is decorated in various shades of blue. Blue streamers and balloons; my favorite color, of course. Even the cake is cobalt blue. It's in the shape of a book, which is quite adorable.

"Happy twentieth birthday, Evalina." My dad wraps me in his arms.

"Thanks, Dad." I let go of my father to make it to my mom who waits patiently beside us.

I engulf her in a big hug as well. "Thank you." I pull away from my mother to face both of them. "I love you both so much."

"We love you too, Alina," they answer in unison. I proceed to greet the rest of my guests.

I chat with some friends for a while before making my way outside, in need of some fresh air. I take in the scent of petrichor in the air from the rain earlier this afternoon, which I did not mind. I really appreciate the rain; it makes the best reading days, and it helps my garden grow.

I don't mean to leave my own birthday party, which I haven't. I'm simply taking a quick walk. I can get by in crowds and at events, though I always need a few minutes to myself for a quick recharge so that I don't get overwhelmed. I direct myself home, then passed the house through the forest. I'm always greeted with comfort here. I have a habit of getting enraptured by the sounds of the animals, and the earthy smells of pine and grass.

I'm taken aback by the rustling sound of leaves up ahead. I know it must be the wind, but it also sounds like someone is walking across them. More like running, judging by the oncoming noise. I hide behind a large rock near the river and wait, listening. But it's gone quiet. I crane my neck and nearly have a heart attack in the process. There, standing atop the rock on all four legs, is a giant, furry white dog. He sniffs the top of my head, then licks my cheek.

I remove myself from my hiding place.

"*Woof*," is his greeting. I make note of his collar. The plaque reads *Saint.* Wait a minute…that's the name Julian told me. This is *his* dog. I look at his collar once again and then I notice it: a small box dangling like a pendant on a necklace. I crouch down and remove it carefully.

"What's this?" I hold it out for him to sniff. My name is written on the box in elegant calligraphy. I proceed to open it and gasp when I see what's inside. Two tiny book-shaped earrings that just so happen to be my favorite color. But these are unique because they aren't just any shade of blue. They are cerulean, the same color as my eyes.

I look up, hoping to see Julian around. "Where's Julian? Is he here?" Saint doesn't bark this time. "If he is, can you take me to him?" I ask the dog at my side. He starts running the second I finish my request.

"Hold up, Saint, wait!" I call after him, trying my best to keep a quick pace behind him.

We venture deeper into the woods until he stops abruptly between a field of pine trees. "Where is he? Is he here, Saint?" I look all around me. Saint starts barking at the trees, "Julian," I call. "Are you here?" He must be on his way. Saint is a fast runner, after all. Julian must have stayed behind. Or he's probably already arrived at the book shop while I'm here chasing after his dog.

I crouch down and pet Saint. "There's no one here, Saint. Let's get back to the party, alright?"

"*Woof.*"

"I'll take that as a yes. Let's go." But instead of following me back, Saint heads in the opposite direction. It's pointless to call after him, so I don't.

I return to the party assuming I'll see Julian. He's not here. Though it is still early; maybe he'll arrive later in the evening.

The celebration continues well into the night, and as everyone sings "Happy Birthday" to me, I glance at the front door of the shop expecting him to walk through. He never does.

The next day, I'm getting ready to close up the shop after a long day of work and studies when the front door opens. I start to say the same welcome I extend to every customer who arrives but pause when I see the tall frame by the door.

Holding out a box, he says, "I brought muffins."

I frown. "Well, hello to you too. 'How are you, Evalina? I'm sorry I missed your birthday party yesterday.'" I lace my voice with as much sarcasm as I can muster. "'But I promise I have a reasonable explanation as to why I couldn't make it.'" I imitate him using a deep voice.

"You jumped ahead; I was getting to that." He sets the box on the counter. "But I do, in fact, have a reasonable explanation. I was put on military patrol, which is what I feared might happen. Though I should have told you there was a possibility I wouldn't make it. I'm sorry. That's on me.

"For that reason, I went ahead and sent Saint to find you. I assume he delivered your present?" He quirks an eyebrow, and I deliberately tuck a lock of hair behind my ear to show off one of my earrings.

"He did. They're beautiful, by the way. Thank you," I say before emerging from behind the counter to close the gap between us. He hugs me first and I can't help but breathe in his scent. "I accept your apology. Only because the outcome of the day was out of your control," I say against his chest. I lift up my head and grin at him. "You said you brought muffins." I point to the box sitting on the counter.

He chuckles and I can feel the light rumble as his ab muscles constrict against my own chest. "Is that all that matters to you?"

"Well, to be honest I am quite hungry."

"Noted. Next time I'll just have Saint send the muffins instead and not visit," he jokes and steps away, walking towards the door while laughing.

"Muffin time," I exclaim.

"Indeed. I brought a dozen," he informs me.

"Just for the two of us?" I say in disbelief, grabbing the box. I open the lid to find an assortment: banana, crème filled, chocolate, blueberry, chocolate chip, and lemon poppy seed. "We have a feast, then. Let us go to the kids' section and enjoy these delicacies." I begin marching to the back of the shop, carrying the box of pastries.

"I love that section," he teases.

I wink back at him. "I know you do; the seats are divine."

Julian and I have the time of our lives. Between eating muffins and reading children's books out loud, we can't contain our laughter. We get crumbs all over the floor, which we have to clean afterwards.

Now, ready to leave, Julian pauses by the exit. "How about I take you out next time. As a way to make up for not attending your birthday party."

I smile. "I'd like that a lot."

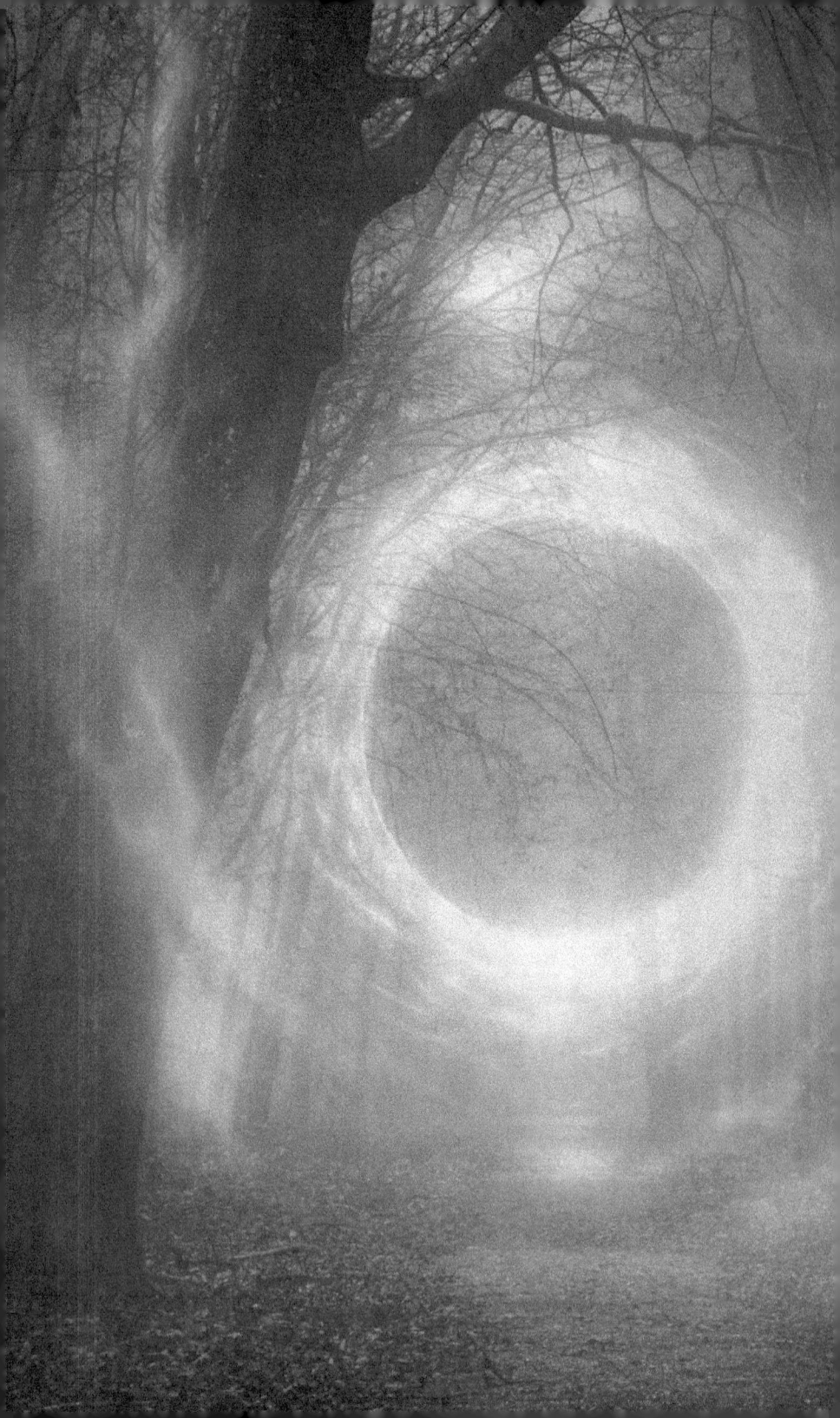

CHAPTER 8
NEW RULES

JULIUS

I return back through the veil with a winning smile. I haven't stopped smiling since I left Evalina at her house. Knowing very well that Soela must be waiting for me to tell her how everything went, I rush to her chambers.

I knock once and proceed to open the door to her room, but I am taken aback by who is sitting on her canopy bed. It's not Soela, but my brother who casually sits with a leg bent over a knee.

"Welcome back, Brother," he says with his usual lack of interest. "How was your visit with my little curse, Evalina? Everything good?"

Something's off. Valec doesn't usually care for details when it comes to my visits with Evalina. As long as I have everything under control. I remain by the door, silent.

"Cat got your tongue, Julius?"

"What's this about, Valec?"

He stands. "Do you truly wish to know?"

67

"Yes, cut to the chase. Why are you here? What do you want?" I say, on the defensive.

I move to the side, letting him pass. He turns, looking straight at me. "I found out something rather interesting and now I am quite intrigued as to what you've been up to with Evalina." *Huh? What is he talking about?*

"Come." He beckons me to follow. "I think you'll be very interested in what I have to show you." He drags me through the hallway, and once the doors to the mansion begin to open, I realize we're going outside to the caves.

We wander even deeper into the caverns, completely veering off the path that leads to the garden. I need to rely on my balance as we pass by a narrow cliff's edge. Countless sharp rocks await at the bottom. It isn't until I spot the crumpled body of a woman at the foot of a boulder that I'm on high alert. As we near, I begin to realize that it's not just any woman—it's Soela. I rush to her in an instant, my heart racing.

"Soela?" I lift her chin. Her eyes are bloodshot. I take her pulse. Thank goodness, she's alive.

My head darts toward Valec's smug stare. "What the fuck did you do to her?"

"She's collateral."

"She's my friend, you bastard."

"You had it coming," Valec says in his signature cold demeanor.

I carefully lift her. She's covered in dirt and dried blood. There are several bruises on her face and her arms have large gashes that appear to have been made by a blade.

"What is that supposed to mean?" I face his front. He makes a gagging sound when the stench of blood hits him, and he takes a few steps back.

"It means, I know exactly how you feel about Evalina." I stop cold. "Oh, yes, Brother. I know." *Impossible.* "I had my suspicions, so I kept watching. I watched how you and Soela interacted with one another. All secretive. The stupid expressions on your faces when you returned from Einalem. I kept a close eye on every little thing you did. Until I finally got the full picture." He circles me, like a hunter waiting to catch its prey. "You're falling for her."

This cannot be possible. My brother is clever, but not this clever. I pegged him as clueless. I was careful, and so was Soela. There's no way. Plus, that's not even true. I'm only keeping an eye on her—I stop myself short. No, that's the exact opposite of what I'm doing. Dominus save me, I even told her I'd take her out on a date. No one does that unless they are somewhat interested in the other person.

"Silent, Brother? Have you got nothing more to say to your king?"

"Why hurt Soela?"

"She was the price for your sins."

"You are despicable," I spit.

"Watch your tone. From now on things will change around here. For instance, after every excursion to the mortal realm, you are to report to me. I want to know everything you say and do with Evalina, and don't you dare think you'll be able to lie. I already have a healer working on a truth serum. So there's nothing you'll be able to hide from me."

That is not fair.

I shake my head, outraged. "That is crossing a line."

Valec grins with malice. "Keep in mind that Evalina is my ticket out. And I will do everything in my power to make sure everything goes according to plan. So, despite your refusal I *will* be making sure you don't tell her anything she does not need to know yet," he says with a tone of finality before he saunters away.

Leaving me with a broken Soela in my arms.

I'm in the infirmary with Soela inside the mansion. She stirs and her eyes begin to twitch. The healer said it would be a couple of hours until she wakes. It's already been five and I refuse to leave her side. I only left for a few minutes to bring food for myself and for her when she wakes. This wasn't her fault and yet she paid for my mistakes.

Her eyes snap open just as I'm adjusting myself in an annoyingly uncomfortable chair. I stand up without further thought.

"Careful," I say when she tries to jerk her head up. "You need rest."

She finds my gaze. "What ha-ppened?" she rasps. I move to the jug of water at her bedside, pouring her a glass.

"Here." I hand it to her.

She swallows the full glass. "Thanks." She hands the empty glass back to me.

"You shouldn't be thanking me when I caused this misfortune upon you." I stare at the ground.

"Julius." Her hand lightly grazes my arm. "None of this is your fault. Your brother is a cruel man. We all know this."

"But it's precisely because of my actions that he acted against you."

"And if it meant seeing you happy I would endure it all over again." This time she lifts herself to sit on the bed. The cuts along her arms have reduced to pink marks, the swelling on her face has gone down as well. Seeing her now, she looks so much better. The healer did wonders.

It's the only thing I can be thankful for in this horrid place. How the herbs that grow in the garden become infused with magic to such an extent that their healing properties are more advanced than anything in the mortal realm. Dominus may have condemned us here, but if we were truly condemned, I doubt we would have been able to make a life for ourselves.

She places her hand over my own. "Jules, it's okay to admit that you're starting to feel something for her."

To hear Soela say so is a pang to my chest. I can't help but wonder if it's true. *Am I falling for Evalina?*

I shake my head. "It doesn't matter now. Valec has just made things more difficult for me."

"How so?" She arches her eyebrow. "What did he say to you?"

"I'm to report to him after all my visits with Evalina. He's having the healer make a truth serum, so that I can't lie. He was uninterested before. Now, he sure as hell wants to know everything. Every moment I share with Evalina will no longer be private." I curse under my breath. "I should have fought him; I should have done something," I yell.

"Then you would be lying in a bed right beside mine. And that's not good; you can't afford to get hurt, Jules. You need to be there for Evalina," she reminds me. "Just play the game, follow Valec's rules, and hopefully no one else gets hurt."

That's the only thing left to do.

I rest my head on her shoulder, the only part of her body that appears unharmed. "Be brave, Julius. Dominus knows we all must be."

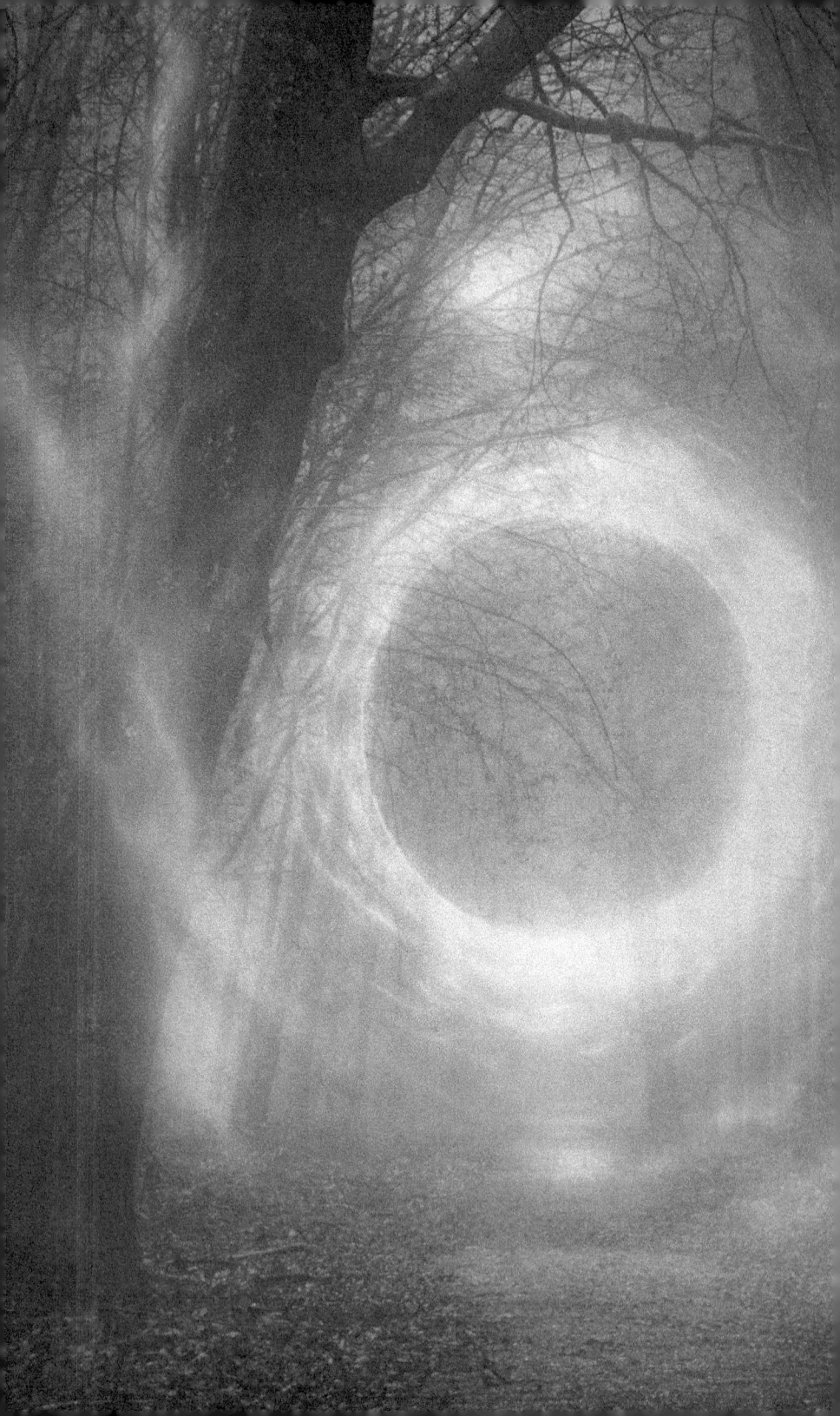

CHAPTER 9
DATE NIGHT

EVALINA

I graduated today. Got my diploma and I couldn't be prouder of myself for achieving my first goal. My second one is to open my own bookshop. Don't get me wrong, I love working at my parents' shop. They literally opened it for me, to find comfort when I had no friends. I'll still take ownership of their shop. Books will always be my safe haven, but now that I'm grown, I'd like to open my own place, where I can earn my own income and save it towards buying a home for myself someday. I just can't wait to get started. I can't wait for this new beginning. For all the possibilities.

I celebrated this milestone earlier in the day with my parents. They took me to Eremat, the capital of Einalem, where we did some sightseeing. I was hoping to spot the military camps while I was there, hoping I'd see Julian. But they must be well hidden from the public eye.

Anyway, Julian promised to take me out tonight. He sent me a message via Saint, who delivered it to my house, much to my amazement. It's our first official date. I was not about to tell my parents that I'll be going out with a thirty-year-old man; instead, I told them I'll be going out with some of my classmates. They were okay with it as long as I promised to be home by midnight. Which is a no-brainer considering Julian has to be back at the camps by that exact hour.

I take my time getting ready and decide to go with a short violet gown with a heart-shaped neckline and puffy sleeves.

I'm applying some rouge to my cheeks when I hear a tap on my window. I draw the curtains and there he is, grinning from ear to ear. He's dressed in a gray, billowy dress shirt, black dress pants, and shoes to match. His hair has been slicked back, giving him a different, more sophisticated look from his usual messy locks.

I proceed to open the window to greet him. "Why hello, Julian," I say in a hushed tone, so as not to alert my parents.

"Good evening, Evalina," he whispers back. "Are you ready for the night I have planned for us?"

"Of course, why wouldn't I be? Just give me one minute." I close the window and rush to the living room, bidding farewell to my parents. Once I'm out the front door, I walk to the side of the house where Julian still waits for me outside my window.

I reach Julian and he stares at me for a long moment with wonder. "You look beautiful." He finally pulls me in for a hug.

"And you're not half bad yourself," I say jokingly. He releases me and I'm quick to ask, "So, where are you taking me?"

"To a place you've never been before," he says enthusiastically. That's when I realize there's a horse drawn carriage up ahead. A man patiently waits for us.

"You rented a carriage?" I'm in disbelief.

"It's a bit far to go on foot. The carriage will be faster." Julian holds out a hand, helping me into the wagon while the driver closes the door for us. Inside it's nice and cozy. Though the night isn't that cold, it's nice to be inside where it's warmer. Julian takes a seat beside me.

"Okay," I say once the driver takes the reins, and the carriage starts to move. "So, you said you're taking me somewhere I've never been to," I reiterate.

His gaze turns to me. "Yes."

"Are you truly certain that I've never been there before?"

"Yes, I am," he says proudly. "I'm quite certain that you have never been to this place before."

I hold my hands up in defeat. "Okay, whatever you say."

We remain in comfortable silence for the rest of the ride. Once we arrive, Julian is the first to step out of the carriage, reaching a hand out to help me. He pays our driver and tells him to return by eleven, giving us a good three hours.

Julian guides me through a narrow pathway, walking ahead of me since we can't both fit side by side. I follow quickly behind him, and it doesn't take long for me to notice the big white structure up ahead. It's a greenhouse. I cannot believe Julian brought me to a greenhouse. I stop walking and Julian notices, turning to look back at me.

"Surprise," he says, pointing towards the building. "I know you love to garden as I do. I discovered this place a few years ago and thought it would be fitting for our first date. What do you think?"

I walk up to him all smiles. "I love it!"

"You ready to see the inside?" he asks.

"Yes!" I say, overexcited. "Wait." I pause in my tracks again, pulling Julian back with me. "Is this a public place? We aren't trespassing, are we?"

"Evalina, I wouldn't take you anywhere we'd be committing a crime. I'm a soldier, remember?" he reminds me.

"You have a point."

"Though it's not open at this hour, so I asked the owner if

he'd make the exception of allowing us to visit tonight. He agreed."

That's good. He takes my hand and the contact of his skin against my own makes my stomach flutter. I'm almost certain this is the first time we're actually holding hands. Or did we hold hands that day we met in the forest? I can't remember. Who cares, anyway? I shake the thought away. This is what's real, the here and now.

I've only set a single foot inside the green house, and I'm already mesmerized. There are loads upon loads of potted plants everywhere, all ranging in height. Small, bushy plants at the front, tall, leafy ones in the back near the large floor-to-ceiling windows. Julian stays behind me as I take in the surroundings, allowing me to explore the vast space. I pass by glass tables of all shapes and sizes, each one holding different types of minia-ture plants. Mostly flowers from what I can tell, though I do spot a table with vegetables like tomatoes and lettuce.

From the walls hang various lanterns that give off just the right amount of illumination to help navigate the greenhouse this time of night. I'm almost at the very back when I see a string of fairy lights flickering like fireflies. They're wrapped around two chairs that just so happen to be facing each other at a table. Though unlike the rest of the tables that have potted plants, this table comes with a meal. Two plates and two glasses are set up for us.

Julian moves ahead of me as he catches me staring. "You didn't think I'd just bring you to a greenhouse and not offer you a romantic dinner, did you?"

"Well, to be honest I knew we had to eat something, but the manner of how or what we would eat never crossed my mind."

"Good." He pulls out a chair for me and I take a seat. I'm greeted by a good-looking plate of roasted chicken, mashed pota-toes, and gravy."

Julian sits across from me and is quick to uncork a bottle of champagne. He pours a generous portion for each of us, and then we dig in.

I'm halfway done with my meal when I decide to ask Julian something I've been curious about for a while. "Julian?"

He strays his attention away from his plate, focusing on me. "Yes, Evalina?"

"Why do you always come to visit me during the evenings?" I've always found it quite odd, but then again, he is a soldier, and they have the huge responsibility of keeping our land safe.

"Because that's the time I'm off-duty." He sets his fork on his now empty plate. "Yes, there are some days when I work late hours, but I still need to remain at the camps during the day. I'm only granted leave on some nights."

"It must bother you, not being in control of your own freedom?" I take my last bite of chicken, savoring the citrusy flavors of the seasoning.

"At first it did." He fills up my empty glass with more champagne. "Then I got used to it. It's my life," he says with a shrug. "Can I ask you something?"

"Go ahead." I take a small sip of champagne before leaning back against my seat.

"I want you to be truthful." *Alright.* I wonder where he's going with his question. "I know you joked about it once, but I need to know... Does my age bother you?" I was not expecting him to ask that.

"No—maybe. I don't know. I've never properly dated anyone," I answer truthfully. "But if it did bother me, I wouldn't be here tonight."

He nods slightly. "Just so you know, I would never try anything with you. Not until you're of age, of course." Which is at the age of twenty-one here in Einalem. "And only if given consent." My eyes widen. Wait, does that include kissing me as well?

He must read the expression on my face because he adds, "I

mean sex, Evalina." Yes, that I got. "I would still very much like to kiss you."

I let out a breath of relief.

Julian waits for a reply, and when I'm unable to give him one, he stands from the table and offers me his hand. Pushing my seat back, I take it and let him lead me through the greenhouse.

He keeps my hand firmly grasped in his own as we navigate through a jungle of vines and trellises. Julian finally pauses, blocking my view up ahead. I tug on his arm and he lets go, ushering me forward. I'm greeted with the sweet floral scent of what looks like hundreds of roses inside the room. Each and every one is a gorgeous shade of bright coral.

"This is beautiful." I pass through the rows of bushes, lining the entire center of the space.

I sense Julian behind me. "The coral rose is said to be the perfect flower for a first date," he says at my back. I pause, looking ahead at the rest of the rose bushes. Julian gets closer until his hands touch my shoulders from behind, turning my skin to gooseflesh.

"The perfect flower for someone you are excited to get to know or who you would like to spend time with," he adds.

I remain very still as Julian drags his hands down to my waist and spins me around until we're facing each other.

I stare into his mysterious blue eyes that never stray from my own. I watch intently as his tongue swipes across his lips. I'm suddenly oblivious to my own actions until I realize I'm biting my lip. This does not go unnoticed by Julian. With his hands firm on my waist, he brings me closer to him, till we're flush together just like the night we first met.

His voice comes out low and sensual. "Can I kiss you?"

"Ever the gentleman." I raise myself onto my tiptoes, trying to reach his ear. He leans closer. "You don't have to ask," I whisper. "Just do it!" That last part might have come out a bit desperate. But that's fine. He should know how I'm feeling.

I lose all sensation in my body the second his lips land on mine. It's nothing like how I thought it would feel. This is—this is magical.

His lips taste of vanilla. His mouth is soft against my own, as his lips move ever so slowly against mine. His tongue lightly graces my mouth and I part my lips slightly. His warmth invades me instantly as his tongue flicks against mine. I moan into his mouth, and that response seems to satisfy him, since he lets out a breathy groan in answer.

I'm lost in his taste, but Julian is the ever proper one and ends the kiss, leaving me winded. I take heavy breaths. That was…goodness, I can't even describe it. But damn, I just had my first kiss.

I'm smiling like an idiot and Julian seems to revel in it. "That smile of yours is contagious, you know." He grins as well.

Everything is great, until in one swift motion Julian shoves me behind him, urging me to run.

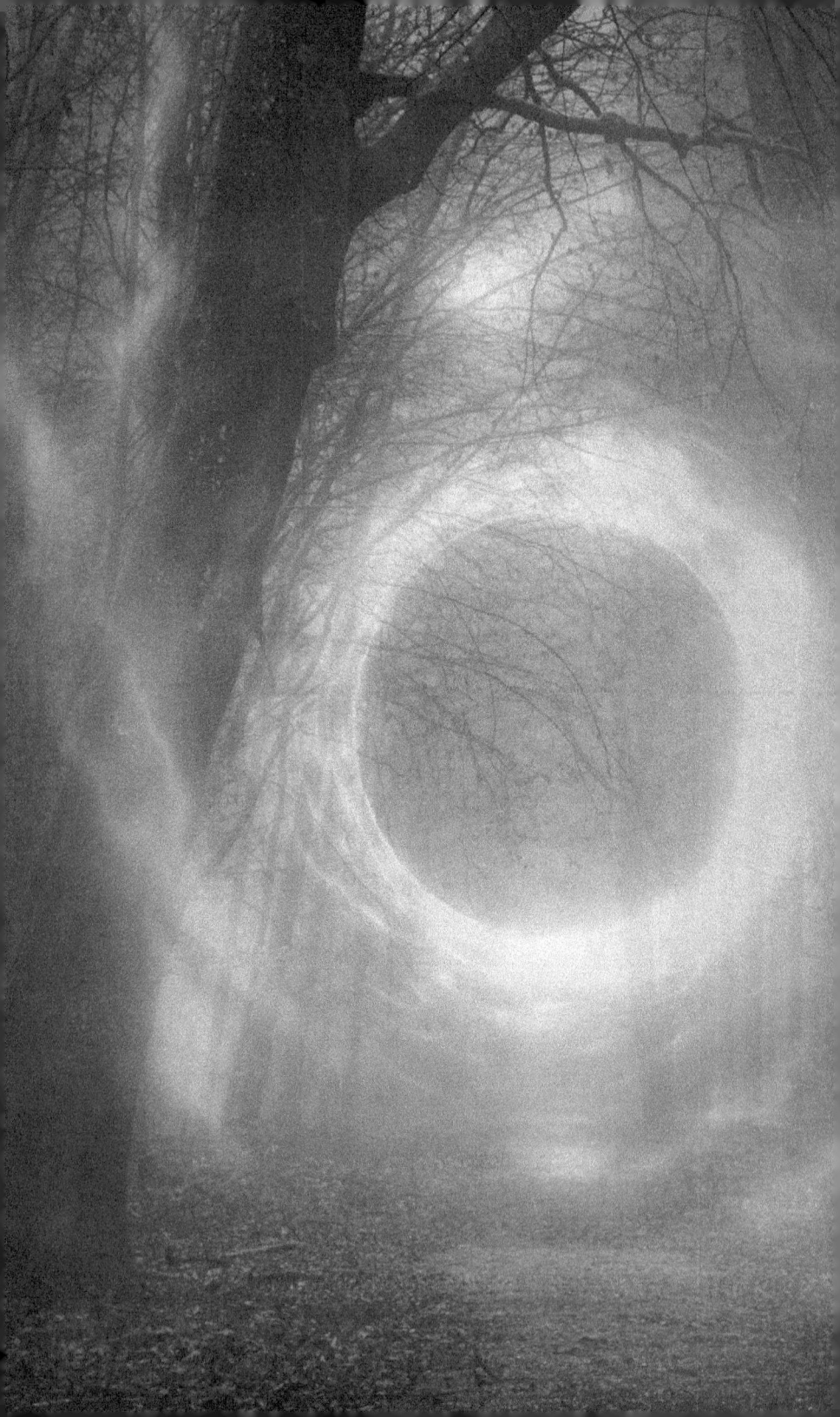

CHAPTER 10
DANGER HERE

JULIUS

I notice the white robed figures outside the greenhouse before she does. That's why I make her run towards the front entrance. I am thankful it's already eleven o'clock; our driver should already be parked outside on the road where he dropped us off. Good, the faster she's out of here the better.

I hastily put out the lanterns, making it pitch black except for the crimson light coming through the glass panels, courtesy of the blood moon.

Ever so slowly I open the door that leads out from the other side of the greenhouse. I need to cause a distraction so that the white nuns remain here, giving Evalina enough time to escape.

I saw the concern in her eyes when I told her she needed to run. I told her it was the same people as last time (a downright lie), that it wasn't safe and that I'd handle it. I promised to return to her when I could get away from my duties and explain everything.

I'm silent on my feet as I follow their trail. There are five white nuns total, each one carrying a lit candle. I can't make out the exact words they're saying, but judging by the symphony of lyrics, they're chanting some kind of prayer. A prayer to Dominus, no doubt. They are circling the building, and with each step they get closer and closer to the front of the greenhouse. So I do what anyone with a brilliant plan would do: I search for a rock and throw it at one of the glass windows. It shatters upon impact.

I remind myself to leave plenty of coins for the man who so graciously lent me the place for the night. Considering the repairs he'll now need to make.

I hide behind a neat row of bushes. The nuns halt and look to one another. They share quick words and blow out their candles at once. With one last glance at each other they all part ways, each walking in a different direction. Thankfully, none of them head towards the main path.

As soon as I know the coast is clear I make my way towards the narrow pathway. I'm hoping and praying that Evalina is long gone by now, but she isn't. The carriage is there, the door open and the driver ready to go. I curse under my breath. She waited for me. After I strictly told her not to.

Her big, beautiful cerulean eyes land on me. Worry lines crease her brows. "I'm sorry, but I couldn't just leave you here." She uncrosses her arms, letting them fall to her sides. "I know that you're a big, strong soldier who can take care of himself," she says, moving forward, "but I just needed to know you were okay." She pauses in front of me, waiting for a reaction.

I'm pissed that she allowed herself to be an easy target by remaining here, but *fuck,* no one has ever checked up on me, save for Soela. The act is so endearing that I don't know what to say. So, instead I say nothing and reel her close to me, planting a soft kiss on her lips.

82

It was a struggle to leave Evalina at her home when all I wanted to do was stay with her and make sure she was alright. But I knew how pointless that would be. It was almost midnight and the veil awaited. I returned to Inferis on time, and waiting for me on the other side was Valec. A sly grin on his face. It was time for my interrogation.

Now here I sit on the silver throne, beside Valec's gold one. He had the throne made for me as the Prince of Inferis, a title I never use. Valec is the King of Inferis, not me. I would never willingly choose to rule beside him. Even as a prince.

The doors to the throne room rustle open, revealing an old woman with silver locks and wearing a healer's robe. She walks slowly, head down, as she passes the ornate golden columns on either side of the entryway. Valec awaits her with his right hand outstretched. She fishes for the truth elixir in her pocket and out comes a small glass vial. She hands it to him without uttering a word and quickly retreats, leaving me alone to face my brother's fate.

"Drink," he orders, shoving the vial at my face. I do as he commands, downing the murky green liquid in one swallow. It burns going down my throat, the taste no better than that of curdled milk. I suppress the urge to throw up.

Valec gives me a few minutes and then stands before me, ready to start his questioning. "What did you and Evalina do tonight?"

The magic from the truth elixir works its way through my body. I feel a distinct hum across all my nerves. I open my mouth to speak, and the words flow freely without effort. "I took her out on a date to a greenhouse."

His eyebrows crease and he cocks his head to the side, studying me. "What did you do at this greenhouse?"

"We talked, ate dinner and—" I try to resist saying the last part. But it's impossible to do so. Resisting gets my throat all dry, as if I swallowed sand. "I kissed her!" I blurt when I feel my throat threatening to close up.

Valec's nostrils flare. "You kissed her?" His hands fist at his sides. He closes his eyes for a brief second, trying to regain his composure.

As long as his shadow magic does not come into play, I'm fine, I remind myself.

"Have you told her anything about me? About her, about what she is?" he demands in a cutting tone.

"No, I haven't told her a thing."

"Your feelings for her are a liability." He glides across the room, staring at me from a different angle. I say nothing as I wait for the next question. "Mark my words, Julius, I may not be an expert on such a sentiment, but if you continue to go down this path, who's to say you won't tell Evalina to move to another continent in order to keep her safe? In order to keep her away from me?"

That's a low blow. "Valec, I would never." He knows I can't lie, so here it is, the confirmation he's always wanted. "I am your brother, Valec. And you may have forgotten what it feels like to experience love, but I haven't. I love you, and that's the only reason I am doing this. That's why I lie to Evalina. Yes, I am falling for her, yet that does not change anything." I rise from the throne. "So don't even think for a second that she is above you. She's not. She is but the pawn in your little game." I shove the empty vial at his chest. His eyes widen in shock.

"Interrogation over," I say, and race for the exit. *I need to get out of here.*

I don't make it to my chambers. Instead, I slump against the dark corridor walls and lower myself to the ground, legs splayed out before me. The tears fall freely down my cheeks, and I can't help the sob that escapes my lips.

My admission to Valec and myself is enough to undo me.

"I'm so sorry, Evalina," I whisper into the empty hallway. "I'm so sorry."

As the days go by and eventually turn to months, I continue to visit Evalina, though I do so less frequently, making up excuses about being on some military mission. I do go out every blood moon night, though I remain hidden some days, only watching, making sure there aren't any threats around. Evalina seems unbothered by my lack of visits. Though I imagine she suspects something. If she does, she never confronts me about it.

I look at myself in the mirror; I look tired. Both physically and emotionally. There are bags under my eyes that weren't there before. I'm leaner, not by much. But I can tell by how my pants hang looser on my hips. This distance I'm putting between myself and Evalina isn't doing me any favors.

Regardless, that all ends tonight, considering today is finally her twenty-first birthday. I'm just about done getting ready when I'm called to the throne room. Strapping on the last of my weapons to my fighting leathers, I make my way to my brother, who waits atop his golden throne. "Tonight's the night, Brother," he says as a way of greeting.

"It is."

"I hope after managing our differences that you finally understand the importance of this evening." I nod. "Good." He leans back into his chair. "Now, have fun, but do keep a watchful eye when retrieving her. Who knows if the high priest and priestess might still have their people lurking."

"I will. You have my word," I promise.

"Excellent. Do not fail me, Julius. Fail and you will uphold the consequences." A threat.

"Trust me, Brother, I know what I'm doing." I can't help

but wonder how things will change now that Evalina will be around. They won't change for the better; everyone knows that.

"I'm pleased to hear that. Now, be on your way. Soela is already tending to the pentagram as we speak." He waves me off. I turn to leave. "Oh, and Julius, a final word." I turn back around. "When you do retrieve her, bring her to me immediately. Understood?"

"Loud and clear, Your Majesty." I bow out of mockery, glad to finally leave his presence.

Soela waits for me by the veil. Neither one of us speaks a word. I keep my focus on Evalina and only her as Soela chants her usual incantation. The veil shimmers, revealing a distinct clearing of trees near a road. The veil is dropping me a little further out from the Nairedian village today, but it's still close by.

"See you soon." I wave goodbye to Soela before passing through the mirror opening.

"Stay safe out there, Julius," she replies, waving back to me.

"I will." I step through and then onward towards Evalina's home. The streets aren't as crowded as I pass through. It's peaceful. I catch an ongoing conversation between two women as I'm passing by.

"Yeah, they're searching here now. There's soldier's everywhere." The hairs on my neck stand on end.

"Do they seriously think the Devil's Curse is in our village?" the other woman asks.

"Who knows? But that's why everyone is tucked safe in their homes earlier this evening."

I lower the hood of my cloak so as not to intimidate them. "Excuse me." Both women look for the source behind the voice. "But where are these soldiers?" I ask in a neutral tone.

"Why, they're at the book shop, the one Lina and Evan own. Books N Baubles."

"Thank you," I answer and break into a run. They've found her. *How on Einalem did they find her?* I was careful.

I arrive at the bookshop in record time and that's when I see them. The men atop their horses, waiting outside the shop. One soldier is blocking the entrance. Real military soldiers wearing the uniform I've worn for all these years, pretending to be one of them. Knowing there's no point in lingering out here, I change directions and move to the back of the building, hoping to get a glimpse of how many men are inside. It's a one-story structure so the windows are low, which makes it no trouble at all for me to see through. I lift my head, getting a clear view of the inside. Evalina stands by the register, the perfect depiction of calm. She seems to be unaware of the threatening situation.

She's speaking to two soldiers. While the other three browse through the shelves, picking up books and looking at the pages, then placing them back on the corresponding shelves. They do this while the other two men engage in idle conversation with her. If only she'd look to her right, then I could get her attention. But there's a possibility that will make the situation worse. The guards will follow her gaze and then they won't hesitate to hurt her.

There's a total of ten men, including the five I spotted outside. To fight against them all is doable, yet a risk all in its own. I need to think clearly before I act. I can't put Evalina's life on the line like this. My job is to get her out of the village safely.

More hoof beats resound from outside. It couldn't possibly be. I move away from the window, rushing back to the front of the shop, and sure enough more soldiers have arrived. They are led by a man and woman dressed in white robes. *No, this can't be.*

There are now fifteen soldiers in total alongside the high priest and priestess of the Grand Church. The very people who banished Valec from Einalem twenty-two years ago. They're here, they found her. They sensed her magic, the hellfire running through her veins. They sensed the darkness within it, and they came for her.

Returning back to the window, I spot Evalina ringing up two purchases. I wonder what in Einalem these soldiers could have purchased. A book on *The Art of Murder*, most likely.

The shop doors open and in rush the others. I count them all; five remain outside. They've caught her off guard, just like they wanted. They start to circle her, and she backs away to the wall. A knickknack falls from the shelf behind her. She says something but I obviously can't hear what it is. Her expression gives her away—she's afraid.

Her eyes fly to the window and that's when our eyes lock. Her lips appear to form my name—well, my fake name—and then the worst possible thing happens. The soldiers look up as well, spotting me by the window.

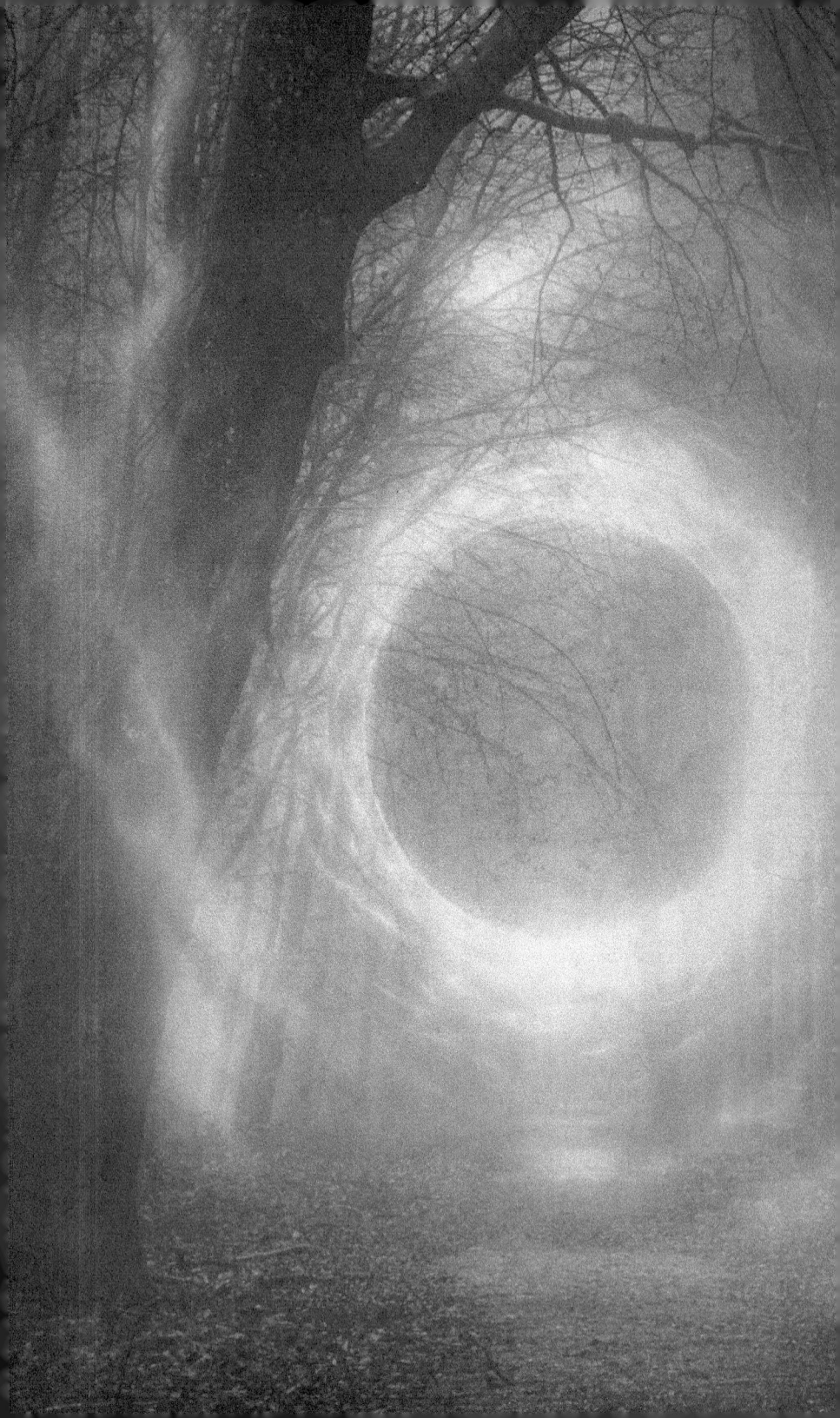

CHAPTER 11
THE ATTACK

EVALINA

I'm being yanked by my arms while I kick and scream.

"Resisting will only make this worse," one of the soldiers says behind me.

"Let go of me!" I yell.

The man at my front pulls on my wrists harder, holding them in place. "We told you to be quiet." I open my mouth to scream again but the man behind me clamps his hand over it. We're almost at the door when the sound of clashing swords and screams stops the men in their tracks. I look out the door and my heart skips. It's Julian. He's really here. I wasn't imagining him earlier. I'm perplexed as I watch him swipe his sword through the air, landing a blow on one of the soldiers.

"Out the back door." A man at the front gives the command to the soldiers who have me apprehended. I nearly trip on my own feet, but their hold on me is strong, which prevents me from collapsing. So strong that tears brim at my eyes because of the force they're using. They have my ponytail in a tight hold and it's excruciating.

They reach the back exit and shove me through. I stare up ahead and find a carriage flanked by two black horses. "Get her in!" the one at my front says. I shake my head in defiance. I want to scream again but the hand over my mouth won't budge, even as I try to bite the soldier. It's no use.

The door to the coach opens and I'm shoved forward. I hear shouting behind me and it's getting closer. One soldier manages to propel me onward and I fall face-first inside the carriage. More screams erupt behind me, and when I lift myself up to see what has happened, I'm met with blood everywhere. Noticing the silence, I peek my head out and there he is, clad in black leaders, sword in hand—Julian.

He doesn't give me time to process what has happened as he grabs onto me, lifting me out of the carriage. He sets me down on the ground, his gaze never straying from me. All around us lie fallen soldiers, their blood pooling on the ground. I stagger back a step.

"We don't have time." Julian places his hands on my shoulders, steadying me. "There's more of them out there. I'm going to need you to run. Run towards the forest outside the village nearest the University. I'll meet you there." Julian's eyes are wild and frantic. "Do you understand me?" I nod.

"Now go!" he urges me. I steal one last glance at him before I break into a run.

I go as fast as my legs can carry me, except I can't just run away. My parents live here; I need to find them. Gasping for breath, I change course and race to my home. I keep to the forest trails, staying off the streets where I'll be noticed.

I spot our front porch and stagger through the door, which happens to be unlocked. Inside the living room, it's as if a tornado hit. Things are smashed on the floor, there is glass everywhere. Now I'm really worried. "Mom, Dad!" I call.

I rush to their room and the door's been left ajar. I push it fully open and the scene before me makes me collapse to the floor at the foot of the bed.

"No!" I scream, shaking my head vigorously. No, this can't be happening. I must be dreaming.

I lift my head, hoping what I saw was a figment of my imagination. But it's not. There, lying side by side on the bed, are my parents. One might assume they're asleep if not for the blades protruding from their chests. Blood coats the front of their bodies. I crawl to them, lifting myself onto the bed between them.

"Mom." I shake her. "Dad." I do the same to him. It's useless, I know, but I still check their pulse. Neither has a heartbeat. The tears stream down my face like a cascading waterfall. "No, please," I beg. "You can't leave me. Don't leave me." Outside, hoofbeats jolt me to my senses. *The soldiers.*

I pick myself up; there's no time for more crying. My life is clearly on the line. I plant a quick kiss on each of their foreheads and send a prayer to whatever god will listen. "I love you. I'm sorry," I say to the lifeless room before making a break for my own. I hate leaving them, they didn't deserve this, but I know they would want me to live, to survive whatever this is. And that's exactly what I'm going to do.

As I used to do when I was younger, I push open the window of my room facing the garden and have no hesitation before jumping.

I'm peeking around the side of the house. The night is fully upon us now. I'm prepared to run in the direction Julian told me to when I hear the shouts of a man behind me. "She's here!"

I sprint for the trees.

"Stop!" he yells. "Stop, in the name of the Lord." *The Lord?* What does Dominus have to do with any of this?

I swerve through the trees, moving as fast as I can. I run through the dark, hoping my knowledge of the village is enough to give me the upper hand. I pass by a few houses nearby, their patio lanterns glowing to illuminate the dark. I can hear the commotion of people rushing out of their homes. Guess the soldiers have drawn a crowd.

Reaching the forest Julian told me to meet him at, I sneak behind a large oak tree. I crouch down and wait. It takes several minutes before I hear footsteps drawing near. I listen for Julian's familiar voice.

I peer out from my hiding spot to see who has followed me here when a tight grip takes hold of me from behind. "Clever girl." It's the same soldier who chased me earlier. "Brothers," he calls, "I've found her. Fall back."

I struggle in the man's arms, but he manages to hold me still. No matter how much I kick or squirm, it's no use. His grip never falters. His filthy hand clamps over my mouth. *Oh no! Not this again.* The stink of his hand makes my eyes water.

He walks, dragging me with him, my back pushed up against his chest. From afar, I hear the sound of clashing swords. This snags the soldier's attention as well, for he stops moving. "Brothers," he calls again. No one seems to be coming. Swords continue to dance in the distance. Men grunt and others yell for help. This sets my captor on high alert.

The leaves crunch, and the man stills. "I suggest you let her go," a gruff voice speaks from behind us. A voice I know all too well.

"And if I don't?" The man presses his hand harder against my mouth. I bite him, but that only causes him to be more aggressive with me. At least I get a response out of this one.

"Then I can assure you, you won't get a quick death like your comrades," Julian answers. Unexpectedly, I'm thrust forward, and pain shoots through my head the second I land on the ground. I try to lift myself up but a weighted boot steps on the back of my neck, forcing my head down.

"You're him, aren't you?" the man snarls. "The brother. You've come to collect the Devil's Curse."

I may not be able to see him, but I can tell this infuriates Julian further. I listen as he takes a step forward. Suddenly, I feel the tip of a sword at my neck and fear overtakes me. "Come any closer and I'll kill her myself. At this rate, who cares what the priest and priestess wish to do with her?"

"I care," Julian barks out. That's when it happens. The man's weight releases me almost immediately. A sword drops and then I hear the loud thud of someone falling to the ground behind me. No longer restrained, I carefully lift myself from the dirt and the movement makes me dizzy. I remain in a sitting position, legs crossed. I reach a hand up to my head. Thankfully, it's clean; I'm not bleeding.

"Evalina." Julian's at my side in seconds. He takes both my arms and lifts me up. My knees wobble a bit and I collapse against his hard muscle. My head is still spinning. He keeps his arms around me, knowing better than to trust my body to keep me upright at this moment.

"Where does it hurt?" he asks, concern adorning his features.

"My head," I reply. He's quick to inspect the back of my head, then my forehead. I wince when he touches the sensitive skin there.

"A lump might form. You'll need ice." He tries his best to be gentle. His eyebrows draw together as if he's just remembered something. "We have to go." His concern for me is immediately replaced with fear. "From where those soldiers came, more will follow. Can you walk?"

I test standing on my own. Once I've got my footing and my head stops hitting me with vertigo, Julian and I commence our trudge through the woods.

"Julian, where are we going?" I question after walking for several minutes.

"Somewhere safe," is his only reply.

"Julian, what is going on? I can't just leave, what about my parents—" The shock hits me again as realization dawns on me.

How did I forget? "Please tell me it isn't true," I beg him, stopping in my tracks.

"Evalina." He tries to comfort me.

"No!" I take a few steps back. "Tell me it isn't true! Tell me that my parents aren't dead," I hiss. Though I saw it clear as day. Their motionless bodies lying on their bed.

"I can't tell you that." He gets closer and this time I don't retreat. "Evalina, you don't know how sorry I am that this is happening to you. I can spend the rest of the night saying those very words over and over again, but the truth is that if we don't exit these woods, things will be much worse. So, I'm going to need you to hold your grief in for a little while. Just until we reach our destination."

I want to say no, to swear at him and say a number of hateful things. Because who is he to distance himself from me, only to return on my birthday wanting to play the hero? "I hate you!" I scream. "I hate you, Julian." Tears fall down my cheeks, and I quickly wipe them away.

Julian actually looks wounded, and I get the urge to slap that expression off his face. "Evalina—"

"Shut up and keep walking." I pass him, even though I have no clue where we're going. "Why were those soldiers after me?" I ask after Julian falls in sync with me. "Weren't those your buddies from the military? And now you've slaughtered them?"

"No, I lied," he admits. "I'm not a soldier. I don't work for the Einalem military."

Okay, now I want to find the most painful way to murder *him*. He lied to me.

"And my name's not Julian, it's Julius, but you can call me Jules."

What! The lies just keep flooding out. I want to close the dam.

"You're not serious, are you?" He stares me straight in the eye and I swear I catch a hint of regret there. But he doesn't say anything; he only nods. I calm myself down, not wanting to cause a scene as I'm in the middle of running for my life. "Okay, then where are you taking me?" I try to read his expression. He doesn't give much away.

"Home."

"You have an actual house?" I say in disbelief. "Well, do you live nearby?" I ask instead, hoping he'll keep talking and not evade any more questions.

"Yes and no." Well, that's a fantastic answer.

This is how it goes for the rest of the way; no one speaks a word. Wherever we're heading, I know we've arrived the moment Julius stops walking. I blink, then wipe my eyes in case I'm not seeing right. But my eyes are not deceiving me. Hovering between the trunks of two massive trees is a large, shimmering black picture frame. Or at least that's what it looks like to me.

"What is that?" I take a step closer to the strange sight.

"That"—he points between the two trunks—"is the veil, the magic source that allows me to cross between worlds." *Did he just say magic?*

"Sure, because magic is a thing." He takes note of my sarcasm as I cross my arms.

"It is," Julius says, dead serious. "And you must believe in it. If not, then why else would you read fantastical stories? If you didn't believe for a second that magic and mayhem could be real."

He has a point. But this…this feels exactly like stepping into a fairytale or a very bizarre dream.

Annoyed, I ask, "What does it do?"

"It's our method of transportation." He grins and I get the urge to strangle him.

"Transportation?" I stare at him with a murderous look on my face. "How on Einalem is that weird thing supposed to get us anywhere?"

"Like this." Julius steps closer, and what was once just a picture frame, has now somehow turned into a...*portal?* I'm not joking. I am clearly staring at another world right through that thing. It's like looking through a painting.

Without even checking to see if I'll follow, Julius steps right through the frame into who knows where. I remain baffled. That is, until I see him beckoning me to follow from the other side. Taking a deep breath, I shove a hand through the frame and it begins to tickle. Julius grasps my hand and pulls me to the other side.

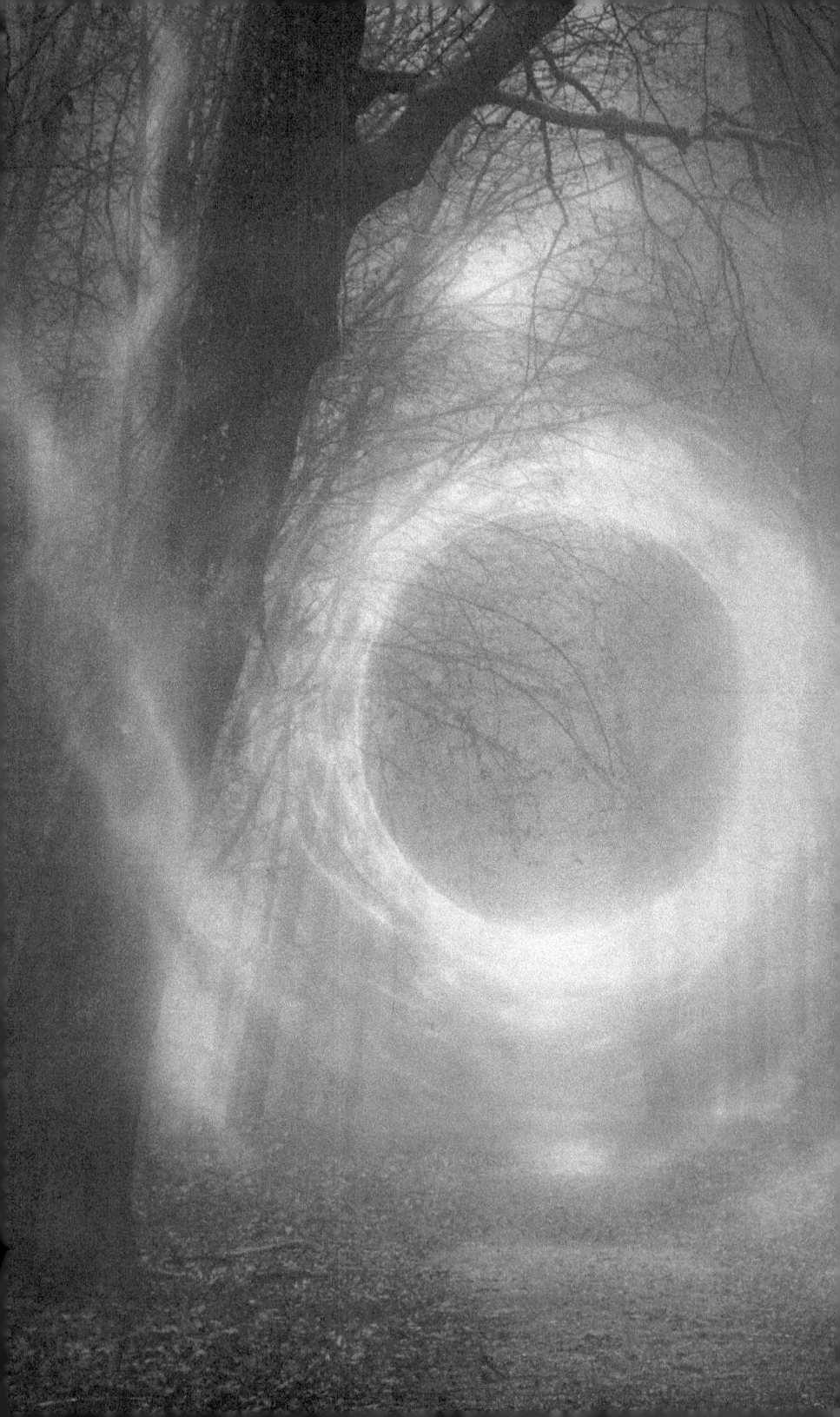

CHAPTER 12
FOREIGN LAND

EVALINA

I crash against Julius's chest, and I pull away almost immediately. That was…that felt unreal. I turn, only to spot the portal—or veil, as Julius called it—showcasing the forest from where we crossed through.

"It's incredible, isn't it," Julius says, now beside me. He pulls out a pocket watch, checking the time. "Give it a minute."

I wish I knew what he was referring to. I continue to stare at the veil until the land on the other side disappears as the portal glazes over, now nothing but a black sparkly painting encased in an oval frame.

I turn to Julius. "What just happened?"

"The veil closed. It happens at midnight after every blood moon."

"What does that mean?" I say, shaking my head. "Julian—Julius," I correct myself. "Where are we?" I turn in a circle, catching every detail of this place. We're inside a cave, nothing but gray stone walls everywhere I look. At my feet is solid rock, yet behind us I spot a lush garden. *There are trees here!*

In this damp, musty place, there is flora. I'm baffled by such a discovery. Back at home I struggled to grow a single plant indoors. The thought of home hits me like a bucket of ice water. My parents, my home, my garden, our bookshop… everything, now gone. Tears prick at my eyes; I try to blink them away.

Julius is about to answer my question about our location when a loud shriek sounds nearby.

"Fuck!" Julius curses at my side. "Fuck, no! Valec!" he calls. "I need to get you out of here. Come on." Julius yanks on my arm, only to scoop me up into his arms instead.

"Julius," I complain. Is he insane? "Put me down. You can't carry me and run. I'm extra weight."

"Trust me, I'm faster than you, despite the extra weight." He isn't wrong. He's quite quick on his feet.

Behind us the awful sounds keep getting louder, and it all happens so fast that I only register what's happening when I'm no longer in Julius's arms, but flying through the air. My body lands against solid rock, my right side taking most of the blow. I hiss at the burn on my skin.

I search for Julius, and there at his feet lies the most hideous thing I've ever seen. A creature with dark scales that appear to be leaking some type of black substance. Nothing but empty sockets where its eyes should be. It's like if a dog morphed into a monster.

It jolts slightly, letting out a loud wail before it collapses, a sword protruding from its chest. Julius retrieves it from its body and scans the space. More horrifying cries echo through the cavern. "We have to go! More are coming." Julius sheaths his sword at his back, where it's concealed. Rushing to my side he lifts me off my feet, carrying me once again.

We trail downward, and it's not long before a giant mansion comes into view. It's as tall as the cave itself, built entirely out of wooden planks and painted black. Tall glass windows surround all sides of the mansion and an onyx staircase leads to a dark marbled portico.

Julius carries me up the stairs and the glass double doors open on their own accord. Inside, I'm met with a long, wide hallway. Beneath Julius's boots is a crimson carpet that stretches the entire length of the hall. Various paintings adorn the maroon-colored walls, mostly all of them depicting nature. Wall sconces, light up our path as we pass by. Julius takes a left and soon enough he's turning a handle that leads into a small room. It's an infirmary.

Julius sets me down on a wooden chair. I take in the space, while he walks over to a large cabinet in the center of the room. The room is painted the same shade of deep red as the hallway. There's a bed at the far corner and another chair beside it. A tall window stands behind, draped by a fine gray curtain.

Julius retrieves a brown bottle from the cabinet. "Take off your shirt," he orders, before kneeling at my feet. I do as told, but nothing can save me from his gaze. Brassiere and all, his eyes linger over my skin for too long. Which, shockingly, does not cause me any discomfort. And that annoys the hell out of me.

Too tired to even want to speak. Least of all to Julius. I remain silent while he takes care of my wound.

His fingers brush at my injury, and I shudder from his cold touch. He removes the lid from the bottle, then lightly trickles ointment over my skin. The liquid is also quite frigid, which makes my stomach clench. It drips down my side, and before it can run down to my pants, Julius slowly rubs the ointment over my wounded skin. The ointment soothes my aching wounds, and I can already feel my side becoming less stiff.

"It should be better by morning." He stands, handing me my shirt before he washes his hands at the sink beside the cabinet. "I'll be back in a minute. I'm just going to get some ice for your head." He leaves and I remain sitting until he returns with a bag of ice.

I keep it pressed to my forehead for a few minutes. Once everything has been taken care of, we make our way through the hallways once again. I lose track of how many turns we take, until we're met with a large gray staircase. We trail upward until we come across a massive set of double doors.

"Evalina, before we go in, I need you to know that whatever happens from today on out has a purpose, and I hope that regardless of the process, you know this was never the life I intended for you, and it was never my choice to decide on a better life for you."

"Where is this coming from?" I feel utterly drained, and Julius being cryptic about everything isn't helping.

He avoids eye contact with me, which unsettles me even more. "Let us go in."

The doors open and the first thing to snag my attention is a set of thrones at the far back of the room. The one in the center glistens, as if carved out of pure gold. The second, much smaller throne is silver and stands tall on the left side of the golden one —a set of thrones built for a king and queen. In comparison to the hallways we walked through, which gave off an eerie, dark vibe, everything in this room screams riches. These walls are painted in a lush golden tone, offering plenty of illumination which the rest of the building lacks. The floors are marble, and I can't help but stare down as they seem to glisten with each step I take. There are even large columns on each side of the room, reaching all the way to the ceiling, that appear to be carved out of the finest of stones. If I wasn't so certain I'm still alive, I could swear I died and went to Caelesti.

"That bastard," Julius curses at my side. "He's not even here."

"Who?" I ask.

"My brother," Julius says, aggravated.

"You have a brother?" I can't help the sinking feeling in my stomach for not knowing such a small yet vital piece of information about him. But given that all he has done is lie to me for the past year and a half, I shouldn't feel bad for not knowing said detail.

"Stay here; I'll go find him. Just so you know, you're safe here. Trust me." I frown. "But if it makes you feel any better"—he removes his sword from his back—"take this."

"You expect me to know how to use this?" I hold the heavy weapon outward, and my arms give out.

"I think anyone faced with danger can figure out how to use it." He pauses at the door. "If you do see my brother before I return and he somehow annoys you, feel free to stab him with it," he finishes before walking away.

I'm speechless. I don't even know what his brother looks like, and Julius casually expresses I'm free to stab him. For one, I have no clue where I am. I traveled through who knows what—and now I'm here, standing in a throne room in a lavish mansion.

"Did Julius leave you here alone?"

I jump, flinging the sword in the direction of whoever spoke. The sword flies out of my hands, landing on the opposite side of the room. Arms raised, I'm met with a well-kept man. "That was quite stupid of you to do."

Judging by his face, the similarities are entirely lacking. It's the way this man carries himself that gives him away as Julius's brother. Icy blue eyes pierce into my own. "You must be her. What's your name?" I don't know how to answer. "Are you deaf?"

I'm too focused on his appearance, on his finely tailored black suit, to register what he's asked me. In Einalem only wealthy men wear suits like that, while the lower class men simply wear embroidered tunics during special occasions.

"Evalina," I answer, snapping my attention away from his body. He's built like Julius, only he's more on the leaner side. This man's hair glistens a rich shade of brown. It's shortly cropped at the sides with loose curls perfectly styled to create a wave shape atop his head. It gives him a mature look, as opposed to Julius, who has a gentler face despite the short beard he now has.

"Where did Julius go?" he questions.

I steady my voice. "He was upset when he didn't see you here and then left to go find you. He did give me permission to stab you if you managed to annoy me." I probably shouldn't have said that last part.

He grins. "I'm delighted. My brother is ever the clever one. Though, I must say I am glad he isn't here. That way we can speak privately, you and I. Allow me to introduce myself." He saunters onto the golden throne, where he lounges freely. I walk a little closer to him. "My name is Valec, Julius's brother. But that last part you already knew. Am I wrong?" He raises an eyebrow.

"No, you're not."

"Did Julius speak about me during your journey here?"

"No, he never even mentioned he had a brother. Not until a second ago."

"Interesting." Valec consistently taps the armrest of his throne. "I'd like to extend an invitation to attend morning breakfast with me."

"And I'd like to know where I am?" I throw his way.

His eyes snap up. "That," he says, lifting a finger, "I cannot do. Not now, at least. If you agree to join me for breakfast in a few hours, then—and only then—will I freely give away our location to you. Amongst other things. What do you say?" He pretends to busy himself with wiping invisible dirt off what I can now assume is *his* throne.

"If I agree to attend this breakfast of yours, do you promise to answer all my questions?"

"No. I'll answer what I feel like. But you"—he motions to me—"on the other hand, will listen to each and every thing I have to say without objection."

I don't like this man. I'm about to answer him when the doors to the throne room open, Julius emerging from behind. His expression is cold.

"You?" Julius points to his brother. "Where were you?"

"Whatever do you mean, Brother?" Valec fakes innocence.

"Bullshit, you were missing like always when I was looking for you."

"Careful, Julius. You wouldn't want to upset our guest. Not after she's agreed to eat breakfast with us."

"I never gave you an answer." I look to the man on the throne. His expression is calm and collected.

"Well, since Julius has clearly not told you the rules of this mansion, I might as well do it myself." He stands and makes his way to me. Julius stops him with a hand pressed to his chest.

"Not another inch," he growls.

"You do not have authority over her. Not in my domain, you don't." Valec pushes past him and is in front of me in an instant. He's even more daunting up close, as I fall witness to his five o'clock shadow. "The rules around here are simple. Rule number one." He holds up a finger, and I notice both his hands are covered in rings. "Everyone who lives or sets foot in my kingdom answers to me, meaning what I say goes. You cannot refuse me. If you do, I can assure you death is inevitable." He claps his hands together. "And those are the rules. Are we clear?"

I nod. This man has a flair for the dramatic as far as I can tell.

"Great." He turns away. "Now, Julius, make yourself useful and escort Miss Evalina to her room."

Many endless hallways and twists and turns later, we come across multiple doors. "These are the guest quarters, most of which are unoccupied." Julius opens the door before us and steps through, while I follow.

The room is decent. Slightly larger than my old one back

home. It's not much different from the dark hallways we walked through. Everything in this mansion seems to be all dark and drab; well, everything except the throne room. "Someone will be here to tend to you shortly. I'll meet you at the breakfast banquet."

"Where are we, Julius?" I snap before he closes the door.

"My brother will tell you soon enough." He lingers by the threshold.

"I don't want to hear it from your brother, I want to hear it from you." I cross my arms over my chest. "You can't keep doing this to me, Julius. Why are you being so distant?" I yell.

"I'm sorry. I promise I'll explain everything, just not right now. You should rest, it's late." He shuts the door on his way out.

All I want to do is scream into the ether. Instead, I fall to the floor, my back against the foot of the bed. Legs curled to my chest, tears run down my cheeks. All my emotions flow free.

My parents are dead. I'll never be able to see them again. I will no longer hear my mother's laugh whenever I make a long-winded summary of the book I recently read. I won't be able to help my father in his fields, nor in the garden. I won't have lunches delivered to me on long days at the shop. I will never again see the two most important people in my life. And the worst part is, I never got to say goodbye. Having seen the life drain from their eyes would have been painful, but at least I would have been there by their sides.

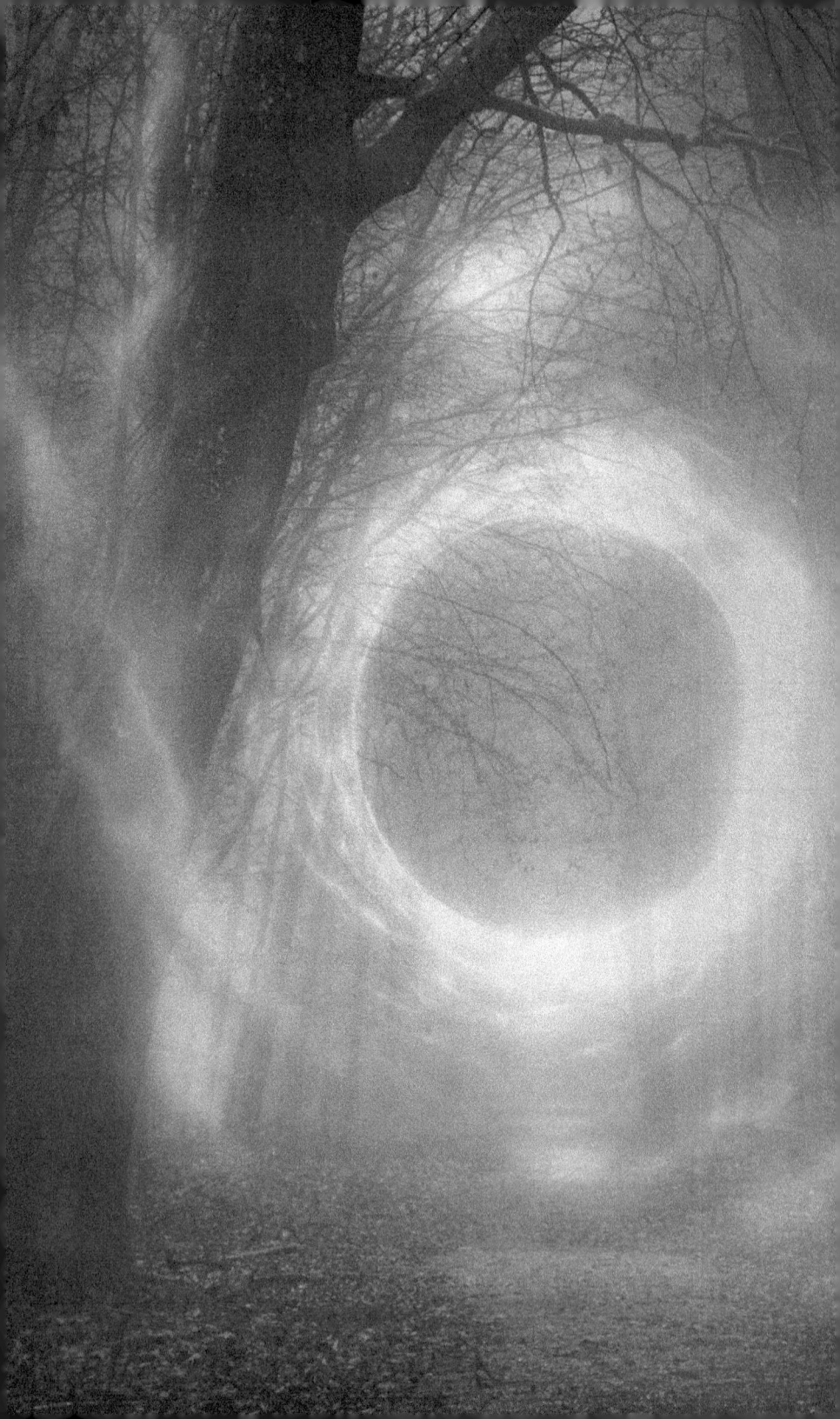

CHAPTER 13
GUILT TRIP

JULIUS

The following morning my heart still aches from my last image of Evalina. I knew this was to come. Knew this was the fate she was destined for. But I wish things could have gone much different. Despite her slight trust in me, I know I've broken all she believed in and she is only abiding me because I'm all she has left.

Vienna approaches me from behind as I debate whether or not to enter Evalina's chambers. "Everything okay, Your Highness?" she asks. Vienna has been working as a servant for many years now. A few days ago Valec promoted her, in a way. She is to become Evalina's lady's maid.

"Everything is fine." I can't possibly leave Evalina alone. Vienna may be a kind woman, but Alina does not know her. Despite Valec's request for Evalina to be escorted to breakfast by one of his guards, she will be escorted by me. I will not leave her side.

Vienna steps into the room and the sight before me shatters all I have inside. Evalina is curled up like a ball on the floor by the foot of the bed. She unfurls herself when she hears our foot-steps. Lifting her gaze to my own, her eyes are puffy and her cheeks show traces of dried tears.

Did she sleep at all? I try my best not to break apart on the very spot. "I'm so sorry," I whisper, crouching at her side and bringing her close to me. I pray she doesn't push me away.

She allows me to hold her. Behind us I hear Vienna making herself busy in the bathing chamber as she prepares Evalina's bath.

"I don't want to cry anymore." She speaks in a hushed tone. "I'm tired of crying."

"You don't have to."

"If I'm not crying, then what am I doing?" She straightens herself, her head moving away from my chest. "I feel like I owe it to them. They gave me everything in my life and I couldn't even be there in their time of death."

"Evalina." I hold her chin in my grip, forcing her to look at me. "You are not at fault for this. You mustn't think in such a way. I know what it's like to feel guilty over something that is not one's fault. It's the easiest way to help explain the *why* of something bad that has occurred. But in the long run it's detri-mental. You're only hurting yourself further."

"Julius, there's no other way to put it." She uncurls her legs. Her head falls back against the foot of the bed.

"Yes, there is. Those soldiers who went after you were sent from the Grand Church. If there's anyone to blame, it's the high priest and priestess."

She keeps shaking her head. "I don't understand," she says, frustrated.

"You will. How are your injuries?" I ask.

She lifts up her shirt to reveal unmarked soft flesh. "Good as new," she answers.

Vienna clears her throat in the background, and Evalina's

attention goes to her. "I'm sorry to interrupt, but your bath is ready Miss Evalina."

I rise and extend a hand to help her stand. "Evalina, I'd like you to meet Vienna. She will be your lady's maid for the time being."

"My lady's maid?"

"Yes, my lady." Vienna bows. "I'll be tending to your needs. Should you need anything, please feel free to ask me." I watch as Evalina takes her in, her stare going from Vienna's jet-black hair and deep chestnut eyes to the lush brown color of her skin.

"Nice to meet you, Vienna. I'm Evalina." Evalina manages a tight-lipped smile.

She nods. "The pleasure is all mine." Vienna beams at Evalina. "How do you take your bath?" her voice echoes from the bathing chamber.

"Um, warm," is all Evalina says.

Vienna lets out a light chuckle. "My apologies, what I meant to say was do you use any bubble bath or just soap?" She peeks her head out to look into the main room.

"Just soap is fine." I walk with Evalina to the bathing chamber where Vienna is crouched on the floor, searching in the cabinet under the basin. She retrieves several bars of soap. "Honey, lavender, or vanilla?" She holds them out for Evalina.

"Vanilla." She takes the creamy white bar in her hands.

Vienna places a robe on one of the hooks on the wall, along with some undergarments "Everything is ready," she says before stepping aside.

Evalina is a ray of sunlight when she walks back into the room, robe tightly wrapped around her. A bath did her good, though it's not enough to erase the dark circles under her eyes from lack of sleep. "Time for measurements." Vienna goes to her side, measuring tape in hand.

Evalina throws me a puzzled look. "You will be expected to dress nice, even if it is just breakfast." I answer. "I'll go make myself busy in the bathroom," I announce. I'm not about to make Evalina uncomfortable by remaining in the room while she's partially naked.

I pace around the room wondering what Valec is going to say to Evalina today. Will he tell her everything? Or will he leave her in the dark? I hate this feeling of not knowing.

There's a light tap on the bathroom door several minutes later, and Evalina peeks through. "We're done. You can come back now."

Vienna is long gone. I can't wait for Evalina to see how quickly her dress will be fashioned. The mansion seamstresses have various patterns at the ready. Gowns and suits are almost entirely confectioned; they alter the garments in accordance with the request. So, it's not about starting from scratch, but rather altering what's already been made.

We remain mostly in silence as Evalina gets a sense of all the furniture in the room. *Her* room now. "This room is a luxury, you know?" She stares at me through the full-length mirror that hangs on the wall beside her closet.

"I do know this," I answer. It's minutes later, and not a moment too soon, that Vienna emerges without warning, a dress in hand.

"I hope you find it to your liking." Evalina touches the delicate turquoise gown. The sleeves are short, much like the gown itself. It's a simple piece; perfect for gardening, she'd probably say. "Now, dress quickly; we need to work on your hair and makeup." Vienna urges her to move.

"How on Einalem did you have this made so quickly?" Evalina seems stunned.

"No time for questions. We must hurry," Vienna announces,

heading for the vanity by the front window. Evalina frowns, most likely irritated that no one seems to answer her questions around here.

"I guess I better tidy up as well," I say, staring at the clock hanging on the wall at the headboard of her canopy bed. "I will be back shortly to escort you," I tell Evalina.

She nods with understanding and I race down the halls, all the way to my own chambers.

Like a ghost, Soela lingers there when I enter the room. A grin adorning her face, she says "Welcome back!" She crushes me in a hug.

I laugh. "I was gone for only a few hours. You were already asleep when we got back. I didn't want to wake you."

"Sorry, I was tired." She shrugs and settles herself on the edge of the mattress. "So, she's finally here."

"She is." I take a seat beside her.

"And...what comes next?" she asks, curiosity taking hold of her.

"What do you mean?"

"Oh, don't play dumb, Julius. I mean what comes next for the both of you. Are you going to tell her the truth of why you were keeping your distance from her, or will you let Valec spill all the beans?"

"Valec is already going to spill the details. He invited her to breakfast. Which I should be getting ready for."

"That sounds like the perfect dismissal to my question. And wait a minute." She holds my arm, preventing me from moving. "Valec already met her?" I nod. "And what was her reaction?"

"Not a pleasant one, but I couldn't exactly ask her what she thought of him. When she was too busy mourning the loss of her parents." Soela lets go of me, sadness evident in her expression.

I walk to the edge of the door that leads to my bathing chamber. "Soela." She snaps her attention back to me. "It all depends on what Valec says to her. Based on whatever information she gains today, I will proceed from there."

"Still, Julius, that wasn't my question. Let me phrase it better: will you try to be with her again? In a romantic way. Will you confess those feelings once again?"

"I don't know." That's the truth. I wouldn't know how to proceed with Evalina in such a way. Not now that she's here. We all know Evalina's purpose for being in Inferis.

"You'll know again when the time is right." She twists the knob, exiting my room and leaving me with many thoughts that weren't there earlier.

I'm freshly bathed and shaved, dressed in a light beige tunic and dark brown hose. I rush through the halls, knocking lightly on her door once I arrive. This morning could go in either direction. That's why I must be prepared for any outcome.

Vienna is the one to answer. "Your Highness, please come in. Evalina," she calls over her shoulder, "Julius is here."

"I'm coming," I hear her say from afar. She must be in the bathroom. Vienna steps aside, letting me pass. I stand by the doorway, hands inside my pockets. When Evalina enters the room, I go completely lax on the spot. She's...*fuck!* I can't even find the right words. I bring my hands to my hair on a nervous impulse. Somehow finding my voice, I say, "You look stunning." I can't help but notice the light flush of her cheeks.

"Thanks," she answers quickly. Her hair is tied in a simple long braid that cascades down her back. Her face is absolutely angelic in every way, her natural beauty shining through.

"Shall we go?" She catches me off guard.

"Come again?" I remove myself from inside my head.

"I said, are you ready to go. Or are we not expected yet?" Evalina wonders.

"No, no." I shake my head. "Yes, let's go." I offer her my arm and she loops her own through. Relieved that one of Valec's men has not yet arrived to escort Evalina.

We're walking through the long halls, and I wonder if she's just as nervous as I am. Given Valec's show of authority last night, who wouldn't be?

We arrive at the dining room and the entrance is opened by the guards. "Miss Evalina Morue has arrived," one of them announces. "Accompanied by His Highness, Prince Julius." My title is what catches her off guard, her neck tilting up in my direction.

"Prince?" she echoes in a soft murmur that only I can hear. I wish I had time to explain but I don't; Valec's already seen us.

"Thank you, Hector," Valec says. "You may leave now." Hector bows and exits. I move across the room in a swift motion with Evalina by my side.

Valec already looks displeased as it is. At the very center of the room looms our table, made entirely out of glass. There's room to sit fourteen people in total. To the left and right corners of the light painted room are two smaller tables made to sit eight. Those tables are usually occupied when Valec's council and their families are invited to a banquet.

"Come." I guide her to the center. Valec sits at the head of the table as usual, wearing his signature colors, black and blacker. A large gem-encrusted chandelier hangs above his head. I take my place at his left side and Evalina takes a seat beside me.

Valec staples his fingers together. "Seems like you failed to adhere to my orders, Brother. Or did you forget my exact words before you left to show her to her chambers last night?"

"I didn't forget, Brother. I simply did not choose to follow said order." Evalina appears confused by my side. "I was not about to let a complete stranger escort her to breakfast."

"Well then, shall we eat?" Valec waves a hand over all the food on the table. "The food will get cold."

The table is full of various breakfast meats, cheeses, breads, and pastries. Valec shifts the direction of his gaze, ignoring me and giving Evalina all his attention. The same kind of attention a predator would offer its prey. I hope she hasn't noticed this, or she'll be even more uncomfortable.

I watch as Evalina serves herself some ham, bread, and eggs. She waits for me to finish serving myself before she begins eating her share. Valec ignores us entirely, already digging into his own plate.

Barely a minute into our meal, Valec clears his throat at my side, setting down his glass of mulberry juice. "Very well. It's time we discuss the matter at hand." Here it comes.

"What exact matter are we discussing, Valec?" I throw the question casually in the air, fork tight in my hand.

"A little impatient, are we, Julius?" He circles the rim of his glass. "All in due time." His cryptic tone is never a good sign. Valec wishes to drag on this conversation for as long as he can. It's his specialty.

"Let us start with Evalina's first question." Her eyes widen at the mention of her name. A piece of bread falls from her hands and back onto her plate. "You wish to know where you are, correct?"

"Yes," she answers without hesitation.

"And what if I told you that in some way, you are still in the mortal realm?" Valec's playing with her.

"I don't believe you," she spurts.

"It's the truth," I say, stepping into the conversation. "This was once a part of the mortal lands. Not anymore."

She throws me a look of annoyance. "Enough with the games! Can someone please tell me where I am?"

"Simple, Evalina." Valec keeps his focus solely on her. "You, my dear, are in Inferis."

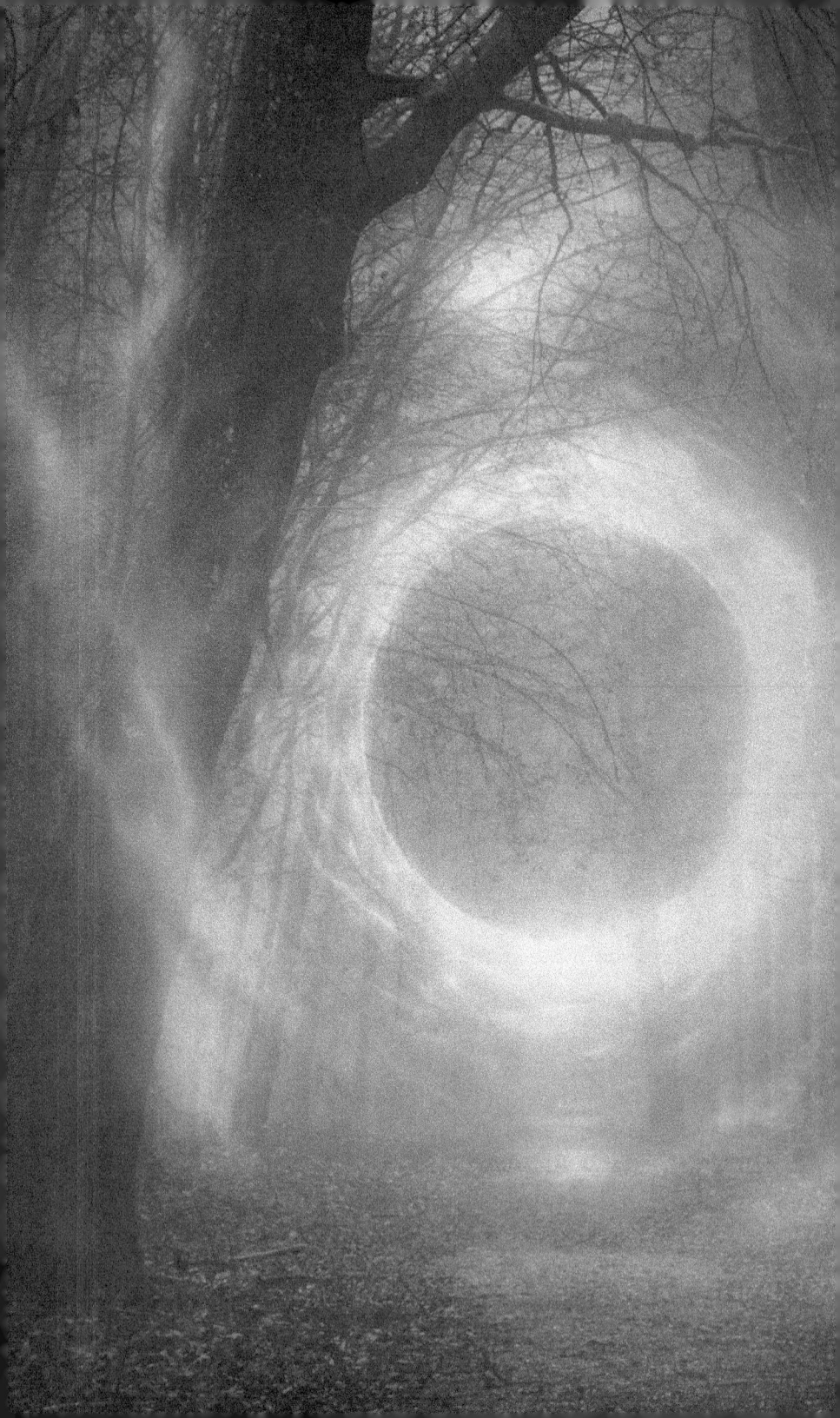

CHAPTER 14
THE BETRAYAL

EVALINA

I should be laughing at Valec's response right now. Instead, I know deep down that what I witnessed along my journey was otherworldly. Something that shouldn't exist but does. It's alarming to think that I'm here in Inferis, as he says. Because only the undeserving of paradise, come here to Inferis after death. Like those who live a life of evil and devotion to the Circle of Impure. Those who loyally follow the Devil. At least, that is what I know to be true. And as far as I know, I am neither of those things.

"I'm in the Underworld?" I call out.

"The *Underworld* is a degrading term used by you humans," says Valec. "I happen to despise every single one of those names. *Hell*, being another. This may be a hell, but this land's true name is Inferis. The land where sinful departed souls descend and are judged accordingly by yours truly." I am uncertain if I've heard correctly. I'm most certain I've misheard him.

My shocked expression says it all.

"Speechless, Evalina?" Valec smirks.

This is all too much.

When I finally find my voice all that comes out is, "You're the Devil?"

"I go by many names: Val to my closest friends, Your Majesty to my subjects, Lucifer to my followers, and the Devil to all those who fear me."

I should be afraid this very second. But the truth is, I always imagined Lucifer to be the color of crimson flowers or with ebony black skin, with sharp horns atop his head and a barbed tail. The ultimate look of dread. Evil incarnate. The man before me looks nothing as I imagined him to be. He is all man. Made of flesh and bone. Truth be told, the ugly creature that attacked me and Julius when we first arrived looked more like how I pictured him, in a sense. So, maybe the man sitting next to Julius is intimidating but at this very second, I do not fear him. At least not in the way I should.

Without looking at Julius, my eyes remain fixed on Valec when I ask my next question. "And why exactly am I in Inferis?"

"Do you truly wish to know?" Valec grins as his eyes go dark, and I suddenly feel the need to take back what I thought two seconds ago about not being afraid of him. Because he sure looks frightening now. I push away my half-eaten plate of food, having lost my appetite entirely.

I suddenly shift my gaze to Julius at my side and his head is down. "You, Evalina, are here because your life is owed to me," says Valec. "It's been owed to me since the day you were born. It took him a few years, but Julius found you. Little Evalina, a ten-year-old little girl who loved to climb trees."

I'm thrown off for the slightest of instances. He's lying...except I remember those light grayish-blue eyes from when I was a child. I begin to backtrack, recalling having met a man when I was ten who looked strikingly a lot like Julius. The resemblance hits me. I remain frozen in place. *No, this can't be.*

Then again, he turned me down each time I mentioned he

looked familiar to me. I pause my own train of thoughts. Julius brought me to Inferis. Of all places. During our trek here I thought we were traveling to the far-off side of Einalem or even to another continent. Instead, he brought me here to where the Devil resides. But how is that even possible? I'm not dead.

My hands fly up to cover my mouth when realization finally kicks in. No, this can't be true. I shake my head vigorously.

"You knew." I'm directing myself at Julius. Who's been like a statue at my side, unmoving, nor paying much attention to our conversation. He finally shifts, sliding his hands back from their place on the arm rest. "You weren't protecting me. You were protecting yourself, you son of a bitch!" He flinches at my curse. "All this time." My hands shoot to my head in distress. "Since I was a little girl. You—we had met before. It's all been a lie."

The betrayal sinks in deeper.

"You brought me here to be a slave, for your own sick amusement, not to keep me safe. Fuck, you sold my soul." I scream, pulling at my hair. "I was so stupid; how did I not see it?"

"Because at some point along the way, you fell for him," Valec interjects.

How he knows this is obvious. Julius must have told him. I feel like such a fool. I genuinely felt safe around him. From the very beginning all I knew of Julius was a false name and career, piled up with countless other lies.

I feel so stupid for having cared so much about receiving one of his nightly visits. And to think he's been using me this whole time. Getting close to me since I was a child, for crying out loud. That bastard. He did all that just to get me to trust him. I'm flooded with countless thoughts, but one particular memory stands out the most to me.

On one of the few occasions I visited the church with my parents, though we weren't really religious types, I spotted a painting of the fallen Lucifer and his brother, hidden away.

Where no congregants could easily spot it. I'd been seated at the right angle to get the slightest glimpse of the full picture. I recall having associated the brother's features with Julius's when we met in the forest. They looked identical, and now I know why. Because he *is* Lucifer's brother.

I stand in a rush, my chair scraping against the tile.

"One final word before you depart, Evalina." Valec says my name like a caress. I despise him for it. "You are here because you have power within you. Hellfire, to be exact. A power I have every intention of using in order to free myself from the confines of this land."

I ignore Valec entirely and turn my gaze towards Julius. "I'd say go to hell," I say with a glare, "but we're already here, aren't we?" Without looking at either one of them I storm out of the room as fast as possible.

"Evalina, wait." I hear Julius call after me. I hear his stomps coming from behind me and I pick up the pace.

I need some place to think, to process everything that has happened. But given that I'm new around here, I don't know where I'm going exactly. I pass by some people, servants wearing brown uniforms. Tears stream down my cheeks. I keep up my speed walking, hoping to lose Julius, who I can no longer hear behind me.

In my sudden haste to get away from him, I manage to find the exit out of the mansion. I run and don't stop until I stumble upon the garden we passed on the way here. I'm amazed that I remembered the way. But slightly fearful that I am completely ignoring the fact that there are monsters out here.

I finally come face to face with the veil. It continues to shine ebony and I instinctively reach a hand forward to touch it. I'm shocked. It's like trying to cross through solid granite. There's nothing there. No pulling, no tingling—it's just a hard surface, impenetrable.

"Evalina." Julius is catching up to me. I make do to hide

behind a bush. His steps become louder as he nears, and if I don't move now, he will find me. But when I try to move, I can't. My dress is caught on a low-hanging branch. I try to pull. It won't budge. *Shit!* Fine, then. I'll just break the piece of fabric off. Ripping a piece of fabric is more difficult than they make it seem in books. In the process, I end up losing my footing and come tumbling down, a sharp pain taking over my ankle. *No, no. Please let it not be broken.*

I get so caught up with my ankle that I fail to register the second a large figure looms behind me. I back away from instinct. "Get the hell away from me!" I cry out.

Not listening, Julius crouches down and scoops me into his arms, and I wince when my ankle grazes his leg. "Where does it hurt?" He crosses the field of flowers and trees with me in his arms. I don't give him an answer. "Evalina, swallow your damn betrayal and tell me where it's hurting." I want to tell him that everything hurts. Because he stabbed me with an invisible knife, and I feel completely used. He takes notice of my left ankle. "Is it broken?"

How should I know? I'm not a medic.

He places me on a carved stone bench nearby and kneels to examine me. Just his touch has me biting my lip, suppressing a scream. "Luckily it's not broken, just sprained." I pull away from him, and cry out as the simple movement of bringing my legs back causes the pain to worsen.

"Stop doing that. You're going to hurt yourself more," he reprimands me.

"I don't care."

"You will once the pain worsens. Let's get you to the infirmary *again*," he states. That's twice already. Apparently, I'm accident-prone. Granted, the first time was not my own fault.

"No!" I say with authority.

"This is not a negotiation." He huffs.

"I don't care if it is. Leave me like this. I can take care of myself. I'm here to die, anyway. Might as well speed the process up." I wave him off. The painful expression he wears will not fool me. No, that ship has sailed.

I try to stand, keeping my weight on one foot. I hop around, looking like an idiot, no doubt. But I can't make it out of the garden with so many plants everywhere. I'll only fall again. Needing a rest, I search for the nearest tree to steady me but find none. Julius is already at my side, planting my hand over his shoulder to steady my weight.

"Just let me take care of you and then you can happily go back to hating me. Since I know you won't want to hear my own explanation on the matter." Once again, I refuse to answer. Taking my silence as confirmation, I'm carried to my room, not the infirmary. "I'll be right back. Don't go anywhere."

This time, miraculously, I obey.

Julius returns with a medical bag. He removes a vial of clear liquid and I squirm, moving to the farthest side of the bed.

Reading my horrified expression, he says, "Calm down."

He tugs on my good leg, yanking me forward towards him. Without protest, he uncaps the vial and pours it over my ankle, not caring about ruining the bedsheets. "There, give it a few minutes, then you'll be as good as new."

I don't thank him.

The moment the pain ebbs from my ankle, I lift myself off the bed and say, "Get out." I practically shove him out the door, slamming it in his face. I crumple to the ground and let the tears flow once more. This time it is not Julius's comfort that will help me. It's the warm memories of my mother and father.

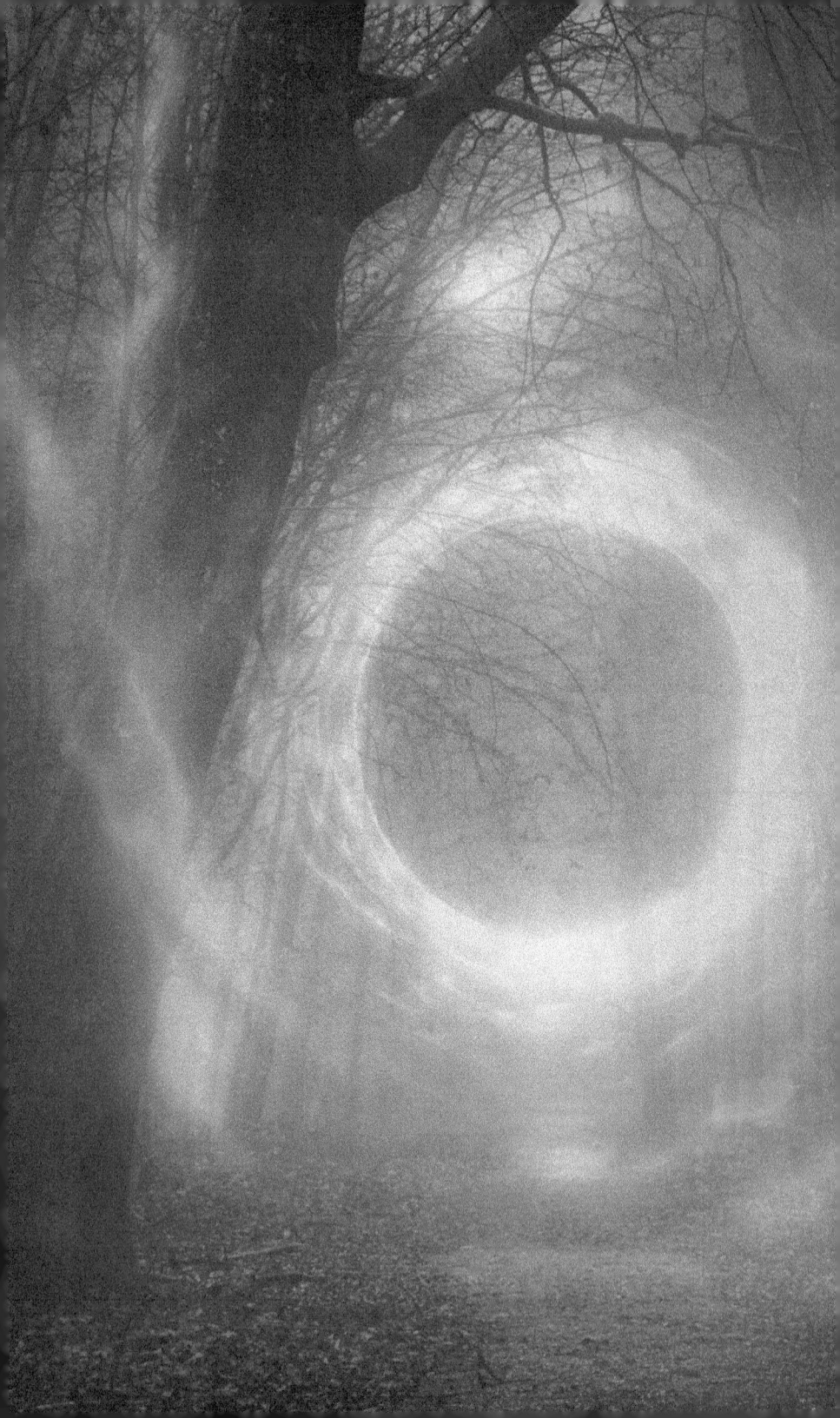

CHAPTER 15

THE TRUTH

JULIUS

The minute Evalina shoves me out of her room I make my way to the throne room where I know Valec must be. He always waltzes back there after breakfast. The guards at the entrance try to stop me, but I play the authority card. "I am your prince, and you do as I say. Now let me pass."

They exchange weary glances but abide, and behind me they say, "We tried to warn you." I walk in, only to find my brother lounging on his throne, a woman between his legs. She's startled when the doors close behind me. Valec's face goes from pleasure to straight up fury.

"Playtime is over," he says to the woman. She stands, adjusting the straps of her gown before exiting.

Valec casually leans back in his seat, and I get an eyeful. "I'd appreciate it if we could have a conversation without your member on display," I express.

"And I'd like a brother who won't interrupt the exact moment I'm getting blown," he snaps, but lucky for me he tucks his dick away, zipping up his trousers. "There, satisfied, Brother?"

"Very much. Now, would you like to explain why you made me out to be the villain? Evalina hates me now." I let my rage seep through. Evalina very much wants nothing to do with me.

"Have you forgotten her purpose, Julius?"

"No, Valec, I have not forgotten. How could I? When I'm reminded by you almost every day," I blurt.

Valec reads the expression on my face. "Don't worry, Jules. You know you can still be with her. That day the truth serum told me with whom your loyalties lie." *Asshole.* "Well, that is, if she ever trusts you again." He laughs.

I've had enough. "You're a real son of a bitch, you know that?"

Valec stands and makes his way to me. "Be very careful with what you say to me, Julius." He raises a hand and from it emerges a puff of smoke. "I advise that you remain in your place or there will be dire consequences. Why, there already are." His clearly amused voice echoes through the room. "Because if memory serves me correct, I was to have one of my men escort Miss Morue to breakfast this morning, but *you* escorted her instead."

That's why I got to her chambers first. Before anyone showed up. "I did what was best for her." I say the truth.

"Because you love her." I keep my mouth shut. "It's precisely because of your careless actions that someone has to pay the consequences. Shall I have someone fetch Evalina and have her pain tolerance tested for myself?"

"No!" I say with a growl.

"Then how about Soela." I squeeze my fists at my side. "I so did enjoy the last time I got to play around with her. Oh, how she screamed and begged for mercy—"

I snap, connecting my fist with his jaw. Valec falls back, landing flat on his ass. I grin in triumph, but it's short-lived the second my oxygen supply is cut off and I'm choking on smoke.

"That was very foolish of you, Julius." Valec stands over my floundering figure on the floor as I cling to my neck, needing this torture to stop. "Guards, retrieve the Four," he calls off into the distance.

I can feel the life slipping away from me. It's agonizing. Suddenly the double doors to the throne room swing open and in walk the four most deadly beings besides my brother.

Their faces are obscured within the hoods of their ebony cloaks, their signature cloth masks concealing most of their faces. Though I can tell them apart just by how they move.

They loom over me like a shadow, and Valec's magic retreats. The black cloud swirling over me vanishes entirely. He directs himself to the Four. "Do as you wish." Through the corner of my eye, I watch Valec return to his throne with the calm elegance of an evil tyrant.

I'm lifted off the floor, two pairs of arms gripping my shoulders. It's Aziel and Sairo who hold me in their grasp. Aziel is the man with pure brute strength, while Sairo is known for his swiftness. He can strike you like a snake, even while Aziel delivers the hardest blow.

"Take off his shirt," Anev orders from the other side of the room. As the only female in the group, she appears fragile but one should never be fooled by her. She's a skilled fighter when it comes to hand-to-hand combat.

She appears beside me with Recifer, who holds a whip in his hands. Recifer is kind of the leader of the group; he's in charge when Valec is not around. Aziel keeps his hands on me as Sairo removes my tunic and then the shirt underneath. He undoes the buttons in a swift motion, exposing my upper body to the cool air of night.

"The floor is all yours," Anev says to Recifer. Aziel and Sairo's grip tightens on my arms. Recifer moves to stand at my back, kicking the backs of my legs and forcing me to fall on my knees. I have no time to prepare, not as the snapping of the whip breaks through the air and lands at the center of my back. Recifer keeps going at it, the pain flaring all across my backside. I'm only thankful that he hasn't broken skin. *Woosh* after woosh as the whip slices through my skin, leaving me breathless and sweaty.

"Recifer, your usual expert technique seems to have diminished," Valec comments from atop his throne. Apparently he's unsatisfied with the damage inflicted upon me. "Those wounds will heal rather quickly, do you not think?"

"Yes, Your Majesty," he answers, like the good slave dog he is.

"Get the knives and bring some shade venom. I want him to spend a little while in agony," Valec orders them.

I remain on my knees for several minutes until I register the cold tip of a knife piercing the skin of my back. I hiss in pain. The knife presses deeper without mercy, as I feel a well of blood rushing down my back. I thrash and squirm the second Anev's calloused hands land on my skin, clutching a handful of venom within her glove. She presses the liquid to each wound Recifer left behind. One by one, cut by cut. They repeat the same action, stopping my immortal ability to heal myself. The substance prevents the wounds from closing. My head is spinning as I try to remain conscious. A pool of blood flows under me, my knees already soaked in it.

"I think that will suffice," Valec tells the four. Aziel and Sairo let me go and I fall flat on my face. "What do you think, Julius? Will your punishment suffice?"

"You're the expert in torture, Your Majesty. You tell me." I sneer his way.

Valec walks down the steps, taking the knife away from Recifer. He lifts me up himself, driving the knife across my arms and legs. I scream in pain; this is the worst he has inflicted upon me so far. He's merciless.

"It will only get worse from here on out, if you continue to challenge me, Brother. I gave you my word when I said that you can be with Evalina. All I'm asking in return is some obedience on your part." Satisfied with the wounds he inflicted, he shoves me back down. A rush of pure agony thrashes through me as I now lay on my back. "Dress him and send him on his way."

I have faint awareness of a pair of arms lifting me, dressing me, and then forcing me to walk. I move through the hallway in slow strides. My mind has no recollection of where I'm headed. I seem to have forgotten the way to my chambers. I arrive at a hallway that I know is not the one that leads to my room. These are the guest quarters, served for visits from the council or any other people of importance.

My legs give out from under me as I slide down the hallway wall. I remain sitting this way, staring down at my now crimson-stained clothes. The pain continues to pulse but by now it's infused in my mind, and I can't tell anymore if it's physical pain or if it's all inside my head. My eyes close and I still, waiting for sleep to claim me.

I eventually awaken, having no recollection of time. My only awareness is of the woman who has me leaning against her as she drags me through the hallway with an audible grunt. Only it's not just any woman, it's Evalina.

I somehow end up in the infirmary. I manage to sit myself on a stool. I'm immediately ordered to undress until I'm in nothing but my undergarments.

Lash marks adorn my thighs and over my arms. Evalina moves behind me, most likely studying the cuts on my back.

"It's the venom of the shades," I say, reading her thoughts. "The ugly monster we faced outside the mansion. The liquid that oozes out of their bodies is a type of toxin. It won't allow my body to heal on its own."

Evalina moves to my front. Her eyes catch my own, her face ashen. I swear I can see pain there, or maybe that's my mind playing tricks on me. Because I'm fairly certain she made her opinions of me quite clear earlier today.

"Who did this to you?" she chokes out as a tear rolls down her cheek. *Wait,* now that I'm surely not imagining. Is she truly crying? "It was your brother, wasn't it?" She fills in the blanks.

"Yes" is my short answer.

"Because of me," she says through wet lashes. "Did he hurt you because of me?" I remain silent, not knowing how to answer her question. Now that I'm awake the pain of my wounds is overriding all my thoughts once again, and I cannot think clearly with the pounding ache of the cuts at my back. The rest of my body is too numb to feel much at all.

"Jules." She says my name like a plea. My gaze snaps back to her piercing cerulean eyes. It's the first time she's ever used my nickname. Grasping my chin lightly, she forces me to look at her. "Jules, tell me. Did your brother hurt you because of me?" A simple nod is all I provide. She chokes on a sob. "Dear gods."

"If only you knew my brother while he still resided in Caelesti," I say to her. "He was a kind man, noble, honorable; he cared so deeply for others. He dedicated his whole life to serving Dominus. And he was the best little brother I could have asked for."

"Then what's changed?" She kneels before me, examining the cuts on my arms and legs.

"Much." She turns away from me, searching for supplies. "The fall took a toll on him. He eventually gave in to the nature of this place."

"But you didn't," she acknowledges, moving to my back. She takes a wet rag and begins to clean the wounds, removing all the poison Anev buried inside. I wince when the cold fabric touches my skin. "I'm sorry," she says.

"It's alright," I reassure her. "To address your statement,

well, that's where you're wrong. I'm not the same man I used to be in Caelesti either." She ceases all movement. The rag simply rests at my back. "Eventually, I found purpose…someone worth fighting for."

She clears her throat. "And who might that be?"

"A girl who captivated me from the very start. She became the sole reason I continued on with this journey."

"But in the end, it was all a lie, anyway." She moves to the next lash. "You didn't actually care for her. She was but a delivery meant to be retrieved for the Devil."

I shift on the seat, turning to face her, which costs me a great deal of discomfort. I take the rag from her and let it drop to my lap. Taking both her hands in my own, I press them to my exposed chest, right where my heart beats underneath. She gasps, feeling how my heart thumps at a speedy pace. "I have only ever had the best of intentions when it came to you, so I only ask that you have an open mind and listen to what I have to say. Can you do that?"

She remains silent for a few seconds, before answering, "alright, as long as you talk while I continue to tend your wounds."

"Deal." I hand her the rag once again and turn back, facing the infirmary door.

"You may speak." She places light steady hands at my back.

"The first thing you must know is that you aren't just some pawn in Lucifer's game. Your existence has a purpose." I pause a moment in case she wishes to interrupt. Greeted with silence, I proceed. "As Valec mentioned, you are the key to freeing him of this place. But in order for him to walk in Einalem once again, he'll need to use the power contained within you."

"What power? I have no powers," she questions.

"Have you ever felt like there was something about you that you couldn't explain? Something that never made sense?" I let her ponder for a few seconds.

"Yes," she answers sheepishly. "There were times when I'd wake up in the middle of the night, burning up, but it was never a fever."

I straighten in the chair. "Those were signs of your power slowly emerging, Evalina."

"You mean the hellfire Valec mentioned?"

I nod. "Are you familiar with the story of the Devil?" I ask carefully.

"Not in its entirety," she admits. "I've heard bits and pieces. But my family isn't exactly religious."

"Well, are you familiar with the day Lucifer walked the mortal lands after his descent to Inferis?"

"You mean the day the priest and priestess banished him from the lands? Yes, I know of that occurrence. Most of us do." She takes a deep breath, exhaling her next statement. "Twenty-two years ago, the Devil threatened to slaughter everyone in Einalem, and the high priest and priestess banished him in the name of Dominus before he could do any harm," she finishes.

"Evalina, that's not what happened. Valec never threatened anyone. He crossed the veil in good faith. He went to the capital searching for a way to contact Dominus because he wanted to explain himself. The Grand Church being the only point of contact with Caelesti, it was the only way."

Evalina moves the rag away. "Your back's all done," she announces and already I can feel the healing taking over. Thank Dominus that my front wounds aren't laced with venom as well, so it's just a matter of cleaning them. "Do you honestly wish for me to believe a story about Lucifer having arrived that day in good faith?" She shifts to her knees, tackling my injured legs first.

"He was an angel once, a god."

"And maybe he was a good man once, but he was corrupted. That's why he fell."

"That's not why he fell, why *we* fell. He was wrongfully

framed by one of the other gods. But that god took hold of Dominus's staff and held control over him and corrupted the mortal lands. That's why he cast us down. I was Valec's consolation prize. So he wouldn't have to rule over Inferis alone. But that night when he crossed over, he did not return the same. The banishment wounded him in such a way that he forced himself to turn into the very man the humans thought him to be. A monster, a tyrant, a killer, the very Devil himself. He snapped.

"He thought that if he could no longer plead his case by showing his innocence, that he might someday appeal to them through his wrath. So, before the banishment took hold of him, he set off a curse. One day a child of Inferis would be born, and on the night of their twenty-first birthday they would descend to Inferis and unlock the power that resides within them, becoming the key to freeing all the damned. Including the Devil himself."

Evalina holds my stare. Her hands cling to the side of my left thigh. "And that child is me," she states. "I'm the Devil's Curse."

"Yes, you are."

"And did my parents know about this? Of what I'd become?"

I shake my head. "The day we first met, I had no clue it was you. Until we touched. My palm heated up and a shockwave hit me. You were too young to have felt it back then. But that's how I knew it was you. On another night I spoke to your parents again. You were already asleep; that's why you never saw me."

"What did you say to them?" She returns to her task, now moving on with my arms. I extend them out for her, my palms facing upward.

"I only told them that you were in danger if they remained in Eremat. That there was a war brewing. Which was somewhat true because the high priest and priestess were on the hunt for you. I told them of a quiet village up north and they surprisingly agreed to move."

"So, my parents agreed to leave the capital without a second thought?"

"They trusted I was a soldier for the Einalem armies."

"You mean, you lied to them, just like you did to me."

"It was the only way," I confess.

"So, what, you watched over me all these years?"

"Yes. I did. But I always kept my distance." That's the truth.

"Out of duty to your brother?"

"Evalina—"

She cuts me off by holding up her palm. But even I know that what she said is the truth. No matter how bad it sounds. No matter how much I hate to acknowledge it. My loyalties lie with Valec. Because I long for the day I get to see my brother whole again.

"Give me a second to understand. Okay, I'm supposed to help free Valec from Inferis with my hellfire. Which I have yet to fully manifest. All in the name of some curse he accidentally cast out of spite for the priest and priestess failing to listen to him?" She's got it right.

"But what I'd like to know, Julius, is what would have been the other alternative? What do the priest and priestess want with me?"

"To prevent the first thing from ever happening, and to do that, they'd have to kill you."

"Then wasn't that the better choice?" she asks. "Have me killed and the Devil will never be freed."

"No!" I say too forcefully, which startles her. "That will never be a choice." I shake my head. "You don't get it. Yes, to Valec it's all about revenge now, but I don't think that's what will actually happen. I have a plan. A way we'll be able to appeal to Dominus this time around."

"You could have done that on your own. I mean, all these years you were roaming the nights in Einalem, spying on me. You could have easily done the same thing Valec did: go to the Grand Church and request a hearing with Dominus." She's right, though she's lacking one vital piece of information.

"Once Valec enacted the curse, my ability to even set foot in any holy landmark turned into an immediate death sentence. Believe me, I tried. So no, I can't go to the Grand Church without our full freedom," I finish explaining.

"How did you cross, anyway?" she asks. "Better yet, how did you initially cross? Aren't both the lands of the living and dead sealed off from one another to begin with? I mean, you don't see me crossing freely to Caelesti. So why is coming here the exception?"

"A woman who died all those years ago came to us one day. Her name is Soela. She showed us a way for Valec to cross during the nights of a blood moon when the veil between realms is at its weakest." I observe as realization dawns on her. "But after Valec was banished, he could no longer cross, so I took his place. I became the one who passed every night of the blood moon, at first in search of you. Then to watch over you."

"Again, out of duty—"

Now it's me who cuts her off. "At first, maybe. Then, not so much." Truth. There's truth laced in those words. Despite what the truth serum made me say a year ago.

"You don't have to lie."

I pause her movements by grasping her chin.

"You agreed you'd listen to me. What I have to say now is of utmost importance." I let go of her once receiving her sign of agreement.

"Night by night, I spent every moment I could by your side. Evalina, I may have had to lie to you a lot in order to get you here. But there is one thing I never did lie about, not even once, and that's about my feelings towards you."

"You grew distant," she comments, finishing the last of my cuts. My legs have now healed and so has my back. My arms follow. "How?" she asks, taking in my healed body.

"I'm immortal. Granted, I can be killed, by blade or by magic. My body, however, can heal itself in rapid succession if the wound is not fatal. But to return back to your first statement, yes, I did lose myself for a bit. I know this. I let my sadness take over. I let my guilt about lying to you take over. It consumed me."

"For a whole year," she states. "You were like a ghost for a whole year and the worst part is, I eventually stopped wondering why you were acting that way. Assuming it was probably the military that was consuming your life. I eventually grew content with just spending time with you every chance I got, even if I didn't get to have you at one hundred percent. For that, I apologize. For not having fought for you, for not communicating with you properly."

"I'm the one who should be apologizing, not you." I take her hands in my own. "I'm sorry. I'm sorry for this fate that was thrust upon you. I'm sorry I had to lie to you about it. I'm sorry for being distant. I'm sorry for everything. I hope now that you've heard me that you understand it was never my choice to stop this from happening, though I wish I could. But now you're here, and all that's left is to see this through."

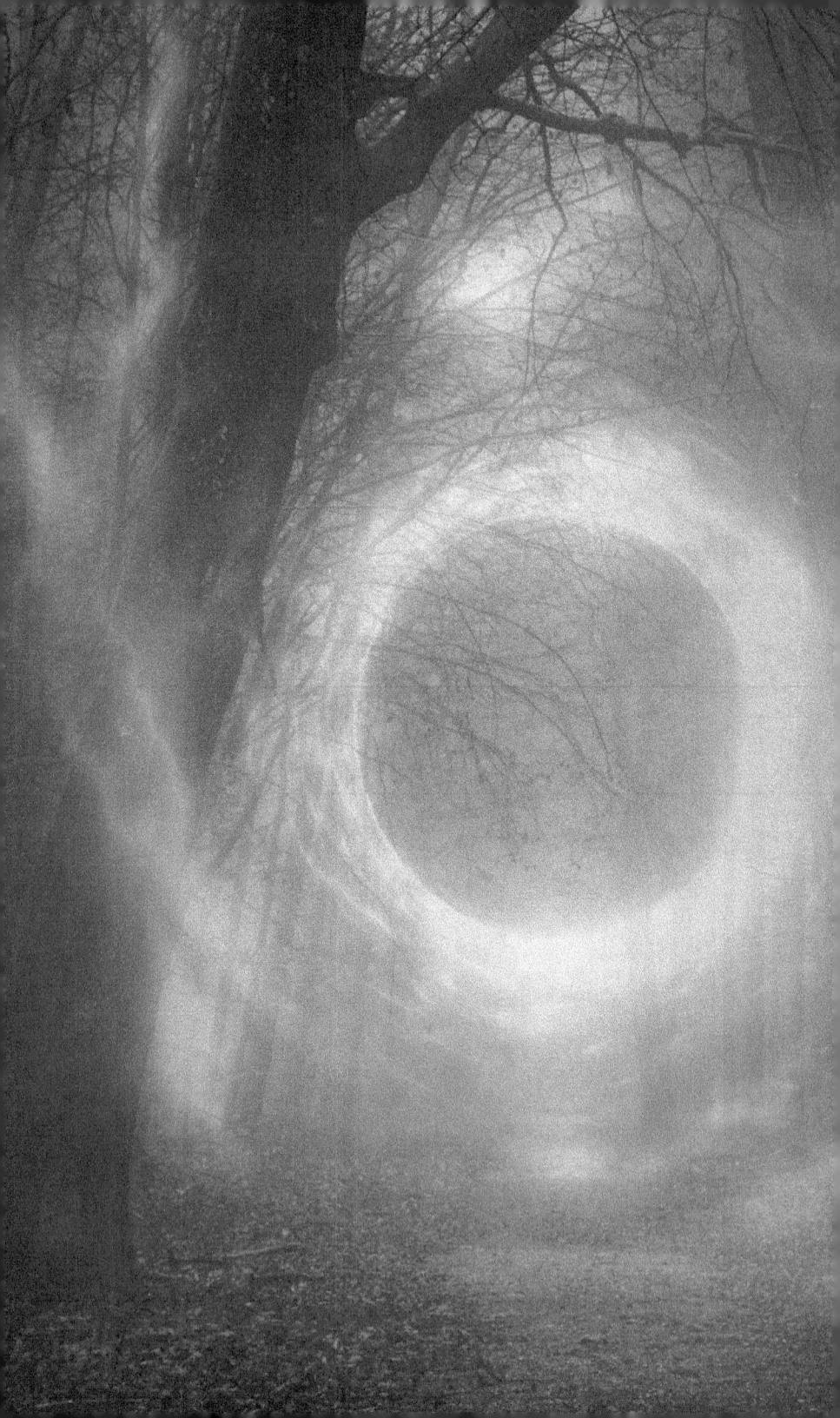

CHAPTER 16
A PLAN

EVALINA

J ulius makes a move to stand and I instinctively try to help
him up, assuming he's still hurt even after watching his
injuries seal up and fade.

"I'm alright." Despite admitting so he leans on me as a
precaution. Once on steady feet I avert my gaze from his body,
now having noticed that he is practically naked in front of me.

He chuckles. "Oh, so now you're shy. You weren't before."

"Before, might I remind you, you were coated in blood, and I
was fearing for your life."

"Well, considering I have no clean clothes on me, I'll have to
make the trip to my chambers in my underwear." He passes me
by, needing no help, and exits the infirmary first. I receive a very
candid view of his glutes against the fit of his tight undergarments. He holds the door open for me to pass through. I move
quickly ahead of him.

"Wait!" Julius grasps my forearm. Spinning me around, my
chest collides with his own. I tilt my head back, trying to read his

expression. Worry lines cross his face. "I need to know where you stand in regard to what I just shared with you."

I take a deep breath before answering him. "I understand where you're coming from, Julius, and I accept your apology. However, I will need time to figure myself out. I still care for you, Jules." I reach a hand out to caress his cheek, and he leans into the touch, tilting his head slightly. "But at least for now, what I need most is a friend."

"I can be that for you," he whispers, even though the hallway is empty at the moment. "Whatever you want, Evalina; it is your choice."

"Thank you." I truly am grateful for his understanding, for giving me the time and space I need to make sense of this life I never knew I was destined for.

I return to my chambers, where I spend the rest my evening, until it's lights out. Julius's admission remains floating around in my head. I'm deep in the middle of processing it. There's no doubt in my mind, I believe every word he said. And because of it, I feel stupid for having raised my voice at him. For saying the nasty things I did. I'd take them all back if I could. He knows this, though he didn't allow me to speak much. The second I began apologizing he stopped me from doing so. And though part of me might still be cross with Julius, everything he did was to protect the people he cares about, me included. So, no matter how unfair what he did may seem, I have much more to consider than just my hurt feelings.

It's the next morning, a knock at my door startles me awake and Vienna comes rushing in, face coated in sweat. "Miss," she addresses me. "His Highness has requested an audience." It takes me a full five seconds to remember who His Highness is, but once I come to my senses that it's Julius she's speaking about, my nerves ease away. Valec is the one addressed as His Majesty.

"Right now?" I say, sliding off the mattress.

"Yes, I'll give you some time to ready yourself. Then I'll escort you to the kitchens."

It only takes me a few minutes to look a bit more presentable in a pair of black trousers and a billowy violet shirt. Vienna opens the door, pleased to find me ready.

It's not far to the kitchens from the guest chambers. They are literally next to one another. Just a quick walk through a small hallway and *boom,* we've arrived. People rush in and out of the room, carrying trays of food. Julius waits for me, standing behind a dark granite counter. Two tall wooden chairs adjacent to one another perch at the front. "Good morning," I say as I approach him, taking a seat on one of the stools.

Behind Jules I spot multiple clay ovens and extra counters where men and women are busy at work. The kitchen is warm and inviting. I'm wrapped in the delicious smell of bread and pastries.

"Morning, Alina." My heart gives a tiny skip at the use of my nickname.

A man walks up to our table with a tray in his hands. He sets the plates down in front of us. "Good morning, Your Highness." He turns from Julius to me. "I believe we have not met." He extends his hand out to me. I grasp it with my own, giving it a firm shake. From this angle I take in the light gray tint of his eyes, a direct contrast to his short hazel locks. "I'm Romar, the chef," he says with a thick accent. I could be wrong, but he looks relatively young, probably in his third decade of life when he passed away.

"Nice to meet you. I'm Evalina, though I suspect you already knew that."

"Guilty." He smiles, placing a plate of food in front of me.

"Turkey bacon, toast, banana muffin, asiago cheese." He places a smaller plate next to the other. "And a side of fruit. Julius mentioned you like muffins, so I made a batch earlier this morning."

My attention snaps back to Julius and that time he brought muffins over to my parents' bookshop. It's one of my favorite memories to this day.

"You remembered." I pick up my fork and dig in.

"Was I supposed to forget?" He arches an eyebrow.

"I can't answer for you." I shrug my shoulders.

Romar leaves us to our breakfast, getting back to work. Julius picks up his own fork and joins me. "Though you never did tell me which kind is your favorite."

"Banana, actually."

"Really?" He's in disbelief.

"Yes, banana muffins are my favorite. So lucky guess."

"Lucky indeed."

After a few moments of eating in silence, nothing but the sounds of cooking utensils in the background, Julius shifts at my side. "Evalina, there's someone I'd like you to meet today."

"Who?" I can't help but wonder.

"The woman I told you about yesterday, Soela."

"Alright. When?" I ask, cleaning my crummy face with a napkin.

"I told her to meet us at noon, so in an hour."

It's exactly twelve o'clock when we arrive at a massive training room. The gloomy walls are covered top to bottom in weapons. I spot padded mats on every corner of the room, for combat and weapon training, I suppose. There are so many mats that I can barely see the tiled floor underneath. This place is actually quite intimidating, if you ask me. There are even targets for dagger throwing. It's a room perfectly made for a warrior like Julius.

The doors to the training room open after us and in walks a

striking woman. Her red hair hangs over her shoulder in a perfect side braid. She looks young, not much older than I am. Her clothes are simple, but immaculate. Wearing a light pink gown that reaches just above her knees, she looks angelic in every way. One could very much mistake her for an angel residing in Inferis.

"Jules." The woman walks to Julius first, engulfing him in a hug.

"Soela." He returns the gesture. "There's someone I'd like you to meet." The woman turns her gaze to me, her wide, grayish-blue eyes staring into mine. "Soela, I'd like you to meet Evalina." He directs himself to me. "Evalina, I'd like you to meet Soela."

In mere seconds the woman is hugging me the same way she did Julius. "Evalina, you have no idea how long I've wanted to meet you." Her admission catches me off guard.

She releases me from her embrace and I'm able to breathe again. "You've wanted to meet me?" I say, dumbfounded.

"Of course. Who do you think has been Julius's wingwoman all this time." She grins.

"Really?" That's interesting to know.

"Of course, you don't know how annoying it was to hear Jules pining over you." She throws him a sly grin.

"Hey!" Julius complains. "So, I was annoying to you? And how come this information has just now reached me?"

"Because I'm a supportive friend who cares deeply and never wanted to make you feel bad about your feelings for the girl you were falling for." She bats her lashes at Jules, and he chuckles.

He wears an annoyed expression. "Good to know I can count on you, Soela."

"Always." She adjusts her skirts. "Now, time for the topic of discussion. What I was called here for." She snaps her attention back to Julius.

"Well." Julius moves to sit on one of the mats on the floor.

Soela and I follow his lead. "I think it's safe to say that Evalina here already knows everything."

"Everything?" Soela questions, taking a seat on Jules's left while I sit to his right.

"Yes. Now, I brought Evalina here so that we may discuss the ideas you've had regarding Evalina's powers and all that's to come." Julius speaks as if I weren't in the room.

"Alright then, but let me start from the top." Soela looks at me. "When Valec created the curse," she says carefully, "he did it in a moment of pure rage and helplessness. I believe that in order for you, Evalina, to unlock your magic you will have to do the same." She pauses. "A likely moment for your powers to have emerged would have been during your parents' passing." I stare at my hands, trying my best to not go back to that image of their stiff bodies on the bed. "So, I wonder what emotional trauma you'd have to face in order for said hellfire to make an appearance. If it didn't do so in that moment."

"Does Valec know this?" I find myself asking.

"I believe he does, but he's being awfully quiet about it. He probably doesn't even know what he wants to subject you to yet." Julius stiffens at my side at Soela's last words.

"He'll think of anything if he's desperate enough," he comments.

"Yes, but let us not ponder on that matter." She inches closer to me. "Your hellfire, Evalina, once manifested and controlled, has the power to do more than just open the veil."

"What do you mean?" I question, curious about the answer and fearful at the same time.

"Julius and I have been discussing this for a few years now and we believe there's a way to bring Valec back. The old Valec. The man who used to be an angel. There's a way for us to return his innocence back to him. You burn with hellfire inside you, and I have reason to believe that if directed at Valec, it will melt through his cold exterior. Melt through the curse, in a way."

"Won't doing so kill him?" I shoot her a concerned look.

"No, not with how far gone he is. I had this thought for a very long time before I shared it with Julius, due to fear of the Four lurking about, and until I was one hundred percent sure my theory was correct, I also couldn't risk giving him false hope. That's why I kept researching."

Knowing I have no idea of these mysterious Four Soela speaks of, Jules elaborates. "The Wicked Four are Valec's henchmen and woman. They're the ones who hurt me yesterday on Valec's command. They're always lurking about when you least expect them."

"You were hurt?" Soela's eyes widen, and she looks to Julius for confirmation, examining to see any wound.

"I'm alright."

"Now, but you scared me to death," I end up saying.

Soela is now staring at me, a ghostly expression in her eyes.

"Evalina helped me," Julius says to her.

"Good, now returning back to the plan. If it fails and Evalina is unable to bring back the old Valec using her power, then we must be prepared to stop him. We can't allow him to set foot on the mortal realm once that veil is opened. All he wants is to wreak havoc upon the land. He wants his revenge for all those who doubted him. He's angry."

"That's why he needs to be stopped," Julius chimes in. "If plan A were to go wrong, then the three of us would have to find a way to get to the capital before Valec and do as he wished all those years ago: appeal to the Grand Church, summon Dominus, and have him release Valec of this curse."

"How do you know Dominus will be able to help without striking him down?" I question. I know I've been asking many questions, but what we're discussing here is the fate of all of Einalem, which is a serious topic to begin with. I need to know everything in order to stop Valec from destroying my home.

"There's no certainty that he won't, but we need to have faith." Soela glances at Julius and places a reassuring hand over his, and it somehow fills my heart with warmth. Seeing someone care so much for Julius. Watching them, I can clearly see that Soela is like a sister to him.

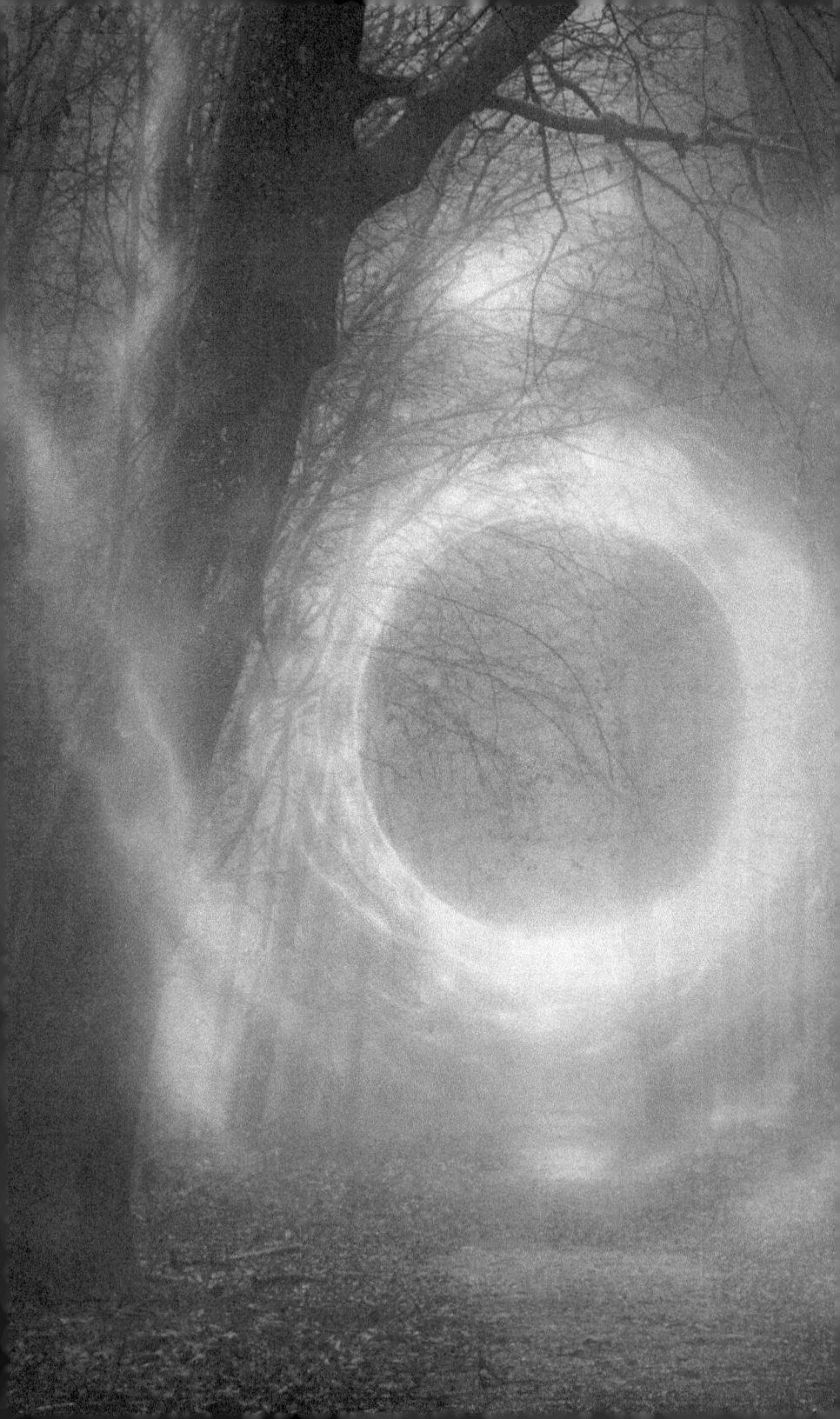

CHAPTER 17
WONDROUS LIBRARY

JULIUS

I t's the middle of the night when I throw a cloak over my night attire and step into some sturdy boots before exiting the mansion.

I walk slowly through the caverns, and most of the houses I pass are pitch black inside. No one is usually awake at this hour.

I take a bit more time than normal to reach the garden to think and simply enjoy the quiet and fresh night air. The garden has always been my happy place. It's the one place I know I can be truly alone, my own sanctuary, of sorts. I know I can always come here when I'm having a bad day or need to get away from Valec.

I hear a bark nearby. *Saint?* I could have sworn he was sleeping peacefully at the foot of my bed before I left. I can't blame him; I did install a door for him to come and go into my chambers whenever he pleased. However, how come he's here at the gardens? Did I somehow leave the mansion door open? Maybe one of the guards let him out. Though he knows he isn't allowed to wander outside without me.

I round a corner and there, sitting on one of the stone benches, is Evalina, petting Saint. He sits by her legs, head lowered in submission. My intention is to be silent, but a twig snaps at my feet. Evalina freezes and Saint jumps into action, growling. Good to see that I can count on him to defend her.

"It's only me." At the sound of my voice Saint calms and runs to me, his tail wagging from side to side. "Hi, buddy." I crouch down to give him a little pat on the head. "Good boy."

I stand and catch Alina staring at me. "Can't sleep either?" she questions.

"No."

She looks down at Saint, who's now moved to rest his head atop her knees. "You know, you never did tell me why Saint doesn't appear to age either. The same rule that applies to you can't possibly apply to him as well."

"He's not an immortal being, if that's what you're asking. But his aging is significantly slowed. You see, animals can cross between worlds."

"They can?" She's amazed by my confession.

"Yes, how else do you think I sent Saint after you when I couldn't go anywhere. Animals can cross because according to the law of life, they have no souls."

"So, for how long can he live?" she asks.

"I can't tell you exact numbers. But he's been with me for a while." I sit beside her. Changing the subject, I say, "Are you okay with what Soela told you?"

"Yes, though I'm worried about what it will take for my hell-fire to make an appearance. Also, about what Valec might subject me to. Do you think he'll torture me to get my powers out?"

"I don't know." I shake my head, getting the image of her beaten body out. "I could say a million times that I hope not but knowing him, nothing can be ruled out, though I don't think that will be the case. You know, I am really sorry, Evalina," I say. She snaps her head to me. "You didn't deserve this kind of fate. You didn't deserve to lose your parents."

"You mentioned before that it was the high priest and priestess's fault. Now I get it. They were after me that night."

"They were actually conducting the search, along with the soldiers. I saw them before I saved you outside the bookshop."

"You said it yourself, Jules: my fate was decided for me before I was even born. No one could stop it, especially you. You've been protecting me all this time. For other reasons, of course." I flinch. "But now it all makes sense. It's finally starting to click. If anything, you were just as fated as I was. Valec couldn't, so he made you do all the dirty work."

"I can't say that it was dirty work in the end. At the beginning, yes. Knowing I was in search of a child I'd one day have to rip away from their family. Then when I met you, it all changed. You were so different from what I expected." Out of fear, I say nothing further. I may be prepared to openly admit my feelings to her. However, I know Evalina needs time to process all she's learned, about me, about herself and her purpose.

I fidget in my seat. "If you don't feel like going back to bed, I have a place I'd like to show you."

"A place?" She arches an eyebrow.

"The library." Her expression lights up.

"Say no more." She leaps to her feet, startling Saint. "Sorry, Saint." She caresses the back of his neck.

"Saint, back to the mansion, go." He obeys, making his way out of the gardens.

We walk side by side. The sound of light water drops falling from a nearby stalactite is our only companion. "You know, you shouldn't be outside the mansion without company. You never know when a shade might pop up out of nowhere."

She throws me a sharp look. "I wasn't alone. Saint was with me."

"That doesn't count."

"It does to me." She saunters on ahead of me. She truly did learn the path from the garden to the mansion well.

We're finally safe behind walls and I happily guide Evalina through the hallway. The library happens to be adjacent to the throne room on the second floor. Once inside, I can't help glance at Evalina's expression, and it's priceless.

The library was one of the first rooms built on the second level. It stands at two floors. On the top floor is the reading area, filled with plenty of tables and chairs to fit as many readers as possible. Below is where the glass cases stand, housing tons of books of all shapes, colors, and sizes. This is the most illuminated room in the entire mansion due to the large, bright crystal chandelier that hangs high on the ceiling, right near the veranda that hangs off the second floor, overlooking the first one. Multiple circular lanterns hang from each beige wall.

"This room is ten times bigger than the throne room," Evalina exclaims and her voice echoes. "It's enormous." I remain by the entrance as she runs towards the shelves. "Forgive me, but this is not a library. This is something else entirely."

"Surprised?" I finally move, following her as she gets lost amongst the books. Her mouth is agape in wonder as her feet glide across the velvet carpet.

"I feel like this is some sort of mirage or I'm dreaming the whole thing." She doesn't take her eyes off the tomes.

I chuckle. "I can assure you, you aren't dreaming." I pop my head between one of the shelves. "This is my second sanctuary. Apart from the garden," I explain. "Valec doesn't have an interest in reading. He's more adventurous. Parties, loud music, sex, and when he can, all of the above at once."

"That statement does not surprise me in the least." She eyes the spines of various tomes, stopping to read the titles. "Any favorites?" she asks.

"Plenty, but I'd like for you to find your own to read first. Then I'll hand you one of my favorites."

"Alright. It's a deal." She walks further into the room.

"If you're looking for a specific genre, the shelves have a hanging banner that state the genre," I call out. "It will make your search much easier."

"Thanks," she shouts back, skipping over shelves containing Contemporary, Historical Fiction, Science Fiction, Romance until she finally reaches the genre I know she's looking for: *Fantasy.*

With a book in hand, she races up the winding staircase, setting the book down at the nearest table. I follow after her.

"Found something you like?" I arch an eyebrow, studying the book in her hands. *The Ballad of Masquerades.* Can't say I ever read that one before.

"Yes, I did." She pulls out one of the wooden chairs and I sit beside her, opening the flap of the dustjacket where the synopsis should be. She sets the book in the middle so we'll both be able to read it.

Huh, I have to admit that sounds quite intriguing. "Okay, the synopsis won me over" she says, her face lighting up with fascination.

"Same," I agree.

"We can read it together if you want?"

"Sounds like a plan." I peruse the pages, arriving at the prologue, and begin to read out loud. "'*Today was as uneventful as any other day...*'"

Evalina and I are both startled awake. I remember us reading for about an hour, just the sound of our voices as we took turns reading a chapter, and then our eyes had gotten tired. We eventually dozed off.

A loud rumbling resounds from outside, most likely coming

from the hallway. I look to my side; Evalina seems as alert as I am. Pushing ourselves from our chairs, we move quickly downstairs.

"What is it?" She comes up behind me.

"I don't know. But I'll go check. You stay here."

"Are you sure you don't want me to come with you?" she questions.

"You're safe in here."

"Surrounded by a bunch of books? I mean, they do make good weapons for flinging at someone, but I'd hardly say they're *that* practical a weapon."

"Please, just stay here! I promise I'll send someone for you if I take too long," I say before exiting the room without waiting to hear her protest.

I move through the halls and the black inky stains covering the floor indicate what exactly lurks inside the mansion. A shade. But how on Inferis did it get inside? There are meant to be guards outside the front doors. The path of ink blotches leads me to the kitchens and, sure enough, the sound of munching greets me.

It seems to be trying to get inside the ice box. Relieved that no one is working in the kitchens at this hour, I unclasp my cloak and remove the dagger from the pocket of my night trousers. I always carry it with me for safety. Glad I've never fallen out of the habit of carrying a weapon with me at all times.

It doesn't hear me as I approach, nor when I lunge for its head. It shrieks the moment I pierce its scaly flesh with the silver tip of the dagger. It fidgets and manages to remove the dagger, tossing it across the room. Blood spurts out of its neck. I move in for the killing blow as it tries to recover and come at me, snapping at me with its razor-sharp teeth. I'm able to move my arm away just in time, grabbing hold of its head. I apply pressure while it screams and kicks. Once I hear the slight rip of flesh, I know I've severed its head and watch as it falls to the floor at my feet.

Something to never forget. There are only two ways to kill a shade: through the head or through the heart.

I clean everything up, disposing properly of the shade's dismembered body outside, deep within the caverns.

Once that has been taken care of, I make my way back to the library. "All is well—" My words linger in the air.

I search both floors of the library just in case. Evalina's not here. I race to her chambers and knock twice; the door is unlocked. An empty room is all that greets me. She's not here either. She couldn't be in the gardens. I had to take that path in order to dispose of the shade's body—I would have seen her if that were the case. Panic takes over. Where could she be?

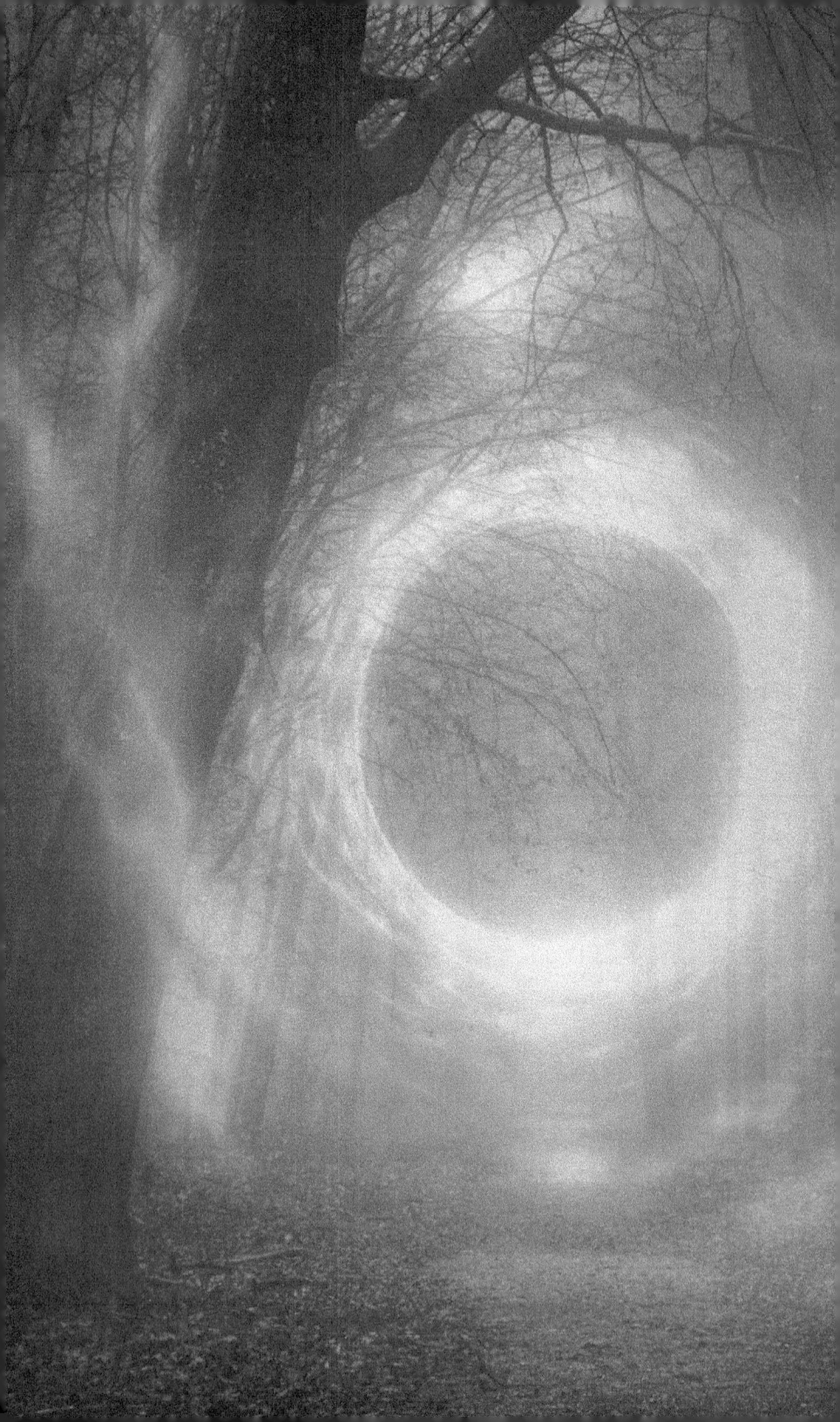

CHAPTER 18
BARGAIN MADE

EVALINA

The strange noise seems to have died down. Everything is silent. Then the coast must be clear. I know Julius said to wait for him in the library, but fifteen minutes have already gone by, and I can't hear anything amiss.

I peek my head through the door, book tucked securely under my arm. There's certainly nothing out of order. Except a few dirty prints on the floor, which I notice as I trudge down the hallway. I pass the dining room, then the throne room, and once I reach an unfamiliar turn I realize I'm heading the wrong way. My room is on the left side of the mansion. And yet I consider myself intelligent. In my defense, who wouldn't get lost in here? This is literally a palace.

I follow the muddy prints back, nearing the servants' quarters, when the door to the training room opens. I jump, my lungs suddenly ceasing their work at the sight of Valec. "What are you doing, Evalina? I thought Julius left you in the library."

How does he know this? Perhaps Julius told him. "Was I meant to stay there the whole night?" I raise my voice at him.

A brave move, I know. But I can't act as if I fear him. "The odd noises stopped so I came out." I place my hands over my hips.

"Well, that was a very bad decision on your part." He yanks me by the arm. "Get in here." I thrash against his hold as he lugs me into the room. No lights are on, so I can't see anything. Soon enough, he's unlocking another door. This house sure has a lot of rooms. We pass through a dimly lit hallway, veering right, then right again until finally making a left. No surprise, there's yet another damn door.

"Let go of me!"

"I will once you get inside." He shoves me through as he turns on a lamp. A large black canopy bed is the first thing to greet me. It takes up most of the room. Only that's not true. There's more open space as one keeps walking, with couches and a coffee table. He has his own living room right in his chambers!

"Take a seat, Evalina." He crosses his arms in front of him. And who am I to disobey him? I sit on the farthest side of the divan.

"Funny how my brother healed himself rather quickly, I might say." Valec crosses the room till he's standing under the archway that leads to his chambers. "Almost as if he had help. Might I assume that help was provided by you?" He looks straight at me.

"You have a lot of nerve saying that."

"My dear, I believe you still don't understand how things work around here. You obey me, and when mistakes are made, disobediences aren't taken lightly. From anyone, not even my brother."

"Why are you like this? Why did you have to transform into such a hateful person? You could have kept trying. Trying to find people in your favor, instead you gave into your wrath and now here we are."

162

His eyes light up with amusement. "It appears that Julius has been talking." Shadows cross his features.

"He has." I return to standing. "He's told me everything I need to know and that's why I'll tell you this. You can do whatever needs to be done in order for my power to surface. If I have to go through emotional or even physical suffering, I will comply as long as you keep Julius out of it. He's had enough torment in his life. You leave him be and I'll do what is needed. Am I understood?" I'm now standing right in front of him.

His icy eyes bore into mine. "Your courage is admirable. But arranging bargains is a dangerous endeavor. Anyone with common sense would know that."

"Call me nonsensical then."

"Very well, I'll accept your offer. Consider Julius spared from all harm. But it will be your job to keep him in line. If he aggravates me once when we commence—"

"I will keep him in check. You have my word."

"Your promise will need to be sealed, as all official oaths are here in Inferis." *Does he mean through blood?* "Come here, my dear." He rummages through one of his drawers and pulls out a thin throwing knife.

With a firm face he brings the blade across his right palm, cutting a small line. Blood immediately begins to ooze out. He grabs a hold of my left hand and does the same to me. I wince at the contact of the sharp blade against my skin and watch the blood leaking out with odd fascination. He links our hands together, our blood mixing.

"There." Valec quickly removes my hand from his. I stare in amazement at how the wound in his palm slowly closes itself. While my hand continues to bleed. He hands me a clean piece of cloth, then proceeds to bandage my palm. "Now your oath is sealed. Break it and know that the consequences will befall Julius."

His threat is clear as day. I made the promise and sealed it with my own blood. There's no turning back now, only moving forward.

A loud thud that comes from outside startles both of us. "Valec, open the fucking door!" Julius yells. "Valec!" He pounds his fist louder against the wood.

Valec walks away to his main chamber, letting Julius in. I can't see either of them since I'm in the living room. But judging by his voice he isn't happy. "Where is she?" Julius is frantic. "What have you done to her?"

"Calm down, Brother." I make my way to them. "She's safe." But they meet me halfway, standing in the middle of Valec's room. "See, perfectly fine," Valec exclaims in my direction.

Julius startles me the moment he picks me up. "Are you alright?" He's got me so tightly pressed to his chest that I can't breathe, nor form a single answer.

"Brother, you're squeezing the life out of her," Valec informs him, and for the first time I'm thankful for his intrusion.

"I'm fine," I say once on solid ground.

"You left the library after I told you not to," he scolds.

"I didn't hear any noise. I thought it was okay."

"But it wasn't." Oh, he's mad, alright. "Not when it was all Valec's doing. With a little encouragement one of the guards sang like a canary." He turns and gives his brother a glare.

"What are you talking about?" I ponder.

"Valec's the one who released the shade inside the mansion just to send me on a wild goose chase. Now I know why." He turns back to me. "To get to you."

"Oh Julius, the ever intelligent one. " Valec claps his hands. "Even if you are correct, none of that is of importance now. Because while you were gone," he sits on the edge of his bed, crossing a leg over his knee, "Evalina and I had the most stimu-lating conversation."

"Well, conversation over." Julius takes my hand in his. I flinch at the contact of his skin on my bandaged hand. Studying my palm closely, Julius's features go dark. Rage flashes across his eyes.

"You did not," he whispers. "To hell with this." He launches at Valec. But Julius doesn't get far before Valec has him suspended in midair within seconds. A puff of black smoke emanating from his hands keeps Julius rooted in place.

"She chose this, Julius," Valec says.

"No, she didn't; you set her up," Julius spits.

"It may have started out that way. But it was Evalina who made the oath out of her own free will. I make no bargains by force. That's the one liberty I grant."

"Let him go, Valec. You promised. Now hold your end of the bargain," I say, keeping my voice steady.

"As you wish." Julius is released, landing gracefully on his feet.

Now I'm the one at his side in an instant. "Are we free to leave?" I ask Valec.

With a flick of his hand the door swings wide open. "I'll be seeing you soon, Evalina. So that we may commence our affairs. I know just the trick to start up that hellfire in you."

I have a hard time keeping up with Julius, as he moves at an alarming pace.

We arrive at my chambers and he's the first to step inside. "Julius." I try to snag his attention. "I only did it to save you," I confess.

Julius ceases his pacing along the room. "How on all of Einalem could making a bargain with my brother be for my benefit!" he yells. This is the first time I've ever seen him this angry before.

"Because I agreed to comply with whatever tactic he could think of in order for my power to emerge." He pauses in the middle of the room. "I agreed to all of it as long as he never lays another hand on you." His eyes seem to soften at my words.

"Evalina." He walks up to me, shaking his head. "You shouldn't have done that. I'm used to enduring Valec's wrath."

"But you shouldn't. I can handle myself too, Julius." Worry lines appear on his forehead. I press a hand to Julius's shoulder.

"Evalina, what you are doing is a huge sacrifice. You asked me a few hours ago whether or not Valec would subject you to torture and now you've willingly planted that idea in his head."

"I know." I look him straight in the eyes. "But for some reason I was chosen, wasn't I? I need to get the ball rolling; this is what is expected of me."

"You never cease to amaze me," he murmurs.

"How come?"

"Because you have a strong will inside you. And you have no clue how much I admire that." He lightly glides his hand to rest on my wounded one. He leans in, planting a light kiss to the palm. "Remind me to get you some ointment for that hand." I nod. "I best be going. I know you said you couldn't sleep before but try to get some rest. Now that you've made this bargain with Valec I have no doubt he'll call you within a few hours."

I watch him leave. Then I fling myself onto the bed. Our nightly events have exhausted me.

Apparently, I'm going to have to get used to people waking me up in the mornings. Vienna walks right in. I yawn and stretch my arms in the air, still feeling tired. This is what I get for waking up in the middle of the night.

"His Majesty and his Highness request an audience," is her way of greeting. "They expect you to wear something more formal for today." Alright.

In minutes, I'm strapped into a lace gown and ready to go. As soon as the double doors showcase the interior of the throne room, I can't avoid the lump that forms in my throat. Both thrones are occupied. Valec is dressed to match his throne in all gold and Julius wears all silver. Seeing them on their thrones in formal attire and crowns upon their heads is intimidating. Well, Valec more so than Julius.

"Welcome, Evalina." Valec is the one to greet me. Julius was right; he is eager to start my torment. "You already know why you're here. Though I wished to conduct this little experiment by myself, my brother here will not allow it." I direct my attention to Julius, whose eyes are solely focused on me. "Though he knows his place. As long as he does not interfere all is well." Valec stands from his throne, Julius doing the same. "Come." He extends a hand to me, but I ignore it, taking Julius's instead. This does not go unnoticed by him.

Along the way I whisper to Julius, "Do you know what he has planned?"

"No, he wouldn't tell me." We try to keep a safe distance from Valec, who walks up ahead.

It shocks Julius just as much as me when Valec leads us out the front entrance of the mansion. Julius's grip on my hand tightens. A sign that he does not like where this situation is headed. We take a left through an enclosed cavernous tunnel, then a sharp right. This certainly is not the trail that leads to the veil, so I can already cross that possible location from my mental list.

"Welcome to the heart of Inferis." Valec stops among cold stone walls and echoey space.

"Why are we here, Valec?" Julius says at my side.

"Glad you asked, Brother." Valec walks closer to us. "I've brought Evalina here to spend the day outside of the mansion." Julius frowns, which prompts Valec to continue. "She will stay here for exactly twenty-four hours with no assistance, nor access to the mansion."

"No!" Julius says automatically. "Valec, that's dangerous. What if she comes across a shade?"

"I'm sure she's perfectly capable of handling herself, Julius."

"Julius." I tug on his arm. Gaining his attention, I shake my head. "It's no big deal. I'll try to find my way to the gardens, then back to the mansion, even if I have to remain outside. I can do this!"

"But you don't have to, Evalina." I ignore his comment, taking Valec's side. *Fuck, this feels weird.*

"Valec, what will this prove, anyway?" Julius asks.

"A lot. When faced with the need to defend herself, I think Evalina's hellfire will be released." Valec stares at Julius long and hard. "Brother, Evalina knows what she signed up for. Now, with that said, off we go." He shoves Julius forward. "We'll be back for you in the morning, dear," he tells me, then walks away without stopping to make sure Julius follows.

Julius quickly walks back to me. He takes a deep breath, then shakes his head, pulling out something from his pocket. "Take this," he says, handing me a dagger. "Hide it." I shove it inside the front of my dress. "If shades come, aim for the head or the heart." He starts walking away, but he steals one last glance at me, then disappears the same way we came. While I'm left alone to face possible danger.

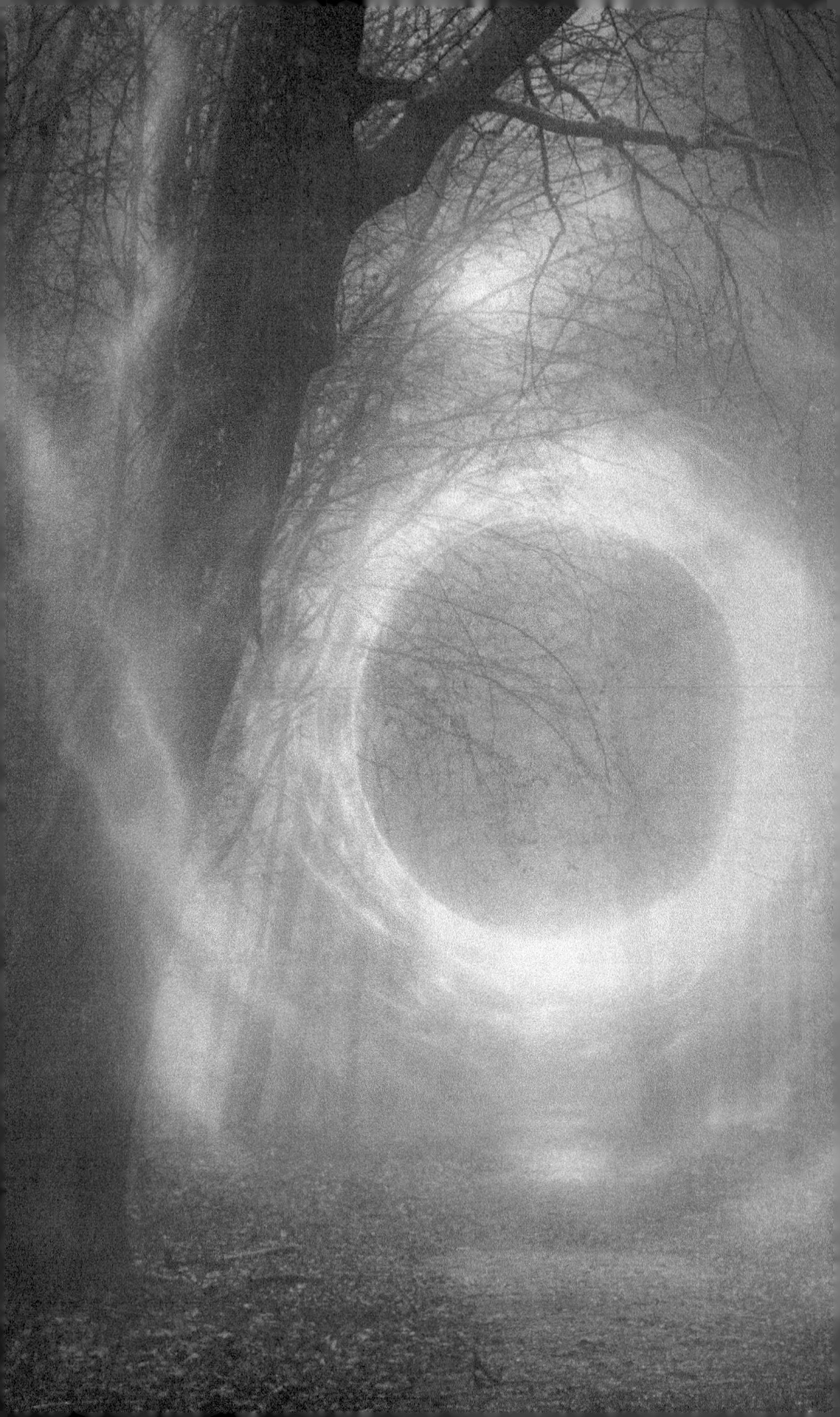

CHAPTER 19
MY FAULT

JULIUS

I t takes every ounce of my willpower to walk away from Evalina. Leaving her there in the cold caverns wounds me, but not as badly as finding out she made a deal with my brother as a means to protect me.

I'm enraged. How could I not be? Everything I've tried to stop from happening is now taking place. Instead of me being the protector, she's switched the roles. And who am I to say I didn't feel a tug at my heart knowing she's done this because she still cares for me. Seeing me bloodied and broken that night must have awoken something in her. It's as if she saw who I was when she first met me that night in the forest. As if it was our first time acknowledging one another. That's why I cannot leave her helpless, no matter what. Though I cannot directly intervene with Valec's plans, I can provide her with help.

The dagger was the first move, now I have to act quickly if I'm going to make it back before Valec suspects anything. Reaching my desired destination beyond what Valec calls the heart of Inferis, I move like a ghost through this part of the land. Knowing exactly what I must do.

I arrive at the throne room minutes later. The Wicked Four wait for me. Recifer, Sairo, Anev, and Aziel stand at attention with those damn hoods over their heads, their faces concealed once again. My back stiffens at the memory of a few nights ago. Their torturous acts nearly killed me.

Valec appears from behind me. "Julius, at ease, Brother." He tries to reassure me. "The Wicked Four are not here to harm you. On the contrary, for the next twenty-four hours, they shall be your security detail."

"Is that not another word for babysitter?" I grimace. It's evident Valec does not trust me. He knows very well that if given the chance, I'll go back for Evalina in a heartbeat.

"Semantics. Regardless, they shall watch over you. They are to tail you during every hour of the day. Your chambers as well."

"What, so they're going to watch over me while I sleep too?" In a way, this is ridiculous.

"During night watch they will take turns."

"Alright, then." I wave him off. "Better commence my day." When I move four shadows lurk behind me. This is going to be a long day, especially since I don't have much to do. Guess I'll try training to get my mind off the woman locked in the caverns.

The day is bland as all the days were before Evalina arrived here. I find myself constantly thinking of her. Wondering if she is okay, if she needs food, water, anything. But I can't allow my mind to drift that far. She'll be okay, I keep repeating to myself. She's strong, I believe in her. I have to. Plus, she's got someone on her side.

Finally glad to retire for the night, I fix myself a bath and return to my room with my two unwanted guests. The other two are stationed outside my door. In case I try anything during the night. Anev lounges by the door, twirling her short wavy locks with her finger. Her hood is finally down, but her mask is still in place. Sairo paces back and forth across the room, deep in concentration. I walk with a towel around my waist, happily letting it fall to the floor the moment I reach my bed. They shift their gazes away from me. I sleep naked, after all. And just because they're here does not mean I am about to change my sleeping habits to make them feel comfortable.

It's the noises coming from outside my chambers that first alert me. "Let me through!" I hear someone yell from the hallway.

"He's asleep," I hear Recifer answer, and that jolts me further from my slumber. Someone is looking for me. I yank on my robe, careful not to trip over Anev who's fast asleep by the door. While Sairo remains by my bed like a statue, his pale complexion feeding into the illusion, I open the door and startle Aziel in the process.

"Soela." I'm at her side in an instant. "What's wrong?"

"Evalina—" I don't allow her to say more as I move like a crazed man about to burn down the world.

"The twenty-four hours are not up yet," Recifer says to my back.

Soela stops, placing her hands over her hips. "The twenty-four hours were up three hours ago."

Three hours ago? I overslept. I'm running for the entryway, but Soela redirects me toward the throne room.

I stomp through the corridor. A guard tries to stop me, but I ignore his request as I usually do and stride right in. There's about a dozen men inside. Valec is right in the middle of a council meeting. "Where is she?" All their focus snaps to me.

Valec appears one look away from murdering me. He could try. "Outside." *Bastard.* He never went to retrieve her. I jolt past Soela on my way, sprinting for the entryway.

"Julius." I hear Evalina's melodious voice in front of me. The guards at the entrance, shut the door behind her. I nearly lose it at the sight of her. She's covered in dust and black ink, her dress nothing more than ribbons of lace hanging around her frame. I lift her off the ground in one swoop, wrapping her in my arms.

"You're okay," I whisper to her.

"I am," she exclaims.

I lower her to the ground. "You are incredible." I place my fingers on her chin. She stares at me through lowered lashes. "You are, Evalina." I scan her body from head to toe, searching for injuries. But given all the stains of shade ink it's hard to get a clear view of her skin.

"I'm alright. I promise. The dress is making it seem worse than it actually is," she reassures me, then hands me something. It's the dagger I gave her, stained as well. "Thank you," she says and that's all the confirmation I need before I scoop her up in my arms and carry her to my room.

By the time we arrive steam is rising from the full tub. I'm guessing I have Soela to thank for that. I leave Evalina by the tub, and step back into the bedroom, allowing her all the privacy she needs. I take the opportunity to change out of this robe and into my leather work attire.

She emerges several minutes later wearing a shirt that reaches her knees and a pair of trousers that are three seconds away from falling down her hips. "Sorry about the outfit." I motion to her attire. One minor detail Soela forgot, something for her to wear.

"It's fine." She waves me off.

I inspect her from head to toe, wondering if I should ask her to tell me about her experience outside the mansion. I eventually give in to my curiosity, once I've assessed that she's told me the truth and isn't harmed. "What happened?" I ask. I can accept if she refuses to talk about it. I won't hold it against her. Instead, she surprises me by responding.

"After you left not much happened. Besides me getting hungry and thirsty." I shoot to my feet, remembering to provide such vital necessities. "Julius, it's alright. I already ate and drank. I'm good."

I settle back down on the bed.

"As I was saying," she continues. "Not much happened. I got bored, started reminiscing about the good days you and I had in Einalem. I tried to find my way around, hoping to reach the garden, but all I did was get lost in the process. I had to backtrack and eventually I returned to where Valec originally left me. Then as the night settled in, that's when they came." I don't need for her to say who *they* were. It's evident she speaks of the shades.

"Three of them. They emerged from different parts of the cavern. Their bodies all contorted. I kept silent at first, remembering they relied on their hearing since they have no eyes. It worked," she says, taking a seat beside me. "They wandered around, then they heard a sound. It came from afar and yet they didn't move in the direction it came from; no, they lunged straight for me." She pauses. "I quickly took hold of the dagger and prepared to strike if need be."

"And did you?" I know the answer. Of course, she did, the dagger is completely coated in their blood and venom.

"I did, but I also had some help. You sent someone to help me, didn't you?" My body instantly warms knowing that the woman I sought out, Anise, helped Evalina. "You interfered without even being there."

"I couldn't just leave you there helpless."

"Julius," she stops me. "Valec may be a monster, but I have to play by his rules if we even stand a chance of making it back to Einalem." Evalina is more sensical than I am. She's willing to face whatever it takes to get her magic flowing, meanwhile here I am trying to make it easier for her, and possibly delaying our exit.

"I don't want to see you get hurt in any way," I admit, because it's the truth.

Evalina leans her head on my shoulder and sighs. "I know. Anyway," she shrugs, "it didn't work. No hellfire." She frowns.

I turn my neck, kissing the top of her head. "Is that pine and musk?" I ask, getting a whiff of her hair now that it's been washed.

"Yep, it is. I mean, it was the only shampoo I saw in your bathroom. It's your scent." She brings a strand of her hair to her nose. "Pine and musk; the scent I've always associated with you," she admits, and I can't help the grin that spreads across my face.

"You know that's how I hid you?" I blurt.

"What?" she says, confused.

"That night in the forest. Getting close to you. It was the only way to make sure those black nuns didn't sense your power, by masking it with my own scent. That's how I've kept you protected for so long."

"Wow," she exclaims, a small smile forming on her face. "To think that if it weren't for you, I'd probably be dead."

"Oh, so now you care for your life?" I tease. "Because if I recall, you mentioned death being the best outcome, given your situation."

"Alright." She rolls her eyes. "I probably deserved that one."

"She was kind, you know," she says after a while.

"Who?" I ask.

"The woman who saved me. Though I did manage to stab a shade in the heart all on my own, like you told me."

"Good." I applaud her. "Then you did good."

"The woman spoke of you like a son."

"In a way, Anise has felt like a mother to me. Considering I don't have one. Valec and I were created by Dominus, so we weren't born the way humans are."

"That's sweet. To have a motherly figure around. But why doesn't she live here with you?"

"That's what she chose. Valec doesn't know about her anyway. Granted, Valec doesn't know much about anyone in Inferis except the people that work for him. Everyone else is practically nonexistent to him."

She's quiet for a moment. "Jules, do you think my parents are in Caelesti? I mean, I told you before, we aren't religious."

"I'd like to think they are," I answer truthfully.

"They birthed the Devil's Curse; I hardly think that's worthy of entering the promised land."

"Well, they never arrived here, so I think you already have your answer."

"You're right." She gazes at the ceiling, a small smile on her face.

"Guess I ruined Valec's experiment," I declare.

"I know you may not like any of this, and I'm not defending his actions, but—" She pauses for a brief moment. "You love your brother, the old one at least, right?" She shifts her gaze back to me.

"Of course," I say with all the sincerity in the world.

"Then you have to find a way to trust the process." I let out an exhale. "I don't like this any more than you do." She stands up, now giving me her full attention. "You think I was prepared to find out I'm some cursed girl who's been hunted by the white church all these years?"

Fair point.

"You were once a god. Act like one. Be courageous. I'm trying and so should you," she says.

I burst into laughter. "Hate to break it to you but Valec was the god, I was just an angel. Granted, I didn't even have wings. So basically, I'd say I was but a humble farmer."

"You were a farmer?" I nod. "While you lived in Caelesti?"

"I was."

"Really?"

"Why so disbelieving?"

"I'm not in disbelief, it's just interesting. I mean, I know you like to garden, I just never expected that you actually had a farm up in the sky."

"You would have loved it."

"Tell me about it. What sort of crops did you grow?" She settles once again beside me on the bed, except she occupies the other side and inches slightly closer to me.

"Well, I had many fruit trees. Lemons, apples, oranges. I grew strawberries and watermelons as well. I had walnut trees too. When it came to vegetables, I had tomatoes and lettuce, and grew potatoes, carrots, corn, and I planted some rice."

"Wow, you had it all." She seems amazed.

"I did. Back then I only relied on what my garden supplied for me. So, I never found much desire to eat meat, but I ate fish on occasion."

"I've seen you eat several strips of bacon, so it's safe to say you're a fellow meat lover now."

I chuckle. "Yeah, I am. It's a good source of protein."

"Well, if you look like that," she scans my body from head to toe, "from eating bacon, who am I to complain?"

I laugh. "I'll have you know, my body is the result of very rigorous training sessions. If it was only because of eating bacon, I would have quit my job a long time ago."

"And what, you'd sit on a couch all day eating pig?" She lightly punches my arm.

"Most likely," I joke and she smiles with all her teeth.

"What is your job here exactly?" she asks. "I mean, only if you're going to be truthful this time." She raises an eyebrow. I had that coming.

"I'm Valec's Official Shade Hunter. Although, I do work with his soldiers and guards every now and then. But my main job is going out to kill shades."

"So, what, you don't rule beside Valec?" I can tell how she'd be confused, considering I was sitting on my throne beside Valec when she was called to the throne room.

"I try to keep up appearances whenever I need to. But no, I don't rule Inferis. That's all Valec." I check the clock on my wall and realize I have to get started on my day. "Err, I actually have to go. Duty calls. I know you must be tired, so feel free to stay here unless you'd rather be in your own room."

"I'll stay," she says and flops down on the mattress. "Your bed is cozy."

I chuckle. "Fine, I'll see you later, then."

She waves me off, and I can't help the grin that spreads across my face the second I close the door behind me.

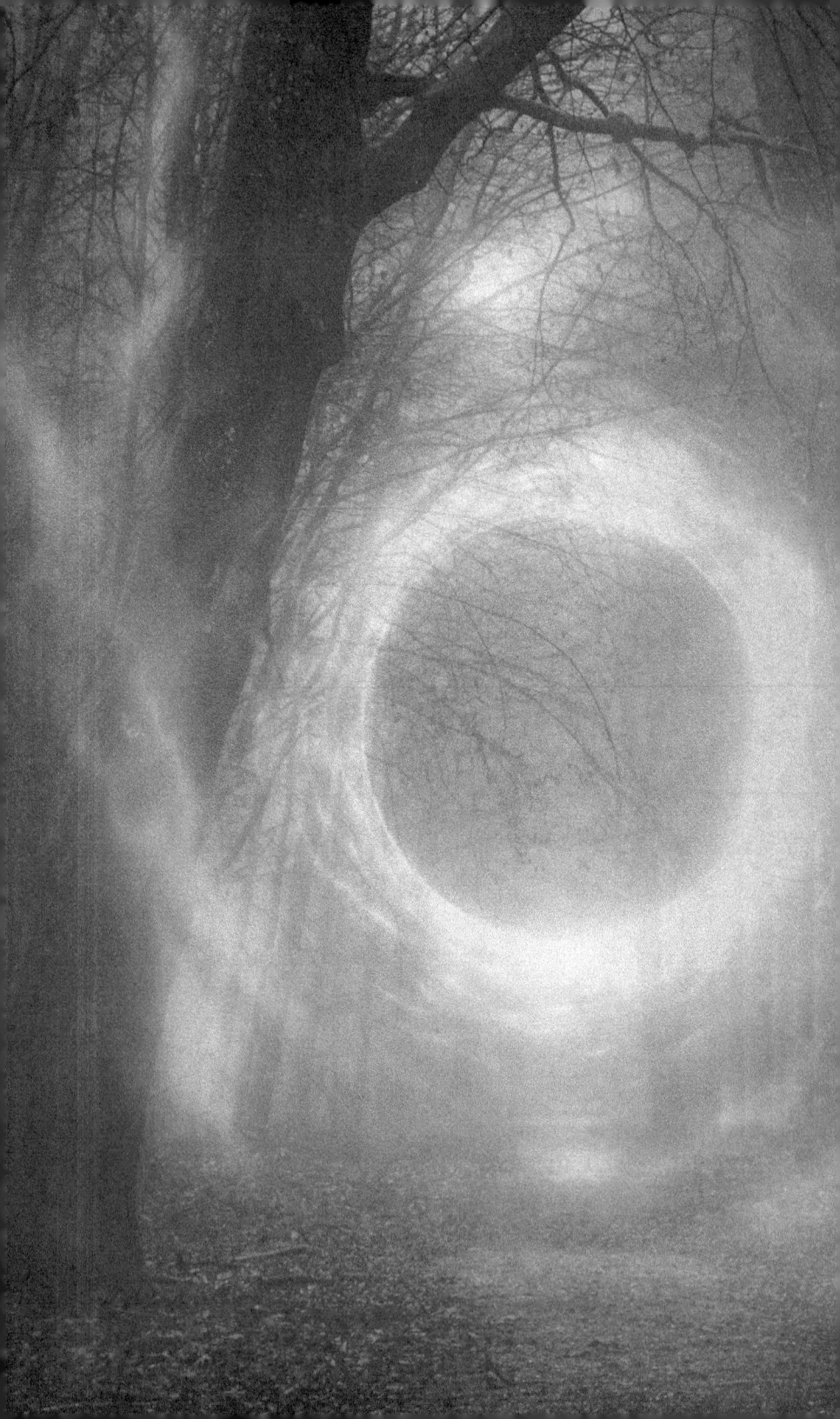

CHAPTER 20
DEVIL'S FEAST

EVALINA

My eyes snap open, and I raise myself to a sitting position. I forgot I never did make it back to my own chambers. Julius sits beside me. What time is it?

I take in my surroundings. Julius's room is almost identical to Valec's. From the placement of the furniture to the subtle color of the walls, it's like they made them to be identical. What differentiates one from the other are the mere possessions they own. Like the record player I spotted sitting on a trunk at the far side of Valec's room. Instead, Julius has two piles of books stacked on his trunk. He catches me studying the room.

"They are quite similar, aren't they." I snap my attention back to him. "Valec and I began building these rooms very early on. They started off as humble chambers back then, not nearly as lavish. Just a place for us to rest and feel at home. Then they became what they are now. Extravagant, just like him."

His story stirs something in me. "It's amazing to me how you've never lost hope for him. Despite all he's done," I say.

"This isn't him. When I look at my brother now, I always say to myself that he is simply possessed by an evil spirit and that someday he'll be released and returned back to me." His admission is admirable. He still cares for someone who's been long gone for years. When you look at it, it's the same as still caring for someone who's died. One never loses that love; it always remains.

"At any moment did you ever think Valec could end your life?" I ask out of the blue. Because the wounds Julius sustained that night were close to doing just that.

"Many times. And on all occasions, I've been okay with accepting my death. But in the end, I never gave in. I always had fight left in me. Do you want to know why?" he inquires, shifting on the bed beside me.

I think I already know his answer, but I don't get to hear it because Vienna is calling us both from outside his chambers. We are to go to the throne room immediately at Valec's request. We make haste to change into something more presentable.

In less than five minutes we're standing in the throne room. Four threatening figures stand at Valec's side. These must be the Wicked Four, Valec's torture crew.

Julius briefly told me about them, but I honestly can't say who's who.

"They usually wear cloaks and masks to conceal their identities," he murmurs at my side.

"Then should I be alarmed at their lack of concealment?" I worry.

"No, that means they're off duty." I let out a breath of relief.

"That's Anev," Julius whispers pointing to a woman with light skin and short dark hair. Her expression is cool and calm, not a hint of emotion anywhere. "By her side stands Aziel." Aziel looks like a full-blown barbarian, from his long locks to the scruffy beard on his face. I look away immediately; just staring at him brings a chill to my bones.

"At Valec's left is Recifer." This man seems less threatening in a way. His expression is more humanistic. His hair is cropped quite short, but his eyes are what stand out from his appearance, a deep green. They almost seem to glow.

"And finally, that's Sairo," Julius finishes off. I stare at the remaining member of the Wicked Four, his messy locks pointing in every direction. His bushy eyebrows crease when he catches me staring. Standing this close to them gives me a perfect view, and out of all of them, Sairo has the smallest frame which makes him less threatening. Plus, he doesn't look as serious and composed as all the others do. Though that does not make him any less of a monster.

Julius keeps a steady hand on my back. "You called, Val." Julius jumps right to the point. I can tell he's just as eager to leave as I am. He holds tension in his stance, unmoving, but with one hand tucked beneath his jacket where his dagger is hidden. After I gave it back to him last night, he wanted me to have it, but I declined. I hope I'll never need to use it again.

Valec taps his foot against the side of the throne. "I did. I wish to ask Evalina how her stay at the caverns went."

"Swimmingly," I answer, irritated.

"Feel any unusual sensations or occurrences while you were there?" he asks, shooting me a look of disinterest. I know for a fact he's feigning nonchalance. "Any fire?"

"Truth be told, Valec, I felt nothing. It didn't work," I say with indifference. I just hope he doesn't suspect that Julius interfered with his experiment.

I made a deal with him, and I must uphold it. But that does not mean I'll give him the satisfaction of watching my torment. Because yes, truth be told the shades that came after me did scare me a little, but not enough so I truly feared for my life. Though maybe that was Valec's goal all along: for me to feel true fear, hoping it's enough to kick start my power.

No matter how grateful I am for Julius having interfered in the matter, it can't happen again. I need to face this on my own.

"Then your situation calls for more drastic measures. Maybe fear wasn't enough when you expected the outcome. Perhaps I'll have to play into your emotions while you do not expect anything."

"Perhaps that's true." Now, please tell me this conversation is over.

"One more thing before you go." Valec notices the hand Julius has slid from my back to my side, curling his fingers on my arm, ready to haul me out of here. "The Devil's Feast is upon us within three nights. I of course expect you to attend, Evalina." He grins mischievously.

I find myself asking, "What's the Devil's Feast?"

"Why, it's my annual celebration. It marks another year since the day Julius and I fell from the heavens and landed in disgrace." That's one way to say it.

"What is required of me?" I ask, prepared for the worst.

"Your attendance. It's a night of merriment. The night where we're all allowed to let down our hair. Music, dancing, utter extravagance, exquisite delicacies fit for any palate, and my most favorite...giving into one's truest desires. It's the night we revel in sin. And you, Evalina, are not the exception. Besides your attendance, I will require you to give in to any sin of your choosing. You will let me know which sin you've chosen prior to executing it. Have I made myself clear?"

"Crystal, Your Majesty." I bow out of mockery.

It's the afternoon of the feast and knowing that Valec expects me to participate in today's events does very little to ease my nerves.

Julius advised me to pick the sin that appears less daunting to me. The one that appeals to me. If I could say such a thing.

I spent the last two days with Soela trying to find other methods to help with my magic problem. None have worked.

Starling me from my thoughts, Vienna waltzes into my chambers as per usual with a large garment bag in her hands. "Evalina, your gown is complete." I gave her my request a few days ago, knowing that a larger gown would no doubt take longer to fashion. "Are you ready to see it?" She sets the bag down on my bed.

"Yes, is that even a question?" I'm way too excited, despite my unease for tonight's events. It's Julius seeing me in said gown that thrills me. I shake my head. Curse my emotions and their inability to stop thinking about Julius in a romantic way.

Vienna unzips the bag and I gasp. It's the most gorgeous dress I've ever seen. Without further thought I get myself ready for the event.

I arrive at the ballroom on the first floor of the mansion an hour later. This is where the main celebration is being held and I'm seeing it for the first time. Golden chandeliers hang from the ceiling. The tables sparkle with silk tablecloths, large flower vases filled with roses at the center of each one. Lush red and silver curtains hang on every wall. There are already people dancing in beautiful gowns and suits. I look down at my own attire, knowing I blend right in. I am no outsider tonight.

Stepping out of the shadows I scan the room for Julius, but there's no need. He's already seen me. I quickly make my descent down the staircase. He's speaking to a couple near the dancefloor and his expression is of pure shock and adoration as he takes me in. He seems to trail every swish of my hips with each step I take. He excuses himself from the conversation and heads toward the bottom of the stairway. Waiting for me.

The royal seamstress surely outdid herself with my gown. It's an off-the-shoulder dress with a sweetheart neckline in the most stunning shade of royal blue. As for my hair, Vienna let my natural waves cascade down my shoulders.

I'm awed by Julius's attire as well. I cannot believe Vienna never told me that Julius and I would be matching. He's wearing a silk coat in royal blue with black trim, and a white shirt underneath and a black tie to match his shoes and trousers. His hair is in its usual slightly messy state, his beard shortly trimmed, and atop his head sits his silver crown, which makes him look the part of a ruler. Just seeing him like this has me in a trance.

Julius grins when my hand is in his grasp, and I'm stunned the moment someone comes to stand on my other side. I look to my right and see Valec grinning as well. He looks stunning, I have to admit. The deep plum suit is a nice contrast to his icy blue eyes. His five o'clock shadow is on display, and despite not wanting to say it, it makes him appear exactly how I would picture the Devil *now*. Pure seduction. The curls at the top of his head are messy and untamed for the night. Very different from Valec's usual polished appearance. He wears his own crown as well, the gold shimmering atop his head.

Many of the guests have ceased all conversation, their full attention on us as we walk between them until we arrive at a small table at the back of the room meant to sit four people. "You look incredible," Julius whispers in my ear, brushing his lips across my cheek.

I take a seat and Julius follows, seating himself right beside me, while Valec remains standing.

"I hope you've already chosen your sin," Valec says from behind me, his hands resting on the back of my chair.

"I have." Truth be told, choosing a sin proved more difficult than I expected.

"Well, what would it be?" He seems impatient.

I let out a breath and urge him to lean forward so that I may whisper my reply in his ear. I don't want Julius to hear what I'm about to say. I feel embarrassed to admit my sin out loud.

"I've chosen lust," I murmur.

Valec seems pleased. "An excellent choice. I'll be announcing the commencement of the celebration soon. In the meantime, enjoy the feast." He leaves to welcome other guests.

"You can breathe now," Julius says from his seat beside mine. He can say that again. Valec is as frightening as they come. "I'm not about to ask you which sin you chose because I got the hint that you don't want me to know. Though I am curious to know why that is?"

"Embarrassment, really."

"You know that you never have to feel ashamed of anything, especially around me," he says calmly.

"I know." I shrug, now feeling guilty for not having told him. I shift my attention to the people dancing to the slow melody of the orchestra playing at the back of the room. A waiter passes by carrying a tray of sweets and I help myself to a few. Minutes later, I'm already bored, fidgeting in my chair.

As if noticing my sudden change in mood, Julius whispers in my ear, "Would you rather we went somewhere else?"

Glad for the interruption and the excuse to leave, I say, "I'd like that, but only for a little while."

"If you're worried about Valec, he won't care as long as we return before he announces the celebration. Knowing this party by memory, he usually announces it at nine. We have time."

With that said, we make our way to the library. Along the way I notice that we aren't the only ones removed from the festivities. I spot various couples making out in dark corners of the corridor, some less decent than others. I can't help wondering if any of these people have chosen lust as their sin for tonight as well.

We wander inside the library. The scent of paper and dust clings to me like a second skin. I run up the stairs to the second floor, careful to not trip over my dress in the process.

Julius and I sit side by side, near the veranda that overlooks the downstairs area. A wave of calm settles over me. In the comfort of books, I feel complete. "Large crowds aren't really my scene," Julius comments.

"I don't think they're mine either." Julius stares at me closely. I resist the urge to touch his face. But I can't help it, he looks so handsome. In the end, I lose the battle and bring my hand across his cheek. My action catches him off guard, but his eyes close on instinct.

With closed eyes Julius says, "What sin have you chosen, Alina?" I quickly move my hand away, his eyes snapping open.

I reel myself back. "Does it matter which one I chose? It's done," I snap.

"Not particularly, no. But it does matter if you're going to choose me as the man you will be doing it with. Or did you plan on going solo?"

I stay silent. There's no way he knows. Not in a million years. *Can he?* Suddenly, he casually leans from his chair. His lips brushing my ear, he says, "I know you've chosen lust, Alina." I'm taken aback for the slightest of instances. Julius knows. He truly knows.

"How?" I find myself asking, my voice hoarse.

"It was written across your face when you looked at me after Valec left. But it was your nerves and your refusal to tell me before that gave it away." Nothing goes by him.

"Jules, I—" I try to find something clever to say. Nothing comes out. All I do is stare at the table before me. I told him that I needed a friend, yet here I admit to wanting to be with him. I am such a liar.

"Evalina, look at me." I gaze back at him. "Do you truly want to be intimate with me?" My eyes grow round like saucers. "I don't want you to feel pressured to do anything for the sake of my brother. You can choose another sin if that's what you want. Valec will be pissed, but it won't matter, as long as you participate in the celebration."

"I don't want to choose another sin," I say. "I chose lust as my sin because it's the one that makes sense to me. It's the one sin I know I can feel at ease with." There's no going back from my words. They're already out in the open. "But I was afraid to tell you, because I don't know where we stand on the matter, and I was embarrassed to downright ask you to have sex with me when I told you all I needed was—"

"A friend." He sucks in a breath, his features hard to read. "Evalina, you have the right to say things, then change your mind about them. I told you I would be patient. Whatever time you need, I'd happily give to you. But you are certain this is what you want?" I nod. "Then I'd be more than honored to give it to you."

Letting out a breath, I relax into my seat. "So, what now?" I say when I feel Julius's hand on my knee. Forgetting all coherent thought, I remain still as Julius gently lifts my skirts with his free hand, trailing a finger up my thigh.

"Now, we do whatever you want," he whispers in my ear. I turn my head to stare at him. His pupils are dilated.

"We should wait until the celebration," I caution, though it comes out as a whimper.

"And we will, but it doesn't mean we can't do something else." His hand slides through my dress, grazing the side of my underwear. Shit. My head tilts back a little. "Only if you want to, of course." He presses his body so close to mine that we're practically seated in the same chair.

"Yes." I nod in agreement, "I want to." Who am I kidding? I've wanted this man from the moment I met him. And in one swift motion his fingers are pushing my underwear to the side, finding sensitive skin. I try to stifle a moan as his fingers move in slow circles. He keeps stroking me at a lazy pace, pressing lightly over my bundle of nerves and fuck, it feels amazing. I've never felt anything like this. Not even when I'm touching myself in the darkness of my room does it feel this good.

His fingers pinch and pull, and I completely lose it, my back arching against the chair. His free hand cups the back of my head, and he crashes his lips to mine. The kiss isn't slow by any means. On the contrary, it's all consuming. His tongue teases my lips, forcing me to open for him. This feels incredible; it's even better than our first kiss in the greenhouse.

The same moment his tongue graces my own is when he plunges another finger into me, and I cry out. He's stretching me with his two digits and I'm writhing against his hand like a worm, rocking my hips to the beat of his fingers inside me.

"Fuck!" He grunts and I'm about to lose it with the sounds he makes alone.

As if two fingers aren't enough, he adds a third to press against my clit. *My god!* He curves the other two inside me, and I yank at his tie, bringing him closer to me, as if we aren't already close enough. All these delicious sensations are killing me. His finger is hitting the right spot and I'm this close to going numb. I'm already a puddle of sin at his feet.

"You're close, Alina," he coos in my ear. My body sprouts with goosebumps at his voice.

"Fuck, yes," I hiss through clenched teeth. His gentle strokes are driving me over the edge. He picks up the pace. His fingers are moving faster, and I can't anymore. Julius hovers over me, his mouth coming down on mine, stifling my cries as I come undone.

I ride my high and come out a complete a mess. My legs feel like gelatin. Beads of sweat coat my face and I try to lightly wipe them away with my hand, not wanting to mess up my makeup.

"It's almost nine," says Julius, looking at the clock by the library entrance. "We should get back."

Jules helps me up. My legs wobble slightly as I descend the stairs. He breathes at the back of my neck. "Is there something wrong?" he says knowingly. "Do you need me to carry you?" It's the first time I've seen this side of Jules. And I'll admit, I like it a lot.

"No, I can walk perfectly fine. Thank you." I saunter past him once we reach the first floor.

"Just so you know," he says behind me, "I chose lust as well."

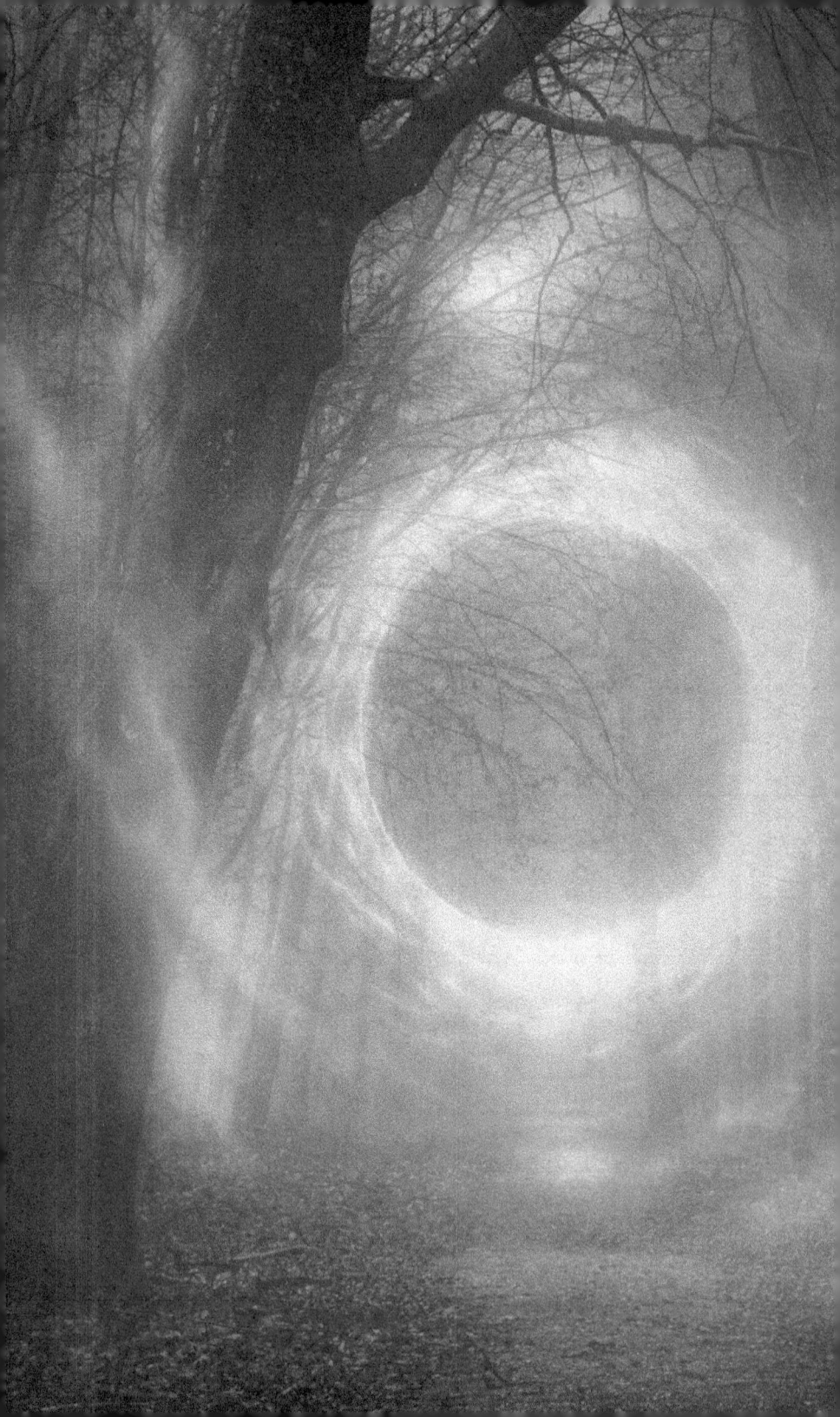

CHAPTER 21
SINFUL DESIRES

JULIUS

E valina and I return right on time.

I search for Valec in the crowd, and surely there he is, making his way to the stage. The orchestra ceases all music at his appearance and the room quiets down.

"Good evening, ladies and gentlemen. As you all know, today marks yet another delightful celebration of our annual Devil's Feast. And like every year, the rooms have been prepared for the sin of your choosing. Tonight," he holds up his champagne flute, "we give Dominus a reason to look upon us in disgrace." Valec says and the crowd begins to cheer. "Now, let us all sin with pleasure." He dismisses the guests and people begin to file out of the ballroom.

"Brother," Valec calls as he makes his way towards us. "Evalina, the lust room is all prepared for you." He snakes an arm over each of our shoulders. "Come. I shall personally escort you there."

When it comes to this part of the gala, Valec tends to delve into all seven sins. He used to want me to do the same and I refuse every time. I would personally not participate at all if that were an option but given his constant threats against not only myself but Soela as well, I've had no choice but to pick a sin every year. I've always chosen lust. It's the least harmful sin, in my opinion. No emotional repercussions. At least tonight, I have a reason to enjoy myself.

Valec doesn't let us out of his sight, not until we reach the guests rooms that have been altered for the night. Each door has the name of its corresponding sin on the front. Valec stops at the final door at the end of the hallway. The word *Lust is* written in large lettering. He opens the door to reveal already fully naked partygoers dancing around the dimly lit room. Their bodies move to the soft melodious keys of a piano playing in the background. Inside the walls are the texture of velvet, giving off a sensual undertone. Those who aren't dancing sit on plush divans, partaking in other activities with their selected partners. It's on the small side, considering Valec always selects more than one room for each sin. The scent of sweat and incense blends together. I instinctively cover my nose.

Valec practically shoves us inside. "Just so you know, you both may have chosen lust but that does not mean you are allowed to act on that sin with each other."

My head snaps back at him. "Come again?"

"You heard me loud and clear: you and Evalina cannot do anything together. It must be with someone else. And I may not be here, but Sairo has taken the liberty of watching over this room. Fail to accomplish what is expected on such a day and there will be consequences. Consider this experiment two." He winks at Evalina.

The door shuts behind him, the lock falling into place. No one is to leave this room until they've partaken in the festivities. People are already eyeing me and Evalina with hungry expressions. No shit! This cannot be happening. How did I not see this coming? It's Valec we're talking about. Of course he couldn't give us a break, not even on a holiday. This must have been his plan all along.

"Julius." Evalina turns to me with sad eyes. "We have no choice."

I know. Fuck, if I didn't know. This is what Valec meant by catching Evalina off guard. This is yet another test, to get her to sin with a stranger. It's almost as if he knew that she would choose lust. He managed to find the perfect way to wound me emotionally. By forcing me to watch the woman I love be intimate with another man.

I stop my train of thoughts, having just realized what I've admitted to myself.

Fuck! I've finally admitted that I'm in love with Evalina.

"Who are we going to choose?" I ask her, trying to disrupt my spiral.

"I don't know." She scans the room, trying to get a good look at the faces that haven't yet started their activities. I search around and there beside the piano is *Soela.* What is she doing here? She usually goes for gluttony, it's her one excuse to eat to her heart's content. She's known for her love of all things sweet. It's as if she can sense me, her head turning in my direction at that exact moment.

"Jules," she says as she walks over to where Evalina and I stand in the center of the room. Her ruby skirts shifting from side to side. "I'd say funny seeing you here, but this has always been your scene."

"I should be saying that to you. What happened to gluttony?" I throw her way.

"I needed a break, wanted to let my hair down for a bit. And this is the sin that temporarily numbs you from your responsibilities." She's not wrong. She turns to Evalina. "I can see that Julius convinced you to join."

"Actually, I chose without his knowledge," she says.

She looks back at me, a smile sprouting on her face. "You

two were made for each other. Well, I'll leave you to it, then. There's no one interesting here. I think I might head to one of the other rooms."

"Wait." Evalina is the one to stop her. "Soela, Valec played us. Jules and I can't do anything together."

"Classic Lucifer," she mutters.

"I can't refuse even if I wanted to. It's all part of the deal I made with him." Evalina lets out a breath. "That's why I would feel much better if Julius were with someone I trust. Someone who wouldn't go out of line." Her words shock me just as much as they do Soela. Because we both know where Alina is going with this. "Would you be willing to be Julius's partner?"

One: it's good to know she feels as uncomfortable as I do on the matter. Two: her idea is clever, but still unsettling. Three: that solves my problem, but then who is she going to be with?

"And for you?" I ask. "Who will you choose?" She looks from person to person until her eyes lock with someone. She can't be serious. As if an unspoken thought passes between them, Sairo makes his way through the crowd. His crimson suit blends right in with the decor.

"Ladies, Your Highness." He bows to me. I snicker. He clearly only has respect for me when Valec is not around. "Is something the matter?"

"No," Evalina chimes in. "I simply wanted to ask if you would do me the honor of dedicating me your night." She sounds so calm and collected that I'm having a hard time associating this Evalina with the one who first arrived in Inferis.

Sairo doesn't even blink, nor does he look towards me. He keeps his expression solely focused on her. "Certainly." He offers her his arm.

Before taking it, she whispers in my ear, "Trust me." Then she walks away with him. Leaving me and Soela. I do trust her, it's him I don't trust. But trust is a two-way street. I have to believe she is capable of handling the situation on her own. She's chosen to trust me with a friend, and I need to extend her the same courtesy. This will all be over soon. I hope.

I let Soela drag me to the darkest corner of the room. Away from as many prying eyes as possible.

"Jules, if you feel uncomfortable, we don't have to do anything," Soela offers.

"Soela, you know I have no other choice. But I need you to block my view of her or I'll lose it," I say, pointing at Evalina and Sairo getting cozy on one of the large couches.

"I promise. Now, let's get this over with." Without thinking I immediately crash my lips into hers. She's taken by surprise but is quick to return the kiss.

I try my best to remain inside my head, pretending that tonight is another of those mindless nights I used to spend at the pubs in Einalem. And that Soela is a random woman I just happened to meet there. If I keep believing that I'll be okay. I'll make it through.

I spin us around, pinning her against the wall but not before sliding a glance at Alina. The one thing I said I wouldn't do. Sairo's got her wrapped in his arms as they make out. I go still, returning my attention to Soela, but she follows my line of sight.

"Jules? Maybe we shouldn't be doing this?" She straightens herself.

"Wait, what?" I come out of my daze.

"This is wrong, Julius, and you know it. It doesn't matter what your brother wants. But if you do this, there's no going back from it. And I know more than anyone that Evalina is the woman you want to be with. You said you were immune to his punishments—"

"Only if Evalina abides by his rules. She's with Sairo, for crying out loud. All I have to do is yank her away and he'll report us to Valec. I can't do that; he said there would be a cost to us refusing."

"There always is!" she yells, clearly exasperated. "Living

here in Inferis is a risk. Why? Because the land is ruled by a monster, Julius. I once told you to play his game, but enough is enough. You make your own rules, not him." She points at Evalina, who for some reason has her eyes open and is staring directly at me. "You want her." I nod. "Then I say fuck it, Jules. Life is meant to be short, and you've lived more than any being, but never to the fullest." She grips my shoulder. "Go fucking be with her. Consequences be damned." She shoves me in Evalina's direction, and I nearly stumble.

"It's time you stand up for yourself. For what you want," she offers as a final encouragement.

Evalina keeps staring as Sairo attacks her neck, completely unaware of my presence at his back. "Ahem," I say with my usual tone. But I know he's purposefully choosing not to turn around. So instead, I grab him by the collar of his suit.

"Hey, what the fuck!" he complains, and is immediately silenced once he's gotten a look at me. I grasp him by the arm and shove him against the nearest wall.

"I'm going to be spending the night with her and you are going to keep your pretty little mouth shut. You might be afraid of Valec, but I can assure you his shade hunter is much worse. And though you've seen me crumble at his mercy and your own, if you haven't noticed," I close the distance, whispering in his ear, "I'm still standing, you fucker."

I'm done. Soela is right. I can't keep living in this state of fear. It's my own personal torture. He stares at me with terror in his eyes. I always knew deep down that Sairo was the weakest of the four. "Have I made myself clear?"

He nods repeatedly.

"If Valec asks what happened tonight?" I question, wanting to hear his new version of the story.

"I'll tell him that you got with the redhead while I did Evalina," he answers.

"Atta boy." I smack the back of his head, letting him go.

"Now, by all means go get yourself laid, just not with my girl." I give him a slight push in the opposite direction.

"Jules." The sound of her voice is music to my ears. I'm an agitated mess when she comes to stand at my side.

"That was…" She pauses. "That was…" She can't seem to find her words. She places her hands on my arms, trailing their way upward. "I don't know if I should thank you or slap you. Because now you've put yourself at risk. Yet again. Julius, this won't end well," she warns.

"I'm tired of playing by Valec's games." I can't believe it took the wise words of my best friend to help me see reason. "And you shouldn't have to play them either."

She stares at me for a long pause, not saying a word. "Then what? What happens next?"

I curl my fingers under her chin. Keeping her gaze locked to mine. "We do whatever we want."

"That sounds dangerous," she jokes. More silence, followed by, "I told my mind to block you out." My expression morphs into confusion at her words. "But I couldn't."

Her confession forces me to close the distance between us. Even though we are already as close as we can get. "There's no one else for me, Evalina." My hands glide to her back, pressing her body firmly against mine. "It's always been you."

Evalina's lip curl then part. "I could say the same. Even when I was nineteen, I couldn't see anyone in the same light that I saw you. The way I feel for you has not changed since that very moment, Julius. On the contrary, it has grown more." I'm rendered speechless by her words.

She tries to loop her arms around my neck, but given the height difference, it's a struggle for her. I pick her up with one swift motion. Her legs wrap around both sides of my torso. I move us towards the piano that's no longer being played. I close the piano lid and carefully set her down on the smooth surface.

I watch her closely, her expression full of desire. "Are you sure Sairo won't snitch?" she asks, concern taking over.

"He won't. I will kill him myself if he does." What a twist of events. And with that said, I bunch up some of the fabric of her gown and dive straight under. I make no hesitation when tugging her underwear down her legs in one swift motion before discarding the piece of lacy fabric onto the floor. I resurface from under her skirts. Dragging her body closer towards me, I happily stand between her legs. I claim her mouth with my own, catching her off guard and manage to slip my tongue past her parted lips. I move away just as quickly, ending the kiss as I get on my knees, positioning myself back between her legs.

Her eyes remain on me until my head vanishes inside her skirts. I yank at the many layers of silk, ripping them till they tear away completely. Evalina gasps at the sight of her dress flying around everywhere. I toss it all to the floor, leaving her with a shorter gown than before.

I watch through my lashes as she closes her eyes the second my breath coats her core. Her body trembles and wriggles without me even laying a hand on her. I let out a heavy breath just to watch her reaction to the warm air against her sensitive skin. With a heavy groan, she bucks her hips. "Jules," she says my name like a plea. Taking her reaction as my cue, I get started.

My lips touch sensitive skin, and she yelps the second my mouth closes around her bundle of nerves. She tries to suppress her scream by bringing her hand to her mouth, but it fails her. If only she knew how many nights I dreamt of this moment, wanting to taste her all hot and needy for me. It's like ecstasy.

During my nightly excursions out in Einalem, though I would fuck, I never allowed myself to give like this. I've always pinned it as deeply intimate, to such an extent that I only wanted to do it and have it done to me by the right person. So, to this particular type of experience, I closed myself off. Until tonight. I've saved myself specifically for this moment. Imagining what it would feel like to have her essence against my tongue, to feel her slickness through my lips. To taste every inch of her, wanting to see how easily she could come with just my mouth alone. Judging by how she's writhing and her back's arching, I'd say she's in heaven.

I suck on her bud, driving her wild. *Oh,* she's coming undone. As if her trembling legs aren't a clear enough sign, she keeps bucking her hips and I have to force them down with my hands.

I watch how a bead of liquid drips from inside her, and I catch it on my tongue, driving it upward, licking every inch of her. The movement is her ultimate undoing.

She's tumbling into the abyss, her eyes closed, her head tipped backwards.

I delve into the beauty of it all. Of the image of her riding my tongue.

Her breathing is still heavy when her eyes fully open.

I give her a few seconds to recover from her high, my head still between her legs.

Her expression is one of pure bliss when she stares down at me, until it isn't. Panic spreads across her features when she stares straight ahead. I quickly bring myself to stand, following her line of sight toward the very front of the room. There standing by the entrance to the lust room is Valec, two members of the Wicked Four standing at each side. Sairo's gaze connects with my own and it's of pure guilt.

That *motherfucker!* I should have known better.

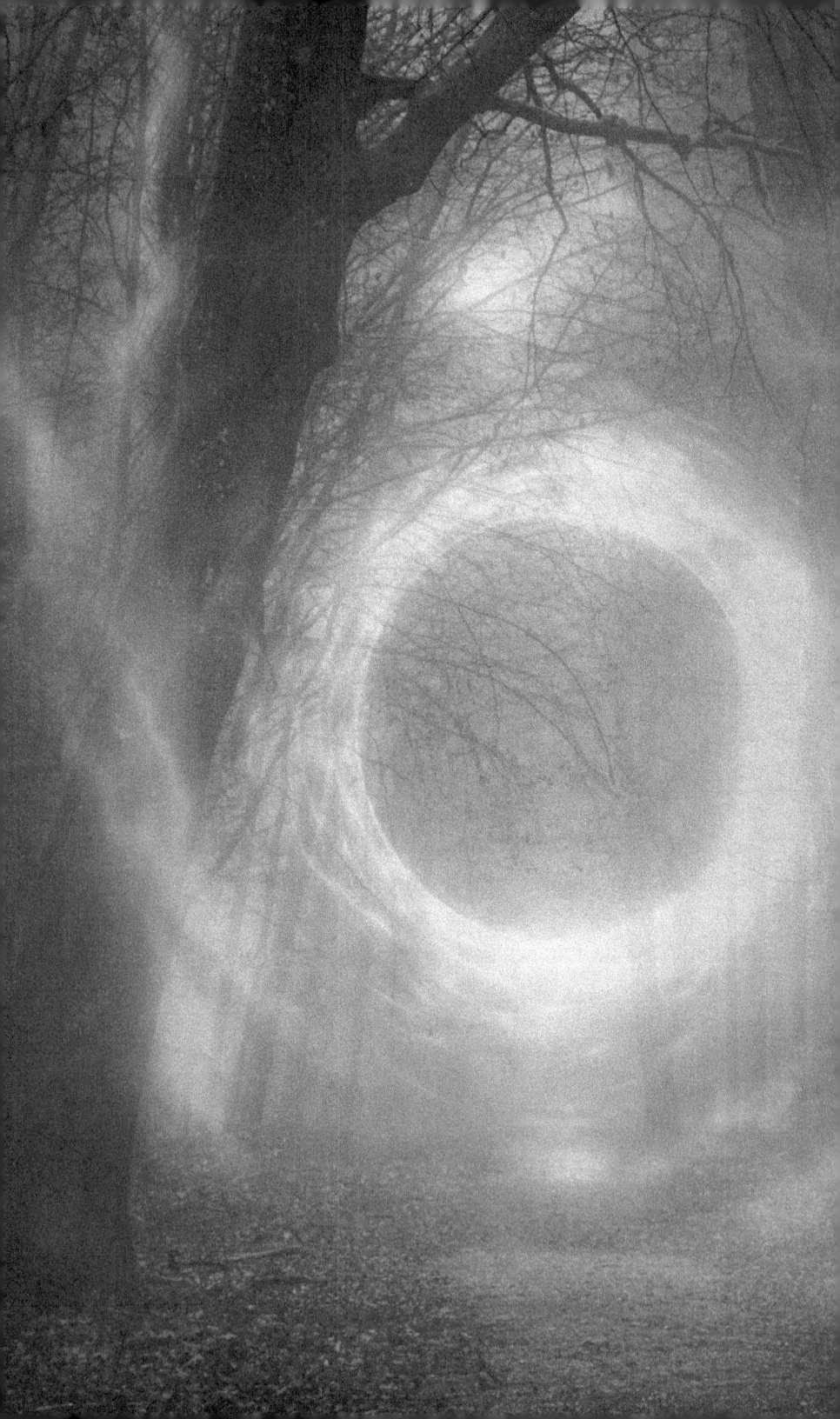

CHAPTER 22
THE AWAKENING

EVALINA

J ulius helps me down from the piano, handing me my undergarment from off the floor. I adjust my gown, or what's left of it, as every person in the room stops what they're doing. I mean it in every literal sense. Men who are deeply buried inside certain women halt their thrusts at the sight of Valec in the room. I find it strange that they'd do so, considering it's normal for him to be here. After all, Julius did express that Valec takes part in all sins during the celebration. Guess the tension can be felt throughout the entire room.

"You motherfucker." Julius points a finger at Sairo, crossing the distance till he's shoving him back against the wall for the second time today. But Anev interferes, yanking Julius off Sairo and shoving him backwards with little to no effort. His body barrels towards me. Julius manages to gain his footing before crashing into me.

"Careful how you use your words, Julius," says Valec. "For it wasn't Sairo who told me of your endeavors." If not Sairo, then who? "Anev saw the whole incident take place. You've got a lot of nerve, dear brother, threatening one of my own."

Oh god, this is not good. Not only did I disobey Valec's orders, but Julius did as well. Now, there's only one way this can go. "Walk with me," he orders. Anev and Recifer move behind us, making sure Jules and I follow.

Julius curls his fingers around mine and I swallow drily, fearing what is to come. We keep a close pace behind Valec, Aziel and Sairo walking in front. They lead us inside the throne room. Anev is the one to separate Julius and I by force. I nearly fall to the floor before Valec swoops in to grab me by the arm. Seeing that I'm steady on my feet, he walks away from me without a care.

"You disobeyed me, Evalina. And here I thought we made a deal. An oath—one that you sealed by blood. You broke said oath and now drastic measures will be taken."

"Fine, but if you have to punish someone let it be me. I'm the one who broke the oath, not Julius."

"Oh, Evalina." Valec smirks. "The punishment is not for you, regardless if it was your fault or not. It's precisely because of your carelessness that my brother shall be the one to pay the price."

"No!" I say with authority.

"No?" Valec lifts a finger. A cloud of smoke appears and suddenly it's harder for me to breathe.

"Valec, let her go," I hear Julius say. "We both know you won't kill her. You need her." Julius's words have the desired effect. The ties to my lungs cease and I can breathe normally again.

"You are correct, Julius, I do need her. You"—he maneuvers his magic over Julius this time—"not so much." The cloud of smoke emanating from his hands seems to grow bigger until it takes on the appearance of something as frightening as the shades that attacked me.

I watch in horror at how the smoke monster enters through Julius's mouth, choking him. All the fumes enter his body. Valec's going to kill him if I don't do something. He's truly going to kill his own brother before my very eyes. I feel helpless with the barrier the Wicked Four have created around me.

I could try fighting them off, but that won't do anything. If only I had a weapon…*wait,* my dagger. The one Julius gifted me. In the end, he wouldn't take no for an answer. He suggested I have it on me at all times, and Vienna was stealthy when she placed it in the back of my dress. Tucked away for no one to see.

This is reckless, but it's my only shot at creating a distraction. With one swift move I grasp the handle and bring the blade to my neck.

The room rapidly goes still; even Valec pauses to stare at me. I back away from the Wicked Four, as they've created an opening for me to escape. All they do is stare at me, none of them showing signs of attacking. I can tell they're assessing me. Cautious of taking one single step towards me, for fear that it might serve as encouragement for me to take my own life.

"If either one of you so much as takes one step in my direction, I'll slice my skin right open. I'll end my life right here and then you can never get your precious freedom back," I say, staring Valec straight in the eyes.

"Evalina, no!" Julius rasps.

I ignore his plea. "Let Julius go." I bring my attention back to Valec. "Pardon my actions against you and all will be well."

I'm too focused on Valec that I fail to notice the shadow looming at my back, until it's too late. I look to my front, only to see three of the Four, Recifer clearly having slipped away.

He lands a blow to my side, which sends the dagger flying across the room as my body lands with a loud thud on the floor.

"Thank you, Recifer." Valec moves to stand in front of me. His foot is only an inch away from my face. "For pulling that little stunt, I have a more rewarding compensation for you." He walks away like the tyrant he is, setting himself comfortably on his throne. "Gentlemen, Anev, do as you please." I expect them to approach me. Instead, it's Julius who they approach.

"No!" I yell desperately, trying to lift myself off the floor. My eyes can barely register what Valec's doing, given how far away he is from me. But the black trail of smoke that leads my way says it all. He's rendered me immobile. The only thing I can do is lift my head slightly and that's how I'm able to see Julius on his knees, while Aziel and Recifer start undressing his upper body. *No,* not this again.

They haven't even started the torture, and tears are already streaming down my face. I keep telling myself that Julius can fight. I've seen him fight. Then how come he isn't doing anything? Why is he being complacent? I thought we were done with obedience. "Jules," my voice breaks, and his beautiful eyes snap to me.

He brings a finger to his lips, as though to silence me. He mouths, *"It's going –to –be okay."* But it's not. Nothing is going to be okay.

But I can't take my eyes off him, not even for a second. Not when Aziel opens a bag full of various weapons. I spot a few knives and daggers, even a throwing star. Once Julius's upper body is completely exposed, Anev grabs his arms and twists them behind his back. The double doors rattle from outside the room. I hear some guards yell, then the doors fly wide open to reveal a very familiar dog. Saint comes running in so fast, I barely have time to register the moment I'm able to move again. Valec must have lost focus on his magic to take in the furry intruder. Julius thrusts his hands out from behind his back, smacking Anev in the process.

Saint tries to approach me, but Valec only needs to lift a single finger and the dog's suspended in the air. Saint yelps in pain.

"Valec, please don't hurt a poor animal!" I exclaim. The

sound of battle forces me to look behind me. The Wicked Four circle Julius as he is now on his feet. A weapon in hand. Ready to fight. I thank whoever it is I should be thanking at this moment. But Valec sure isn't it.

"I hurt whomever I please, Evalina. And it's about time you understand that." Valec sneers at me, then flings his hands forward and sends Saint flying across the room. He smacks against one of the entryway columns. I stop breathing, fearing the worst, until I notice the animal move a paw. he's alive. The dog's alive.

In my moment of distraction, a thin frame barrels into me. It's so sudden that I can't steady myself, and I faceplant against the cold tile. Anev looms over me.

I'm forced to watch in horror as Valec gets closer to Julius. Followed by sounds of his pain. It's like watching a conductor direct an orchestra. Hands outstretched, Valec waves them through the air, except there's no music. Only the anguished sounds of my lover.

Valec doesn't stop; he keeps lifting him higher and higher in the air, until Julius's head touches the ceiling. Smoke hovers all around him. His arms flail, reaching for his neck, as he desperately tries to get oxygen into his lungs. The sight of him in need has me doing something incredibly brave, yet stupid.

I lunge for Valec, but Anev grasps my gown in seconds, pulling me back once again. The sight of Julius in pain and defenseless is killing me. "Valec stop this," I scream.

Valec doesn't break concentration when he addresses me. "You caused this, Evalina." His words hit me like a brick .

As Julius keeps thrashing, Saint barks from his side of the room. But he must be badly hurt if he's having trouble trying to stand. It's when Julius's body jolts, his back arching backwards, excessive smoke entering his mouth, when my worst fear is taken right out of me. His body suddenly calms, and that's when I scream.

It's unlike any scream I've ever heard. The ground seems to rumble at our feet. Everyone loses their balance. Even Valec's magic falters. I'm still wailing but whoever was restraining me from behind has let me go, and that's when it happens. That's when the flames erupt. First from my hands and then from my entire body. I'm completely lit with fire. Sairo, Aziel, and Recifer all take a step back, Anev having joined them. Valec lowers Julius to the floor. Blinking, unbelieving of what I've just done.

Unconcerned by their stares, I rush to Julius's now limp form on the floor. Tears leak from my eyes. *No, this did not happen.* Completely ignoring the fire erupting from my skin, I touch a hand to his cheek. He's not gone. I refuse to believe such a thing.

Can a man truly be as emotionless as Valec right now?

It sickens me to believe what Julius said was true. Valec is *that* far gone.

The flames from my hands begin to spread rapidly till they engulf Julius's body. They spark bright orange and remain over his form like a cocoon. *Oh gods,* what have I done?

Much to my relief, my powers don't burn him. Like Valec's ability, the fire seeps through his mouth like a vapor, until there's not a single flame left on his skin nor on mine. Saint manages to make it to my side on wobbly paws, nudging my hand with his nose. I pat him lightly on the head and he relaxes. Staring down at Julius, Saint curls himself against him, resting his head on his lap. The action alone has me crying all over again.

I remain on my knees in front of Julius for what feels like hours. But in reality, I know it's only been a couple of minutes. Losing hope with each passing second.

The realization has me sobbing. He never wanted this, he did all that was asked of him, played by all Valec's rules, just so I wouldn't be alone to face all this. And now he's gone. There's nothing I can do. I lay my head against his chest and sniffle. I never got to tell him how I feel. I never told him the truth. I was always so afraid to admit it that it never passed my lips.

As I lay against his chest, something feels odd. There seems to be a slight shift in the air, or maybe I'm only imagining it. Until a firm hand lands on my back. I stiffen and immediately straighten myself. That's when I see it, that's when I see *him*. The bluish gray of his eyes stare at me in wonder.

"Jules?" I cup his face in my hands.

"Alina." His hand brushes the side of my cheek.

I won't waste my time; I won't keep my words locked up. Not anymore. If the fates have given him another chance, given us another chance, I won't waste it. That's why, when I open my mouth, it's to say the three words Julius least expects. "I love you."

His eyes flash with emotion, but he remains quiet for a few seconds. He brings his arms to his sides to lift himself off the floor, bringing me with him to a seated position. I remain with my legs on each side of his torso. I barely have time to register his actions when his lips connect with my own. His mouth feels like a feather over my lips. This kiss isn't rushed by any means. It's tender and sweet, a soft and steady brush of lips against lips. I savor every second, till Julius pulls away. His forehead rests against mine.

He clears his throat. "I've been waiting a while for you to say that." I break into a smile. "I love you, Evalina Morue. And I will continue to love you every minute of my existence."

Tears flow down my cheeks once more, but for all the right reasons this time. Behind us I get the sense Valec and the rest are lingering close by. I'm scared to look behind me, thinking they might be holding weapons, ready to attack, while Valec prepares to unleash his power again. I hold Julius close to me.

Jules stares behind me. "It's okay," he says. *What's okay?* Because as far as I know nothing is okay. He was dead and now he's not. Saint nudges his hand and Julius happily smiles down at him, petting his head. "My boy."

I allow Julius some room to stand, but the second we're both on our feet, I stick back to him like glue. Grabbing at his arm, curling against his side—I won't let Valec hurt him again.

"Brother," Julius says casually, staring into Valec's cold expression. "Thought you could get rid of me that easily."

"It appears that my efforts were quite useful, considering she unlocked her power," he says with a wicked smile," triumph in his gaze. *I what?* "Such an exquisite spectacle we witnessed here today. What a pity that you missed it, Julius. She was magnificent." Julius stares down at me. "But given you were dead and all—"

"I died?" Jules says quietly to me. I nod without looking at him. Did he not see his entire life flash before his eyes?

"Oh, how I've waited for this day to come. Hellfire in its most primitive form. You see, Brother, while I possess death magic through my shadows, your dear Evalina's hellfire has necromantic properties." Valec motions towards me. "She brought you back to life." The instant those words leave his brother's mouth, Julius's hold on me loosens.

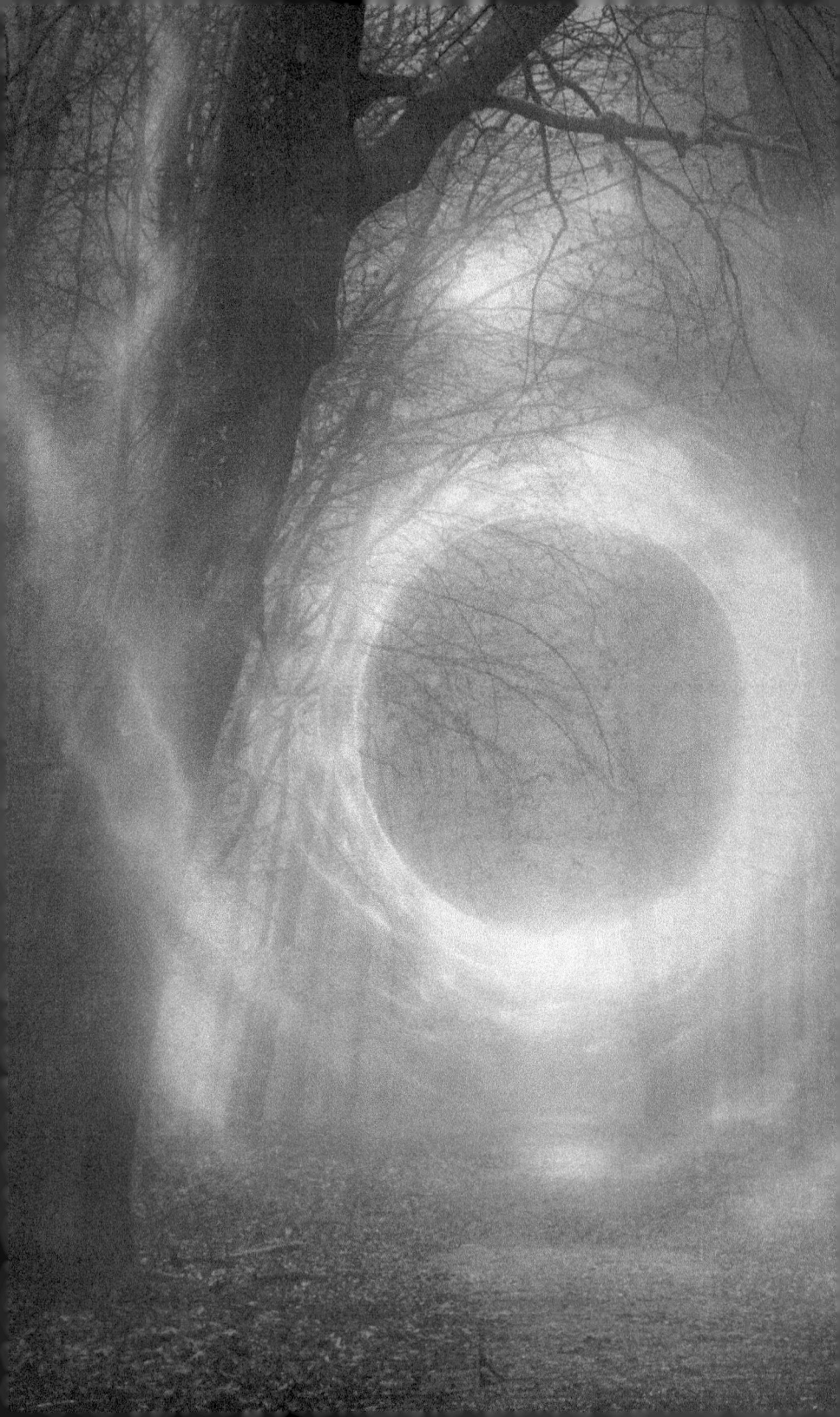

CHAPTER 23
NEW LIVES

JULIUS

I remain stiff by Evalina's side, shocked by the news Valec just delivered. Valec was always quiet when it came to Evalina's power. I knew it was hellfire, but not in a million years did I expect hellfire could bring back the dead. Nor that I would be the first person Evalina tested her abilities on. Did she even know what she was doing?

I thought I was unconscious; I was certain that I was still alive. But my brother truly murdered me. He was merciless, as always, though this time he went there. To the place I always feared he'd get to someday. He breached the very thin border we share, the one that bonds us as brothers. Soela was right: he doesn't care, and he never will if he continues to be Lucifer.

Evalina hangs on to me, clearly afraid that if she lets go, she'll somehow lose me again. I want to reassure her that I'm not going anywhere. But not here, not in front of Valec, nor the Wicked Four.

"Congratulations, then," I express. "You are one step away from freedom, what you've always wanted."

Valec seems pleased. "I hope there are no hard feelings, Julius." *Is he serious?* "As you can see, your death prompted Evalina to manifest her abilities. And she brought you back. All is well. She barely even suffered. I consider that a win." *Sure thing.*

"Now, all that's left is for Soela to train her for a while, and once she's properly able to wield her hellfire, we will be out of here by the following blood moon. Consider yourselves lucky. You now have my full blessing. Though you did always have it," Valec says to us. "I will no longer be a disturbance in your lives. The deed has been done. Train, learn, then unlock the veil, and you and Julius are free to live out the rest of your lives as you see fit. As long as none of you try to stop me." He directs his last sentence at Evalina. "Enjoy your immortality, my dear."

"What do you mean?" Evalina shifts her grip on my arm.

"What I mean, dear Evalina, is that you are no longer mortal. Besides necromancy, your hellfire awoke your immortality. You are now like Julius and I, purely immortal. You will so graciously live on forever. Now," Valec waves a hand in the air, "leave. I have some unfinished business to take care off." He looks at Sairo, and I already know what he's going to do.

I tug on Evalina's arms, tucking her against me as I lead her out of the room. Valec doesn't wait for the doors to properly close until Sairo's scream echoes from the room. He protected Evalina and I. He never snitched. He kept his word. Though now he's paying the price.

I steer Evalina in the direction of my chambers. There's no way I'm leaving her alone for the rest of the night. Not with what's happened. I unlock the door and she hesitates by the entrance. I pick her up off the ground in one swoop. Carrying her inside, I shut the door with my foot. I think what we both need is a bath. I place her on the bed and proceed to prepare the tub for us. When I return, she has her eyes trained on the wall.

"I'm immortal," she says under her breath. I sit beside her

while the tub fills up. "I can't decide if that's a good thing or if it's bad."

I rest a hand on her thigh. "Does it appeal to you? The fact that you no longer have an expiration date?" I question.

"In a way it does because that means I get to be with you forever. No aging, no dying of an illnesses." Her answer brings me joy.

"There's nothing that will make me happier than spending the rest of my days by your side," I express. She nuzzles her face to my chest.

"Then I guess I should say it is a good thing I get to live forever now." She giggles.

"Yes." I plant a kiss on the crown of her head. "It is." I stand and extend my hand to her. "Bath?"

"Yes," she says, and takes my hand.

We've bathed, and now it's late in the night. We're laying in the dark, neither one of us able to fall asleep. "Jules." She shifts to the side, facing me. "Did you truly not feel yourself die?"

"No," I say with honesty. "I felt nothing. I thought Valec rendered me unconscious. I simply felt myself slip away but not in a permanent way. I only thought I was sleeping in a comatose state." I pull her closer to me. "What was it like for you?"

"Horrible," she answers. "It felt like my entire life flashed before my eyes. I screamed and it was so unlike any ordinary cry of pain. It was something different and before I knew it, I was on fire. My entire body erupted with flames. I went to you and the second I touched you, the flames consumed you. You were covered in them. I thought it would kill you. That I had only made it worse."

Hearing her tell the story leaves me incredulous. Much like

her, I'm in disbelief over my death while she's in disbelief over my resurrection.

"I don't think I'll ever get the image out of my head. Seeing that you were gone killed me. It was like reliving my parents' death all over again."

"Hey." I press a thumb to her cheek, caressing her. "I'm here, aren't I? You brought me back. I'm here right beside you, and in case you forgot, Valec will no longer be a problem for us. He gave us his word, and his word is as good as his oath. We're free."

"Once I unlock the veil," she states.

"No, once you bring *him* back," I remind her. Now it all makes sense. I never understood why Soela thought Evalina's magic could kill the new Valec and bring back the old one, but it is clear as day now. Her necromancy can revive the Valec that has been dead for years. "After that, you're more than welcome to open the veil. But not a second before. I *will* have my brother back first."

"You will," she promises. "I'll do whatever it takes to bring him back to you."

"No, Evalina." I stop her. "Please, don't you dare do anything reckless like you did when you placed that dagger to your throat."

"Julius." She reaches for me. "It was to get Valec to stop hurting you."

"I know, but you have no idea how frightened I was seeing you like that."

"So, you're the only one who gets to be the hero?" She brings herself to a seated position on the bed. "I don't think so. Julius, I love you, and by now you have to know that I will do anything for no harm to come your way. We are both the same in that regard. So don't ask that of me. I will continue to be reckless if need be." She's right. Though I dislike and admire that aspect about her. Who am I kidding? We are both one and the same.

I reel her close to me. "I love you. My beautiful and brave Alina."

○

The following morning, I tell Evalina I'll be taking her somewhere this afternoon and leave her to prepare. Given that Valec instructed her to begin training with Soela tomorrow, it means we have today all to ourselves. I checked up on Saint earlier; he's doing well. He had no broken bones, only bruises that have already faded. I have our wonderful healers to thank for that. Having finished all my tasks for today, I knock on Evalina's door twice and Vienna answers. "Good evening, Your Highness," she greets me in her usual manner.

"Good evening, Vienna. Is Evalina ready?"

She lets out a light giggle. No one could know where we're going, so I simply told Vienna to find something practical for Evalina to wear. "She'll be right out," she lets me know before scurrying off.

I remain by the door, but nothing prepares me for when she steps out of the bathing chamber. The seamstresses managed to mirror my own outfit and fashion it for her frame. We are dressed identically. Black trousers and black boots. Belts complete with a holster for our daggers. Gray billowy shirts with the top buttons undone, much like how I wear it. And to top it off, Vienna has styled her hair in a long side-braid. She looks stunning and deadly all at once. Anyone who sees her would steer clear of her for sure.

"Are you going to say something? Or are you just going to keep gawking at me?" She crosses her arms over her chest. Her appearance becomes even more lethal.

"It is a crime to stare?" I comment.

"No, unless you do it creepily, the way you are right now."

"I am not staring at you creepily." I jump to my defense. "I'm simply admiring you."

"Vienna thought the outfit would be fitting. What she regretted to inform me was that you would be dressed the exact same way."

"Why do you think she chose it?"

She grins. "It's quite hilarious if you ask me. Us dressed alike."

"I like it."

"I didn't say that I didn't like it." She approaches me.

"You didn't say you liked it either." I can't help but curl my arms around her. "You look beautiful." I plant a quick kiss on her lips. "As you always do. Are you ready for today?"

"Of course, though I'd like it even more if you weren't so secretive about it," she complains.

We begin to walk out of the room. "We're going to visit Anise, the woman who rescued you that night in the caves," I say in a hushed tone.

"We are?" She seems dubious.

"Since the day you arrived, she's wanted nothing more than to meet you properly. I figured now that the worst is behind us, it's only fitting she get to know the woman I can't seem to shut up about."

"You talk to her about me?"

"I did say she's like a mother to me, so yes. I tell her more than I'd like to, actually." I lead her outside the borders of the mansion. "Though she never complains. Anise likes hearing all I have to say. She loves a good romance story."

"I wouldn't say our story qualifies as your typical romance. It's more tragic to me." She isn't wrong.

"Try to look at it through a happier lens. That's what I've been doing all this time. It's worked for me so far."

Alina keeps a steady pace beside me. "I guess you'll have to teach me your ways."

"Guess I will." We fall into silence as we near the heart. I hate the fact that we have to pass through these secluded caverns to reach Anise's house, but it's the closest route. That's why I keep Evalina close to me. Guiding her with a steady hand on her back, I hope she realizes that she's safe with me.

I pause once we're inside another tunnel that will lead us to the depths. Here it's a bit trickier to navigate. The rocky terrain becomes unpredictable. There are too many stalagmites that make it difficult to cross through to the next cave. For a moment, I notice a shift in Evalina's mood. "Hey, what's wrong?" I place my hands on her shoulders.

"Nothing's wrong. I was just thinking about something. Not the shades. Something else."

"Well, what is it?" She seems to overthink her response. "Hey, whatever it is, you can tell me."

"It's not important now. Just my brain being dumb."

"Your brain isn't dumb, Alina. Trust me," I assure her.

She appears to give up her internal fight, her shoulders sagging a bit. "Okay, like I said, it's not really important at the moment..." She unconsciously bites her lower lip. "I was just thinking about what life will be like when we eventually go back to Einalem."

"That's not dumb, Alina."

"There's more. I was picturing a life for us. The both of us living in a cabin in the middle of a forest, having our own farm and maybe a bookstore as well..." She trails off, likely scared of my reaction. "Forget I said anything." She dismisses her thoughts.

"Alina." I circle my arms around her waist. "Your thoughts are valid. I would love nothing more than to share such a life with you. You mean everything to me. We've expressed our love for each other, by now you should know that."

"I do, I just thought it silly to be thinking such a thing when we aren't one hundred percent certain that Soela's plan will work."

"Have faith that it will. Just wait and see. That life you want for us will come true." I press a quick kiss to her lips to reassure her. "Now, come on. I have a friendly woman I want to introduce you to." We continue our walk.

It doesn't take long for Evalina to notice the tiny little homes carved into the stones of the cavern walls. "They're so cute!" she exclaims. "These are much smaller than the ones I've seen in the other caves."

"Depends on how much space you want. Many people only want a safe place to call home."

"Did you make them?" she asks once we're walking past the houses. Some of the people inside hear us and peek through the windows.

"I helped a little." I reach Anise's familiar gray home. A few potted plants and a welcome mat greet us at the entryway. I knock on the front door, and we wait.

The door swings open to reveal a white-haired elderly woman. Her small frame makes it easier for her to stand in the narrow entryway. "Welcome, Evalina. I've been expecting you." She smiles, expression lines forming. "It's so good to see you again, dear. I'm glad that you are well."

"It's good to see you again as well. Thank you again. I will forever be in debt to you," Alina expresses.

Anise shakes her head. "That won't be necessary. The best payment you could have given me is this, a visit. Come." She links Evalina's arm with her own. I follow them inside. "It's not much," she comments.

I know she's saying it for Evalina's benefit. I've been inside Anise's home plenty of times, and though it is small, it has heart. Anise made do with the little she had. The small structure consists of a kitchen and living area within the same room, a bathroom that can only fit exactly one person at a time, and then her bedroom, which fits her bed and a small wardrobe, nothing else. But the space is heavily decorated with pink curtains at each window and flower vases around each surface, giving the place a homey feel.

She leads us to the living room. "Please take a seat." There are exactly three chairs. I take a seat beside Evalina.

"I know life here is not ideal, so I won't ask you about that. But rather, what was your life like back in Einalem? Julius has told me many stories, but I'd like to hear them from you." Anise smiles. "So, tell me dear, what interesting stories do you have?"

Alina seems to shrink into her seat. "Well, there was this one time Julius and I were working in my garden. It started raining but we ended up making a mess of each other, having a full-on mud war."

Anise's smile grows wider. I remember that night clear as day; it's one of my favorites, and funnily enough, I've never told Anise about it before. Only Soela knows all of my and Evalina's encounters, and with vivid detail.

"It kept raining, and we were a mess," she continues. "My parents would have killed me if we got mud inside the house, so we went to hose off. Except that Julius decided to strip." I swallow, recalling how pale she'd looked when she saw me in nothing but my undergarments. "I couldn't stop my cheeks from blushing. He looked..." She turns to direct her words at me. "You looked way too sexy." I let out a low chuckle, enjoying her use of the word *sexy* to describe me for the first time. "I literally froze." Her attention is back to Anise. "I'm pretty sure Julius had to break me out of my trance. Because I wouldn't stop staring at him."

"Would you say that was one of the moments when you started falling for Julius?" Anise asks in her warm tone.

"I would say that yes, it was. I mean, I never dated anyone before Julius. So, I can't say for sure. Though, it was always him, I guess." I drape a hand behind her chair.

"You mean to tell me that you are now twenty-one, and you never dated anyone before?" Anise is amazed.

"No one," she answers. "There was just Julius." From the corner of my eyes, I notice the little girl who's walked into the room. Evalina hasn't noticed her yet.

"Pia," I say with enthusiasm, and she comes running towards me.

"Jules!" She runs into my arms. I feel Alina's eyes on me. "Pia is our youngest," I say. "She's ten." I watch Evalina regard Pia with warmth. I imagine she reminds Evalina of herself when she was that age. Same curly brown hair and bright charisma. The only difference between them is Pia's eyes that shine green like an emerald.

"Pia," I say to the girl. "I'd like you to meet someone." The girl has just now noticed that I am accompanied by someone. She's so used to me coming to visit alone that I can see how it's a shock to see someone else with me. "This is Evalina, my girl-friend." Evalina's eyes flash with a look of surprise as I intro-duce her to Pia.

"Evalina, meet Pia."

"You're very pretty," she says to Alina.

Evalina smiles. "Why thank you. You are very pretty as well." Evalina shoots me a look and I know exactly what she wants to ask. *How did she die?*

"Fever. Her father was too late with the medication she need-ed," I explain.

Pia moves to sit on Anise's lap. Evalina stares at her, then brings her gaze back to me. "I thought children had no sin. Why did she end up here?"

"Her mother died in childbirth. So, maybe it was her father's misdeeds she paid for," I guess.

"Just because of her father?" I nod. "How could Dominus overlook such a thing?"

"The same way he overlooked Valec's innocence and trusted

the word of a lying god. If Dominus is still being controlled, then there are a number of things he'll disregard. Pia being one of them."

Someone taps on the front door. "I'll get it," Pia says and runs to answer the door. "Anise!" she yells from the other side of the room. Anise scurries off. It only takes her seconds to return, her face ashen.

"Anise, what's wrong?" I immediately jump to my feet and so does Evalina.

"Shades," she says. "Loads of them. We're being surrounded."

Outside, all chaos breaks loose.

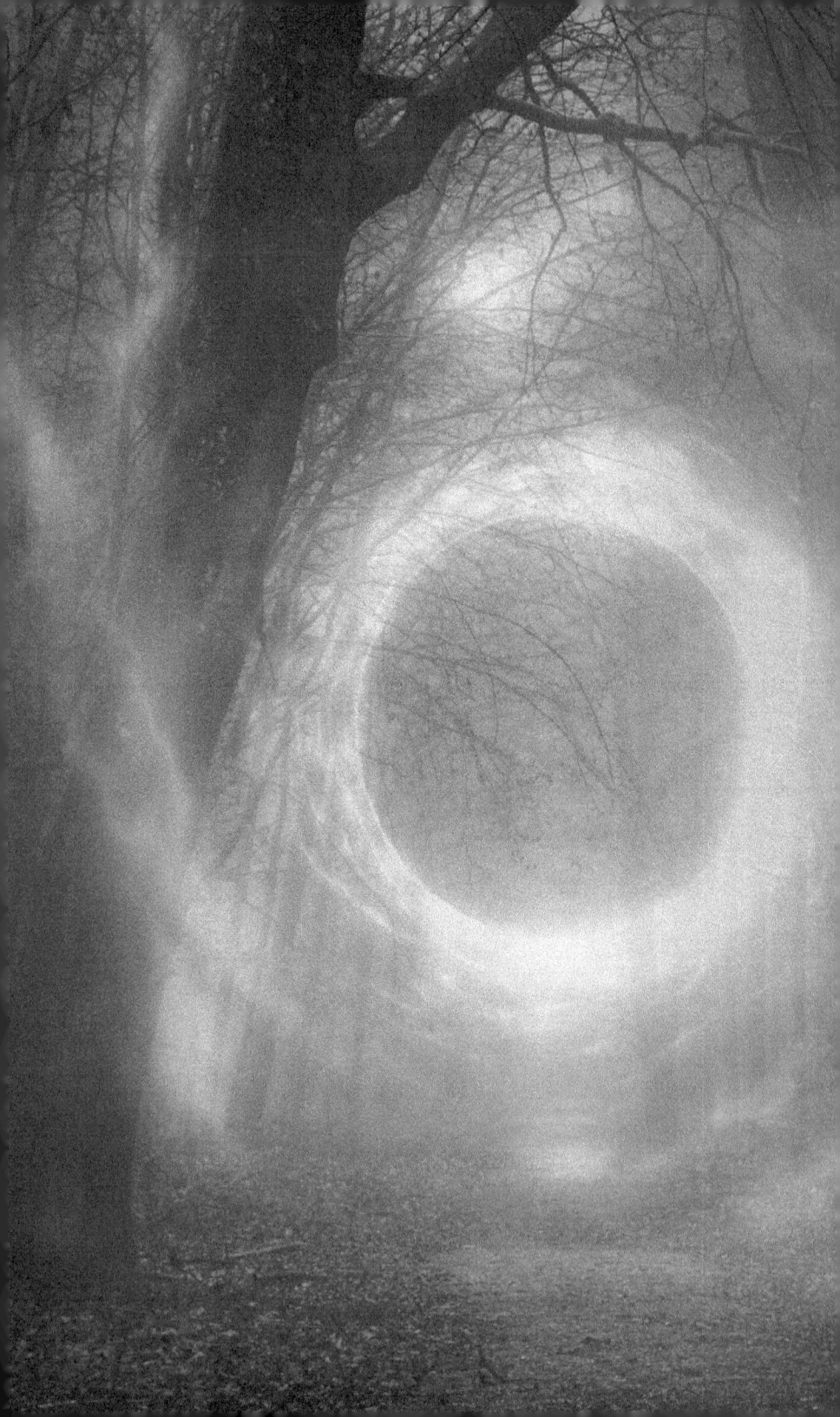

CHAPTER 24
UNDER ATTACK

EVALINA

"Get Evalina out of here!" Julius orders, shoving me towards Anise. "Go! I'll take care of the shades."

I barely have time to protest before Anise is pulling me by the arm, taking Pia with us as she guides us through a back door.

We're running through tunnels, but we aren't the only ones. Many others run ahead of us. As we pass by, I don't recognize a thing. It doesn't look anything like the caves Julius and I came through. Which means we must be heading further out.

"Evalina," Anise says, dragging me out of my thoughts. "Through here." I follow her and Pia as they duck into a smaller cavern of smooth rock. Other people have retreated to the same space too. "This is our bunker," she tells us. "We built it as a refuge from the shades. Everyone," Anise says, addressing the whole congregation. "We'll keep the doors open for a few more minutes, but after that we'll have to close them. Can't risk those monsters reaching us."

"What do you mean by close the doors?" I direct my question only to her.

"The bunker walls will seal everyone for as long as need be."

"I can't." I back away as more people gather inside the hollow.

"Evalina!" Anise calls. "You're safer in here."

I shake my head. "I'm thankful, truly Anise, but I can't remain locked up while Julius is out there fighting those things."

"Julius will know where to find you."

I shake my head. This is crazy. Staying here is insane, and to think that Julius knows this, and yet he still told Anise to drag me here. No, he promised no more playing the hero. I won't leave him alone. Not now, not ever.

"I'm sorry. But my boyfriend needs me." I offer Pia one last smile as she stares at me wide-eyed.

Thankful to be wearing pants I run through the cavern as fast as I can. I can do this. I can make my way back. I just have to concentrate. In my haste to get to Julius, I end up bumping into someone through the tunnels, and that someone just so happens to be one of the Wicked Four. Anev. *Shit!* I take out my dagger faster than she reaches for her own. She's not wearing any other weapons but I notice that her face is bloody. She's got a nasty cut that runs from the side of her left eye and ends at her chin. Her clothes are dirty and stained with blood as well. Anev was in a fight and if she somehow did have more weapons, they were most likely taken from her during the blow. My hope is that it was with Julius.

"You're a long way from your master," I spit, holding the dagger steady in my grasp the way Julius taught me.

"Valec can take care of himself. He's having the time of his life with Julius." *Why is Valec here?* I try to block out her words. She could be lying just to get a rise out of me. Hoping I let my guard down. "Who do you think rounded up those shades and sent them on the loose right where you were? Valec's orders." She sneers.

"It was you?" I'm at a loss for words. I wield hellfire now. Valec promised no more games. Then why on Inferis did he send shades after us?

"Me and what's left of our group, of course," she says as we circle each other like predators.

I hope she doesn't notice how shaky my hand is as I hold the weapon. I steady myself. *Concentrate, Evalina.* I've got this. She strikes and I duck right on time. All I need to do is knock her dagger from her grasp. I hope having both daggers will be enough to scare her. But even I know that's wishful thinking, especially since Anev is good at hand-to-hand combat.

We remain circling each other as I try desperately to dodge her attacks.

I could try to strike her, but most likely she'll attack in a matter of seconds, and then I'll be under her mercy. "This cat and mouse game is getting pretty tiring, if you ask me. Just give up and I'll take you to Julius."

I laugh. "As if I'll ever trust you. You sold us out."

"You broke the rules." As if I need a reminder.

"Here's an even better idea. Get out of my way and go run into some of those shades you wrangled."

"If I let you go, Valec will have my head."

"What, does Valec now want to kill me?" I question.

"No, but he wants you and Julius apprehended."

"For?"

"For Julius having aided you during Valec's first experiment." He found out. How? Someone must have seen Anise come to my aid. Someone who also lives outside the mansion and is loyal to Valec. There is no other explanation.

"Valec truly is a monster." A muscle in her jaw ticks. "You know this, don't you, and yet you chose to work for him."

"I serve the man who spared my life."

"Look around you," I look up to the cavern walls. "This isn't living. This is a prison. You say Valec spared you, but did you ever even meet the old Valec, the kind leader, the one Julius has told me so much about?"

"I did not."

"Then that's your answer right there."

"That Valec you speak of is dead; he is not the man I serve," she snaps.

"How many lies has Valec had to feed you in order for you to take his side—"

"None," she cuts me off. I stop moving and so does she. "Valec has not fed me a single lie. I chose to stand by him on my own. It was either that or second death. He knew I was a good fighter, that's why he chose me. I initially refused, then the threat came, and I chose life over death." Of course he threatened her as well.

"That wasn't a choice." I motion to her attire. To her hooded cloak. "This life of misery and suffering. Being subjected to his every wickedness. Having to do all Valec's dirty work for him. That's not living."

"Is it not the same life your beloved Julius has chosen for himself." She lowers her dagger, but I keep my own arms raised just in case. "He's had plenty of opportunities to die, but he's always played the savior because he never wanted to leave you alone to your fate." Julius has told me this several times, but somehow hearing Anev say it takes a completely different undertone.

I'm at a loss for words, though my fury gets hold of me. "Do not compare what Julius has gone through with your own struggle. You are not the same. You've done nothing but torture him for all these years." I'm aware of how close I've gotten to Anev and how she now holds her dagger at the ready, anticipating my approach. I know I should back away, though that's the complete opposite of what I do.

"We are all but one and the same," she mocks.

One second my skin is its normal pale sheen, and the next it's covered entirely in flames.

Anev's eyes flash with surprise. "Pretty neat parlor trick, huh?" I question. She takes a step back. "Maybe you're right, and Valec did spare you, but I'm not going to." I fling myself at her, one of my hands touching her skin. She yells in pain, and I watch as the dagger slips from her hand. Every inch of her skin is covered in my hellfire.

I snatch her weapon off the ground and that's when I notice my skin has returned to normal. Anev still screams, her flesh melting off bone. I quickly avert my gaze and make the decision to walk away, not wanting to look back. A chill takes over my body over what I just did. Clearly my power can do so much more than resurrect the dead. It's dangerous in the same way Valec's shadows are.

I don't know how I manage to do it; it feels like I've been walking forever. But I return to the exact location of Anise's house. The once gray floor is now covered in the bodies of dead shades. I count about eight in total. I walk the deserted cavern, searching. There isn't a single sound, just silence. Looks like everyone fled to the bunker. The depths are completely empty.

Suddenly I feel an urge to enter Anise's house. I stop short of the entrance. There standing in the very narrow hallway is Julius. Giving me space to enter the house. He walks to the tiny living area that connects with the kitchen. I don't care that he's filthy and caked in blood. I sprint for him. He holds me with ease. He doesn't grunt, nor make any sound of pain, which is a good sign. It means he isn't hurt, which is all I was hoping for.

Tears spill from my eyes, and I guess I'm not the only one. I hear a sob coming from the man that holds me. "I thought you left for the bunker," he scolds.

"I wasn't going to leave you," I cry, burying my head in the crook of his shoulder. "I hate that you sent me away, though. You promised me, we're in this together."

"I know. I'm sorry. Some selfish part of me knew you wouldn't stay with them. But the more protective side of me hoped you would." He sniffles, letting go of me to wipe at his tear-stained face. "I don't know what I was thinking. I was already going mad without you here by my side."

I chuckle and raise my hands to touch his face. I have to stand on my tiptoes and even that's a struggle, so he lowers himself to me. I wipe at his tears with my thumb. "You know, you're beautiful when you cry," I whisper.

"Am I?" he doubts.

"A man who cries in the presence of others is a man who isn't afraid to show emotion." He takes my hand in his, pressing it to his lips.

We let the tenderness of the moment keep us locked together. Until it's time to get serious.

"Did everyone make it to safety?" Julius asks me minutes later once we're both seated by the kitchen table.

"Yes, I think so."

He nods. "That's good." Julius stares at his hands resting on his lap.

"What happened here, Jules?"

"The second I knew that you, Anise, and Pia were on the run, I went out. Valec appeared. You aren't going to like what I have to say next."

"If you're going to tell me that Valec is responsible for the shade attack, then I already know."

He doesn't seem the least bit surprise by my statement. He breathes out. "That's not the worst of it. Valec locked us out of the mansion."

Come again. "He what? Why?"

"I bet you already know why." I do.

"He found out you sent someone to help me that day."

"Yes, he would have killed me but saw no point considering you'd only revive me again."

"What about training with Soela?" I ask.

"He said that he'd gladly send Soela to us. We aren't to set foot inside the mansion until it's time to knock down the veil."

"That son of a bitch." I pound my fists on the table. "He needs to be stopped."

"And he will." A reassuring hand squeezes my own on the table, and I squeeze his back.

Now standing, I walk around the room. "What now?"

"We remain here. Anise is most likely a target now because of me. I wouldn't want her to return here now that he knows where she lives. I'll find her a new home for the time being. She will likely remain under the bunker's protection for the night, but tomorrow I'll go find her."

"I'll go with you," I say as I pick up some pots and pans from under Anise's cabinet.

"Of course. Now what are you doing?" he questions.

"Making dinner; are we meant to starve?"

"Not at all. But please allow me to offer some assistance." Julius rummages through the ice box in search of food to cook.

After an hour of cooking and eating, we are both satiated and tired. Julius prepares the bed while I finish washing the dirty dishes. "You really know how to cook a good meal," he says from the other room.

"Were you doubting my cooking skills?"

"Never." He pokes his head out from the hallway. "I'd simply never tried anything that you've cooked before. It was a new experience for me. An enjoyable one, at that." He lifts his shirt and pats his well-defined stomach. "Guess what they say is true."

"What?" I remain staring at his ab muscles.

"That a way to a man's heart is through his stomach."

I let out a loud chuckle. "You know, my mother used to say that."

"She did?" He walks into the kitchen, leaning against the table.

"Yeah, she said that's how she and my dad actually met."

"Lina cooked a meal for Evan. Did she work at a restaurant or something?"

"Close, my dad was an orphan when they first met. She was nineteen when she started volunteering at the kitchens of her local orphanage. My dad was brought there after his parents died in a horrible carriage accident. He was twenty, considered still too young to live on his own. My mom happened to be working that day. She told me that with one glance his way she immediately knew he was the one."

"I can relate." I smile at his comment.

"Anyway, they talked mostly about their love of books. Passing the time together reading."

"Like us," Julius comments.

"Much like us. Until my dad came of age and asked my mom if she wanted to marry him."

"That young?"

"That young." I grin. "My dad had a small fortune my grandparents had left him. Just enough coins to last him a few good years without having to work. He bought his first house with that money. Which was the house I first grew up in. Till I was ten and this brooding man barged into my life, changing it forever."

The corners of his lips tug upward. "For better or for worse?" he inquires, taking a seat at the edge of the bed. I happily move to sit on his lap.

"Definitely for better." I circle my arms around his neck. "No matter what, my answer will always be for better." I plant a tender kiss on his lips. Julius returns the kiss but with more force. His hands cupping my face, he retracts slowly, his eyes closed.

"Have I told you that I love you?" He snaps them open, and the beauty of his irises still take my breath away.

"Yes, several times. Have I told *you* that I love you?"

"I'll never get tired of hearing you say that." He beams.

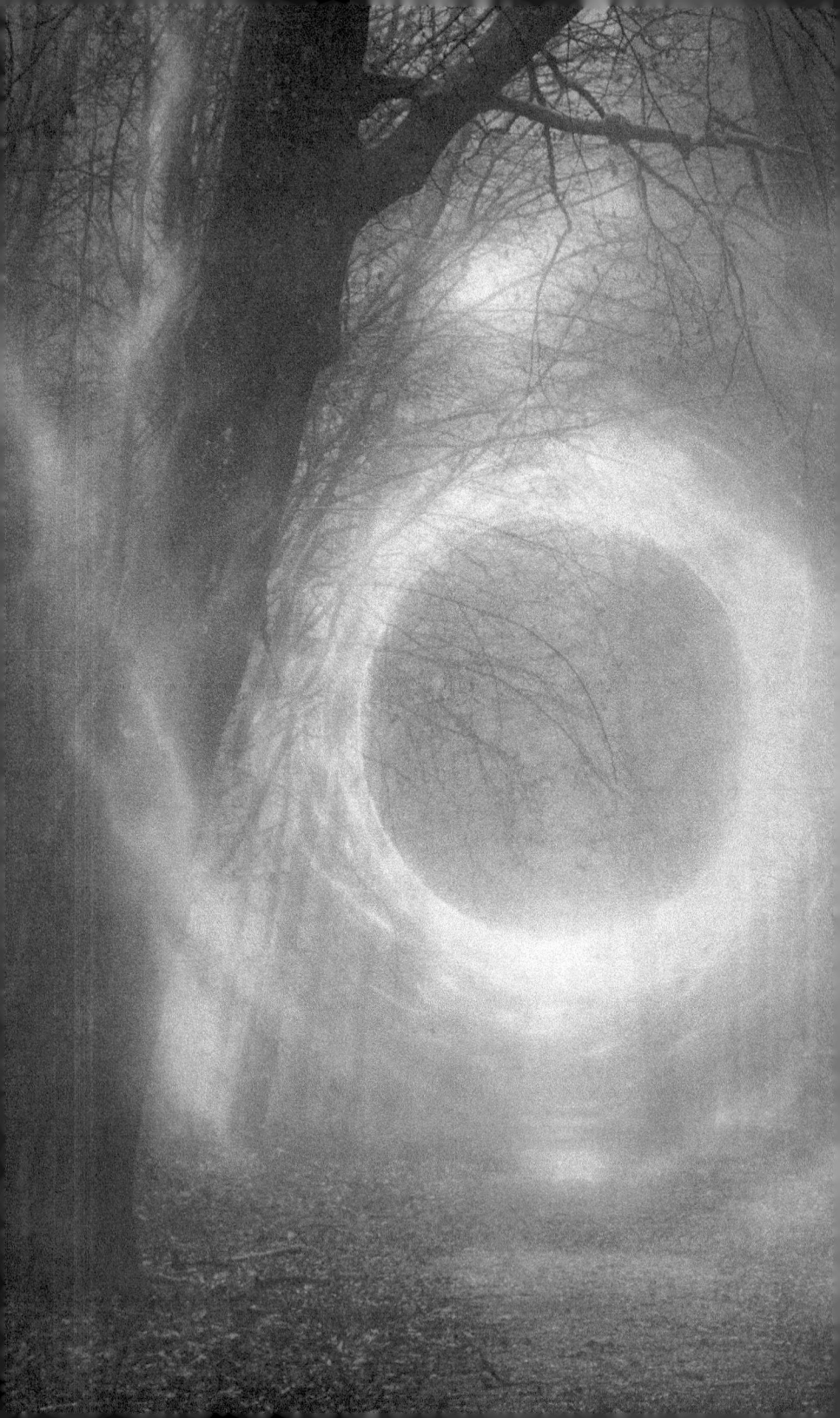

CHAPTER 25
POWER WITHIN

JULIUS

"You need to concentrate, Evalina." Soela has been trying to get Evalina to focus for the last half hour.

"I can't. That was one of the worst nights of my life."

"Why?" Soela asks as a way to get Alina to release some semblance of emotion.

"Are you actually asking me that?" Alina walks to the nearest rock and takes a seat. "You know why, Julius died. I lost the man I love." Soela's eyes spark when she notices a tear rolling down Evalina's cheek.

I grab my friend by the arm. "Soela, please don't tell me you're going to use *that* tactic."

"There's something I need to tell you both." Evalina interrupts my conversation with Soela. We both turn around to face her. "I killed Anev yesterday." For a minute I assume I've heard wrong. But it's written all over her face, every bit of truth.

"You what?" Soela asks in shock.

"It's a long story." Evalina moves on to tell us everything

that went down between her and Anev prior to finding me in Anise's house. No wonder she already knew the shade attack was Valec's doing. Anev was the one who told her.

"So, you're telling us that your anger, which was triggered by Anev comparing herself to Julius, was what got your hellfire to emerge?" Soela questions after Evalina has finished telling her story.

"Yes," she says shyly.

"Then we obviously now know what the trigger is. It's Julius. Valec killed Julius, you reacted from a place of sadness and hurt, and then Anev mocked Julius and you reacted from a place of anger and fury. He's the answer." I don't particularly like where Soela might be going with her statement.

"What do you suppose we do then?" I find myself asking.

"I need to prompt Evalina to evoke those same emotions. Like for instance, the sight of you in pain."

"Soela," I warn, "you're playing a dangerous game."

"I know, Julius, but we could at least try."

I'm given no warning when Soela connects her fist to my jaw. It doesn't hurt, though I'm pretty certain it's caused her pain. But if it does, she isn't showing it. Evalina's eyes flash with irritation.

"What on Inferis are you doing?" She directs her question at Soela.

"A test."

"Stop!" says Evalina. "This is not how I want to manage my powers."

"Like I said, it's only a test," Soela reassures her.

"Soela," I caution. "Don't test her like this. She's already gone through enough."

"It needs to be done." Soela shoves me against the stone wall, but instead of hitting me, she lands a kiss on my lips. *Okay, now that's one way to do it.* She's only just initiated the kiss when a pair of hands yank Soela off me and she falls to the ground. Replacing her in front of me is my beautiful girlfriend, flames dancing across her whole body. And damn if I didn't admit, she's quite the sight.

"I told you to stop," she shouts at Soela.

"Evalina, look at you. You touched me and I didn't go up in flames." Soela looks down at her perfectly normal arms, no burns in sight. "I evoked something in you, but you didn't go after me with the desire to harm. See, your hellfire is good. That's what we need."

Soela is right. Nothing happened to her. Thank Dominus.

"That was risky," Evalina points out. "What if I had hurt you."

"But you didn't. And I'm almost certain that if you had killed me, Julius would have begged you to bring me back to life." She's not wrong.

"Hurting Julius and kissing him are two very unnecessary tactics. I like you, Soela. But please don't ever do that again. I don't want you turning into Valec." Evalina takes one step forward and I remain in place, despite the intense heat emanating from her body.

"Don't be afraid," she says, probably having noticed a sliver of panic cross my face. She skims her thumb across my cheek, and I'm surprised to admit I feel no heat, except from the soft contact of her skin. Her fiery thumb traces the shape of my lips.

"I could never be afraid of you." To prove it I lock lips with hers. There's absolutely no difference. Though I do feel the heat, it's bearable. I'm not burning alive, and neither is she by the looks of it. I open my eyes to see the tiny flames dance across her cheeks. I reach a hand to touch one. Nothing happens except the fire parts and returns back to its place as I pull my hand back.

"You're absolutely beautiful," I whisper in her ear, nipping lightly at her lobe. She makes a tiny noise at the back of her throat that ignites me to full force. I look down and sure enough I'm already hard.

A throat clears behind us. "Make out session is over. Time to train." I try to break away but it's Evalina who refuses to part from me. With one last press of her lips, she moves to Soela's side.

With a huff of annoyance she says, "What's next?" Glad to see I'm not the only one bothered by Soela's interruption.

After a hard day of training, Evalina is finally able to rest. I sent her to bathe a few minutes ago. I would have joined her but, alas, the tub only fits one. Later in the day, she managed to switch her hellfire on and off without needing any *motivation*. Next, she'll have to learn to use her power. She needs to know how to attack with it, to shoot it out of her hands the way Valec does with his shadows. I have no doubt she can do it. Alina is stronger than she gives herself credit.

Once the training session was over and Soela retreated to the mansion, Evalina and I found Anise already on her way home. We told her the shade attack was Valec's responsibility. She somehow already had her suspicions. Showing no signs of panic, she agreed to stay at a friends' house who lives near the veil. She would take Pia with her as well.

For what's left of the night, Evalina and I read in bed together. Considering we have long hours of hellfire training awaiting us.

"This is pointless!" Evalina yells at the rocky ceiling.

"You were doing great before. What's changed today?" Soela asks her. It's been five days since Evalina first started training, but today it somehow feels like she's gone backwards with her progress.

"I don't know. Today my power won't turn on," Evalina growls in frustration.

"Please don't tell me that you'll need to be prompted to use your fire." Soela points a finger at me.

"Don't you even try," Evalina warns, knowing Soela will use me as bait again if need be.

I raise my hand like a child would during a school lecture. "What if I volunteer; would that ease your worries?" Evalina shakes her head. "Alina, we need to do something." We've been here for two hours, and nothing has happened.

"Time is running out," Soela reminds us all. "Valec is already breathing down my neck. His patience won't last forever, and today, instead of progressing, we've gone backwards." I knew Valec's word was too good to be true. He can't wait, he's itching to get his revenge. Which means that each second we waste is less time for Evalina to prepare properly.

"I'll be fine," I assure her. "You've done this before. Just concentrate and visualize yourself reaching for your flames."

"I'm not shooting you with hellfire," she shouts.

"I never said that," I correct myself.

"Aim for the rock," Soela says at my side.

"Okay, fine," Evalina huffs. "Go do your thing. Go kiss Julius," she says to Soela.

Soela grabs my shoulders and crashes her lips into mine. We wait and wait. Nothing happens. We break apart from each other, knowing how uncomfortable this is for the both of us. Meanwhile, Evalina is irritated in a corner trying to get her magic to appear. "This is useless," she yells. "It won't start."

"Should I try something else?" Soela suggests.

Soela doesn't give Evalina enough time to answer when she lands a kick to my shins. No harm done.

"No," Evalina warns. "I said no harming Jules." I'm not prepared for the blow that follows, Soela's knee connecting to my groin. I hear Evalina shout as I'm doubling over in pain. "Jules!" Alina runs towards me.

Shit, Soela has a knee of steel. The rest of my body may be

hard muscle, but she went for the most vulnerable part of me. I'm glad I can't bear children because if I was able to, I'm most certain I wouldn't after this. I'm on my knees with my hands between my legs when Alina drops to the ground before me. "Are you okay?"

I want to say yes, but that would be a lie. "I think I need ice."

Evalina snaps her head in Soela's direction and that's when the flames blaze on her skin. "I told you not to hurt him!" she yells. "Julius has had enough of this shit and so have I." I haven't seen Evalina this angry since the day Valec told her she was in Inferis. "I won't have it. I know your intentions are good, Soela, but you just did what I told you not to do when we started these training sessions, and that was to turn to Valec's teaching methods."

"Evalina, I'm trying not to. My methods are nothing like his." She raises her voice. "I kick and punch like a child. I don't have Valec's smoke magic—"

Evalina cuts her off. "I don't care if you don't. You went ahead and did the one thing I told you not to do."

"Evalina we're all desperate—" Soela tries to state her claim.

"I said no…" It happens so quickly that I'm almost afraid I conjured it from my mind. However, the evidence doesn't lie. Behind Soela, a rock has ignited in flames. A light trickle of smoke now pours out of Alina's palm.

Evalina doesn't even acknowledge what she just did, she simply looks at me and helps me to my feet. "Can you walk?"

"I'm alright." One of my hands still cups my groin.

"Let's get some ice on you." She turns to face Soela "Same time tomorrow," she barks. "Without Julius."

I smile, teeth exposed.

"What?" She blinks.

"I find your need to protect me quite alluring."

Her eyes widen. "Tell me the truth: how hard did she hit you?"

"Hard enough," I complain. "But that has nothing to do with what you said."

"What I said was the truth. You will not suffer a second more on my behalf. That is done for. That's why you are not going to attend tomorrow's training session or any other, for that matter." She opens the front door to Anise's house. Our home for the past few days.

"Now, go lie down on the bed," she instructs. "I'll fetch something cold from ice box." I move to the bedroom, following her orders.

I climb on, groaning in the process. Fuck, how hard did Soela kick me? Evalina arrives with a bag of ice. "Why have you still got your trousers on? Take them off."

She sits at the foot of the bed while I'm dragging my legs back to the floor to slide my trousers down my body. "Seriously, Jules!"

"What?" I panic.

"Your second layer of clothing as well." She points to my undergarments. For some reason this is turning out to be *quite* the experience. Regardless, I obey her command.

I watch her expression as she gets the full image of me. I expect her cheeks to flush like they did when she accidentally saw me naked the other day. I see none of that today. She's stock serious.

I lie back with my head against the headboard. Evalina scoots closer, and she spares me no mercy when the bag of ice connects with my member. "*Shit!*" I curse under my breath. I couldn't even get a good look at it to see if it was that bad before she placed the bag over it.

"I know it's cold, okay. But it will help with the swelling."

"I trust you," I remind her.

Several minutes later, all is well. Thanks to my immortal healing, of course. But what neither of us is prepared for is how erect and ready I am to take part in not so innocent actions.

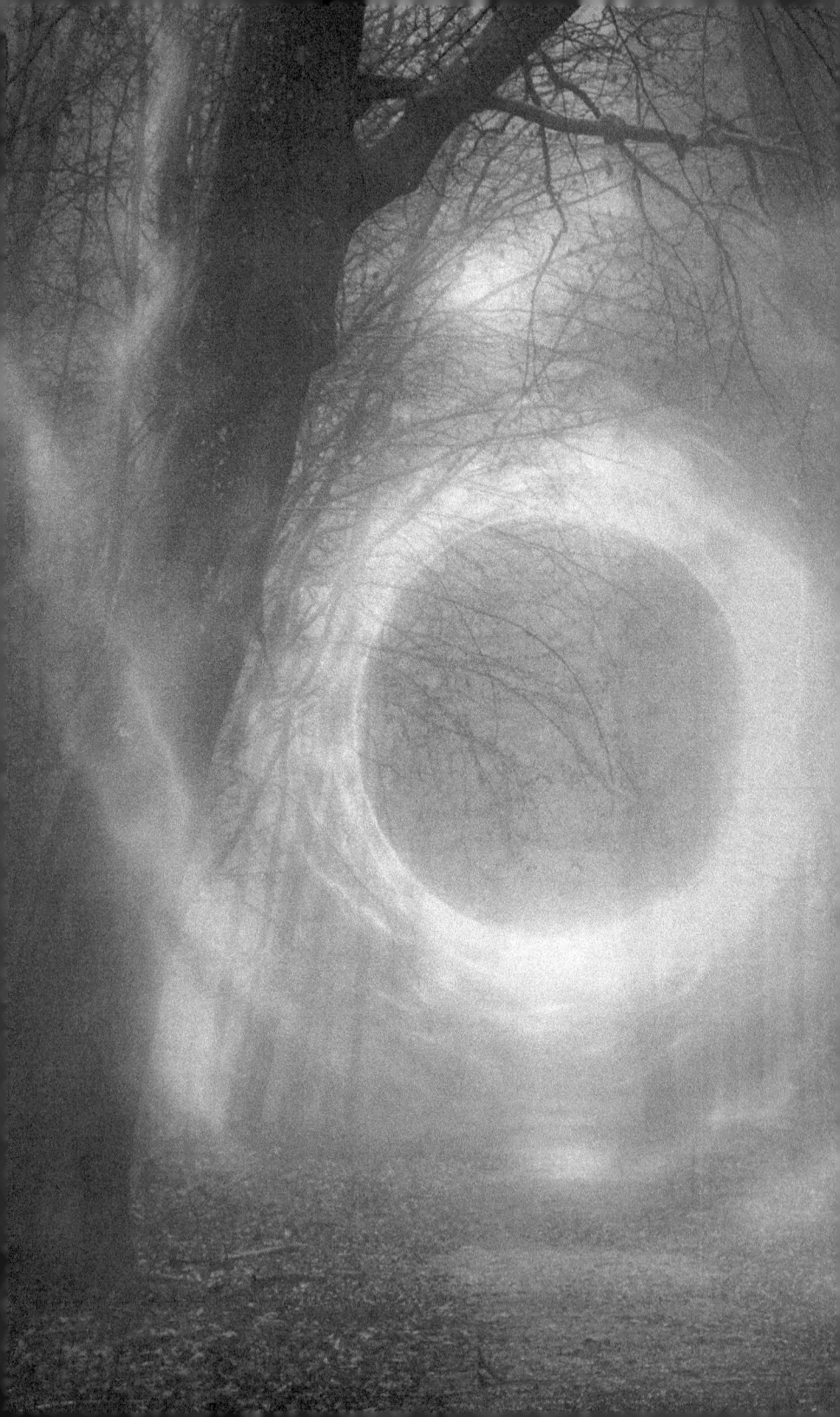

CHAPTER 26
OUR LOVE

EVALINA

I stare at Julius's throbbing member before me, and I can't help the sudden fluttering in my lower belly. This need that has my throat dry and my body wanting. Julius was injured for crying out loud, and now here I am lusting for him.

"I'm sorry," he says. As if it's his fault.

"For what?"

"For being hard."

"That's a natural reaction," I say, as my eyes undoubtedly darken a bit. I debate if I should give into what my body desperately wants. I set the bag of ice aside. Testing the waters, I carefully slide my right hand over him. His breath catches at my touch. I have no idea if I'm doing this right. I'm going with what I've read from romance novels. Moving my hand up and down the base of his shaft, his heavy breathing is my only indication that I must be doing something right.

I pause my movements to adjust myself on the bed and lie belly down, my elbows propped. Julius stares at me through half-hooded eyes. "Alina," he issues a warning.

"Does it still hurt? Should I stop?" I ask as a precaution.

"Fuck no, don't stop," he barks and that's all I need to bring my mouth down on him. He hisses, his head tipping back. "Damn it!"

I repeat the motion over and over. One hand is at his base, the other is cupping his sack. "Evalina," he says my name like a plea. "I beg you to stop." I freeze. He just told me not to stop.

Seeing the horror in my expression he clarifies. "That's not what I meant. I mean, I refuse to come unless it's inside you." He stares at me through lowered lashes. "Only if you want to, of course," he adds. "If you're not ready, then—"

"Jules." I climb over his chest, sitting on his torso. "I want to. You know I do."

"You're certain?"

"I'm certain. Now, stop stalling," I complain.

"I'm not stalling."

"Yeah? Then prove it!" I challenge.

He flips us over with one shift of his legs. I fall head-first onto the mattress. Julius hovers over me, not wasting any time as his mouth and hands skim my collarbone all the way down to my hips. His fingers drag till he's bunching up the gown I borrowed from Anise's wardrobe. Thank goodness it's a loose fit or I never would have been able to fit my breasts into it.

Julius dives under, letting the length of the dress conceal his head. I jump when his breath is at my center. His lips plant kisses at every corner and I just might combust.

"Julius," I say through parted lips. He pops his head up from under the dress. "Take it off; I want to see your face. I want to see what you're doing to me." Saying those words is apparently a turn-on for him. *Hell,* it even feels foreign to me.

He eagerly lifts the garment over my arms, tossing it somewhere across the room.

The dress isn't the only thing to go. Julius pulls down on my underwear and I might as well unlatch my brassiere as well. I lean forward, my fingers hooking on his shirt, tugging it upward over his chest. He raises his arms for me before his shirt flies through the room, landing who knows where. Instead of lying back down, I take the opportunity to explore his body while remaining on my knees against the mattress.

Cold air grazes my skin and I shudder. It's not cold, to be honest. But the sensation on my exposed skin does feel delightful. I skim my hand over his collarbone, leaving a trail of light kisses over his skin. My palms lightly press on his sides, my head lowering to kiss every inch of his chest and stomach.

Julius pulls me closer. "My turn," he rasps. He plants a warm kiss on my stomach, then lowers me back onto the bed. As his lips brush my navel, tiny bursts of pleasure surge through me.

Julius takes me by surprise, spreading my legs apart with a nudge of his knee. He dives in without warning. My scream pierces the entire room when his teeth lightly scrape up against my sensitive flesh, my legs twitching in the process.

His mouth sucks on every inch of me and I'm a complete mess. Julius all but grins at me, his lips glistening with my essence. I want to kiss him. I have an urge to taste myself on his tongue. Julius apparently knows what I want as he lifts himself up, his hands brushing my shoulders, before he crushes his lips against my own. He groans because I've taken the liberty of brushing my hands across his shaft. Keeping them there, I squeeze lightly.

"Fuck, Evalina!" he growls, and I'm dazed by his taunting lips. He musters enough strength to separate us. "I can't, you're going to make me come before I even get inside you." He leans closer, propping my hips up slightly so that I'm at a better angle. His tongue happily slides inside me once more.

"Julius," I moan. This is heavenly.

"That's right, Evalina, say my name." Now it's not just his tongue. He's placed a finger inside me as well. Curving it to reach the right spot. My body moves and Julius uses his free hand to pin my hips that keep bucking. I can't help it—it's too much all at once and I can feel my release climbing.

I shut my eyes for the slightest of instances. Waiting, climbing my way up a mountain of pleasure, and when I reach that point, I shatter into a million pieces. Every inch of my body gives out. I look down to see Julius having his last fill of me. It's an image I want to memorize for the rest of my days. Him, this strong powerful male, worshiping me. It's a stunning picture. There's no doubt about it. Julius licks his lips, cleaning himself off, and I delight in the view.

I'm not given much time to compose myself before he tugs on my hips. Bringing me closer to him. Angling our bodies. My breath hitches in my lungs. His tip grazes my entrance and I'm already a whimpering mess. "If it hurts let me know," he says.

"I will," I promise him.

"I don't want to hurt you, Alina. I only want to make you feel good."

"And believe me, you are." I nudge myself closer so that his tip dips in slightly.

"Fuck," he cries. And I clench my teeth. He inches himself forward slowly and I can feel myself stretching to accommodate his size. He's only halfway in, and my body's trying really hard not to let the tension take over. "Alina, does it hurt?" He ceases all movement.

"No, it's just a bit uncomfortable," I respond, being completely honest.

"Do you want me to stop?" Concern flashes in his expression.

I shake my head. "No, keep going."

He hesitates for a few seconds, then he's pressing back into me. A slight ache rushes through me like an electric current. But I try not to tense up. To keep myself distracted I cup my breasts and squeeze, letting the pleasure override the discomfort.

"That's it, Alina. Touch yourself," Julius praises.

I'm hit with a wave of desire as Julius fills me entirely. "Are you okay?" he asks.

"Yes." I'm more than okay.

"Let me know when I can move." He remains propped on his arms.

I give it a few seconds before giving him the okay. "Now," I whimper as I continue to pinch my nipples with my fingers. Julius lets out a low snarl and removes my hands, his mouth closing in on one of my breasts. I scream. He moves quickly between one and the other, giving each breast the attention it deserves. He kneads each bud with his fingers. I'm so lost in Julius's attack on my nipples that I fail to notice him pull out of me, only to crash back in, shockwaves striking my entire body. It's plunge after glorious plunge.

I eventually find the ability to cross my legs behind his back. My nails dig into the skin of his shoulders, no doubt leaving scratch marks behind. I just hope I don't draw any blood. I'd be mortified if that happened.

I moan into his neck as my body arches backwards as far as my back will allow.

I've never felt anything like this. Boy, was I missing out. Now I know why all those book heroines described sex as a holy experience. Surely this is as close to Caelesti as I'll ever get.

Pressure begins to build in my core and I'm a writhing mess underneath him. Julius speeds up his thrusts, his cock twitching inside me, and that action alone has me convulsing. My body contracts, every muscle going lax. Stars dance through my vision and Jules comes crashing down as well. His body collides with my side as he struggles to control his breathing.

We wait for our high to pass. "The wait was worth it," Julius voices into the room.

I crack an eye open. "You exceeded all my expectations."

"I did?" Julius rolls onto his side. His chest brushes up

against my back, his hand lazily skimming my ribs. My body instantly comes back to life.

"You did!" I confirm.

"I'm glad my girlfriend approves of my skills."

I snort.

"You know, you tend to call me your girlfriend quite a lot for someone who hasn't even asked me the question yet." I turn my face an inch away from his.

"I was finding the right moment."

I giggle. "I think we've had many right moments by now, don't you think."

"Also plenty of wrong ones."

"Those as well." I lightly skim his arm with the back of my hand. "And now? Is now not the right time?"

"It is." He shifts on the bed, swinging his legs off the mattress to bring himself to stand. He doesn't cover up, but rather walks to my side of the bed in all his glory. I can't help staring at his ass as he rounds the bed. I move into a sitting position, waiting. My legs dangle off the side. Julius lowers himself onto his knees and the act alone is endearing, and quite the turn on.

Taking both my hands in his, he says, "Evalina Morue, will you do me the extraordinary honor of being my girlfriend?"

"Yes, I will." I'm smiling from ear to ear, even as Julius picks me up off the bed and carries me across the room, bridal style. "Julius, we're not engaged. That wasn't a proposal," I squeal as he paces back and forth with me in his arms.

"Someday it will be."

"You're awfully confident. Who's to say you won't break up with me?"

"I would never do that," he reassures me.

"Okay, what if I break up with you?" I inquire.

He stops and contemplates this for a second. "Would you?"

"No, you idiot. Not in a million years. For heaven's sake, I was never involved with anyone romantically before I met you." The admission rolls off my tongue with ease. I remember a time when I wondered why I never went out on dates. It was when Julius was being cold and distant. Why did I never even contemplate the idea of being with someone else? Not even for a one-night stand. Not even to spite him for acting that way. I thought maybe it was just me.

No, that was never the reason. Julius was. Even when I didn't know it, it's always been him.

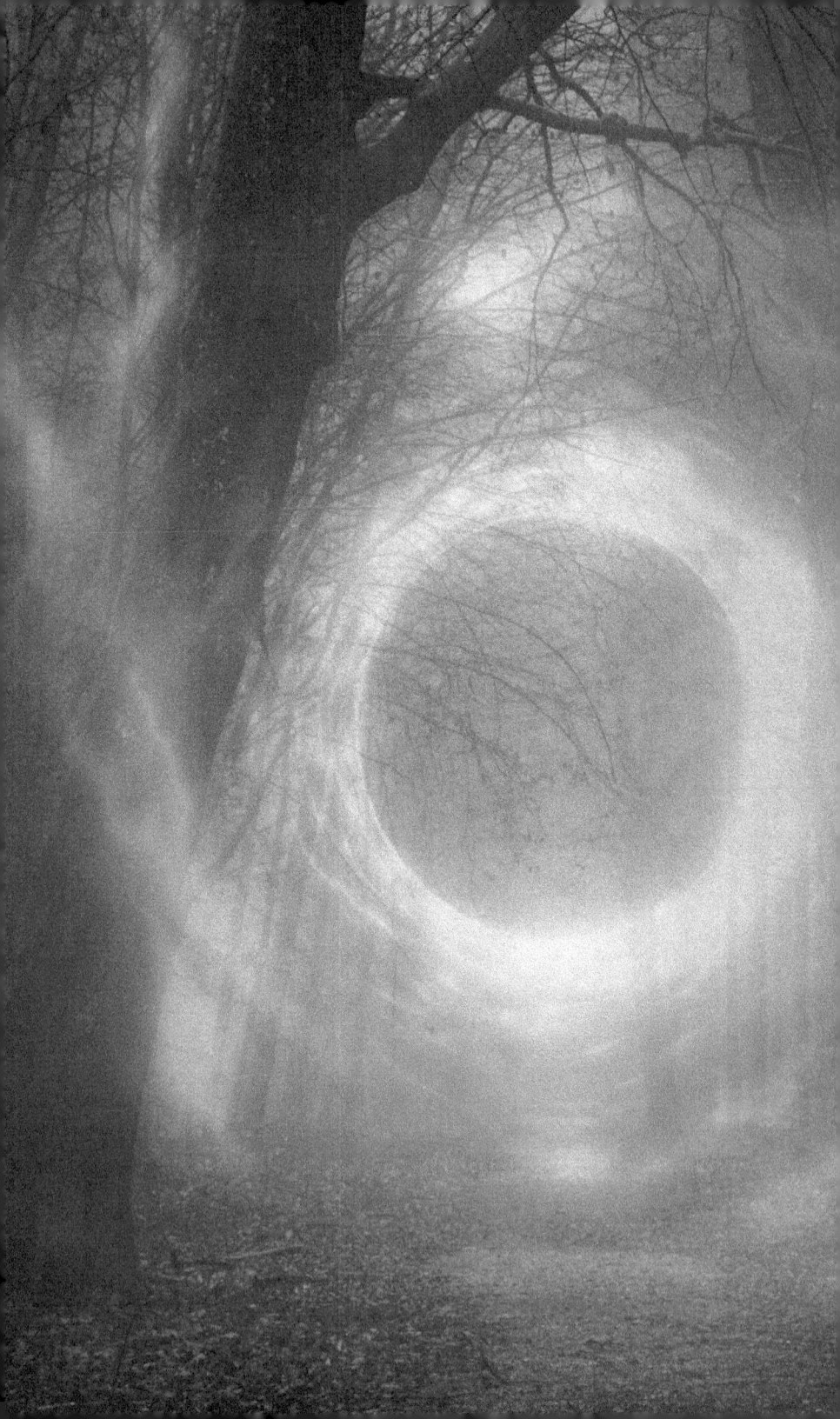

CHAPTER 27
FIRE POWER

EVALINA

"Someone looks happy. I'm guessing you had a good night," is Soela's way of greeting me the next morning.

I can't help it. I woke up giddy. Julius gave me the best orgasm of my life when I awoke. We both knew I was too sore to go at it again, but that didn't stop him from doing other things. Now, here I am: a walking puddle of total bliss.

"Is it that obvious?" I meet her where she sits on one of the flatter stones in the heart.

"Evalina, please. You have the post-orgasmic glow." She gestures to my face.

"Is that a thing? That is not a thing." I shake my head.

"It is."

"No, it's not." She makes room for me beside her.

She smiles as I take a seat. "I already told you that it is."

"And I'm choosing to not believe you." The conversation dies down.

We sit like this, neither of us saying a word for a few

seconds. "I'm sorry," she blurts, breaking the sudden tension. "For hurting Julius and pushing you too far. It was never my intention to use Valec's sick ways for my teachings. So, there's really no excuse for using Julius as a punching bag."

"I understand." She moves her head to face me. "And you're forgiven." I pat her on the shoulder. "He still won't be present for the remainder of our sessions, though."

"Fair. Was the damage a lot?"

"Not really. He healed up pretty quickly."

"Based on your expression alone I can imagine how well it healed up."

"Very well." I beam.

"Well, enough is enough. Come on." She rises. "Time to do what we came here for. Show me what you've got."

One hour turned into two, and two later ended with three, and after that I lost count of how long I trained in the heart with Soela.

I'm making my way to the depths. It isn't so far from the heart, except it's a deep descent. It's called the depths for a reason. I'm almost there when I hear a distinct sound, much like a cross between a growl and a howl. My insides freeze and I pause in my tracks. There's no mistaking it, that's a shade. And I need to move. I don't run because of how loud my strides will be, but I do walk at a quicker pace. I see Anise's house and the man standing outside near the entrance.

Julius's face morphs, terror fillings his eyes as he notices whatever horror has followed me here. He opens his arms for me, signaling to hurry up. I make my last jump, and he scoops me in his arms, then places me back on the floor. "Get in the house. I'll take care of this." He removes his dagger from inside his tunic.

I give one last glance to the advancing shade. This one walks a little off balance, but it's as gruesome as all the others. Its black slimy skin peels off as it moves from side to side. I race deeper into the house the second I hear Julius's attack on the beast. I expect him to return as soon as the shade is dead. Instead, I hear the sounds of more monsters approaching.

No! I open the door, peeking my head through. Where the first shade came from more follow. There's got to be about six, and I am not about to leave Julius to fight them all on his own. He's given me a few extra lessons since we've been down here, in case I ever run into one and he isn't around. I will not let fear force me into hiding. That's why I pull my dagger from my holster and open the front door.

Julius notices me but quickly switches his attention back to the shades, who are slowly advancing on him. I expect him to tell me to go back inside. He doesn't. Either he realizes he can't fight them all on his own or he knows I can handle myself to some extent. Maybe it's a mix of both.

Seeing the determination in my expression, he says, "You know what to do. You've got this." Words of encouragement. Guess it was the latter.

"We've got this," I scream over the roar of the shades running towards us.

The first shade arrives, and Julius slices through it as easily as he would a piece of fruit. I hadn't realized earlier that he was carrying his sword as well. He strays a little farther from me, swinging his sword and striking home.

I spot a shade coming for me from the side and I prepare. Its jaw is crooked, black marble teeth fixed on taking a bite out of me. I won't allow it. Its gangly legs somehow tangle with my own. I fall to the ground, and it reels me in. Its mouth drips ooze, ready for its next meal: *me.* I thrash against it, stabbing at its legs. Trying to cut my way free.

"Get off me, you son of a bitch." I successfully chop one of its legs off. It blares an ear-piercing shriek. My movements are sloppy as I'm mostly fixated on saving my own life rather than properly wounding the shade as Julius taught me. I do the same to its other leg, stabbing repeatedly. That leg gives out, falling to the ground as well. And I scramble as I try to get up.

I look at what's left of the beast, unable to move. It screams in agony. "Allow me to end your suffering, you heathen." With all my might I jab my dagger through its head. Its body goes limp immediately.

I turn around and spot Julius near the cavern entrance of the depths. He's being attacked by three shades. I run for them. Not anticipating my presence, I decide last minute to do something stupid. I jump and attack the monster from behind. Landing on its back, its skin is so slick, despite the scales, that I have a hard time holding on. It thrashes, trying to get me off. It succeeds, throwing me off its body. I land on the ground several feet away, but I still need to help Julius. Another shade has just joined the other three he's fighting off.

From the corner of my eyes, I see my hands flicker with sparks. My hellfire. I can fry these bastards to a crisp. Soela and I practiced the exercises for so long, on stone and whatever else she could find around the heart, that I'm certain I'm ready to try with a real target. My first victim doesn't have to be Valec. These shades will do.

"Hey, ugly," I call, and the four remaining shades crane their heads in my direction.

"No, Alina, what are you doing?"

"Julius, trust me." I close my eyes and will my magic to emerge. It doesn't take long for the faint sparks to transform into a full blaze.

"You want me," I say to the creatures, "come and get me." They break into a run, but they only make it so far. I bring my hands back like Soela taught me, so that I'll have a farther reach, and then I launch them forward, releasing the flames. The shades scream as their skin melts away. Even in suffering, they're still trying to get to me. I prepare one last time and I ignite myself with full force. Concentrating as hard as I can, I let my power flow. They barely have time to register my second attack when they shatter right on the spot. Their bodies turn to nothing but ashes on the ground.

I did it.

Julius stares at me. His mouth opens to say, "That's my girl."

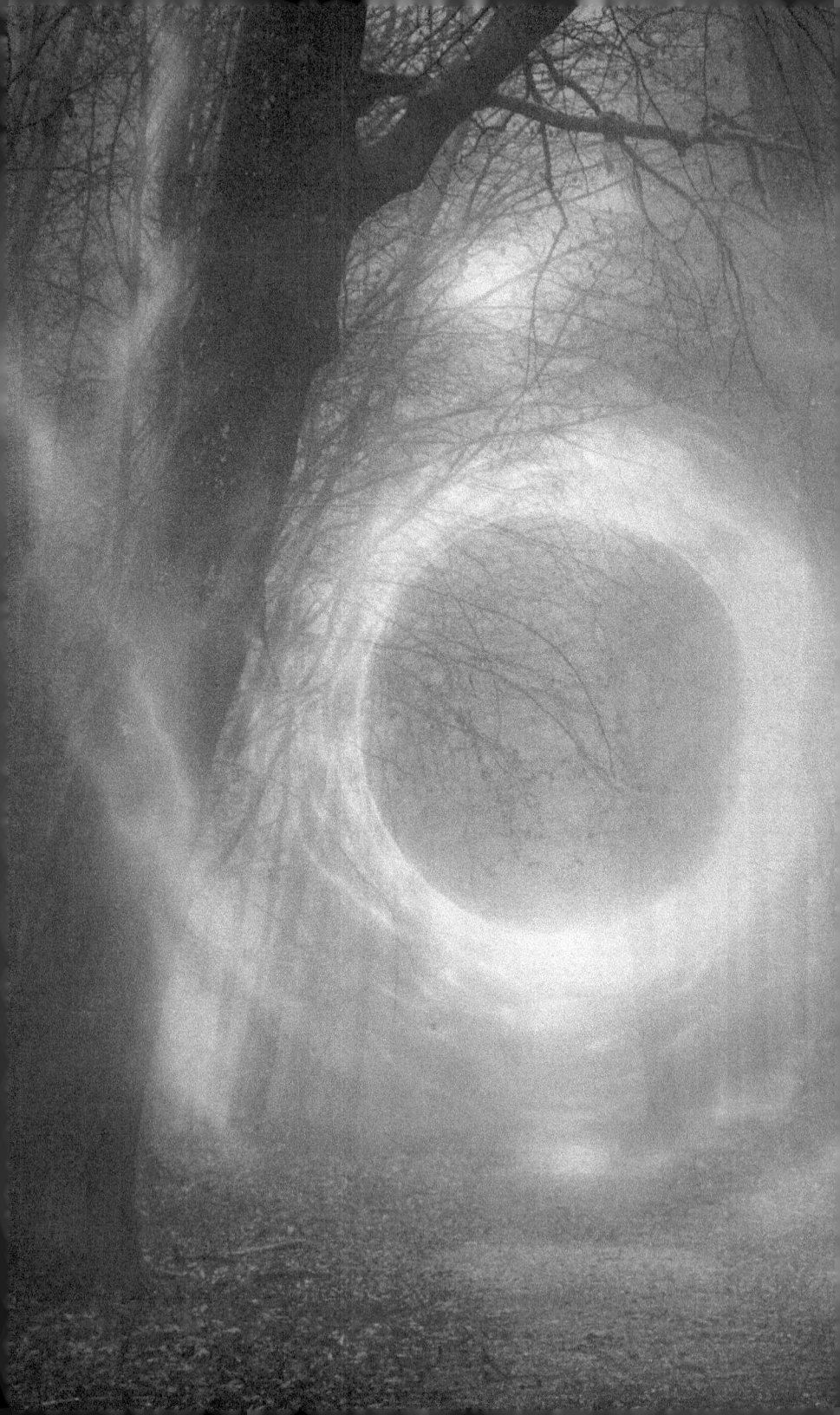

CHAPTER 28
THE VEIL

JULIUS

There are two knocks on the door, and I have an inkling as to who it might be. I rush to the entryway in an instant. Sure, my guess is confirmed once I spot Aziel and Recifer, who have apparently arrived to collect us. The time has come. Evalina's short window of training is over. Tonight's the blood moon, and even if it's hours away, we must prepare.

We're brought into the throne room after Valec so graciously allowed us to bathe in our rooms and change our clothing. Evalina and I went our separate ways just to speed up the process and not get caught up in each other. We met up in the hallway and now here we are.

Valec appears to be in mourning. I've never seen him wear so much black in his life. Nor have I ever seen him in battle gear before. He reminds me of myself when I wear my uniform while shade hunting.

"I heard you made progress." Valec steeples his fingers together as he speaks to Evalina. "I'm glad. Now there's only one last thing for you to do and then you and Julius can live the fairytale life." He says the last part with distaste.

Evalina doesn't budge; she keeps her expression stone cold. It seems she does not want to show an ounce of emotion. Valec motions for Aziel and Recifer to move forward. "Although there is one more thing." Valec raises a hand and Evalina begins to choke. Aziel and Recifer hold her back, making sure she isn't able to use her power. I take but one step and I'm airborne as well.

"You killed Anev," he hisses through clenched teeth. "May this serve as a warning to never cross me again. This is your second strike. I will not hesitate at the third."

He lets us go and we fall flat on our asses. Evalina shakes her head and laughs. Genuinely laughs. "You can't kill me Valec. You *need* me."

"I won't need you for much longer. You may be able to bring back the dead but I'm quite certain you aren't capable of bringing yourself back from death. Heed my warning, Evalina Morue, or this will be the end of the line for you." He inches closer to her, till he's standing right in front of her. "You break the veil and then you and Julius get out of my sight," he spits at her. "If you so much as try to stop me, it will be the end for you."

He spins on his heels, marching up to his throne. "I'll see you all in the gardens at seven. Rest up, my little Devil's Curse." He inclines his head toward Alina. "You're going to need it."

Once again, Evalina and I go our separate ways. She saunters on to the kitchens; apparently Romar made us a banquet. I told her I'd join her shortly. With that, I make my way to the gardens, the new cobblestones steps I just added guiding me there. Since I spent so many days outside the mansion, I kept busy with the garden while Evalina trained.

I find Soela crouched on the ground, some chalk in her hand. "Does it ever get easier to draw?" I lean against the side of the veil, it's center an empty black pit as usual.

Her head snaps up. "You mean since I've drawn it a million times already? No, it's still complicated as fuck."

"Glad to see my vocabulary has rubbed off on you." I put on a smile and make my way to her.

"I'd find it strange if it didn't." She looks behind me. "Where's Evalina?"

"The kitchens, Romar cooked up a storm."

She chuckles. "He always does."

"I need some advice." I look to the ground before meeting her eyes.

Soela dusts off her hands. "Okay, but first let me apologize for hurting you during Evalina's training session."

"Apology accepted, Soela. I know you were only trying to speed up the process."

She nods. "So, you said you needed advice." She veers the topic back on track. "Honestly your timing is perfect, I'm in need of a break." She gets off the ground and I follow her to sit on one of the stone benches. "What's on your mind?"

"Evalina."

Her eyebrows crease, her smile faltering. "I thought everything was going well between you two."

I correct her before she misunderstands me. "Everything is well, Soela. That's not what I meant." I adjust myself on the bench. "Tonight, if all goes well our lives are going to change significantly. Evalina has already spoken to me about what she wants, and I love the idea."

"Jules, I'm failing to see where the problem is."

"The problem is I don't know what to expect from said life. I've lived so many years in torment, surrounded by darkness and bloodshed. I'm afraid that I won't know how to live a peaceful life again." Understanding crosses her features. "Unlike Valec, who will hopefully return to us, the Julius who once lived in Caelesti is long dead. I don't know how to be him anymore."

"Julius," Soela says as she squeezes my shoulder. "Your fears are valid. But you need to know one thing. Evalina never met Julius the Saint, she met Julius the Prince and Official Shade Hunter of Inferis." I wince. "Yes, I know how much you hate those titles but that's not where I'm going with this. My point is, she fell in love with this man. The one who sits beside me. The other one only ever existed to yourself."

"That's a lie. You got to meet him."

"And he was lovely, but the Julius that exists now... he's the one I consider a brother, like a best friend. You need to forget about the past life you had in Caelesti and focus on the one you're about to commence with the woman you love. Believe me, this life," he waves at all the empty walls surrounding us, "this won't ever come to mind again once you've lived in the utter beauty that is the mortal realm. You'll be happy in Einalem."

"Thank you, Soela." I give her hand a light squeeze before returning back to the mansion. I arrive at the kitchens, the scent of warm spices awakening my senses.

Evalina doesn't hear me approach, too consumed with her giant stack of waffles. Till she sees the figure sitting beside her on the stool. She tries to smile with her mouth full and somehow it's the cutest thing she can possibly do.

She finishes swallowing her fill of waffles. "You came! The food was starting to get cold."

"That's alright. I simply needed to have a last-minute talk with Soela."

"About Valec?"

"About you, actually." I take my first bite out of the stack. She stares at me, confusion written across her face.

"What about me?"

"Oh, you know, I was simply asking for advice on how to break up with you," I joke.

Her hollow eyes tell me she is anything but amused. But then she says, "Is that so?" And that's when I feel it. Her foot skimming the side of my leg. I remain still. "Well, I planned on having some fun before I was called to serve the Devil. But considering you want to break up, I guess those plans are off the table." Her foot climbs higher, brushing the inside of my right thigh. I suck in a breath. "Something wrong?"

Evalina sure has come a long way, wearing her newfound confidence like a second skin. I still can't get over how she fried those shades the other night. She looked like a goddess in her element. And then I'd shown her just how much I appreciated her for saving my life.

I'm out of my thoughts when I feel her foot brush a very sensitive area. *Okay,* this woman knows how to play dirty. I let her foot drop to the floor and swing my legs away from the high chair.

I walk to her side and offer her my hand. "How about I show you just how much I want us to break up." She eyes me cautiously but then her smile grows.

"By all means." She takes my hand and I gladly lead her to my chambers.

It's later in the afternoon, when a light tap on the door has us both jolting to a sitting position. The door's locked so whoever's knocking can't come inside. "It's me, Your Highness." Vienna. "His Majesty sent me to retrieve you and miss Evalina. He and his companions are on their way to the veil." By companions she means Aziel and Recifer.

"Tell him that we're on our way." I sprint for whatever clothes I first spot in my closet. Evalina is in luck that she doesn't have to borrow any of mine. Vienna filled a drawer with her clothing, knowing Evalina would spend nights with me. I take out the first item of clothing I see and hand it to her. In less than a minute we're dressed and have our weapons strapped on.

Outside the mansion I direct her through the empty path. We choose to leave Saint behind as a safety precaution. Mainly out of fear. I don't ever want to see Saint hurt again. We remain silent, walking hand in hand. But it's evident in the tightness of her shoulders that she's dreading this next step as much as I am. We don't stop to admire the plants in bloom as we pass the garden. Instead, we rush through until the portal comes into view, along with four awaiting figures. The gang's all here.

Aziel and Recifer are the first to receive us with blank expressions. Followed by Soela, who keeps away from them, and my brother who stands at the center of the pentagram. His crown rests casually on top of his head.

"Wow," Evalina says, seeing the pentagram in all its glory. "It's beautiful."

"My family invented it." Soela walks to us, ignoring Valec entirely. "Down to every last detail. This is what has allowed Julius to enter Einalem for all these years. He would stand right there." She points at Valec's foot. "While I chanted the old tongue. The magic of the pentagram serves as an anchor between worlds—" she tries to explain when Valec decides to interrupt us.

"Enough of the history lesson, Soela. Let us begin. Evalina, you have the honors." Evalina looks to Soela, then to me. I nod, providing her with all the encouragement she needs. She knows what must be done.

She turns in the direction of the veil and rests her hands over it. With little to no effort, flames spark onto her skin, covering her from head to toe. Almost like a cape of fire. She remains staring at the veil, the portal now glimmering. I take a step forward, reaching my hand out to touch her slightly trembling fingers. Curling them against my own, I whisper in her ear, "You can do this."

I disentangle our fingers and move back. Evalina readies herself by hovering her hands over the veil.

It's Soela's turn now. She begins to chant nonsense. I know it's nonsense because she made me listen to her while she practiced earlier. It's a combination of made-up words mixed with average words from the old tongue. Right now, she just so happens to be mentioning that she will be cooking tomato soup after this. Instinctively, I want to laugh. I can't help the snort that comes out the second she mentions snails dancing the tango. Valec shoots me a glare and that's enough to silence me.

Soela is nearing the end of her *spell* and Evalina takes notice, her back muscles shifting as she tries to loosen up. The ending is said, and I take a few steps back, not wanting to be caught in the line of fire when Evalina shoots Valec.

The veil parts under Alina's touch, revealing the lush landscape of Einalem.

"Now, Evalina." Valec gives the order to proceed.

Yes, Valec. Now, indeed. Evalina spins as fast as a lightning bolt, striking without hesitation and sending a wave of fire in Valec's direction. The pure shock on my brother's face does not go unnoticed. The blaze lands home, knocking Valec backwards out of the pentagram.

Valec's gaze locks onto mine, and that's when his shadows strike.

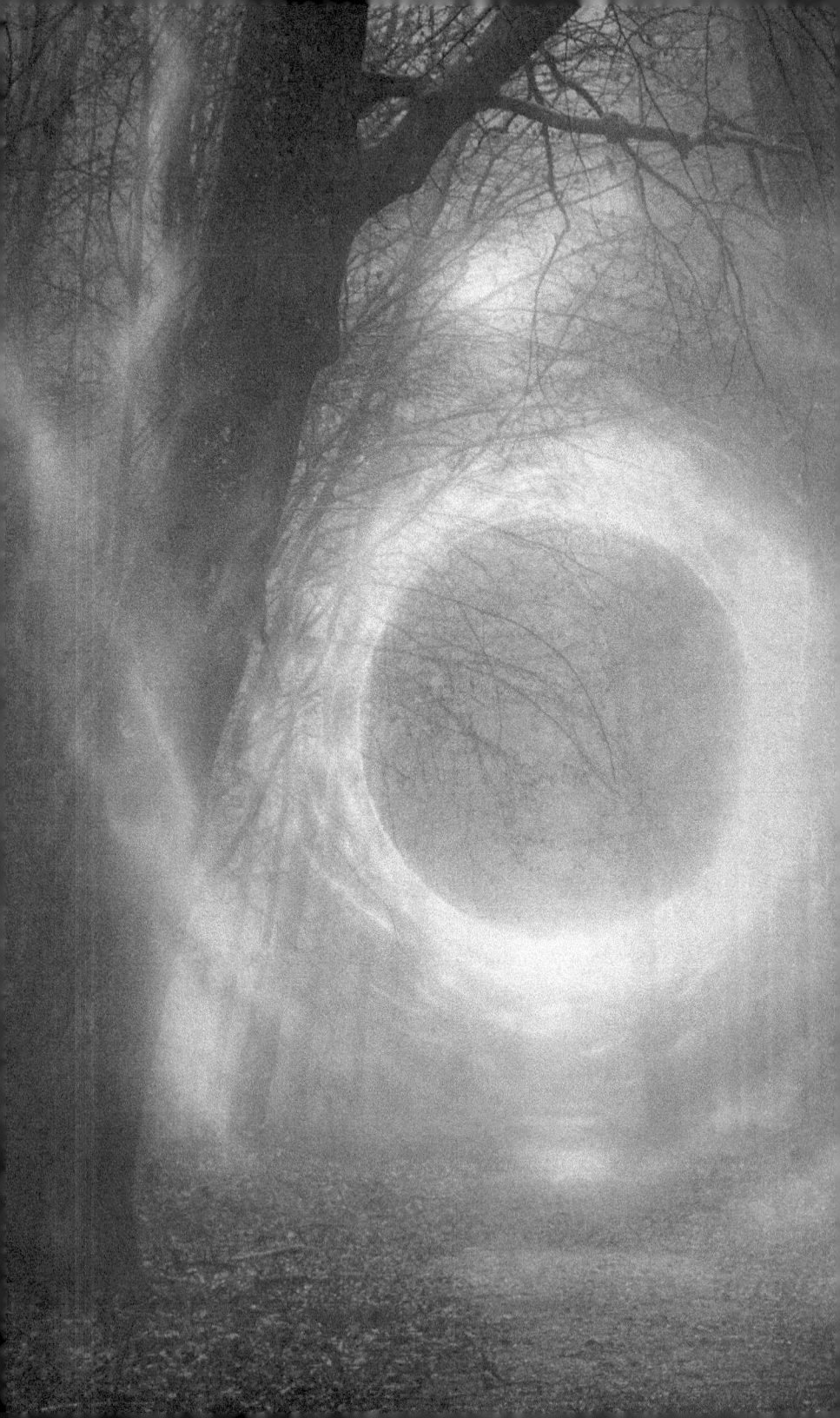

CHAPTER 29

TUMBLING DOWN

EVALINA

I expected to see Valec on the floor unconscious. I wanted to see him lying there, my flames consuming him. Instead, the man I love is at the mercy of his brother. Valec has since stood up from the ground after my fire knocked him down. Smoke lurks dangerously close to me, not going for the blow. With one hand Valec has Julius suspended. His favorite method of attack. To my left Aziel and Recifer have Soela pinned against a rock.

Valec's icy gaze lands on me. "Why am I not surprised, Evalina?" He approaches me with the graceful elegance of a snake. "That was a real show you put on. I'm amazed that you would actually think to harm me." He crosses his arms in front of his chest and that's when his magic retreats, Julius's body landing near Soela. Who remains pinned by the two male brutes.

"You aren't crossing this veil." I look to the portal behind me. "You will not torment my people," I say with authority.

He laughs. "Your people. Those were once my people. They worshiped me like the god I was, and just like that they spat at my feet, cursing the ground I walk on. Wishing me dead. They chose the wrong side, and now I will be the one to help them remember."

Through the corner of my eyes, I catch Julius righting himself. He does not seem hurt, which is always my initial concern. "Valec, there's no point to this," Julius says, making his way to my side. I remain focused on Valec's hands, making sure he isn't baiting Julius to come to my side only to suspend him midair again. But his arms remain at his sides, not a flick of movement. "She won't let you pass. And you can kill me as many times as you'd like, but she won't budge. It's best you surrender now."

Valec studies Julius with utter calm. His expression is happily fixated on his brother's every move as Julius leans closer to me. "You're right," Valec says, and surely that's not what I expected the king of Inferis to say. "It is pointless. Given that the veil isn't actually shattered." I gape at him. "What, you didn't think I'd notice Soela utter nonsense out of her own amuse- ment." Another predatory step my way. Julius inches closer, a hand reaching for his sword. "So, if my two men would be so gracious as to bring Soela forward." Aziel and Recifer keep their hold on my fiery friend.

I don't wait for them to reach us when I strike with all my might. Julius yells, Soela cries out, but all I can hear are the anguished sounds of the two men whose bodies have ignited in flames. They thrash against the ground, some of the garden flowers catching sparks along the way.

Soela tries to run from her burning assailants, only to be caught in Valec's snare. He pays little attention to his men begging for his help. He's too busy circling Soela with his power. It's like there's a tornado wrapped around her. I can barely make out her features as she becomes wholly incased in his shadows. Julius is set to attack Valec, his sword gleaming with all its might. Until the weapon is flung from his hands. The king is busy between keeping Julius apprehended and Soela caught in a battle of life and death.

I won't have it. I will go down swinging even if it's the last thing I do. I let my palms ignite. The heat like a second skin. It warms me from the inside out. Julius notices what Valec has not, considering he's too busy torturing Soela. "Evalina, stop!" I let Julius's warning pass right through me. I will not stop. I will not yield. This ends now.

I fling myself forward with all my might. Crossing the remaining distance between us until my hands connect with Valec's. Dousing his shadows with my hellfire. His hold on my friend ceases, her delicate body falling to the floor. Julius is already rushing to her side.

Valec looks behind me at the two piles of ash that were once the remaining members of the Wicked Four. With our hands still locked he tries to force my grip off him.

Grunting, he kicks and jerks violently. I keep my hold steady. Despite Julius being a trained soldier, he revealed to me that Valec has all but lounged on his throne for all these years. Leaving all the heavy lifting to Julius and his torture crew. So, I know for a fact Valec can't fight without his magic. Julius may have taught me how to defend myself against shades, but an unarmed immortal male with a taste for vengeance will have to suffice.

I try my best to pin him to the ground, arms at his back, but it's hard when I'm also trying to channel my power into Valec's hands. In seconds Julius is at my side, bringing a knee down to pin his brother as my palms continue to snuff out his power.

"Soela," I yell. I catch a strip of red hair in my vision. "It's either now or never. We need to leave. Chant the spell." I feel the last of my flames sinking into his palms. *This better work, please let this work.* Valec continues to struggle in Julius's grasp. That is until his body goes completely limp. Valec's hands loosen in my own, and I let them drop to the floor on either side of him.

"Is he?" Soela gapes at Valec's prone body. "Is he dead?"

"I don't know. Maybe." I'm lifting myself up, Julius helping me to my feet, when a pair of delicate hands grab Julius's ankle.

Icy blue eyes threaten to glue me to the spot. Then Julius is thrust across the cavern by a lingering shadow. "Soela!" I scream. "Now!" Soela chants, trying her best to keep her concentration on the veil.

Behind me Valec desperately tries to cling to his power, but it only comes out in tiny puffs of smoke. His last able burst of power was wasted on dragging Julius across the cavern.

I ready myself, igniting my flames while pressing my hands firmly over the veil again. This better work.

There's an instant where I don't feel my right hand over the portal. I can see it, but I've lost all sensation. And that scares me, but I try my hardest to remain focused. I switch between staring at the veil and craning my neck to the side, as Valec tries to catch his footing and fails. Doubling over.

It doesn't take long for me to recover all feeling in my hand, and when that happens, I press them both forward. But instead of going through like when I first arrived with Julius, my hands find resistance. It's like being separated by glass. I tap lightly on the portal that has frozen over. Knowing what I must do I punch my flame-covered fist against the glass. It shatters upon impact, the shards falling to the ground.

"Now it is done," Valec rejoices at my back.

It isn't until I've taken a step back from the veil that the ground starts shaking. Julius is rushing towards me while Valec again makes his way over to us. I fire up my hand for the last shot.

"You will not set foot in Einalem," I warn. He lifts a tentative hand and I silence him with a feral blaze to his heart. He cries out as my power engulfs him in his own heat prison. His shouts do not cease, and with each of his cries, the cavern seems to grow more unstable.

I nearly lose my balance. "What's happening!" I shout over the rumbling noise. Behind us stalactites fall one by one, smashing everything in their wake. The screams of the land's people jolt me to my senses.

"I don't know, but we have to go!" Julius bellows.

"People live here, Julius. We have to save them. We have to help them cross." I failed to notice the moment Valec's voice no longer echoed through the space. His body remains incased in flames, though it's unmoving. Eyes closed, hands resting perfectly atop his stomach, almost as if someone placed him that way. It's like staring into the casket of a dead man.

I jolt as the ground under Soela's feet trembles, and she sprints away toward the veil. "Time to bolt." She crosses our path, entangling both Julius and I in a hug. "Thank you for everything."

Julius is the first to pull away, and he stares at Soela, incredulous. "This feels a lot like a goodbye."

"Because it is," she cries as we all try our best to balance on the wobbly terrain. Julius is too focused on Soela to register the old woman and young girl walking hand in hand toward us. It's Anise and Pia. "Julius, I can't cross. No one in this land can. We're dead remember? We've already lived our lives, but you and Evalina..." Soela brings her attention to me. "You both have lives to live."

"No." Julius shakes his head. He takes a step back, his gaze darting to Anise and Pia who have finally reached us.

"Do not be alarmed, Julius," Anise says in her sweet, motherly tone. "You made our stay here pleasant. You cared deeply for all those you could. But Inferis was never meant to exist in the first place. We were all meant to exult in Caelesti. This is the balance of life."

Julius snaps his attention to Soela. "You knew, didn't you? All these years you knew that this would happen, and you didn't tell me." I know that Julius is hurting, but I understand why

Soela hid this information from him, so that he wouldn't try to find a way where there was none.

"Valec's life is linked to this land. Thus, the land will be gone once he is." She points at the flames that have since died down around his brother.

The caverns jolt with force. Rocks tumble down all around us.

"Go!" Soela urges.

Julius pulls her to his chest. "I love you." I stare with tears in my eyes as Julius says goodbye to the only family he's ever known in Inferis.

I do the same, thanking Soela and Anise over and over again. I give a last warm smile to little Pia. My composure breaks, and a cascade of tears flows down my cheeks. Julius looks no better than me. It pains me to even look at him. So broken.

He places a steady hand on my back. "After you," he says, trying his best not to fall apart. I guide myself forward through the veil. Now, it's like stepping through an archway. Magic no longer separates the two lands. I let out a sigh of relief once I'm back on mortal soil.

I give myself a few seconds to measure my surroundings. I forgot what it's like to breathe fresh air. It's cleaner, less heavy than in Inferis. I look up at the sky, having missed seeing the stars at night, and having this abundance of natural beauty all around me. I spin around, delighted to be back. I wait for Julius to cross. He was right behind me, so it shouldn't take him long. When he's a no-show, I begin to worry.

"Where are you?" I call out. "Julius!" Something must have happened. What if the cavern caved in, what if he got stuck under a piece of debris?

That's it, I'm going back. I force my feet to move forward. Welcoming the dusty air back into my lungs, I call for Julius as the ground starts cracking. The cavern wall descends like a waterfall of falling stone. "Julius?" He isn't here. Where did he go? I call out for Soela, for Anise, for anyone who can hear me.

What I receive in answer is the high-pitched screech of a shade nearby. It's climbing up one of the fallen stones, its focus on the sound of my voice. Behind it more follow. Their howls are the only sound I can pick up besides the crashing of stone.

There's truly no one here. I have to leave but, when I reach out for the veil there's nothing there. The portal is gone. Vanished, like the man I love.

Not knowing what else to do I ready myself to attack. The first shade whirls on me and I let all my hellfire consume it. It burns into a pile of ashes before my eyes. I do so with each monster that approaches me. Many more come and I feel my power slipping which each blow. I wobble as a crack forms on the ground, where Julius's garden once stood. I prepare to take down the last of the monsters when my whole body erupts. Fire coating the entirety of my skin, I whirl around and let out every-thing I've got. By the time the final shade is nothing more than cinders, I also collapse.

My eyes close the second I hit the ground.

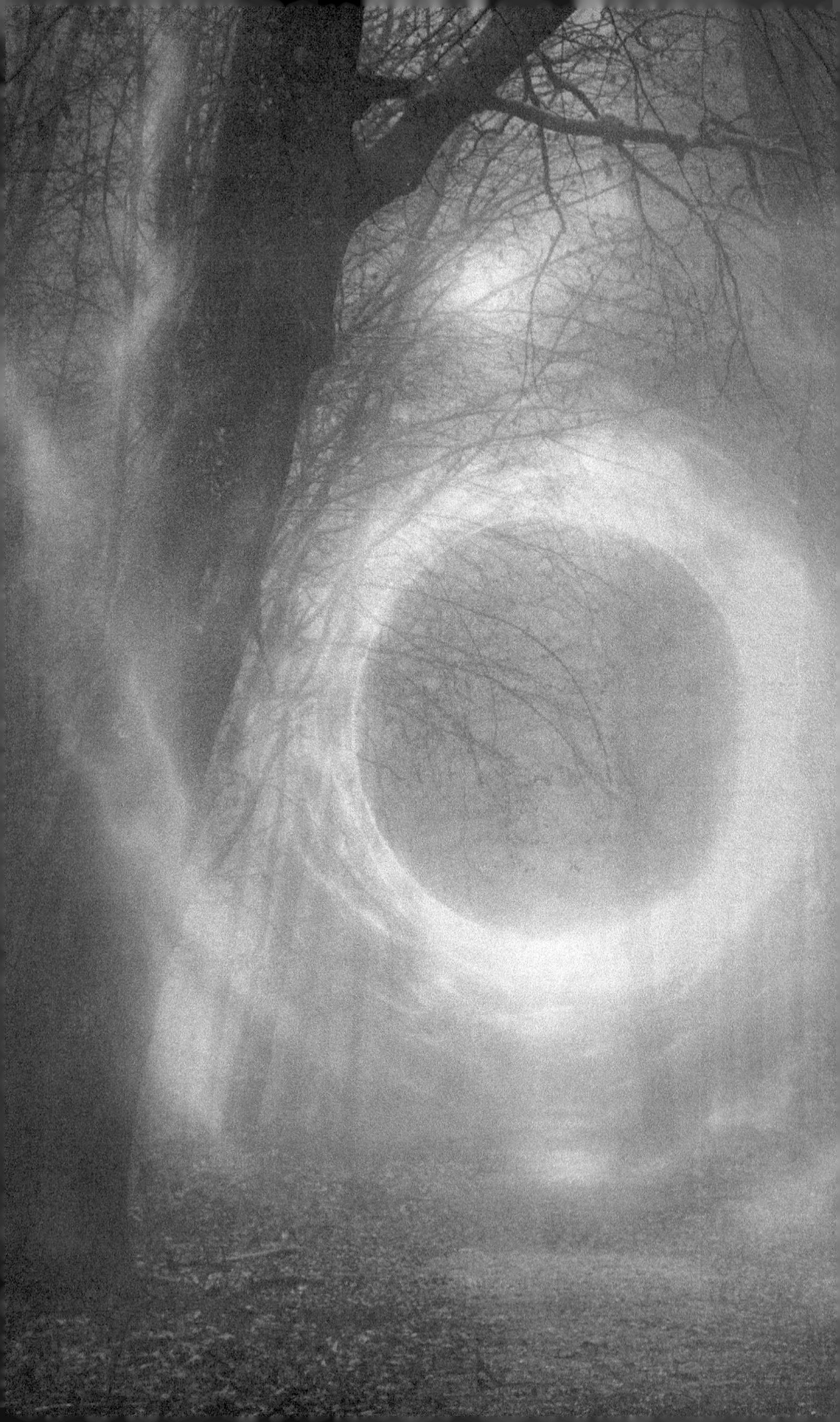

CHAPTER 30
WAKE UP

EVALINA

I have this vague sense of someone looming over me. Well, actually, a few someones. I can tell by the many hushed voices. I try to open my eyes, but they won't budge. It's as if they are sealed shut.

I sense someone approach. "Children, what are you doing in here? Have I not told you to let her rest." I know that voice. The tone, not so much. The man I knew with that voice was none other than the Devil. Whoever this is, he surely isn't him.

"We know, we were just curious," a child answers. "Pia saw her moving her eyes and thought she was waking, and she called us all to see."

The man seems to be leaning over me because I can feel his breath fan over my face. I try to open my eyes again. It's no use. The rest of my body is dormant as well.

"Sorry, children, but she's not waking any time soon." I hear shouts of disappointment.

"When will she wake?" another child asks the man looming over me.

"Only Dominus knows." *Dominus?* Why would Dominus, the ruler of Caelesti, know when I'll wake up. I'm awake. I can hear, I just can't move.

"Run along, children, I'm sure my brother Julius could use a hand at the fields." I remain there, listening as tiny footsteps resound on the floor as the children run off. I expect the man to leave as well. Instead, I hear a chair scrape against the floor.

"This is my fifth time coming to visit you, Evalina. Now, I know you don't know me. You only knew the cursed side of me." My breath stops. What did this man just say? *No,* it can't be. That's too far off. "But I want you to know that I'm praying for you every day. Julius isn't the same man without you."

Julius? My heart constricts. I couldn't find him. I went back through the veil, and I couldn't find him.

"I honestly wish I could do more. Visiting him once a week is not enough. He's not himself. And he won't be until you're back by his side."

He takes my hand and a jolt of something hits me. Something familiar coursing through my veins. "Come back to him, Evalina. He's waiting." He presses a warm kiss to my hands before setting them down at my sides again. "I will be back next week to see you. Hopefully you will be awake and well by then."

As he walks away, I swear I can hear the flapping of wings in the background.

My face is wet. Something is wetting it. There it goes again. I reach my hand up to my cheek. Yes, it's wet and sticky. I freeze, realizing what I just did.

I can move. I try my other arm. It moves as well. Now my legs. They both kick upward. My toes wiggle as well, and they accidentally touch something soft. Maybe it's a blanket. The blanket somehow moves to my other side. I reach out a hand to feel it. I was right, it is soft, but this is no blanket. It's an animal.

"*Woof.*" I jump. I'd know that bark anywhere.

"Saint, is that you?" My throat feels like it swallowed sandpaper.

"*Woof.*" I try desperately for my eyes to open. It works, to an extent. Though I am still unable to see. I blink several times, hoping that does the job. It doesn't. Saint licks my face and now I know why my cheeks are wet. I keep petting him, even as I shift to a sitting position. My legs feel like jelly.

Somehow, I sense a presence in the room, but I'm certain I haven't heard anyone enter. Saint lets out a low bark, but apart from that he's relatively calm.

"Evalina Morue," someone says at my side. The hairs on the back of my neck rise. "At last, we finally meet." The bed dips, a sure sign that someone is sitting beside me. "I'm happy to see that you've finally awoken." The voice is thick and slightly intimidating. Though I find it odd that I feel no fear.

"Who are you?" I ask into the void.

"That depends." He laughs. "I go by many names. Though most like to call me Dominus."

I'm not sure if I heard the man correctly. "Come again?"

"You heard correct, Evalina. I am Dominus."

"You're—" My mouth hangs opens. "How?"

"How am I Dominus?" I can see how my question might sound stupid. "Allow me to ease your worries, dear child. For one, you are not dead. You took a hard blow, but I got to you in time. You are very much alive." *He* saved me. Dominus, the ruler of Caelesti, saved me?

I press my hands to my cheeks, feeling the moisture there. A few tears flow down my face, my emotions running free. "Do not cry, child, you are safe in Einalem. You are home."

"But how? Everyone vanished. I lost Julius." I choke on a sob. "Everything was falling apart; I couldn't find him. There was no one," I cry, shaking my head frantically. "I don't know what happened. I—" A hand comes to rest on my shoulder. I blink several times, trying to get myself to stop crying. Then I see them, the tips of my fingers as I wipe my tears away. Am I hallucinating?

"I said that you are safe, and now you are whole." I turn to see the man I've been speaking to. Light brown eyes greet me with a welcoming smile. His dark hair hangs above his shoulders. He wears a simple bone-white tunic that seems to shine in the light. I look to the floor and notice that he happens to be barefoot as well.

"Hi." I offer him a shy smile.

He chuckles. "Hello, Evalina." Okay, now I'm scared. Suddenly everything I've done in my life comes rushing back to me, starting with my lack of belief.

As if reading my thoughts Dominus says, "Evalina, listen to me." He takes my hand in his. "I am in no way offended that you do not take part in religion. You will not be punished for such nonsense. You are a kind woman, with good morals. You are neither cruel nor wicked. You saved us all. And when your time comes, room will be made for you in Caelesti." I stare at him, dumbfounded.

"Let's say I've been doing some redecorating up there since Valec's return." *Valec.* I want to ask the man a million questions, but I don't interrupt him. "We're preparing a very special location for people who identify as you do. Somewhere you will feel at ease after your passing."

I'm speechless. All I can say at the moment is *thank you.* "Truly, thank you. For saving me, for healing me."

"It is not only I who deserves your gratitude. Valec and Julius have been crucial to your healing process as well. Their kindness knows no bounds. You are lucky to have them in your life."

"I—" I can't say the words.

"I know you have many questions regarding what's happened

to you. I wish I could be the one to ease your mind. But I am needed back home. However, I'm sure Julius can fill you in. I'll send for Valec as well. Once he's finished his work for the day." He gives my hand a light squeeze before he stands. I do so as well, realizing I have no difficulty standing at all. Saint hops down from the bed and I give him a tight hug. "How's my boy? I missed you."

I turn around to thank Dominus one last time and find that he's no longer in the room.

I face Saint again. "Hey, boy, can you take me to Julius?" He wags his tail all energetically and barely gives me enough time to open the door before he's darting out. "Wait up." I move quickly, though it's hard to navigate a home I'm not familiar with. "Saint, wait." Julius really needs to teach Saint to wait for others.

I manage to exit what happens to be a cottage. I'm dressed in a blue cotton gown, and like Dominus I'm not wearing shoes. I forgot to look for some when I was still inside whoever's house that was. Doesn't matter; if I go back to find a pair, I'll lose sight of Saint. Who hasn't stopped running. Geez, someone's happy today.

Saint has me racing through large fields. The ground is moist against my bare feet. It must have rained yesterday. "Saint!" What's the use in calling him? He's already far away. I can barely make out his form. He is but a white blob moving towards a large figure crouching under a tree.

Saint has already made it to the tree, while I'm still a few feet away. I try to catch up.

"Hey, Saint. What are you doing here?" Julius seems to process the fact that Saint couldn't have left the house on his own and that's when he brings his gaze forward.

His eyes connecting with mine, he drops what he's holding and comes running towards me. I meet him halfway. His hands fold around my waist. "Tell me I'm not dreaming." He presses my body to his, not quite believing I'm awake.

"You're not dreaming." I breathe against his chest.

"You're awake." He holds me close, neither of us moving an inch.

"I am."

"I've missed you." He caresses my hair.

"I've missed you." I grasp both of his arms, not quite believing that I'm in his presence either.

He pulls away slightly. "I love you."

I press a hand to his chin. He lifts me off my feet. "And I love you." I connect my lips to his. I've missed the taste of him, the feel of our bodies flushed together. The sound of his voice, everything.

Saint is the one to separate us. "Hey!" Julius complains. "I get that you missed her too. But I missed her more." Saint doesn't seem to care about what Julius has to say. He simply nudges his head against my side.

"Aww Saint, I already told you I missed you." I give him a good rub behind his ears. Content, he walks in the direction of the crops.

"Come." Julius extends his hand. "There's something I want to show you."

I tug on his arm, gaining his attention. "Julius, how long was I asleep for?" My eyes wander to his slightly leaner frame and undereye circles. Has he taken care of himself at all?

"Forty days," Julius answers.

"Will you tell me what happened?"

"Valec and I will tell you everything you need to know. I promise." He reaches for my hand again and this time I interlace my fingers with his. Bringing his gaze forward he says, "But first —" he walks us towards a massive oak tree. "You caught me as I was about to leave them some flowers."

I'm about to ask Julius who he's leaving flowers for when we arrive under the foliage. In front there's a headstone that reads:

Here lies Evan and Lina Morue. A loving mother and father till the very end.

My heart constricts. I help Julius arrange the flowers on the ground. Then we remain at my parents' grave in silence. The light breeze is the only sound as Julius holds me. As we hold each other.

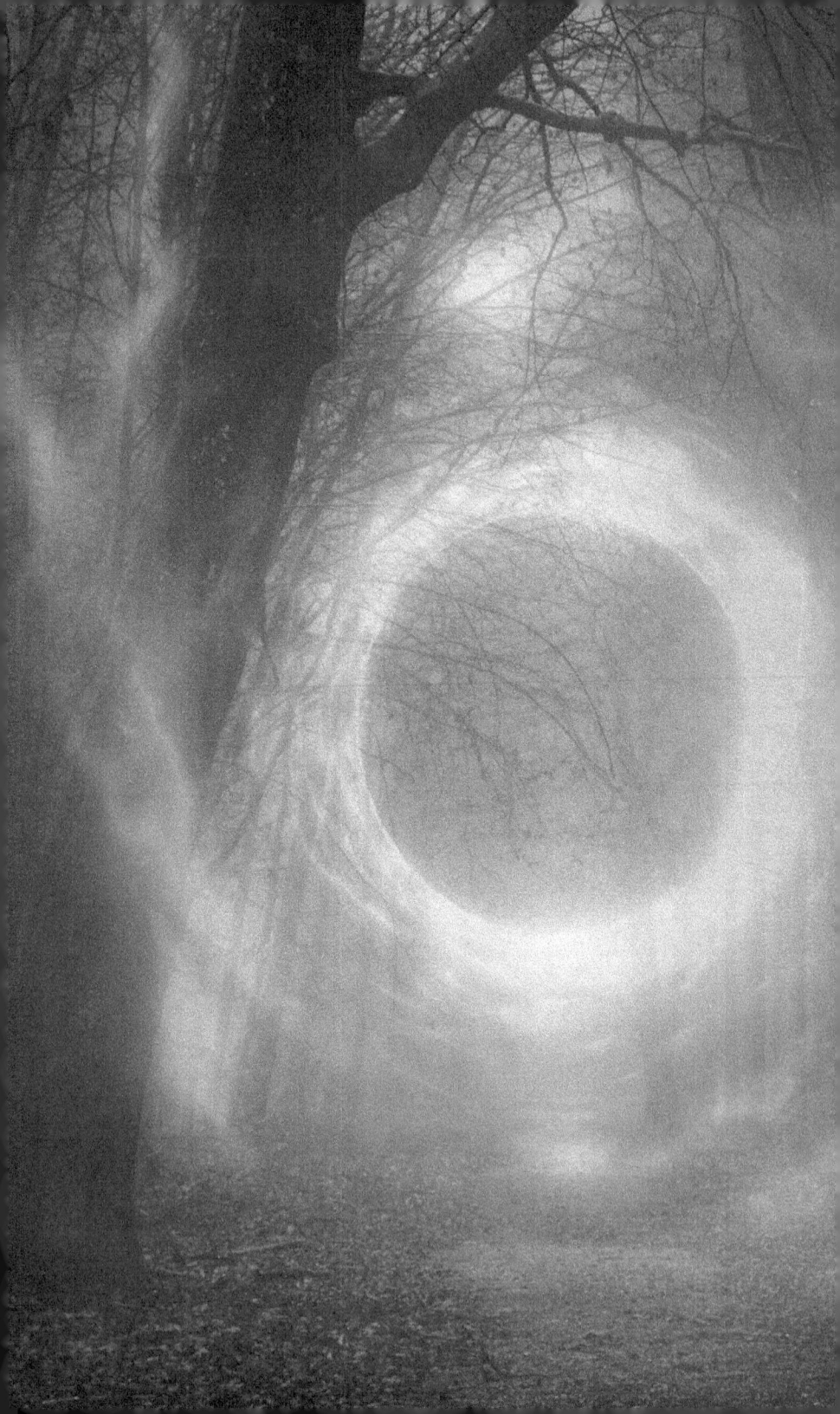

CHAPTER 31
THE STORY

VALEC

T he minute Dominus returns to Caelesti he asks me to go to Einalem. Evalina has awoken. I couldn't be more pleased. I can only imagine the look of pure joy upon my brother's face. *Oh, Julius, I am so happy for you.*

I make my descent to the mortal realm without a single thought. I spot them almost immediately, both of them sitting on their front porch. I land in one swoop. Evalina's shock does not go unnoticed. She's never seen me like this before. With my feathered wings. I tug them closely to me, not wanting them to get in the way.

Julius comes to me first. "She came back to you," I say as a way of greeting.

"Yes, she did." We embrace and I watch as Evalina stares at us, perplexed.

Julius pulls away from me and turns to her. "Alina, there's someone I'd like you to meet." She rises. "This is my brother, Valec. Valec, this is Evalina, my girlfriend." Finally, our first proper introduction.

"Valec?" I know she's confused, searching for the other man. The cruel one, the one who abused her and Julius, the one who made them go through such unspeakable suffering.

"It's nice to finally meet you, Evalina. Please let me be the first to tell you how sorry I am for my actions. I let rage get the better of me, and in doing so, condemned you to a horrid fate."

"I—" she stutters. "I don't know what to say."

"You don't have to say anything. I know it will take time for me to earn your forgiveness. Just know that I am not the same man you got to know. I'm back to being the man I used to be before the curse took over myself, and you." She nods lightly.

I go on. "Dominus told me you had questions. I'm here to answer them."

"Then let us go inside." Julius leads us inside their new home. He walks into the living room, proceeding to occupy the brown settee fit for two, Evalina sitting right beside him. I take a seat on the single couch near the unlit fireplace.

"The stage is all yours," I say to Evalina. "Ask me anything you want to know."

"Well, Julius told me I was asleep for forty days, but I'd like to know how I ended up that way?" She places her hands on her lap.

"What do you remember last?" Julius questions her. His left arm circles her shoulder.

Evalina looks to me instead. "I remember crossing the veil because Inferis was falling apart, and when Julius didn't cross after me, I went back for him. But I found no one, except for a bunch of shades who came after me. I couldn't cross back through the veil even if I wanted to. It was gone, vanished some-how. The last thing I remember was collapsing to the ground after fighting off the shades."

"First of all, I believe I should clarify what happened with me," I begin to explain. "After you landed your final shot, my body became trapped within your flames. In that very moment I felt myself slip away. According to Dominus, my cursed self died instantly. It was like a tree branch snapping in half. Which I'm guessing was the plan all along." She looks away. "Evalina, are you aware that I am not mad? On the contrary, I am grateful for your and Julius's actions. Because of it, Dominus finally saw the truth."

"How?" she asks.

"Your power broke whatever hold the angel Esveld had over him when you shot me. Your magic reached Dominus through me. He saw my virtue. He felt my angelic power again. And that's how everything flashed before him. The memories. They all came flooding back to him. That's why he came to me."

"How? Inferis was an unholy land. How was Dominus even able to enter?" I can see why Evalina's confused.

"He couldn't. But he could destroy it. After all, it was a land of his own making. And that's exactly what he did."

She gasps. "The ground shaking. That was him?"

"Yes, he came for me. And when you came back for Julius, he'd already taken him and every other resident of Inferis he deemed worthy of a second chance at life. He brought them back here to Einalem so that they may pick up where they left off."

"What about members of the Circle of Impure?" She straightens slightly on her seat.

"Some, like Soela, were spared," Julius answers her. Indeed, it was Julius's friends' belief in my innocence from the start that brought us here. Her family saw, they knew the truth, and they gave everything they had to become members of a hateful group. All to find a way to save my soul. I will be forever grateful to them.

"After he saved everyone, all was done," I continue. "That was until he saw you return to Inferis just before the veil closed permanently."

"He got me out," she comments.

"Not before you over-exerted your power on the shades. You burned yourself out."

"I—what?"

"I was beside myself," says Julius. Evalina turns to him. "I thought I was going to lose you. You were in such bad shape that Dominus had to take you to Caelesti. And I had to stay behind. Valec went with him."

"Why? You were a part of Caelesti just as much as Valec," Evalina jumps in. "Granted, you weren't a god, but—"

"And Dominus would have taken me back to Caelesti if I didn't relinquish my immortality," Julius says carefully.

"You what?" Evalina jerks her head, now facing him entirely.

"The minute I was saved Dominus gave me two options. Return to my life in Caelesti as I was. As the man I used to be before I met you," he says to Evalina. "Or remain in the mortal realm with you as I am now. Sans immortality."

"And you chose me." Evalina seems to be in disbelief. How could she ever think Julius capable of leaving her? He loves her. She's his everything. The man suffered time and time again for her.

"And I'd choose you every single day for the rest of my life." He brings her hands to his lips in an endearing gesture.

Breaking the sweet moment, Evalina brings her attention back to me. "What happened after I was taken to Caelesti? Was I healed?"

"Yes, I was there to look after you. On the fifteenth day you were stable enough to return to Einalem. I brought you here. To Julius."

"What about my powers; what happened to them?"

"Dominus extracted the hellfire from you. It was extinguished from the lands permanently. You are no longer immortal either," I add. "Like Julius, the ability to live forever is only granted to those upon their second life." I stand, knowing Dominus may have granted me the time to come and see her, but

I must return immediately. There's always much to do in Caelesti. A god's work is never done.

"Wait." She stands as well. "So, Inferis is gone?"

"Yes." I grin.

"Our friends were brought back," Julius exclaims with joy. "Like I mentioned before, Soela, Vienna, Romar, Anise, Pia, and Saint. They're all here. They were saved." I know she's happy to hear that.

She asks one more question as I reach for the door. "What does Dominus do, then? Does he judge the souls? Or is the world back to how it used to be before the fall, with no wickedness."

I shake my head. "What has been done at the behest of another cannot be undone. Esveld opened the eyes of mortals and led them to sin. Dominus can't erase that. But he can judge people's souls accordingly. Those who do not deserve a place in Caelesti live only one life. Their soul is then released to the ether." I cross the threshold.

"I'm glad you are well, Evalina," I offer as my farewell to her.

"It was nice to meet you, Valec. And thank you," she says at my back.

I turn, offering her a smile. "Likewise, Evalina. I'll be seeing you again soon. Goodbye, Brother." I nod in Julius's direction.

"Goodbye, Val. See you soon."

I let my wings spread and then shoot for the skies.

Today's the day. Dominus chose to wait for Evalina to recover before he enacted punishment on Esveld. I remain seated at my place while two of my brothers bring him in. We had no use for shackles before, but now we do. We were even forced to build a prison cell specifically to hold him in.

I expect to see Esveld cowering. Quite the opposite, he's gleeful. Staring at us through lowered lashes. His usually pristine self is quite the disheveled mess.

My brothers let him drop to his knees at the foot of Dominus's throne. Dominus rises and the rest of us do the same. "Esveld." The Lord's voice echoes through the whole temple. "You stand guilty of many infractions against my being, against Valec, my Second in Command, against the land of Caelesti and the Mortal realm. What do you have to say for yourself?"

Esveld raises his head, some of his white locks sticking to his forehead. "That I'd do it all again and I wouldn't bat a lash," he says with no emotion. "The people of Einalem are being lied to and you know it. I only opened their eyes to a fraction of the truth. Truth that you are denying them. But you can't keep up this charade forever, Dominus." The god tugs on his chains before continuing. "I only did what these cowards wouldn't. Especially him." Esveld looks towards me. "As a god he is undeserving. He is unworthy. He is void of all the harsh realities of life, my Lord."

Dominus has had it; I can tell by his rigid posture. "Silence. I've heard enough. I always knew one of my seven would betray me. Though I was never granted the knowledge of who it would come to be." He brings down his staff. "You, Esveld, shall be sentenced to a lifetime of misery in the mortal realm. May you live out the rest of your years enduring hard labor and knowing that no second life awaits you." He raises his staff into the air and when it taps against the floor, a hole opens up within the temple floor. The clouds part beneath it and Esveld falls through.

Seeing Esveld fall from the skies brings back some unwanted memories for me. I quickly shake my head, not wanting to relive that day ever again.

It's been a month since Esveld was cast down to Einalem. I still think about him from time to time. About what he said about the people of Einalem being lied to. It's a feeling I can't quite shake. However, not wanting to ruin the mood, I place those thoughts away as I stride through a green field. I'm in Einalem, visiting my brother and his girlfriend.

Everyone from the neighborhood is outside in their backyard, which is technically a large plot of land they use to harvest their crops. Tables have been set up on their lush farming land. For what reason, I do not know. All I know is that everyone who once resided in Inferis, who once feared me, now smiles at me when they see me arrive.

"Valec." Romar waves at me. The once cook of Inferis is now a proud restaurant owner.

"Romar, good to see you again. How's the restaurant going?" Romar opened up the restaurant in memory of his late wife Ava, whom he died protecting. Thus, how he ended up in Inferis.

"It's going well. Thanks for asking. You can swing by anytime, free of charge. I've got strawberry pie on the menu for you." The passing wind rustles his hair, and I can't help chuckling as he tries to tame it.

"My favorite. I will definitely be taking you up on your offer." I smile and continue to walk around the tables, greeting everyone I see.

"Vienna," I say, greeting the most hardworking servant Inferis ever had.

"Hi, Valec." She sits beside the son of her once lover. As Vienna's story goes, she died one night sneaking out of her home in Eremat to meet him. That night, the carriage crashed, and she drowned in the riverbank. Much like Soela, who was thrown off a cliff into the sea at the hands of the Order of Divine.

I did not know any of their stories before. It's now as I've gotten acquainted with them, learning the tales of how they ended up in Inferis. Many for unreasonable mistakes that

Dominus overlooked due to Esveld's constant influence over him.

I find an empty chair beside Soela. "Have they told you why we're all here?" she asks me. Her vibrant red hair matches her floral gown.

"No clue." I take a seat at the white round table. There are no centerpieces, though plates have been set up for the evening.

"But you're his brother!" she says, raising an eyebrow.

"Regardless, Julius doesn't tell me everything." I look behind me at Evalina and Julius, who've just now joined us, dressed head to toe in white. Interesting that we're matching, considering white and gold are my signature colors up in Caelesti.

"Good evening, everyone." Julius reaches the end of the tables in his pristine suit and slacks. "I've gathered you all here today because Evalina and I have some exciting news to share with you all." Evalina leans on him, her above-the-knee gown flowing with the breeze.

"You're getting married," Soela hollers at my side.

"Way to ruin the surprise, Soela," Julius grunts.

"So, it's true!" she rises.

"It is." Julius nods. "I have asked Evalina to marry me." Evalina shows off her ring and all the guests rise from their seats to congratulate them. I wait for last, coming up to hug my brother and my soon to be sister-in-law.

"Congratulations." I embrace them both at the same time. "May your union bring you both true happiness for all the years to come."

"Thank you, Brother." Julius pats me on the back.

"Thanks, Valec." Evalina offers me a bright smile.

"But that's not all." Julius snags everyone's attention again. "Our family of three is expanding."

"What!" Soela jumps to her feet again, quickly looking at Evalina's stomach.

"No, I am not pregnant, Soela," Evalina says quickly. "You

know I don't want children." I've never quite understood Evalina's reason for not becoming a mother, but I respect it, nonetheless. Julius has never been keen on the idea of being a father either. Though they are both quite the parental figures, looking after the children of the local orphanage and occasionally taking care of Pia when Anise has to work. Still, it's their decision and it should be respected.

It's through them that I've been able to see there's so much more to a union than procreation.

"Then what is it?" Soela grows impatient.

"Saint," Evalina calls for their Siberian Husky, who has now also been given a mortal lifespan like his parents.

We all crane our heads to see Saint carrying a little pup on his back. He's mixed color and very fluffy. Saint kneels and Evalina bends down to grab the puppy. "Everyone, meet Muffin, the new addition to our family."

"He's adorable," someone says from behind me.

"What breed is he?" Vienna asks.

"He's a Shih Tzu," Julius answers. I notice something quite unusual about the pup. Though he is many colors, black and white are the most predominant. But what I find curious is that his right leg looks as if he were wearing a white shoe, while the left resembles a white boot. I don't know if Julius and Evalina have noticed this. But the patterns are quite adorable, if you ask me.

I extend my hand out to pet him. Soon enough all the guests take turns petting the new addition to Evalina and Julius's family.

At some point Evalina leaves the pup with Julius as she takes me by the arm, leading me away from the crowd. "How are my parents?" she asks. The day Evalina found out her mother and father were in Caelesti was a joyous one.

"They're doing well. They ask about you all the time."

"Will you do me a favor?"

"Of course."

"Ask my mother in what shop I can buy the nicest gown for the wedding." She beams. "I know she has a favorite dress shop, but she never told me which one."

I laugh. "Will do, Evalina. Anything else?"

"Tell them I love them and that I miss them every day."

I nod.

"They love you too, Evalina. Very much."

The celebration is in full swing when Evalina and I return. I spend the rest of the evening amongst friends. Until it's time for me to return to the clouds.

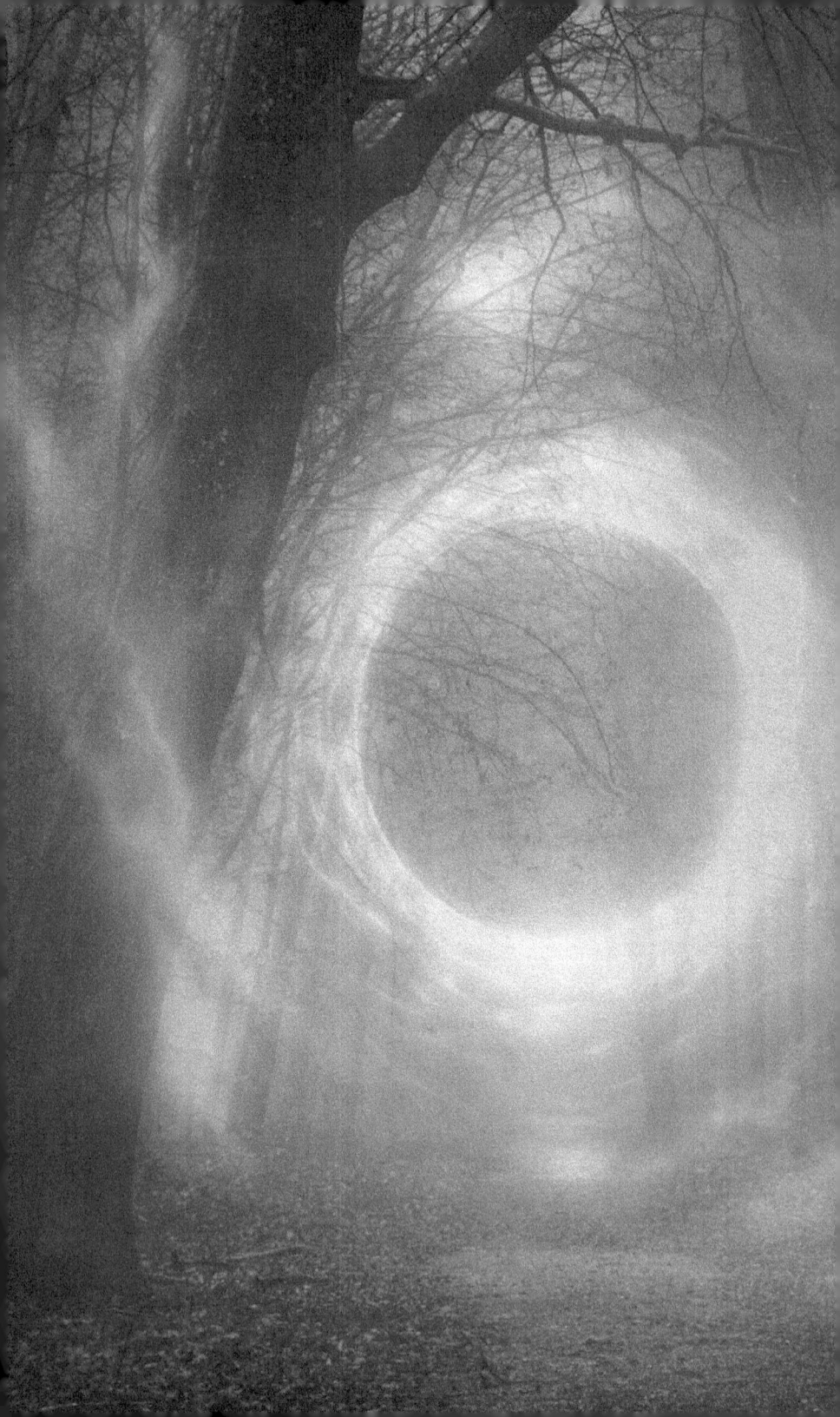

EPILOGUE
THE END

JULIUS

"Where are you taking me?" Evalina remains blindfolded as I guide her towards her birthday surprise. "Are we there yet, Jules?"

"We're almost there, relax. Just one more second…" I keep my hands on her shoulders, guiding her in the right direction. "We're here," I announce and proceed to remove her blindfold. "Happy twenty-second birthday, Alina," I whisper in her ear, raising goosebumps on her skin.

I had Evalina stay at Anise's house while Soela, Valec, and I, alongside the dogs, worked day and night to get this room fixed up for her.

It takes Evalina a second to register the light that surrounds us. The moment she does, her hands come up to her mouth. "Julius!" She spins around, getting a better view of the room. "You built me a library." We had a spare room in our cottage that Alina hadn't gotten around to doing anything with it. Though she always told me she wanted it to be a library room.

She finally moves through the space. Taking in all the wooden shelves lining the oak-colored walls, displaying plenty of books for her to choose from. "How did you get all these in here?" She is absolutely mystified.

"I had a bit of help from Anise and little Pia. But it was Valec and Soela who helped me paint and build the shelves," I say before wrapping my arms around her waist from behind. She stares ahead at the cushioned armchair in front of the floor-to-ceiling window, the perfect spot for curling up with a warm mug of tea and a good book.

It's nothing like the library back in the mansion at Inferis. But it's beautiful, nonetheless. Homey, inviting. Our special space inside our wonderful home.

She cranes her neck to look up at me. "I love it. I love you." I loosen my hold on her to allow her to turn completely in my arms. She happily kisses each of my cheeks, leaving my lips for last. "Thank you," she whispers against my mouth.

"Anything for you, Alina. Consider this your place to retreat to after a long day of working at Books N Baubles."

"Yes." She laughs. "What better way to escape a long day surrounded by books but with more books?"

I flash her a warm smile. "I love you, more than you can comprehend. And I will continue to love you for as long as my mortal years will allow." We embrace, getting lost in the moment. In our moment, and for once I'm not fearful of what the future holds.

ACKNOWLEDGMENTS

My journey with *Kingdom of the Forsaken Saint* began back in 2021. Though the idea for it was explored long before that. To be honest I always dreamt of publishing my own book, but I never thought it possible. I always saw it as nothing but an illusion, something that other people could do, but not me. It took me a while to convince myself that the career I always wanted was possible, I just had to be patient and work hard enough. Now here I am three years later, a published author.

Despite the long process, I am so thankful for having gone through it. It's a journey I'll gladly go on again and again. Until there are no more stories left to tell (which won't be any time soon). I'm also thankful for the people who formed part of this experience.

To God: All of this was possible because of you. Thank you for your constant presence in my life. For your unconditional love and for always believing in me.

To my Mom and Dad: I remember the day I told the both of you that I no longer wanted to pursue criminal justice, and that I wanted to be a writer. You supported me in my decision, despite how scared I was to take the leap. I love you both immensely. Mom, thank you for buying me books as a kid, and for taking me to the school library book fairs. My love of books started because of you. Dad, thank you for listening to me, for being there for me, but most importantly for understanding me and my dream of writing. You've been the best book marketer an author could ask for.

To my dog, Rocky: Even though you're no longer here. You were a part of this journey from the very start. From the beginning stages of draft one you were there sitting beside me on the floor as I typed away at my keyboard.

To Angie: You are the best cousin and parabatai a girl could ask for. Thank you for being so supportive of my dream and for listening to all my crazy ideas. I love you to the moon and back.

To Keila: My forever friend. Even when we haven't seen each other in a while, you've always been present throughout this process. Always asking me how the book was coming along. So genuinely excited for publication date. You have no idea how much I appreciate you. Thank you for everything sis.

To Erica: You have always been my greatest supporter, my cheerleader. Thank you for believing in me since day one.

To my coworkers and my bosses at La Gran Vía: You guys are the best. Thank you for constantly asking me how the book was coming along.

To my beta readers, Hanne, Aisha, and Nicole: Ladies thank you so much for choosing to read *Kingdom of the Forsaken Saint* when it was in its earliest stages. Your feedback was extremely helpful. Without it the book wouldn't have gotten to where it is today.

To Rachel: You were the reason I went ahead with publishing this book in the first place, after I'd initially given up on it. So thank you for pushing me out of my comfort zone.

To my high school English teacher, Sara Torres: Thank you for believing in my writing since the beginning. Your class was always the highlight of my day. Though I never want to write a single essay ever again, I'm grateful for the work. Because it made me a better writer.

To my therapist Marie Lloyd: Thank you for helping me see the uniqueness of my thoughts, and for being completely mesmerized over the concept of my book. I'll never forget the day you told me how incredible I was for thinking outside the box.

To Sky Regina: Sky you are the best editor I could have asked for. Thank you for saying *yes* to my project. You truly helped shape this story for the better. It was a pleasure working with you.

To Danielle Greaves: My cover designer and extraordinary map maker. You did such an amazing job bringing my cover and map concepts to life. I am forever grateful.

To Marina Ceban: My beautiful character artist. You are incredible. Thank you for bringing Evalina, Julius, and Valec to life. Your work speaks for itself.

To Melissa Hawkes: My fantastic website designer. You have no idea how little I knew about running a website let alone creating one. Thank you for making the process easier for me.

To Mallory Kent (The Nutty Formatter): Thank you, Mallory for formatting *Kingdom of the Forsaken Saint*. I'm grateful to have come across your name within the acknowledgments of another book.

Lastly, thank you to everyone holding this book in their hands. I hope that the story resonated with you in some way, and that you were able to escape from reality even if it was for a little while. Thanks for visiting the land of Einalem and I hope you stick around for my next adventure!

ABOUT THE AUTHOR

 Melanie Cardona Vélez is a graduate of the Criminal Justice program at the Interamerican University of Puerto Rico. During her time as an undergrad student, she earned three certifications within the field of writing. In 2022, she had her first article published in *Panochazine's* Food Issue for the month of September. Melanie currently lives in the city of Camuy, PR with her family. When not writing, she can be found obsessing over K-pop, baking, listening to music, or reading a good book. Kingdom of the Forsaken Saint is her debut romantic fantasy novel.